MY BROTHER'S DESTROYER

Clayton Lindemuth

Hardgrave Enterprises
Chesterfield, Missouri

Publisher's Note: This is a work of fiction. Names, characters, places, and incidents are
a product of the author's imagination. Locales and public names are sometimes used
for atmospheric purposes. Any resemblance to actual people, living or dead, or to businesses, companies, events, institutions, or locales is completely coincidental.

Book Layout ©2013 BookDesignTemplates.com

MY BROTHER'S DESTROYER/Clayton Lindemuth -- 1st ed.
ISBN-13: 978-0615938240

For Donald Lindemuth, the most virtuous father and role model a son could want.

OCTOBER

I moved the lantern close to Fred's head. His eyes was broke open and red. I stood there looking at him. Wondered if I was man enough to put him down, if I had to.

Fred said, How 'bout you murder the evil cowards threw me in that ring instead?

—*Baer Creighton*

ONE

I see the bastards ahead, fractured by dark and trees. Twenty—
more. They voices led me this far. I touch the Smith and Wesson
on my hip. They's a nip in the air, harvest near over. Longer I'm
still, colder I get.

One of these shitheads stole Fred.

Problems for him.

I'm crouched behind an elm, pressed agin smooth bark.

It's dark enough I could stand and wiggle my pecker at em and
they wouldn't see. They's occupied around a pit. Place swims in
orange kerosene light with so many moths the glow flickers.
Hoots and hollers, catcalls like they's looking at naked women.
Can't see in the circle from here, but two sorry brutes inside are
gutting and gouging each other. Two dogs bred for it, or stole
from some kid maybe, or some shit like me.

All my life I got out the way so the liars and cheats could go
on lying and cheating one another. I can spot a liar like nobody.
But these men is well past deceit.

One of these devils got hell to pay.

Fifty yards, me to them. I stand, touch Smith one more time. Step from the tree. A twig snaps. I freeze. Crunch on dry leaves to the next tree, and the next. Ten yards. If someone takes a gander he'll see me—but these boys got they minds on blood sport.

Sport.

I test old muscles and old bones on a maple. Standing in a hip-high crotch, I reach the lowest limb and shinny. Want some elevation. See men's faces, other side of the ring—and if I don't see dogs killing each other, that'll be fine.

I know some of these men—George from the lumber yard, and the Mexican runs his forklift. They's Big Ted; his restaurant connects him to other big men from Chicago and New York. Ted's always ready to do a favor, and tell you he done it, and send a monthly statement so you know your debt. Kind of on the outskirts, Mick Fleming. And beside him is Jenkins. Didn't expect to see the pastor here.

"Lookit that bastard! Kill 'im, Achilles! Kill 'im!"

Why looky looky.

That's Cory Smylie, the police chief's son, shouting loudest. Cory—piece a shit stuffed in a rusted can, buried in a septic field under a black cherry tree, where birds perch and shit berry juice all day.

I make the profile of Lucky Jim Graves, a card player with nothing but red in his ledger.

The branch is bouncy now, saggy. Stiff breeze and I'll be picking myself off the ground.

I think that's Lou Buzzard. The branch rides up my ass like a two-inch saddle and each time I move, leaves rustle. But I want to know if that's Lou 'cause he's a ten-year customer. Be real helpful if these devils was already drinking my likker. Little farther out and I'll see.

Snapped limb pops like a rifle. I'm on the ground and the noise of the fight wanes, save the dogs. Hands move at holsters and silver tubes sparkle like moonlight on a brook. These men come prepared to defend the sport, and got more dexterity than I could muster on two sobers.

"You there!"

Voice belongs to a fella I know by reputation, Joe Stipe. We've howdied but we ain't shook. A man with a finger on every sort of business you can imagine, including mine. Got a truck company, the dog fights, making book, and a few year ago sent thugs to muscle me out of my stilling operation. We ain't exactly friendly.

Men gather at Stipe's flanks as he tromps my way. "Grab a lantern there, George. We got company."

I sit like a crab. The light gets in my face.

"Why, that's Baer Creighton," a man says.

"Baer Creighton, huh? Lemme see." Stipe thrusts the lantern closer.

"That's right."

"Don't tell Larry," another says.

"He ain't here tonight," Stipe says. "What the hell you doing, Baer? Mighta got your dumb ass shot."

"I was hanging in the tree because you's a bunch a no-count assholes and I'd rather talk to a bag of shit."

They's quiet, waiting for something let em understand which way things'll break.

Not tonight, boys. But I'll goddamn let you know.

The hair on my arms floats up and static buzzes through me. I look for the man with a red hue to his eyes. Ain't hard to see at night—it's always easier at night—and it's the one said, "Don't tell Larry."

I don't try to see the red, or feel the electric. Gift or curse, I subdue it with the likker. Got it damn near stamped out.

"It's just Baer," Stipe says.

The men disperse back the fight circle, where a pair of dogs still tries to kill each other. Stipe lingers, and when it's just him and me, he braces hands on knees so his face is two feet from mine. I smell the likker on him.

My likker.

"Come watch the fight with us assholes." Stipe looks straight in my eyes. "And later… you breathe a word of this place, I'll burn you down."

"Didn't come so I could write a story in the paper." I crawl back a couple steps and work to my feet. My back and hips feel like a grease monkey worked em with a tire tool, but I won't show it. We's face to face and Stipe's a big somebody; got me by a rain barrel. The fella give me the electric stares from the fight circle, that circle of piss and blood and shit and clay.

Expected to see Larry here. After thirty years of meditation, I don't know whether to blame myself for stealing Ruth or him for stealing her back.

"I believe what you said about the newspaper, Baer," Stipe says. "So what brought you to my woods?"

I meet his eye for a second or two and take note of his bony brow. "Nothing to say on that." I turn and after a step he drops his hand on my shoulder. Spins me. I get the juice like I stuck my tongue on a nine-volt. His eyes pertineer shoot fireworks. He's so fulla deceit and trickery, he's liable to shoot me straight.

I lurch free.

"You remember what I said. I'm going to burn you down. I'll find every sore spot you got and smack it with a twenty-pound sledge. You'll pull your head from a hole in the ground, Baer, just to see that awful sledge coming down one last time. You best get savvy real quick. Don't mess with a man's livelihood."

Heard rumors on Stipe going way back—how his truck company made lots of money after his competition died under a broke hydraulic lift with a sheared pin. Curious, is all. Got them lugnuts by his side when you see him in town, like he's some president got a private secret service. Always some jailhound on the work release with a mug like a fight dog after a three-hour bruiser.

"They's no such thing as impunity, Stipe."

His look says he don't ken my meaning and that's fine as water. You'll smack me down and every time I look up, I'll see Fred. I'll shove that impunity down your throat and you won't know you're filling up on poison. That's what I'm thinking, but words ain't worth a bucket a piss. I back away. His eyes is plain-spoke menace.

I'm so torqued I got to look for my voice. "Ain't quite time to call it war. But I'll let you know."

I tramp into the woods and every square inch of my back crawls. I get far enough the static don't bother me; bullets do, and if I was twenty years younger I'd run in spite of low-hanging limbs. But I'm fifty and my hipbone feels like it was dipped in dirt, so I stomp along and eventually I'm deep enough into the woods I turn.

Stipe still looks my way, but him and his boys is all shadows, demons.

Farther out, when the fight circle's a slight glow through distant trees, I rest a minute on a log. They know I live and work at home. Wasn't thinking I'd tip my hand just yet, but part of the curse of seeing lies is not being worth a shit at telling them. And knowing the bastard who stole Fred was in that crowd works agin my better judgment. It's hard to hold your tongue while the plan sorts out—you want to let the bastard know something god-awful brutal is coming his way.

I stand, work my joints loose. I come to Mill Crick and follow south a mile, and pause at my homestead, a tarp strung tree to ground, a row of fifty-five gallon drums, a boiler and copper tube.

Fred growls.

"It's me, you fucking brute."

Fred's in shadows under the tarp. His tail taps the diesel turbine shipping crate he sleeps in. I hammered over the nails and reinforced the corners with small blocks, and it's been home to four generations. If I was to pick the hairs between the boards, they'd be white like Fred, red like George, brown like Loretta, and brindle like Phil. All relations of his, though I couldn't name the begats.

His voice turns quiet.

He's got words and I got words and we know each other well enough to talk without losing hardly anything to translation. He knew it was me tramping into camp when I was a half mile out, most likely. He only growled to show disapproval, and now it's done, he can go back to sleep.

Poor son of a bitch needs it.

Fred's one of them pit bulls they like to fight so much.

It was October third, the night that cleaved summer and fall. I gathered apples at the Brown place across the road in an orchard strangled in grapevine and hauled buckets back and forth to my still. Farmer Brown died a dozen years back and no one claimed the property. I was thinking on Fred, how uncommon he is, how he'd yammer for hours on any manner of subjects. He'd been missing three days.

Neighbor farmers tilled the fields. I'd scrounged inside the house a dozen times, stripped some plumbing and recoppered my still, and helped myself to a few shingles—the loose ones at the edges. I stole Brown's cast-iron bathtub and hauled it on his wheelbarrow to the brook below my camp. Then I carted enough lumber to build a platform above the mud and strike a post for a small mirror off'n Brown's wall. Every night 'fore I turn in I scoop crick water into the tub, and haul a leather satchel of stones from the fire pit to take away the chill.

I stole all that but me and Brown was tight and hell, he's dead.

They was a full moon that October third night but the clouds kept it smothered. I came around the house hauling two buckets of apples and headlamps flashed from the forest a half mile off, bright like God Almighty made em on the spot. They turned on the dirt road headed my way.

I know them woods. Nothing there save a logger's doubletrack that curves around a side hill where Joe Weintraub cut the hemlock to let the hardwood grow in. Seven year ago. Lost money on it, he said.

The headlights came closer. Truck had a regular gasoline engine, not diesel. Swung onto the driveway.

I dropped my buckets and dove. Headlights passed above. I crawled a dozen feet and scanned over the grass. The vehicle reversed, swung onto the yard, lurched forward and stopped. I couldn't scope the make but the truck was full-size, white or silver. The left side of the tailgate glowed like a layer of dirt was wiped clean.

A man jumped from the driver's side, dropped the tailgate and pitched a white ghost, maybe a burlap sack of grain to the weeds beside the driveway. The door slammed, the engine roared and the rear wheels spat dirt.

I waited.

Taillights disappeared around the bend toward town. I dusted my sleeves and knees, grabbed a couple spilled apples. I looked at the white clump beside the driveway, then back at the house, then to the hill where the truck came from.

Couldn't pull my eyes from the ghost. It took the shape of a small body, hips, shoulder.

I hurried, then stood with buckets straining my forearms and shoulders. Fred was slicked in blood, had a dark slash across his chest. Caked blood blacked his eye and his neck was splotchy. Blood smell cut the whiskey numb in my mouth and I could almost taste Fred's bleeding. Could almost taste my dead dog.

I dropped to my knees. Fred growled—he said, I'm alive you son of a bitch but you got to do something 'cause I'm pretty well whupped.

I looked at the moon, shifted my shadow off Fred and catalogued the wounds. None looked fatal but he was almost dead. Them slashes was moist but the bleeding'd stopped—most sopped in his coat. He'd likely been defeated by running out of air. Temporary suffocation. Maybe they'd called the fight out of boredom.

I looked to the road where the truck come out. Headlights glowed single-file in the forest. Stipe and his boys. I vowed right then every one of em would meet a cruel end.

I carried Fred in my arms with his feet straight up and his head agin my shoulder and now and again dropped a kiss on his muzzle. It maybe pissed him off but that was okay. Give him a reason to stay alive. "You're some kind of ugly," I said, and Fred said, They's no cure for stupid either.

My house is across the road from Brown's. I don't go there but to store my likker in the basement. I put Fred on the kitchen table. Struck a match, lit a kerosene lantern that cast a wicked shadow on the wall. It was the first time I was in the house and didn't ponder what Ruth touched last. Where she last stood. What she thought while she was standing there. Almost thirty year ago.

I moved the lantern close to Fred's head. His eyes was broke open and red.

I stood there looking at him. Wondered if I was man enough to put him down, if I had to.

Fred said, How 'bout you murder the evil cowards threw me in that ring instead?

"You're going to mend," I said. "But I got work to do."

I carried the lantern back down the hall to the medicine closet. Filled my arms with cleaners, antiseptics, bandages. Set em on the table by Fred. In the big bedroom I dug up a pink tackle box sewing kit.

My hands shook. I found a jug of corn whiskey and gulped. Spent three minutes putting thread in the needle. I cupped my hand and poured a half-shot of shine, then shifted to Fred's side and held my hand over the big slash across his chest. Dripped whiskey on it.

Fred growled.

I emptied my hand into the cut and touched the ragged edge. "You hang in there a little while and I'll patch you up right. Yes-sir."

I touched my wet fingers to the clots and clumps of dirt stuck to his coat near the wound. Gash put me in mind of a cut of meat from the butcher. I grabbed a clean cloth from a drawer, a bucket from under the sink. Went to the well out front and worked it 'til cool water splashed, then washed my hands and filled the bucket.

Inside, I held a soaked rag to the gaping cut. Fred's throat rumbled but he understood if only one creature on the planet gave a shit for him it was me.

I worked the cloth across ratty knots and clumps of blood. I soaked the rag in the bucket again and dripped water into the slash. Crust adhered to the edges like scorched meat to the bottom of a skillet, but the water worked it loose.

"I'm going to find who stole you," I said.

Fred said, Uh-huh.

"And they's going to be an eye for an eye come out of it."

Fred's a survivor and he's spent the last two week growing stronger. I step under the tarp and hunker beside him. "You doing good tonight?"

Fred sleeps with his head on the left and his body curled to the right. I scratch between his ears, careful the scabs. I want to look over his cuts and slashes, his smashed-in eyes—but it's night and I settle for feeling his busted body. Lot of heat from the slash across his chest.

I pop the cork from a jug, cup my hand, pour a little. Work the wound. Fred growls—that hurts you ignorant bastard—and I say, "Easy, Fred. You know I love you."

I work shine into every wound save his eyes. Both is smashed so bad I shake when I look at em. Black jelly starting to scab. He sleeps with that mess agin the blankets like to get infected, but he about took off my hand last I daubed likker on his sockets. I'll check again come morning.

I got to see about the mash before I wash off the day's stink.

Anything with sugar makes shine. Fermented grain or fruit—apples, plums, strawberries—keeps the air stinky sweet. I lift the plywood lid from the first fifty-five gallon drum. Smell washes over me so thick it almost sticks to my clothes. The mash is apples and pears from dead Farmer Brown's orchard. These big yellow apples got so much sugar you don't have to add any to the mash. Just a cake of yeast and in almost no time you got to still or you'll have thirty gallon of vinegar.

Men don't pay near as much on vinegar.

I lift the lid on each barrel. They's three of corn, and it takes longer. Different mechanics entirely. Them sugars is bound up tight. Got to cook the mash and stir it, keep it agitated, and if something goes wrong you got to add a five-pound bag of Pillsbury cane—but no more'n one. Two bags and you're in sugarpop territory. The men that drink sugarpop'll come for your ass, once they get over the evilest headaches they ever had.

The final fifty-fiver sits a dozen yards from the rest. It's empty, but I got an idea for it.

They's no sound but whispers from trees and water rolling over rocks at the brook a few yards into the dark. I gather smooth oval crick stones from the fire—anything but sandstone. They's still warm, but not hot. Tonight's bath won't be a slow soak. I roll em into a leather sack and tote em to the tub. Rest em easy on the bottom. I skim crick water into a five-gallon bucket.

I got something in mind for that barrel, is why it's away from the rest. Something Stipe and his boys won't like.

Stipe and his boys sure appreciate shine, though.

TWO

Joe Stipe sucked in the sweet smells of battle. The last match had taken forty-five minutes, and even the victorious dog was barely upright. Stipe tucked his thumbs under his waistband. The deepest scent was the earth. The ground was black with centuries of accumulated humus, matter once alive and now dead. The scent of trees hung above that, then sweet engine exhaust as revelers fired their trucks and motored off.

Stipe stepped to the pit and leaned against an oak shipping pallet standing on end that formed part of the ring's perimeter. His most trusted employees were breaking down the fight circle, lifting pallets vertically over the steel pickets that held them erect. They'd leave the pickets—this circle had many fights left before the dogs wouldn't willingly enter. Stipe's men guffawed as they retold moments from the night's spectacle.

How Achilles had turned and placed his stunning career in jeopardy. The men had gasped. He'd never been a coward. But his turn quickly became a spin, a feint; Achilles had whirled around his opponent in a flash of teeth and fury. He'd snapped his jaws to the other's neck and the move proved the winning gambit. For the next twenty-five minutes he never released, and the men watched in silent awe until his opponent finally wheezed, trembled, and died. Far from being a coward, Achilles had demonstrated that his bravery matched his cunning. He would someday be a grand champion. It was worth reliving a dozen times, from every conceivable viewpoint.

Stipe listened to his men and smiled.

He studied the ground where Achilles's opponent had bled. The dog's bladder and sphincter had released. The odors were still there, trampled into the black dirt. Stipe's nostrils flared and he thought for a moment he detected the very evidence of Achilles's inspirational performance. He released his breath and leaned closer, inhaled deeper, savoring the stink.

That was the last scent. Death.

Stipe was alone with his three closest workers and two hangers-on. Lou Royal, Stan Lucas, and Mitch Freeman disassembled the fight ring. In minutes the pallets would be stacked four high on the beds of three trucks so as to remain below the bed walls. Although insulated by the attendance of local police chief Horace Smylie, Stipe insisted his operation remain clandestine. Girly men—and there were a lot of them around Asheville—would raise a stink. Until a man stood beside the ring and felt adrenaline gallop through his veins, he wouldn't understand the service Stipe provided.

A fourth man, Ernie Gadwal, loitered at the edge of the lantern light. He was half Stipe's height and possessed a weasely aura, always lurking, always spying. He wanted a piece of the action but had nothing to offer.

A fifth man, Burly Worley, stood with his hands crossed at his groin. Stipe knew Worley, going back years and years.

"You staying out late," Stipe said.

"Wanted to bend your ear."

"Have at it."

"I got myself unemployed. Didn't know if you could use any help at the garage. Hell, driving even?"

Stipe shook his head. "Shit, that's rough. I feel for you. I'm full up on help."

"And the other sort of help?"

"I don't think you play as rough as these boys." Stipe noticed Stan had stopped lifting a pallet long enough to grin.

"Thanks." Burly turned.

"Hold up, now."

"Yeah?"

"Shit. Just hold up is all I'm saying. I'm thinking."

Burly Worley had a wife and a son and you could be damn sure Burly would raise him right. Burly was the kind of man who wasn't happy unless he went to bed tired and broken from a hard day's labor, and no smart organization turned its back on help like that. Burly had the ethic, and in the modern age of pussified men, it made sense to hire him on principle and build a job underneath him.

"I don't have anything," Stipe said. "But I want to think on this. How long you been without work?"

"Two months."

"Sign up for the unemployment, did you?"

Burly scowled.

Stipe extracted a fifty from his pocket. "For now, help Stan and the boys red up. Come see me at the garage tomorrow. I'll think of something."

Burly looked at Stipe's hand almost as if to reject the money. A battle played out on his face. Pride fought duty, and his wife and son won. Burly grabbed the bill, nodded to Stipe, and spun to the other men.

Stipe watched him for a moment. Burly was an example of an honest American, raised with decent principles, getting screwed by the system. He was tough, ornery, and prideful, and probably said meaningful prayers every night. Not like these others Stipe saw around town, the girly men.

Even in Gleason, city ways had crept in. Gentlemanly behavior aroused more dirty looks than thank-yous. It demeaned a gal; as if she couldn't open the door herself. And correcting a woman was equally obtuse—what right did any man have to correct a woman? Whether they'd read the Good Book or not the fact remained that the order of things was written: these girly men were failing their divine charge. Children weren't merely tolerated, they were coddled. Self-esteem was more important than competence. Rights were more important than achievements. Even the last sanctuary of manhood, a Sunday football game, failed against the universal assault on masculinity. Enviro-whackos selling cars. Sitcoms featuring dull men and dominant women. Nowhere in society except Stipe's fight ring could men go for a truly gritty thrill. Nothing else filled men's nostrils with the rich odor of blood. Nothing fulfilled their innate lust for carnage. Stipe alone was willing to battle for the old ways.

Stipe noticed Burly Worley staring toward the remaining trucks. Stipe turned.

Cory Smylie sat on a tailgate, hands on his knees, head low like a calculating dog. Cory had a wrestler's build, thick shoulders atop a wiry frame. His smooth face and greasy hair combed to a duck's ass in the back. Put Cory in a t-shirt and fold a deck of Marlboros into his shoulder, you'd never know he was a half-century removed from his atavistic decade of choice.

His father was Horace Smylie, Gleason police chief. Cory had been raised by a modern woman and a spineless man, and neither had the inclination or gumption to keep him on a short leash, set some boundaries, by God. Cory had enjoyed every toy, pursued every whim, had been guaranteed the world owed him his dreams. Stipe could tell just to look at him. That's what the schools taught nowadays. Cory was a perfect example of modern flawed thinking.

Since taking an interest in him, Stipe had learned Cory's history from his father, and his present from other men in their mutual orbit. Stipe knew things Chief Smylie didn't.

Cory had rejected higher education. When economic realities slammed him to the dirt, he'd chosen the easiest path. He used connections forged as the child of a well-traveled mother and began a small-time hook and crook operation. He stole. He sold drugs. He lived for intoxication. And then he lived in jail. His father knew most of what had landed him in the slammer, and being a Christian who believed in second chances, Chief Smylie had waged a personal campaign to get him accepted at UNC Asheville. But Chief Smylie was unaware that his son didn't attend classes and only set foot on the university grounds to deliver drugs.

Cory Smylie was irredeemable, but given the vastness of Stipe's enterprise, odd jobs presented that were uniquely suited to irredeemable men.

Cory had adequately performed his recent assignments, and unlike Burly Worley, Stipe didn't care if Cory Smylie ended up dead or in jail or just plain disappeared. However, although Cory's general demeanor was arrogance and entitlement, if Stipe could turn Cory into a man he'd be striking a blow for mankind.

Thinking of his problem with Baer, Stipe lifted his arm and stepped toward Smylie as if to take him under wing.

"Tell me. You got an eye for the rifle?"

THREE

"What the fuck'd you say?" Baer stepped into the group—they were all in Larry's grade, a year ahead. They were the boys Larry jawed about getting in with. They were cool.

Burly Worley said, "You heard me—"

Baer launched, swung left and right. Connected with skull and jaw, and as he reared for a third swift blow one of the other boys grabbed his arm. Another joined with a knee to his groin. Baer doubled over and a fourth boy drove him to the floor with an elbow to his shoulder.

They were beside the lockers, twenty feet from the principal's office.

Boys shouted and cursed. Girls screamed and wilted. Inched closer. That blonde Larry was all crazy about leaned against a wall locker, shifted sideways for an unobstructed view.

Baer absorbed kicks at the bottom of the pile. Burly Worley sat on Baer's ass and pummeled his kidneys. Baer spat blood, struggled to breathe. At last only Burly was hitting him, in the same section of his back over and over. His stomach turned. Kids shouted. The blows ceased and the crowd parted. Baer rolled to his side and stared at patent leather shoes and cuffed trousers. Principal Doolittle had lifted Burly by his lapels and slammed him into a locker.

The girl was there, the blonde. Ruth Jackson, the snotty daughter of the Asheville judge.

"What you get yourself into?" Larry said, kneeling at his back. "Come on, get up."

"You heard what Burly said," Baer said.

"My office, Creighton." Principal Doolittle pointed the way, as if Baer hadn't had a dozen visits in the last month. "This is the last time."

"You're out permanent? Permanent?" Larry said.

They walked home. Baer dragged his feet, kicked loose rocks.

"'Expelled', Doolittle said."

"Why you always starting shit?"

"You heard what Burly said about Ma. Why wasn't you in there with me?"

"Because she *is* a whore."

Both boys were skeletons with skin stretched by growth spurts into gangly knots of knees and elbows. Larry had Baer in size, but not moxie.

Larry had been acting acutely aware of their poverty; every disdainful smirk on another kid's face aroused shame on his. His pants ended before reaching his ankles. His wrists extended beyond his sleeves and he'd taken the habit of rolling them, even in winter. He talked of wealth and mused out loud that his penchant for mathematics might carry him beyond his beginnings. Larry watched the cliques that roamed as units, intimidating like stampeding cattle—and Baer knew Larry wanted to join them.

Ever aloof, Baer saw the herd and scoffed at its noise.

Their father worked in Asheville but lived with another woman and took his earnings to her. Their mother sewed, cleaned, catered.

And performed other services to put food on the table.

"She ain't a whore, damn you! She's your mother!"

Baer swung. His fist glanced Larry's shoulder, smashed into his ear. Baer connected shoulder to shoulder and drove Larry to the field. On the ground, he landed a punch to Larry's gut before his brother wrestled sideways. Larry jumped to his feet with a pocketknife in his hand. Baer led with a left before Larry could open the blade. Caught Larry in the nose.

He stood dazed. Baer brought another. Larry fell, but not without grasping Baer's shirt and dragging him along.

On the ground Larry used his weight advantage to straddle Baer. Pinned, Baer brought his knee up hard.

Larry toppled to the side, hands cupped over his groin. His mouth was open like he wanted to speak or breathe and could do neither.

"You heard him say it, and you know she ain't," Baer said. "And even if she was you got to stand up for her. Asshole."

Mother didn't understand why her boys were always at sixes and sevens. Baer made sure she didn't know why they'd fought this time. They'd entered the house sullen, bruised and bleeding. Mother trotted from the kitchen and cuffed each.

"What the sam hell happened?"

Neither brother responded. Larry, leaning forward and breathing shallowly, eased into a seat at a desk closest the door. Baer dropped Larry's books in front of him.

"Fine. You got homework? Sit and do your homework."

"Ain't got any," Baer said.

"Sit at that desk and read something," Mother said. "Here, read this."

"The Constitution? Again?"

She pointed.

Baer turned on a lamp with a green dome and a brass base, the only item in the house that suggested money. He opened the pamphlet to "We the People."

Larry remained hunched with his hands at his groin, showing immense concentration.

The brothers sat at opposite sides of the room with a glass-topped coffee table between. A painting of no particular ocean hung on the wall above Baer. Mother returned to the kitchen and trussed a chicken.

Baer read until his eyes flitted ahead, skipping words, lines; his hands joined the revolt and flipped two pages at a time. Three. Behind, Larry mumbled and growled. Whimpered. Baer closed the pamphlet. Mother appeared.

"Where you think you're going?"

"Take a piss."

She grimaced.

"What?"

"You come right back."

He entered the bathroom and stood above the bowl. At the bottom of the water, colored the same yellow as the stained porcelain, lay a rubber. He flushed the toilet and urinated into clean water. Rinsed his hands and splashed water into his eyes. Came out wiping his hands on his pants—

The lamp was off.

Larry watched, mouth flat, eyes hollow. Baer returned his glazed look and lifted the cord from the floor below the outlet.

"Thought you was supposed to be the grown-up," Baer said. "Asshole."

He shoved the plug into the socket—thinking as he did that the cord felt shaved to bare copper.

Electric flashed through him. He crashed backward on the coffee table; the thick glass held but the legs collapsed. He quivered on the floor, eyes open, unseeing. His lungs shook and his heart rippled. He was aware, detached.

A dormant cluster of cells awoke deep within a corner of his mind.

Mother beat his chest with paired fists.

Baer batted her arms. "Ma!" he choked. "You're going to kill me!"

She rocked back and sat on her legs, skirt crumpled above her knees. He saw rug burns.

"Oh baby," Mother said. She took his hand.

Electricity trickled through him as if from the room, like he was an antenna.

She got to her feet and stalked to the lamp. Lifted the unplugged cord at the base, hand over hand like a rope. She studied the burned plug where it met the cord.

"It's been whittled down," she said.

Baer watched her eyes fall on him, then shift to Larry.

Baer felt the shock again, strong.

"I didn't do it," Larry said. His eyes pulsed red. He collapsed. "My balls are like lemons."

Mother drove her sons to the hospital. They watched Baer a few hours and released him.

First time I saw the red light in a fella's eyes was after Larry tried to electrocute me.

The glow wasn't particularly strong, but my sense of it was. Whether I get the electric first or the red depends on if I'm standing next to the liar, or can't see his eyes.

That's all I know about my curse, except it started when I beat Larry's ass and he tried to murder me for it. After that it was hard to trust folks when I could see they was all the time deceiving.

S'pose I'm like a rat. Every time I try to cross the cage they shock the shit out of me.

The curse wanes with age and drink. Sometimes I think it's gone on account of me not seeing anybody for a week, and then someone shows up for likker and I know I still got it.

Everybody lies, and I see every one.

FOUR

Cory Smylie slugged a can of Coors and tossed the empty behind the seat of his F-150. He'd had speed for breakfast and was deep into the rush. It was time to moderate things.

He lifted a .30-06 from the window rack. He'd followed an old logging trail a quarter mile off the road and parked in an overgrown thicket of blackberry brambles. He locked the truck; a leather gym bag below the seat stored items he didn't want found.

Stipe had given him this task and though Cory hadn't been looking for work, it aggravated a part of him that he innately wanted aggravated. The thought appealed like the sting of pulling off a scab. Stipe had intimated that this next assignment would do far more than elevate him in Stipe's esteem.

It would make him feel like a man.

Cory placed his hand in his pocket and felt the folded piece of paper Stipe had given him. "Get his attention, and make sure he finds it."

Stipe had said his dogs weren't natural-born killers. They only developed into brutes through the patient application of training, conditioning. Nurturing. A man was no different. You take this task and help me solve a problem, your nuts'll swell into cannonballs and you'll walk with an honest swagger, not this pimp-punk-bitch thing you got now.

Cory had hunted these woods years ago after his father bought him a rifle and four-wheeler at the age of fourteen. He'd been up and down these trails and knew where he was going.

At fourteen it was difficult to score alcohol, especially as the son of the police chief. Cory had heard of a man who lived in the woods and distilled hooch. He'd stalked the man with binoculars and ingratiated himself with the man's niece. He'd even approached his camp while the surly bastard was absent—only to be stopped cold by a bristling brindle pit bull.

That was years ago, but Cory Smylie was not one to forget being thwarted.

He used the rifle barrel to forge a path through a ten-foot barrier of leafless briars, then set off at a brisk pace. The woods had changed in the intervening years; trees had grown, some had died. A giant stump that had been rotted in the center was now a jagged pillar on one side, with the rest crumbled. He came to a flat rock that sloped downward, eventually coming to a steep drop-off.

He could take a prone shooting position at the edge, but if he engaged Creighton from the top of the rock, Creighton would never find Stipe's note.

Cory stopped and thought. If Creighton was a thorn in Stipe's side, how much more appreciative would he be if Cory took matters into his own hands? Maybe stepped a foot or two off the reservation? Cory had seen Stipe's altercation with Creighton. He'd heard the threat. In giving Cory his instructions, hadn't Stipe almost implied that Cory would be that awful sledgehammer?

Nodding, Cory slung his rifle and urinated over the edge of the rock. Hell yeah. He'd do it.

It would be a military operation, like a video game. The crag below where he stood sported a cave-like recess. He'd observed Creighton from there years before while awaiting an opportunity to steal moonshine. When he'd crept to Creighton's still and been warned off by the dog, he'd chanced a look back to where he'd been hiding. It was an open firing lane, and even at high noon shadows masked the cave. It was a perfect blind.

Cory circled to the back of the rock and followed the terrain lower around the face. A well-worn trail cut below the rock and led up a steep incline to the dark cavern. Cory grabbed a rope hanging from the ledge and pulled himself up. He hesitated at the opening. The cave was only ten feet deep, but who knew what strange animals the pervasive shadows hid? A bobcat? A bear? He unslung his rifle and pointed into the depths while his eyes adjusted. In a moment he saw ancient fissures. Bones from a small animal. A crumpled Schlitz can—a relic of the famous Schlitz Indians.

He sat on a rock positioned behind two boulders that blocked most of the cave's opening. The place felt contrived, as if nature couldn't have deposited these rocks in such a convenient position. Creighton had probably done all this so he could hunt deer without walking very far. It would be funny if he ended up getting shot from his own blind. There was a word for that. I—yeah, it'd be funny as hell.

Cory leaned against the boulders, placed the rifle barrel in the V-shaped slot formed where they met and sighted through the scope. Two hundred yards away, half of Creighton's camp was exposed. Creighton sat on a log beside a fire. No way he'd expect to be hit so soon. It was only morning. Seven o'clock. Shit.

He was going to kill a man. He'd thought about it—who doesn't think about killing men? Right? You see the dogs go at it and you have to wonder what it'd be like to cross the line. To really do it. Because there's no looking back—if you kill someone you can't bullshit an apology. You have to know beforehand that every angle's covered. There can be no mistakes. You can't get caught because you can't flash your dimples at a judge.

Would he really do it? His heart thudded and he realized he was pulling the trigger already, without aiming, without taking the safety off. Damn... was it loaded? Yeah. This was the real shit. Cool down. Smoke another joint. It helps your reflexes.

Yeah.

He fished a baggie and a book of cigarette papers from his front pocket. He leaned the rifle on the rock and, with dexterity born more of experience than sobriety, expertly pinched mariju-ana into the paper and rolled it. Shit yeah, he was going to kill a man. Fuckin' A.

He could shoot. Lord, how he could shoot. When he was four-teen his father took him to the range and couldn't believe the tar-gets he was hitting. From fifty yards there wasn't a ten-inch bulls-eye he couldn't nail every time. Then his senior year he'd returned to the range with his buddies and refined his skill. He was a sniper.

Cory lit the joint. Sucked in the smoke and held it in his lungs until the burn felt good. In a moment, normalcy. He was cool. Creighton was just a man. He could kill a man.

Last night could've spoiled a lot of work.

Joe Stipe was none too happy seeing me; those fights is by invitation. Lou Buzzard had a couple my jugs with him and maybe Stipe had enough he wasn't thinking too clear. Don't take much. But I get the feeling Stipe won't let my challenge go unanswered.

I got a little fire on and coffee percolating. Me and Fred split a few eggs. Been two week since I hauled him home. He's timid crawling out of bed and when he does he's slow poking his way about. Both his eyes is scabs.

I keep him up to date but he's reluctant to talk and his speech got an edge. He sniffs around the crate, crawls back inside and licks his jowls. Finally he cants his head and while I look at his eyes he says, What are you doing about it?

I'd like to say something stronger than "My wheels is turning."

Fred perks up, jabs his nose high in the air.

"What you smell?"

Don't know.

"Well, I'm a little on edge. You holler if you whiff something funny."

My still sits in a little hemlock cathedral, the lowest limbs thirty feet up. A couple black cherry nose through but nothing else got the gumption. Hemlock keeps the air fresh, and when a breeze comes through and wipes away the mash barrel smell, they ain't a place on the planet smells cleaner. These trees sway with the wind and it ain't uncommon for a bad storm to blow one over. Six year ago I sat under the tarp thrilling in the belly of a tornado's baby brother. Wind boomed like thunder. Thunder sounded like God. This hemlock a hundred yards off let out a yell. Roots popped out the ground and the whole thing pitched over. But hemlock grows thick and other trees caught it. To this day it grows at a sixty-degree slant, its limbs tangled in the arms of five other.

I climbed to the canopy and it was another world. Birds you never see up close. I looked down and them green pine needles looked soft as pillows. A breeze got everything swaying. All of a sudden the whole damn thing was ready to come down and jumping at them pillows seemed credible agin riding a sixty-foot hemlock to the ground. Hell of a spooky place.

More so drunk.

I'd like it much if none of this shit with Fred ever happened. I don't want to be a five-year-old pointing my finger saying, "He started it." If they's a fight, let's not stand around with our thumbs up our asses.

But what's the Good Book say about being slow to anger? Ain't that a virtue?

Most times I sit on a stump next the fire. Water gurgles over rocks at the brook; wind rustles leaves. One time when the humidity was thick as week-old cream I sat so long I saw a mushroom grow. It's best when all the woods works to keep me occupied—a red squirrel chatters, the wind blows, a pinecone drops, a sparrow darts limb to limb, a moth lands on a stump and his wings don't match—that'll take a good ten minute to adequately marvel…

A leaf pops up off the ground.

I no more than wrinkle my brow and I hear a rifle report, must be two hundred yard off. I spin around on my log and peer between trunks.

Some fool hunter wandered in on my posted land—though I got a sign up every ten feet the whole damn way around. That, or Stipe's boys is making war. Either way I'll set somebody straight. Way the ground lays, all wavy and such, they ain't but a single place a hunter could sit two hundred yard off and reach me through all the trees.

They's a rock overhang with a pair of boulders in front makes it look like a Hun machine gun nest. From the still site it's a narrow aperture—some freak phenomenon lined the trees right—so I can see it when I stand just so.

I don't see anybody up there, but I wouldn't. It's a natural blind. I set off to my left, make a wide circle up there and

Crack!

I dive to dirt. Two shots ain't accident. I look back at the tarp, confirm they's hemlock between Fred and the Hun blind. Fred's safe.

"You stay where you're at, Fred. I'll sort this out."

Fred says, This about last night?

"That's the question."

I'm just saying, Fred says. That sounds like a sniper to me.

I crawl to tree cover and then run. One more shot rings out and the bullet sings like it bounced off a rock. I'm moving fast as old beat legs and hips can carry me. I slow when I wheeze. Pull out Smith and rotate the cylinder. Keep it pointed ahead.

Shit, I'm not playing games—I'm going straight in.

At fifty yards from the Hun blind, things get exposed. They must be a hundred firing lanes. I hunker behind a tree and catch my breath. Rethink. I'm royal torqued, getting sniped at in my own woods, but I get myself killed on account of being angry-stupid, old Fred'll starve to death.

I breathe slow 'til my anger settles.

When I can't make out the rocks of the Hun blind between the trees I continue the circle I started on. Seventy-eighty yards farther, I'm partly behind him. But it's been minutes and minutes since he last fired. He saw me take off through the woods—only a fool'd get pinned in a blind. He's prob'ly slipped away and got me in his scope right now.

I squat and look out between the tree trunks far as I can see, and scan leftward from the Hun blind. He's behind one of them trees. He's got a rifle barrel pointed and enough of his head sticking out to line his eye behind the sights. If I could only see him. I cover the whole swath and back again 'til my eyes stop at the blind. I got no electric. No red. He's maybe lit out, but hell I don't know.

Maybe he didn't take off.

Maybe it was coincidence, a hunter popping shots off at a running squirrel and me running behind thinking it's me getting aimed at. That would make sense—except it's stupid.

I slip from tree to tree, closer and closer to the Hun blind. Twenty feet out, I pause. Peek from behind the rough bark of an oak. My heart thuds and neck sweat chills me.

The overhang sits upslope and the last ten feet is steep. I got a rope tied off to a tree trunk on top, hangs down to the trail. The blind is two rocks and it's the fissure between that makes a perfect place to poke a rifle. Got the overhang casting everything in a deep ugly shadow, trapping your scent from any animal wanders by. If I shoot inside the blind I'll have to hit a one-inch gap, or maybe ricochet lead from the rock ceiling and hope it keeps him low while I charge.

"Come on out! 'Fore I come in and get you!"

Silence.

I point Smith in the air. I fire.

I look out through the forest again and wonder if he's already gone. Maybe shoot me in the back as soon as I get to the rocks? I feel like I got sights on me right now but I don't know where or which way from. I take slow aim at the overhang slope so my lead'll ricochet inside.

I fire.

And run. I'm low. Boots thudding. Smith firing. I shoot the ceiling once, twice. Each discharge sparks and smokes and zings like a Yosemite Sam gunshow. I point at the crack between the rocks and fire again. Got one shot left. I charge up the final slope. Don't even grab the rope—I just scramble my winded ass forward. At the last second I dodge left to right. Swing my gun arm inside. I follow, ready to plant my last bullet in some sniper or die from his.

Smells like dope up here.

Cavern's empty save a piece of paper on a log seat and three shell casings. I pick em up. .Thirty-aught-six. That ain't a hello gun. That's a fuck you gun.

I swipe the paper. Sit on the log and look a clean line to my still site. This has to be where the shooter drew his bead. I catch my breath a minute. Pull out a flask that's been flapping in my ass pocket and take a long, steadying pull. I feel the paper in my fingers but my eyes point out there… wonder if I'm the sitting duck now.

I unfold the paper.

It's easy to kill a man who lives in the woods.

Of course he didn't sign the damn thing.

I damn near got steam coming out my eyes. I stew a minute. Sure, you sit this far from my camp and you got the patience, you can take me out. But it won't be as easy up close. Fred'll catch your scent, or I'll see you, day or night. No. You want to visit again, you'll come right back here to the Hun blind.

I'll have something for you.

I stand outside the blind, looking in. Looking above. Slope of the rock give me an idea. The nearby trees—a four-inch birch not thirty feet off—give me another.

I'm back after twenty-five minute. I got a hundred feet of barbed wire from the fenced-off plot behind Farmer Brown's. I got my ax, thirty feet of rope and a twenty-pound burlap sack full of pissed off.

Somebody want to send me a message?

Come on back for my answer.

First off I climb around the crag to the top where I got the rope. It's a steep angle and slippy. I find a boulder the size of a carving pumpkin. I cradle it between my knees and scoot across the top, and leave it where the rock is flat.

Next I gather smaller rocks—about fifty. Scavenge all over and finally pull most out the crick. I want em round and smooth. I make the bottom of my shirt a bucket and fill it. Five trips. Finally, I ax an eight-inch piece of maple, each end at a harsh cant.

Years ago I hung a rope over the ledge to help me get up the trail. It's tied to a tree on top. I scout a faint bowl in the nearby surface and set my pumpkin rock there and prop it in place with the eight-inch maple. Wary, I stand back a pace. That'll work. I carry the smaller rocks by twos and stack em against the upslope side of the pumpkin 'til it's the only thing holding back an avalanche. I cut the rope hanging over the ledge, weave it under the maple strut and tie it off. And careful as all hell, lower the rope back over the ledge.

Let it go, asshole. It's easy to kill a man who lives in the woods.

It's easy to kill one visiting, too.

Next, the barbed wire. I study my resources. Birch tree. Rope. Wire. Plenty of sticks and rocks. A hemlock right close to the trail.

I head back to the homestead, pass the house and stop at the shed. Grab an auger with a one-inch bit.

At the Hun blind I drill three holes into the side of the hemlock closest the crag. Chop a six-foot branch from a distant hemlock and whittle three pegs so they'll stick four inches proud of the tree, and one more peg that'll act like a trigger. One more for a stake.

With the back of my ax-head I drive the stake into the ground about twenty feet from the birch tree. Loop the rope over it and jam the other end between my belt and britches. I climb the birch hand over hand 'til the tree bends, then kick out my feet and let my weight bow the tree to the ground. I tie off the rope.

The tree fixed, I loop one end of the barbed wire around the top and arm the trigger, pulling taut as I can. The hemlock branch goes across the trail so anybody wants access to the Hun blind has to push it aside. That'll pop the trigger and release the bowed birch. I string the rest of the wire across the trail.

Anybody pushes that branch aside'll get castrated with rusted barbed wire. Then he'll pull the rope for support and get buried in rocks.

Let it go, asshole. It's easy to kill a man who lives in the woods.

Yeah? Well it's easy to maim a dumbass wants to snipe at a man in his home.

FIVE

They's times Ruth flirts at the edges of my thoughts and they's only two ways to drive her off. I write her a letter, or drown her in shine.

After seeing Larry last night and getting shot at today my distrust of mankind's all but confirmed and I got to mope on Ruth. Can't sit in the woods and hope a conspiracy of squirrels and butterflies'll hold disgust at bay.

I keep a notepad in a plastic box under the tarp, and a pen right next.

Ruth—

I don't call you Dear no more. But we been over that, so I don't got to say it again. I thought maybe I hadn't told you in such a long time why I write that I oughta refresh you, and maybe that way you'll get the fuck out my head for just a little while.

Fred is better than he was at least. Still don't like to move around, but he eats and he shits and that's two-thirds what a dog is for.

You know I can tell a liar. Well, I remember sitting with you and thinking you was the only person in the world who told the truth. Even after a little likker!

Aw hell. This don't work so good—knowing you won't ever say anything back. You know where I live. You come here, just honk the horn.

Baer

I tear the love note from the pad, fold it, tuck it in my pocket. Got to swing by the house later anyway, so may as well put it with the rest 'til I mail em. Only thing I go in there for is storing letters and likker and patching up Fred. House has history.

I wrote in the letter that she told the truth because I never called her out on the giant lie she told that set me on this path, and her on hers, and Larry his. It's ridiculous how we pretend, can't get along honest because little things pop up. Pride. Shame.

Ruth and me scrogged enough to make a jackrabbit blush, and didn't talk about much else. We was young. By the time she told me her lie, I'd been set thinking she was the only one in the world who'd never flash red or give me sparks. And so these last thirty years has been all about disbelief. If I ever let the truth about her lie take hold, they's no way avoiding the absolute fact that everybody—everybody—is a damned liar.

Druther stoke an imaginary love affair.

I stow the pen and look through the trees, and back at Fred. He's no more interested in what's going on than I am, and I spend a minute shaking Ruth loose from my head. They's one thing that works even better'n writing letters.

Looking at Fred.

Poor bastard still ain't right. His eyes is black crust and flies land on em 'til he starts twitching and grinding his head on the ground. The rip across his chest—I sewed it shut that first night at the house, and I keep it pretty well likkered. He breathes better now, but I believe his windpipe is still half-crushed because he'll wheeze after no more effort than licking his sac. Fred's ornery like that hound the two old-timers was looking at. They watch the dog lick his nuts and one says, "Boy I wish I could do that," and the other says, "I doubt he'd much care for it."

Fair to say I look at Fred and I don't think on Ruth.

Three blasts from a car horn filter through the trees and arrive at the still without a note of urgency. Someone's waiting on the likkerman. Sounds like Pete.

I check the Smith on my hip and gander off through the woods before getting off my stump. I sit real quiet. If they's a sniper out there, getting ready to move, I want to see him.

I shoulda fixed a whistle to that birch tree, or a string-pull fire-cracker so I wouldn't all the time be wondering if it went off.

Come on the house from behind, enter through the basement. Up the stairs, through the front door like I'd been inside napping. A Ford with half the front fender rusted off sits in the drive. The bed's intact and this's Pete Bleau. He'll be after a dozen jugs so I carry four on the first trip. He sits behind the wheel in a cloud of stogie smoke, and rolls down his window. He's so fat if he was an inch taller he'd be round. I hold up the jugs. He nods. I rest em in the straw lining the truck bed. Nestle em down separate like they was nitro.

"The usual," he says.

I bring four at a time, and snug em in. Finally I stand beside his window and he shells a handful of bills from a wallet looks like he pulled it from a shipwrecked corpse.

Bleau's quiet a minute and his eyes glow red. "Henderson says you been cutting your likker."

"Henderson's fulla shit. Tell him I said so."

"I know he's fulla shit, but his shot house moves half this likker. He's put the pressure on my price. Told him I'd ask if we could come down a notch."

"You tell him if he's cutting my shine he better not sell it with my name. Any more talk on the subject, I'll raise the price. Fuck him. Fuck you too."

I snatch the bills from Pete's hand and static pops through me. I tuck the money in my pocket, and studying the red hue in his eyes, think to pull the green out and count it.

"All there," he says. "Don't trust me no more?"

I hope they's a dollar or two missing because that'd account for the red and the juice. I hate to know they's deceit and not dig it up. But the count comes out. So it's something funny about him and Henderson. Or who knows what. That's the point I hate, not knowing.

"Henderson says I cut my squeezins?"

"Uh-huh."

"Henderson says?"

"He kind of danced around it."

The hair on my arm stands. "He said me or you, one, cut it? That it?"

"What you saying, exactly?"

"I always trusted you because thieving's work and you's too damn lazy for it. But I was wrong. Shaving a little off the top each jug gives you what? An extra gallon? Two?"

"Hold on 'fore you say something you'll regret. If you ain't already."

"More'n that, huh? Three? That it?"

"Come on. Easy now."

"So you fuck him out of hundred-sixty proof, and got the gall to come jew me down on account a lying to him. I never see such optimism. But it don't make sense, you and me to keep working together, Pete."

"Hell, Baer. Don't be so damn uptight. This is a misunderstanding is all."

"Don't think so."

Pete drags on his cigar and the cherry burns hot. He exhales. Smiles. "Yeah, I cut it. Shit."

"Now you're saying you cut it."

"Shit yeah I cut it, but I won't no more. You got me. You got some wiles, is what. I dunno. But they ain't no reason we can't have a new understanding."

"Like 'fore we had this conversation, we both understood you'd cut my likker and kick my name in the dirt?"

"That's awful strong. I got the wife to feed."

"It'd be a favor, make her miss a meal." I step to the truck. Drop my hand at the open window, a few inches shy of Pete. Stare into his eyes. "You saying you won't ever cut my likker?"

"Scout's honor."

I wait. Pete sweats, but his eyes ain't red no more. "Guess I'll see you end of the week."

Pete sighs. Nods. "You're a good man, Baer. And we understand each other now."

If I didn't work with liars and cheats, I wouldn't have work. I slap the Ford's roof and back away.

It's four mile to Gleason—or two flask.

Road to Gleason—they's places more eye-pleasing than others. The bridge over the crick—the spill tube shoots water fast and heavy, and years of current's opened a hole where trout grow the size of pond bass. They hang back in the shadows and watch. Wily, far as fish go. Rest the road's just a place for cars to cut across a field or forest. On the left, most the way, is corn or wheat. Starts with Brown's land. Craddock tills it, then goes on and tills his own land too. Mile and a half later is Werner's land, then Sinkey's. On the right they's woods all the way except a quarter-mile stretch of cow pasture belongs to Sidell.

I'm in the post office. Slap six singles on the counter. Harry takes the letters I saved for Ruth. Seems dishonest to put more'n one to an envelope, and I speculate she keeps em separate, each with its own postmark, so she can find the one she's looking for easy. I write the date by the return address, case it helps her.

Harry holds the stack edgewise, raps em on the counter, tosses em in a bin.

"How long 'til they get there?" I say.

He grins, and says the same words as the last hundred times. "Couple day. Only going Mars Hill."

"Right." I push my stack of singles to him. He rings me out and drops the change in the jar for the three-year-old angel named Susan Wilkes, got the leukemia.

I nod.

"See you in a couple," Harry says.

The Second National Bank's across the street and down Main a few block. I watch the sidewalk and brood on them letters, and how they's prob'ly four five I'd rewrite different. All these years I must've spent two thousand dollars on stamps. It's no differ-ent'n being in the woods and saying "hello" to yourself, and say-ing "why, hello, how are you" right back. Ain't nobody in the whole woods, and the trees don't care. Them squirrel bark no mat-ter what you say or do. Sending letters to Ruth is like that and I write things maybe I wouldn't say at all if I knew she might ever write word one back.

Wonder if I'm writing letters to someone else—

I step into a man who don't move.

Joe Stipe.

"Stipe—"

"Didn't see you, Baer."

"Had my eyes on my feet."

"Glad I run into you. Wanted to talk about our misunderstanding last night, and it's just providential you're here, and I run into you just now."

"Yeah. Something I might ask you, too."

He lands his hand on my shoulder. Stipe's the size of three mules' asses and about as slow. His arm weighs like a bucket of lard and he leans as he talks. I got my eyes on his free hand.

"Let's sit a minute," Stipe says. "What are you looking at?"

"That awful sledgehammer you promised, I guess."

Stipe pulls me to a bench and the three lugnuts he was jawing with hold back like our privacy was ordained. I'm thinking this is the bastard behind the bullets and the note but I got to play it cool.

"You come on us kind of sudden, in the woods," Stipe says.

"Well—"

"We're an exclusive group, you know, with the dogs… "

"Picked up on that when you said you'd burn me down. Something change?"

"No, that threat's good as gold."

I twist the cap on my second flask and his eyes follow. I offer the shine and he pours it down his gullet; stops the flow with his tongue. He hands the flask back and I gurgle some.

"Lou Buzzard buys from you," Stipe says.

I watch his face. They's no juice running through me—he ain't said nothing but fact.

"I talked to Lou," Stipe says, "and he vouched for you. You got to come spend some time with your brothers-at-arms. Gimme another hit of that." He takes the flask from my hand. "You got to come out with the boys, else I won't be comfortable the way things sit."

"Your comfort's real important to me."

"I want you there, and maybe you oughta fetch a jug o' that shine."

He gulps a half-hour drunk from my flask, takes the cap from my hand and screws it. I nod, but I don't feel it. "Maybe next time Lou stops by, he can let me know when y'all are getting together."

"No need. Every week, same night. You know the place."

"I—uh."

I ain't good at untruth. Ever since I first got the shocks, I'd kife a cookie or raid Gramma's garden and sense I was sending electric all over the place, and had red flames shooting out my eyes. Everyone'd know I was fulla shit. So I was the dumbass fessed every crush to every girl. I was the one told Deputy White we all knew he was gay as a jaybird. I was the one told my first boss his son was robbing him blind. It never settled in my head that no one else in the whole world sees red and feels electric like me, and most folks is happy with untruth, both telling and hearing.

"What's on your mind, Creighton?"

"I don't know about going to them fights."

"That ain't what I wanted to hear."

"I didn't want to say it."

"Sunday next. Bring one o' them jugs. Bring two." Stipe braces his hands on his knees and rocks forward, wobbles. "That's good shit. Gimme another slug o' that."

I hand him the flask. He empties it.

"You know, Stipe, I got a dog named Fred. White pit bull."

"Bring him." He passes the flask to me.

I glance back at his friends.

"Someone already brung him. Telling the truth right now, I'm liable to bust your party, if I come."

Stipe smiles like he's got his grandbaby in his arms. The fucker's got secondary dimples, his cheeks is so fat—but his eyes got dirty mischief like a boy pulling wings off'n flies or sticking firecrackers up a bullfrog's ass. He says, "Next I run into you, it won't be friendly like the middle of town." His cheek twitches but his smile holds. "I'm giving you a chance, but looks like if there's a pile of shit on the floor, you'll walk a country mile to step in it."

"Which one your boys fought my dog?"

"White pit? Star on his chest?" He winks. "I never seen that dog."

SIX

Thought I could've kept myself pertineer sloshed, but Stipe stole my slosh and I'm exercising in the sun with no likker protection.

Stipe's one of a handful of organizers this half the state. He arranges fights, makes book, and guards the sport. Dogmen take it serious as hell. Talk about dead dogs soldiering on in Valhalla.

I heard about him years back—rumors and lies—but he kept his fight business on the other side of town in a swampy draw nobody'd ever wander into without a gun to his head. Seeing that truck come out the woods and drop Fred cued me to his new location, and from the sight of it, new ain't the word.

Been out the loop on those sorts a goings-on.

Running fights every week is only part of Stipe's living. He got his fat hands on every form of commerce in the county, but the bulk of his dough comes from the trucking company. His fleet hauls from here to every city or crossroad-and-church in three states. He don't get the big warehouse business, as they keep they own fleets, but every small company needs connected to the world, Stipe's the connection. One of his drivers runs to Cincinnati and stays fresh on my shine, so I know a little about Stipe.

It's six, eight mile from my operation to Stipe's complex. Truck company sits cattycorner his house on a fifty-acre plot. The quarters sits back, and way off the side is a barn turned mechanic's garage. They work on his semi trucks, and more trucks is parked in rows on a cement pad. All that, surrounded by wood and hills.

He keeps a few lugnuts at his side most the time; these boys do to men what Stipe's dogs do to each other. They's bruisers, wandering around here, somewhere. Maybe one of em was shooting at me from the Hun blind.

Stipe's white GMC pickup sits beside the trailer he uses for an office.

Man could sit in one of these trees and plink bullets on that complex all hour, and the men coming up on him wouldn't have a lick of cover. Man knew how to shoot a rifle'd cause all sorts of hell. But this thing burning in me ain't about getting wicked on men guilty other shit. May as well find an old lady and slap her silly, the moral's the same. Got to keep retribution correlated with the evil deserves it. They's got to be accountability, but more on the part of the man setting things right. I got a rifle with a scope, and an eye that'd drill a piece of lead through a man's ear at a hundred yards if I was sober, but I don't want to wind up in hell over it, and sober just ain't likely. So I brought Smith and a pair of binoculars.

I'm just here to reconnoiter. Last thing I want's more trouble before I'm ready for it.

Don't know what I thought I'd see. I watch through the field glasses and not a lot goes on. Stipe's truck is white and looks brand new. I went back to Brown's looking for clues the day after

I found Fred, and found oil'd brushed off the truck's undercarriage. Stipe's trucks don't likely leak oil—not when the man's got mechanics on the payroll.

I'd like it if it was Stipe that stole Fred because I like him about the same as ass rot. But that ain't the truck I saw. So I wonder how much strictly honorable hell I can park on this man's porch. Sure he's evil, but unless he gave the order to steal Fred he's a secondary target.

A man crosses the lot from the trailer office and drives a rig to the barn. Nothing happens for a while, and I dwell on other things.

Stipe did say he'd burn me down.

I'll burn him down. That's his kennels, off the side his house, way in back. Lined up two-high, got his animals in wire cages where they prob'ly walk in they own shit. They must be ten brutes in there licking wounds, commiserating. Waiting somebody to do the right thing.

Cut em some slack.

Fella comes out the garage and looks this way. Pull your thumb out your yin-yang and get to work. Stipe don't pay his boys to think. I adjust the binoculars and zoom in close. He ain't shaved—prob'ly on account the mole on his chin. I had a mole like that, I'd cut it off. He turns and looks left, then right, across the field. Waves at somebody.

I gander rightward and they's a man on the run, got a rifle. He vectors toward the wood's edge. I zip back to the left, way, way over. Another man's running with another gun.

Crack!

Wood bark stings my cheek. I drop the binoculars. Mechanic's on one knee, taking aim for another shot. I duck and his rifle flashes again. I let go the tree and all of a sudden my shoulder's got a sting like a nest of hornets picked one spot and dive-bombed it. Bounce off limbs and hit the ground. Knee smashes into my binoculars. Good shit, I can't walk. I stretch along the ground sideways, extend my leg. Something pops and I think it'll hold. Don't make sense, them starting a skirmish right after I run into Stipe—unless he left instructions to kill me on sight, and didn't have the brass to do it himself in town. Prick.

Noise in the brush off both flanks. Mechanic pops off another shot, and another. Walking bullets down the tree. Pin me down.

Dry leaves sound like thunder. I wriggle. They's brush cover and these boys won't see me 'til they's on me, sure as shit. But they ain't stupid. They hunt buck, put on drives, sweep the woods and funnel animals so they got to run a gauntlet.

I'm game.

The crunching closes in, both side.

Maybe fifteen feet of brush and trees between me and the field that leads to the mechanic. Big old rhododendron thickets. I crawl best I can, not dragging leaves or making trail. Don't let my shoulder leave a blood mark.

C'mon, you ragged-assed knee! They's coming quick.

Rhododendron grows tight and low. I lead with my left shoulder so the leaves don't drag on the right. Either way they's noise. I bust through. Trunk's only four-inch thick. I hide like a fat boy behind a flagpole.

Pull Smith and wait.

Sounds on the left stop. On the right they come closer. That's right. You fellas shoot each other, and I won't have to.

"He split!"

"Bullshit. I'd have heard him."

"Well, he ain't here."

"Go in and see."

Rifle clicks. I hunker down and a shot cuts leaves above my head.

"Wait! Don't he carry a piece?"

They keep jawing. Don't sound like Stipe's lugnuts at all. They must yet be in town. These boys is damn near comical. Come dark I'll bust out of here with six-inch flames out the Smith tube. They want to dance by God we'll shake it up.

Another shot from the mechanic's barn.

"Hey, Norm? Norm! What the hell you doing?"

"Well, you go in if you want. I'm loyal, but I'm a damn truck driver. I ain't about getting shot."

They's quiet. Whispers. I get electric all through me.

"I guess we'll just go on home, now. Nothing left to do here."

"Yeah, he sure got away real good."

Footsteps on leaves, first one, then the other.

They make sounds with they boots—hell, I can see one by his pant legs. He's tramping up and down, quieter each time. Kind of grabs my cool by the balls. I brace Smith agin the rhododendron trunk and sight on the edge of his pants. Shot'll cut a groove but won't cripple him. The fella on the right stands still, waiting on me to come out I guess. I'll test his conviction.

I squeeze. Slow. Don't pull the trigger—with a pistol you can't even think about breathing, or the shot'll—

Crack! Smith jumps in my hand and dipshit's dancing.

"Shit! Shoot him! He shot me! Shoot him!"

I hit the ground and crawl. Bullets smack branches and leaves. Splinters in my back. Movin-movin! I spy a depression maybe six-inch deep and half as big as me—I slide the good parts in and leave my legs up and out.

Now they's two guns firing. Dirt kicks in my face. Finally one stops, then the other. Hear a lever-action rifle go click twice.

I come out the brush. Gun in the air, steady silver in the shot man's face.

"Howdy."

He holds his rifle sideways, lever open. Empty breech thirsty for one bullet. I gander at the fella on my left, got his rifle trained on me. Eyes got a tinge but I want some electric.

He says, "I got one left, asshole."

"If you did I'd say you better make it count. But I think you's fulla shit." I swing Smith. "Let's trade off and see who's left standing."

He drags his front foot back an inch. I pull the hammer.

He pulls his hammer.

Got electric up and down my arms. Nape of my neck.

"This son of a bitch shot me! Shoot him, Reed!"

"Nah—Reed? That it? Reed? Like blows in the wind, this way and that? Like a pussy willow—that kind of reed? Pull that trigger for me, Reed."

"I will, you keep jawing."

"I don't think so. Take Hopalong with you back to the garage, and when your master gets home, you tell him Baer Creighton was along, and brought his bullets."

He glances sideways. Shot man's got his hands wrapped around his leg and blood soaks his pant. Reed lowers his rifle.

Awkward. You got a gun on a man, it's hard to put it down.

"I didn't come to shoot you." I wave Reed over to the other. "I was sitting in that tree minding Stipe's business, and you boys come out raising hell. More I think, more it torques my ass. Move out 'fore things get ugly."

Reed takes the other fella's shoulder, and keeping an eye on me, they forge through undergrowth.

Wonder where that fella at the garage is.

Well, he ain't behind me—they ain't been noise. Them other two bust through the brush, and with them in the field, it's all quiet. I could sit here by the tree trunk and wait on em to come back, but I got an itchy idea about them dogs in Stipe's crates.

Sun floats on the horizon like it won't ever dip under, but that's my pulse, my nerves.

I trek back the way I come. Get out this neck of woods where it wouldn't take but six men to flush me out for a turkey shoot. Headed east the forest opens up big, just woods and hills, on and on. Nothing safer. I got a half-mile between me and Stipe and my heart settles; got a comfortable sweat on my neck. Find a beech on a side hill with a view of the garage, way the hell off, and drop my haggard ass to the dirt. Lean back and probe the slice on top my shoulder from the mechanic's bullet.

Didn't lose much at all in that scrape.

Birds flutter and red squirrels bark orders at somebody. Not me. Eventually a hawk circles way the hell over the trees, floating down on a dying thermal. Getting shot don't feel too awful good, but the likker helps.

I reckon I won that skirmish. Yessir.

SEVEN

Wake with a chill rippling through my back and dark all around. Lights down the hill—Stipe's operation. Got the purple glow of security lights, and men working in the garage. Prob'ly keep guns handy.

I suspect a guard roams the premises. If it was my operation they would be, after a shootout. But the boys I met earlier didn't have any sense and I got the feeling if Stipe don't give the order, neither of these boys got the gumption to pick his nose.

I'll keep my eyes open. But either way they's dogs in that compound waiting on freedom.

From way off comes the sound of truck motors, that low rumble that lopes through the trees like a cold wind. Engine shuts off and the noise don't end so much as steal into shadows and black.

I got to shiver but not 'til I listen to the woods.

Just like them booby traps at the Hun nest: enemy sends a sniper to harangue you in your own damned house, you strike back. Once you got the advantage, you press him back on his heels.

If I cut them dogs loose, Stipe's cash flow takes the hit. He's got to be fighting some of his own animals every week. He wants new dogs, them cost money. And if I make him shut down his fight circle, maybe them cowards that bet money on his animals will start looking other ways to satisfy they habits. Fight chickens. They ain't got souls—not like dogs.

I get up a little giddy. Brain's like a razor. I'll slip down the hill, circle back of Stipe's joint, ease up on them sad-assed dogs. They's got to be itching for liberty. Hell, they want to come home with me, I'll feed em. Let Stipe wonder where they at, whether they's dead or wandering the hills with a chewed-off foot.

Creep along like they's people nearby, though I'd see they deceitful eyes in the dark.

I find the field a few hundred yards off where we had the showdown and head to the back of Stipe's complex.

The dogs is quiet. I come up slow. Wind picks up at my back and the dogs grumble. Pen's set off thirty yards from Stipe's house. Inside the window they's a chandelier set low. I bet Stipe's at the garage or the headquarters trailer between. I take a slosh out the flask to settle the stomach flutters.

"Hey puppydogs. You take it easy, now."

One snarls and another joins. Now the whole batch is pissed and snooting. Noses bang the chain link and teeth flash white in the purple glow. I glance back to the garage—sound of wrenches on concrete. No alarm.

Up close the pen I try and reason with a brute. "Hey you. Your name Killer, something? Easy now. I'm cutting you some slack, you hear?"

Put my hand flat on the mesh. He gnashes at it. I seen bucktoothed women could eat corn on the cob through a fence like this, but Killer can't pull it off. He gets to sniffing—maybe whiffs Fred—and his tongue wets my hand. Rest of the dogs growl. I poke a finger through the mesh and he licks it. All right. We at peace.

I pull the latch.

Killer pops out like his legs was coiled springs. Lands six feet off, spins. His back is bristled like a wire brush and a snarl pulls his lips back so his face is all teeth and eyes. Voice is low like that truck in the bay.

Well shit.

"Don't you go back on your word."

Other dog barks; now the whole crew's at it. Killer steps closer. Head's low, shoulders like a dozer blade ready to plow me flat. I pull Smith, though I damn sure don't want to use it.

Killer don't know what a gun'll do—he don't even blink. He takes another step and his voice pitches higher.

"Hey! That's a six-time champ, you son of a bitch!"

It's someone from the garage, standing with a tire tool in his hand. I skirt sideways along the kennel. Dogs bang the wire. Killer pivots. I get past him and turn. Killer launches. Knocks me agin the wire. Got my arm in a vise with nails. Shaking my bones even as he falls back to earth.

Don't go down, Baer. That's death for one of us. But Killer's heavy and I'm sporting a buzz. I drop to my knees and he rears hard and topples me to my back.

I'm fucked and I know it.

"Damn you! I thought we was cool."

We struggle.

Out the corner my eye I see that mechanic coming at me with a tool in the air. Killer's let go my arm and he's at my neck. Can't breath, and them teeth feel like knives.

He snarls. Eases a tiny bit and snaps a better hold on my throat. I get a breath and his mouth smells like mud and old cowshit. He's clamped tight again—if I don't get air quick, I'm Alpo. He shakes like to snap my neck. Lowers me and jerks back and I feel every bone in my spine pop. I open my mouth and can't speak. I got terror in my blood, shooting fast through me. Can't breathe!

I'm sorry Killer I'm truly sorry—

I shove Smith agin his head and pull the trigger.

Got blood all on me, and a dog letting out his last air, his last piss. I roll him off and wiggle to the side, get my feet under me. Feel my neck all slippy with dog drool and blood. Man with the wrench stands off twenty yards, stopped cold by the pistol shot. I cough. I bet that's Norm, tried to shoot me in the tree.

I point Smith. Step back. Another.

He drops the tire tool and lifts his hands head-high. I step back again.

Stipe's at the edge of his trailer, hand at his brow to cut the glare from one his security lights. The glow don't reach me, this far out.

"Lou," Stipe says. "What the hell's going on?"

"That's your boy Creighton out there. And that's Achilles by the crates. Shot."

"Shot? Creighton shot Achilles?"

"He's right there!"

Stipe raises his arm and orange explodes from his hand. He can't see me but he come close for guessing. He fires again, and again. He points one way, then another, random. Bullets smack the kennel. He's shooting his own dogs, the dumb shit.

That pistol sounds like a forty-five, big heavy bullets come by so slow you could almost run along beside em and have a conversation. But they's so heavy, one hits you, you're a chock block in front of a downhill freight train.

"I'm going to hunt you down, Creighton! I'm going to crush you!" He's walking toward me, into the darkness. Fires again and again. He pauses and I figure he's out of bullets, but in ten seconds he's firing again.

I'm backing away at a full clip. "Go to hell, Stipe. That's an eye for an eye."

I turn tail and ain't gone three steps before I see I opened up a whole new war. I killed Stipe's champ. Wonder what kind of hell I got coming now.

EIGHT

Bank's fulla assholes and I'm in no mood. Teller's a kid with lawn-mowed hair and Mount Rainier zits. He studies the scarf I wrapped over the bites on my neck. He collects his thoughts and prepares his pitch. He's one step removed from cashiering at McDonald's but thinks he knows all about the central bank and the history of money.

A year ago I was foolish enough to explain my gold strategy to a fella didn't give off any juice. Now every one of em smiles at me. But when it's all done I know my money's safe; whether they lock me up the rest of my life or not, nobody'll get they claws on my dough.

"It's good to see you again, Mister Creighton. We've got a new checking account you might be interested in—"

"Promise I'm not." And why don't you pop that cussed thing on your forehead?

"Why is that, Mister Creighton? Regular money not good enough for you? You know the price of gold keeps going down?

You keep pulling funds away from us, but how much are you losing by avoiding paper?"

"I wish you folks sold gold. You wouldn't be so damned afraid of it."

"We're not in the commodities business."

"Since Nixon dropped the gold standard, you ain't in the money business either."

I take all my cash but a few dollars—a hair shy of seventeen hundred.

With the fiat paper already in my pocket, I got eighteen hundred and forty-eight dollars. I head down the street nervous and suspicious of everyone I see, but nobody minds me. A couple turns and a couple blocks later I'm in Millany's Coin Collectory, a shop that feels academic and conspiratorial at the same time. Millany's got numismatic gems—coins pulled from a dozen shipwrecks, bullion from Africa and Canada, silver from all over. He's got collector guns, memorabilia from every army ever lost a war, and his walls is papered in Confederate bills and the equally debauched Union Greenback.

"Thought you was due," he says. "What'd you do to your neck?"

"I was sucking face with a rattlesnake and goosed her. I need out of some paper cash."

"I can help."

His's been the only place in town to buy gold since 1974.

"I got seventeen hundred." I take the stack of fiat paper from my pocket and rest it on the counter.

"Two maple leafs'll put you at sixteen fifty."

"Two it is."

"Surprised you ain't a seller at these numbers."

"Why's that? Trend's down."

"You been buying since, what? Buck ninety-five, thereabouts?"

"Gold's going to twenty thousand. People'll trade corn and wheat before they give up food for a stack of government paper. Mark my words."

"Not this genetically modified shit. They'll use cod in Boston and tobacco here." He exits to a back room and closes the door. He's gone a few minutes and I don't know if he's got to find his way down a few flights to a vault deep in the ground, or whether he sits behind the door a long time so no one thinks the real money's one wall away. He comes back and I've got a bayonet in my hands that was sitting on a cardboard box.

"Austrian," he says. "See the OEWG on the ricasso? Fits an 1895 Mannlicher. In the market?"

"Got all the edge tools I need."

He passes the coins. They gleam through plastic. He counts the stack of bills on the counter and stops at sixteen fifty, and passes the rest back.

"Pull a seat," he says. "How goes the country commerce?"

I stay standing. "I got a helluva walk."

"Suit yourself."

"Generally do."

I nod and he grins and that ends it. Got one more stop.

Mae's house sits on the low side of town. I cut a field by the pond and pick up the road. She lives in a weathered wood tinderbox with a door got a hole you could pitch a horseshoe through.

I knock. She don't answer right off. The kids inside yell like animals and for a second I think if she'd turn the television off for a year she'd have the money to move out. I rap the door again and hold back so I don't bust it. Then I push it open.

Bree stares at me. Her hair is like straw with winter frost; she smiles and rushes to me on feet ain't used to taking orders. Her sister Morgan comes from the other room and hollers, "Uncle Baaaaaaaar!" Joseph wails.

"Baer?"

"Yeah, honey?"

"Uncle Baer, that you?"

I lift Morgan in one arm and Bree in the other. Shoulder aches like shit. I got to steady myself before turning the corner. Mae looks so much like Ruth I can hardly stand to see her—got the same eyes and nose—they's a dimple on her nose you could almost fall into—and her cheeks is high. I used to tease Ruth she was part Cherokee, and Ruth always hushed me on account of her asshole father. Wouldn't do for a rich man of considerable social standing to 'fess Injun blood. Mae looks like her mother except her mouth, and the streak of hair she's dyed black so she looks like an inside-out skunk. Her mouth is all Creighton.

"What are you doing? Come in. Sit down." She lifts Joseph and smooches him 'til he giggles. "So cold you have to wear a scarf?"

"Started shaving sober and damn near cut off my head. So I quit."

"Quit drinking?"

"Shaving."

I carry Morgan and Bree and drop into a sofa built for people like to feel like they furniture's got emotions or something. Sink so low my eyes is level with my knees. The girls wriggle from my arms and start climbing me.

"So how's Fred?"

"He eats and shits, and that's two-thirds what a dog's for."

"What's the other third?"

"Conversation."

She smirks.

I say, "Anyway, I was in town."

"Buying more coins?"

Her face is all smile without a hint of red, and the only thing uncomfortable is the kids clawing my hair, and the couch that kind of mopes.

"I come in town for a little business is all."

"Stay for supper?" She mutes the television with a remote.

"Got supper in my back pocket." I take her in without letting my eyes wander up and down. She's wearing pink sweatpants with a hole in one knee, and a baseball jersey that don't hide her mams worth a damns. Flip-flop shoes and painted toenails. A crucifix on a choker.

Morgan has a fistful of my hair. She pulls 'til I look at her, and she meets my look with wide eyes and a wider grin, and the baby powder smell—and baby skin—is too much. She points. "Whiskers." I crane my neck and scratch her with my cheek. She giggles and Mae watches.

"Wanted to give you something."

"Oh, Uncle Baer, you don't—"

"I know it, and that's half why I do it." I pull an arm free from Bree and dredge fifty dollars from my pocket. I put it on the end table. "Hell, I don't need it."

Mae unfolds her legs, and with Joseph in one arm comes to me on the sofa and stoops and wraps her other arm around my neck. She smells like watermelon hard candy and when her soft arm is around my neck and her boobs press my shoulder and her hair is up in my face, I don't feel as easy as I might in the woods staring at a campfire.

She pulls back and they's water in her eyes. She smiles like they's good tears but she's fulla shit and she knows I know.

"Where's Cory?"

Her eyes roll. "We aren't together."

"He know, this time?"

"I told him not ten minutes ago. He just left, all pissed off."

"Did it take? Or you want me to tell him?"

"No. I'll handle Cory."

I try another direction. "So who's buying the food?"

She glances at the fifty dollars and back to me. "Food stamps."

"Where the hell's your grandpap? Rich old Preston Forsyth Jackass?"

"You know all about that."

She sits on the couch and the hug never happened.

"None of my business," I say.

"I don't even see him. It's been two years since I tried to visit the Baptist home. You know how he is."

I know how he is. Preston Forsyth Jackson, one of those sons a bitches with three names so blue he's got to use em all.

"I don't care," she says. "I'll make my fortune on my own. You have to let me tell you about my MBA program. The Jacksons can keep their money."

"Hell of a clan."

Bree snuggles agin my chest and makes a tiny fist around a fold in my shirt, and pulls the buttons.

"Cupboards full? You getting by?"

"We're getting by."

I look at the wall behind the television. They's a photo of my brother Larry and Ruth with baby Mae in her arms. The side of the paper is yellow from too much sun. I know when that shot was taken—a few months after I come home for my mother's funeral and my girl met me at the door holding baby Mae. By then Ruth's daddy—the honorable Preston Forsyth Jackson—had booted her out and ran an ad in the paper: this soupcan of dog shit ran an ad in the paper saying the whore known as Ruth Jackson wasn't his daughter. His wife made him pay for another ad the next day retracting the statement but how the hell you tell a town you didn't mean that? Whole town knew it was on account of her holing up with me. But before she holed up with me she did it with Larry… so Mae sits here with a rip in her knee and three hungry kids, while her eighty-four-year-old grampa yells at the wall at the Baptist home waiting for it to say something back, and all his money sits in a vault at the Second National bank instead of buying a couple hamburgers or a fucking can of Similac, and it's all because neither Larry or me backed off Ruth when her daddy laid down the law.

"I don't know what I'm going to do," Mae says.

I fight free of two kids and a needy couch. The kitchen table looks like a floor with aluminum on the sides. The oven is clean but they's a burner missing. I open a cabinet and it's flat empty. So's the next, except a bag of flour and another of rice. In the other room, Mae's silent and Bree and Morgan sit on the sofa watching me with the same eyes that looked happy a minute ago, but now seem sunk.

I slip a hand in my pocket and feel two plastic-sheathed coins.

NINE

I walked into Mae's and I should have known what'd happen. They ought to be a law agin mothers living in decrepitude.

Millany stands at the door, looking out. He's got a stogie in his mouth. He steps back and I come through.

"Changed my mind on one of these coins."

"Flaw? What? Let me see—"

"Nah. Just changed my mind."

He hesitates. A tinge of red escapes his eyes but they's no juice with it. He's a little pissed is all.

"Keep your commission. I don't give a shit. I just need more cash'n I thought."

The red goes away.

"Ah, hell. It's no problem. Gimme the coin."

I flip him the maple leaf and he pulls cash from a box.

"Everything all right?"

"Fine." I stop. Think back to October third. "Who has a white truck? Silver truck?"

"That fella with the deer rifle and the Caterpillar cap."

"Prick."

Walking back to Mae's I pick up a thought I dropped earlier. All those letters I been sending to Ruth, without ever getting word back, was really just to me. I'm no better'n her old man in the Baptist home, cussing at the wall and expecting it to talk back. Coming up on Mae's house I stop dead.

They's an F-150 in the drive. Mae drives a Tercel.

Truck's white.

I glance at the house. Circle for an eyeful of the tailgate, white as the rest of the truck, and shiny. Been washed recent—no dust in the rims. S'pose every kid washes his truck; it ain't necessarily to get rid of evidence. Fact, whoever dropped off Fred that night don't know I watched the whole thing, so whatever was glowing on the tailgate ought to still be there. 'Less it was just one part clean and the other not.

I go to my knees, brace on my hands. Oil pan's dry. Not even a bulb saving up for a drop.

But the truck's white, and Cory Smylie was at the dog fight.

I hesitate on the porch while feet stomp and move inside— heavy feet, boot heels. Got my hand ready to rap but I wait. She said she'd handle Cory Smylie—but I hear anything wild, I'll tear this door down.

Whispers. A shout. Stomping gets louder. I step aside and the door flies open.

He's three feet across the porch with his leg swung over the steps before he turns. Got money in his fist.

"Why hello, shithead."

He does a double-take, misses the step and skids. I get a bolt of the juice real quick. "Piss off," he says on the way to his truck.

Mae's at the door.

"That the money I left you?"

Her face is blushed. Streaming. She nods.

I tramp after Cory and he's already spinning tires. I swoop down for a rock the size of my fist and chuck it. Sandstone clangs on metal and the tires lock. Truck skids. Door flies open. He charges so close I can smell his breath and the hair on my forearms stands so hard it tickles.

Trickery.

I step back and his knee comes up. I kick out his other leg and he's on the ground.

"Gimme that money. Fifty bucks. Then get the hell out of here."

I'm ready to stomp my heel two inch through his nose. I've knocked the red out him. He scowls but his hand shakes. Nothing but a playground bully with a truck. He pulls the green out his pocket and throws it at me. I let it fall.

"Get the hell out of here."

He crabs away, wobbles to his feet. Limps from the kick I give him.

"You know, it's supposed to work the other way. You's supposed to bring her money."

Ten feet away, Cory finds the courage to meet my look. He climbs into his truck. "Yeah, well the word's out about you, Creighton. You're sixteen kinds of fucked. Stipe's got a hard-on and he's liable to bend you over one of your own mash barrels." He slams the door, floats me the bird at a forty-five-degree angle—I guess that's cool nowadays—and guns the engine. "Maybe I'll see if Stipe needs a hand."

"You stay away from Mae."

He fishtails off, waving his middle finger out the window, though he can't keep the angle right, and don't look near as cosmopolitan as a minute ago.

Mae's on the porch. Her cheek's swollen.

"He hit you?"

She won't nod. "He said he needed the money."

"More'n your kids need food?" I hit the wall and wood cracks. Lucky I don't put another hole in it. "All right, damn it."

"Uncle Baer!"

I walk back to town. Was going to give her cash, but fuck it I'll give her food. Let the son of a bitch steal it from her. What this town needs is one good cop, a sheriff ain't afraid to string a hoodlum by his toenails 'til he understands the rules. But ours'd rather watch dogs slaughter each other. Whole miserable country gone crazy. You hear the radios two hundred yards. Feel the music through your feet 'fore you hear it in your ears. No one cares. They's good kids, expressing themselves. And someday they knock they women around just like they daddies did. Whole damn world lost its mind.

I'm at the grocery. "You do a delivery for me?"

Merle looks up. "What's wrong with your neck?"

"Run afoul a gang of gay vampires, just south of Sutton and Main. You do a delivery?"

"Where to?"

"Up the road. Mae. You know, she rents Smotherman's place. It'll be a lot of grub."

"Fit the bed of my truck?"

"If that's the limit."

Merle's an affable son of a bitch and that sits good. I grab a cart and fill it. Six jars of peanut butter, six of jam. About forty pound of pork, chicken, and hamburg. Rice, noodles, potatoes. Fruit. Milk. Eggs. Cheese—six kinds. Can't have too much cheese. Pretzels. Kool-Aid. Canned veggies, fruit, soups. Spices. Frying pan. Two.

They's a woman with a basket comparing two can of fruit. Name's Emmy; she works at the bank where they don't know what money is. Her gaze drifts past her hands and she takes in my feet, then all the way up. Fairly easy on the eyes herself. She says, "Which of these would you pick?"

I take one out her hand and put it in my cart. "You keep that one."

She smiles.

I fill one cart and bring it to Merle at the counter. "You want to tally this while I grab another cart?"

"Sure."

He empties items and I start again. Pass through the same aisles as last time seeking nuggets I missed. Creamed corn. How can a woman raise babies without creamed corn? Tomato soup? Fuck tomato soup. Nobody likes it. But she'll have bread and cheese for grilled sammiches... two can of tomato soup. Formula. Diapers. Soap. Toothpaste. I don't know about the rest of the stuff in this aisle. Lady products—she's on her own.

"You throwing a party?" Emmy says. Her voice is a hair from self-inviting. I recall a time at the bank she looked at me from behind the counter and was batting her eyes like she had dust in em.

"No party, Emmy. Just a bunch of food."

Her face is suspended in that cloudy-water look says she don't know what the hell to do next. She's purty enough, but a liar lurks somewhere inside. They always is.

Finally, last, I stop in the aisle with the antacid and Tylenol. I call to Merle, "What you got that'll put a man to sleep?"

"Melatonin in that aisle." He points. Smiles. "Bullets behind the counter. What kind of sleep, Baer?"

"Mela... "

"It's the bottle with the sleeping woman on the picture, see?"

"Yeah. This work?"

"Guaranteed. Problems sleeping?"

"Sorta precaution, maybe."

Back at the register, Merle works up a grin the size of a small motor home. "You're already at two hundred and fourteen," he says.

"That all?"

I unload and he scans. I pack bags and stick em in the cart. Let him ring the melatonin, and slip it in my pocket.

"Three hundred fifty-eight and thirty-two cents," he says.

I hand over eight hundred dollars. He looks at me funny.

"Put the rest in credit for Mae Creighton. She can't have cash. She can't have cigarettes or liquor. She can't spend a penny if Cory Smylie's with her."

"Let's see. No liquor, no smokes, no Cory Smylie."

"That's right."

"You know we don't ordinarily do this sorta thing."

"I can't be coming back and buying her groceries every damn week."

"I'll handle it myself. Difference is four forty-one, sixty-eight."

"Appreciate it."

He writes the number on a slip of paper and initials it.

I say, "You send word when the money runs out. Them kids need to eat."

"Gimme an excuse to get some of that hooch you make." His eyes twinkle red. Fucker don't drink.

"Running apple tonight." I stop at the door. "And you don't need no excuse."

TEN

Wake from a nap. I'm in the middle the woods, waiting on dark. Shoulder's seeping, blood and lymph trickling down my chest. Teeth punctures in my neck're hot like to start a fire.

If it ain't the holes I already got worrying me, it's the ones I'll get if somebody sneaks close with a rifle and goes to work. It don't feel good, thinking the only reason you's alive is nobody yet got serious about killing you. Not when you got so many flirting with it.

Even feeling like I had a set of eyeballs watching me, I brushed aside the worries and got a couple winks. Dreaming of Mae's a wistful thing. Not some pervert thing—she put me in the mind of Ruth so strong it's like losing thirty years.

Sun's about done for.

I'm leaning on an oak. Got the thirty-thirty across my arm and the Smith on my hip. Looking ahead through undergrowth, I'm close to the edge of a clearing by a pond dates a hundred year. Farmhouse long gone, nothing but toppled foundation stones on the ground, arranged in a twenty-foot square. Got my back to the tree and it's dicey every time I come.

I watch the woods 'til I'm sure no one's out there, but how the hell you ever really know? Not that anybody but Millany'd have a clue it was time. I recall that red glint in his eyes, and the tingle of juice.

The woods is more shadow than light.

I listen.

Chipmunks dash across leaves. Eventually a buck wanders through the meadow and grazes at the edge, not far. I'm downwind. He keeps his eyes my way. Trigger finger's itchy but my apple mash is ready and you don't get much window on perfection. Buck lives another day.

Wind turns and he swings his head around. Looks straight through me like I'm a hundred yards deeper in the woods. Deer eyes don't work too good—it's my smell he's after. Even if we don't communicate, eye to eye with a buck is a majestic thing. He bounds off, and like that, it's dark. I wait 'til the thrill's gone and the black's whole. Shift to the side of the tree; reach inside a two-foot rot hole; feel along the left wall.

I check the darkness behind me. No one. But I got a spooky thought—what if that buck was looking at some man staking me out, looking where I keep the metal? I wait. They's no sound.

Inside the rotted hollow I find a nylon cord hanging from a fifty-penny nail. I lean my rifle agin the tree partway around, lift the cord one hand after the next.

It's a strain.

Inside the tree, a metal bucket hangs eighteen inch down. Never had the nerve to check in daylight to see if a man can get the angle to see sparkles in the shadows. I grab the wire handle and hold the bucket, keeping everything inside the tree. Give it a quick shake.

Drop the gold coin from Millany's inside.
They's twenty-five year of gold in that tree.

ELEVEN

Ernie Gadwal didn't bother to crouch. The forest was almost dark and Ernie stood four foot three. Though prone to mousy twitches and scurrying movements, he forced himself to be calm. Through the trees he watched Joe Stipe's nemesis.

He'd been spying since learning Stipe had launched an operation weeks before. Ernie had been in the shadows across the dirt road, fidgeting with braiding three strands of dried grass when Baer Creighton found his massacred dog. He'd looked in through a window as Creighton drank shine and stitched his dog back together. When Creighton stopped at Millany's Coin Collectory, Ernie had been enjoying a hot dog at George's, across the street. When Baer bought groceries for his niece, Ernie had watched through the store's giant plate-glass window from his Subaru Outback.

Ernie Gadwal was a clinger in Joe Stipe's outer circle, one who attended fights and afterward savored the valor of the dogs, gaining spiritual enrichment from their struggles and triumphs. The fights were awesome spectacles and the man who put them on... Joe Stipe was magnetic, a dynamo. In all Buncombe County, no man save Stipe could quiet a crowd just by grunting, or with a single word banish a reveler from all he held dear.

Stipe's circle was wide at the bottom, but narrow up top.

Ernie thought of Joe Stipe a lot.

Ernie's small stature caused him to perennially compare himself to other men. Early in his life his mother noted his behavior and said it was the root of his mischievousness. Left with no obvious comparator, fate forced him to dissemble. His want of superiority predisposed him to deceit, and he sought the hidden qualities by which he could transcend his peers. He learned to notice minutiae. Flaws. Some men found inspiration in other men's greatness. Ernie Gadwal drew inspiration from unearthing what haunted them.

It was a short leap to trade on these faults.

Ernie studied men like a broker and treated faults like commodities. He traded information for favor like so much specie. He hoarded secrets, ever trading up, ever seeking the exchange that would vault his stature.

By some perverse fate he earned a reputation diametric to his goal. In the overheard words of his mentor, Stipe, he was a conniving little shithead.

Yet Ernie had learned to isolate the weaknesses other men sought to fill, exposing their core motivations and the easiest levers by which to steer them. His guiding calculus was that knowledge of what men craved was fungible, and in the hands of an expert trader it could make men mules. And because the void within him was great, his nature was inevitable. He could not turn from it.

Baer Creighton had been leaning against a tree trunk, dozing. Then he rose, and studied the terrain. Then he reached inside the tree and deposited something from his pocket.

Ernie wondered about that, but in a flash of realization he connected Baer's visit to the bank and the gold dealer.

Now, looking at a tree ostensibly full of money, Ernie thought about what to do with it. He didn't need wealth. A trust left by his grandmother provided a seventy thousand dollar per annum stipend. What Ernie craved was the standing that accompanies men of action. It wasn't by Stipe's dollars that he commanded respect.

What Ernie now saw would be worth something—though not to a man as wealthy as Stipe. This little nugget fit someone else's desires far better.

Who among Ernie's poorest acquaintances was most embarrassed by his poverty? Who dreamed of wealth? Everyone, of course. But which friend had something to offer in return? Who, by his proximity to Joe Stipe, might bolster Ernie in the hierarchy? It was a complicated strategy, but Ernie Gadwal was a complicated man.

He waited. He stepped sideways, whispered "Patience," but his excitement grew. Would it be gold? Or silver?

While observing the enigmatic Creighton over the last few weeks, Ernie had surmised Creighton preferred solitude. He thirsted only for the company of a dog. Sure, Creighton had more than a normal man's allotment of moxie. But Ernie wasn't interested in getting into Baer's good graces. Baer might be an interesting study, but a recluse had little social currency.

A deer broke cover and bounded off, not thirty yards away. Baer reached for his pistol and slowly turned, his eyes searching for some other animal that might have spooked the deer. Creighton was wily, but Ernie wasn't afraid. He had surprise. He was unknown. He was invisible.

Baer Creighton walked away from the tree and Ernie darted to the cover of a wide hemlock. The darkness varied from shadow to shifting shadow. He cocked his ear toward the vanishing sound of Creighton's feet on dry leaves. Ernie stepped closer.

He should wait. Couldn't be too eager, for if he had in truth just discovered Baer Creighton's savings account, danger lurked at every approach. While observing Creighton over the last few weeks, Ernie had seen Cory Smylie fire a few shots at Creighton and haul ass just before Creighton charged, waving a pistol in the air and returning fire into the cave. Cory had been barely able to run a straight line, tripping and stumbling over roots and rocks, and was lucky to have escaped.

Afterward, Ernie had watched from eighty yards as Creighton painstakingly rigged mantraps around the cavern Cory had hidden inside.

What kind of traps had Creighton set around his deciduous bank account? Pits filled with spikes? Deadfalls suspended in the trees?

Ernie leaned against the hemlock. Would it make more sense to approach in daylight and risk being seen? Or dusk, and risk not seeing Baer's inevitable traps?

He knew a man who was close to Stipe, yet unambiguously conscious of his poverty. Burly Worley would be more than happy to go after the gold and he wouldn't fear the dangers.

Burly Worley was close to a mule already. Ernie recalled meeting him. A frustrated dog owner had pulled a pistol and shot an already mortally wounded dog. This was entertaining carnage, but afterward the man fired twice more into the air and called the owner of the victorious dog a cheater. Of all the fear-frozen men, Ernie alone drew the man's gaze—and wrath. Burly Worley had acted upon the man's distraction, and dropped him with a quick punch to the neck. Later, he'd credited Ernie with being the only person there with the stones to act, and had praised his coolness to Stipe, making him welcome to linger after the events while the men stacked pallets.

Worley was honorable enough to edify another man. He was not jealous. He was close to Stipe, and he was unemployed.

Ernie backed from the tree and circled out the way he'd come in. This was good. This was unexpectedly good, the kind of windfall that changed the dynamic of...everything.

TWELVE

First I kindle the fire under the boiler. It'll take a while to get the coals glowing, but not so long I can be idle while the tank sits empty. Every now and again I listen for the sound of a rock avalanche or a tree whip-snapping fifteen feet of barbed wire across some fool's nuts.

"Well Fred, we got to keep the lookout for a sniper."

Fine, Fred says.

"Or maybe you oughta keep an ear out."

Yeah. I'll do that.

The fifty-fiver on the end is apple mash. Sits on blocks high enough to fit a bucket under the nozzle. Ants crawl all over it, sucking up sugar that seeps through no matter how tight I twist the knob. I fill a bucket and dump it in the boiler. Mash is sweet and rich.

Another bucket and that's all she'll take.

The trick is one hundred seventy degree. Keep the mash a quinnyhair above and alcohol boils off while the water stays mostly behind. Vapor escapes in the copper coil, rests in the doubler—nothing but another pot where water condenses faster'n the likker—and out the other side spits some apple brandy a fella could burn in his lawnmower if he was too dense to drink it.

Flames lick around the boiler. I clamp the lid and sit on a stump. Hungry enough to eat the quills off a porcupine's ass, but food's at the house.

S'pose I'll drink.

Been a few hours but part of me's still in Mae's house. She lit up like a deck of firecrackers when the grocery boy Mike backed Merle's truck to the porch so he wouldn't have to carry all them bags so far. Bree and Morgan screamed and ran back and forth. Joseph wanted in on the fun and let out a wail.

"What is this? What did you do? Baer? What's this?"

She had a half-pissed look and I guess it was shock because she about suffocated Joseph between them boobs while she was hugging me hard and beating my back with her fist. Scared me to tell her about the tab I set up with Merle.

I had a woman like that I wouldn't take her money.

The fire's died enough for some of the heavier logs to fit. This's where the coals'll come from. I shove a couple, light a lantern and hang it from a jig in a hemlock. Just enough light to keep the operation efficient. I sit on a stump thinking a watched still don't boil, talking to Fred and generally miserable. Every twig breaks or pinecone falls has me reaching for Smith.

A still makes a particular sound approaching the perfect temperature, like a teapot right before the water boils. You'll hear about all manner of impressive operations where the stiller's welded a thermometer to his cooker, valves all over. Truth is all it takes is a place to cook and a place to condense. My operation's basic as they come, built by an old-timer died long time ago. A ten-gallon kettle with a fitted lid. I use a leather gasket and seal it with ten C clamps. The copper tube's fitted to the lid and coils fifteen feet, with a doubler midway.

The shine that drips out the other end'll generally hit a hundred-sixty proof, plenty high for everyday consumption. Though another run'd refine it almost perfect.

The boiler ticks, expansion sounds. Already vapor twists through the tubes but without the pressure to keep it moving. Little longer.

Ah, hell, Ruth. What's this all about? All these years and not a damn word? Your life ruined and mine nothing but cooking mash in the woods.

I got thrown out of high school in tenth grade. Seemed school was more about telling me what to think than how to think. I had my own mind. They knew when I looked at a teacher I thought he was fulla shit. Only thing worthwhile was Ruth—though I never once said hello. Her hair shined like a sunset off'n water, and her smile'd turn a dick into a baseball bat.

She was Larry's girl and everyone knew it. I left school and didn't think on her. I got a job pumping gas and changing oil—basic maintenance at the garage. Had free rein over the junkers in the back lot and more money than a sixteen-year-old had any right to. Larry and Ruth was together most two years, and by then I wondered if I'd ever do anything more than pump gas and clean windshields. Had a muscle car and an attitude, but couldn't afford to move out my mother's house.

Larry went to college. Ma said he'd marry Ruth.

One day Ruth swung by in the car the honorable Preston Forsyth Jackson bought her. Oh, how she missed Larry. She talked like we'd been pals since God said light. She smiled. Locked her hands and straighted her arms, and poofed them titties between her elbows. She twirled her hair. Rubbed a bare shin agin a bare calf, and my eyes about fell down in the seat with em.

Larry and I looked alike, I told myself. She sure missed him. But they's nothing in the world so beautiful as the curve on a woman's calf.

Aw hell, accourse she knew what she was doing. All women know men is hard-wired. May as well run electrodes from a man's nads straight to a billy goat. She knew that.

Later I heard her father'd warned her off Larry. Only thing for Ruth to do was track down another Creighton, the gas-station greaser with a black Chevy Nova. She knew what she was doing. But I didn't know what she was doing and to me she was a walking, talking pinup girl, but different from every person I'd ever knew. They was never any red. Never any juice. She never give a lick of either. She maybe had a hoor's heart but she was flat unpretentious.

Ruth swings under the gas station canopy in this cherry mustang, paint gleaming. Chrome dripping off both ends. She sits behind the wheel and does that thing with her arms.

"You're Larry's brother," she says.

I don't say a word, and that's what she wants. She wants my eyes buried right where they are.

"I'm empty," she pouts. "You want to fill me up?"

"Uh."

I stumble to the gas tank and I'm looking off the other way because I caught her eye in the rearview scoping me scoping her and adjusting my tool 'cause it's bending my trousers. It's evening and I'm twenty minute from done. They's a drive-in just down the road.

"You want to catch a flick?" I still ain't met her eyes except on accident. I want her so bad I could spring a leak. "They's an Eastwood movie," I say. "Hang em High."

"A Western… "

"I'm done, twenty minute."

She looks at my greasy hands. My clothes with sweat stains at the pits and grime across the belly.

"Maybe I can take off now and meet you in a few."

She looks through the windshield. Purses her lips. "Or maybe we could just meet at the lake."

The lake. We was real young, Larry and me used to go there looking for panties and bras got left in the grass and trees, on the rocky beach.

The lake.

I'm cool now. I got my cool. "The lake?" I croak. Clear my throat. "An hour?"

"Make it two. Those hands better not have any grease on them," she says. "Where they're going."

She drove off. I never collected money for her gas and shelled out for it myself.

Boiler's got a ring says the mash's gleeful and saucy. A spit sound comes out the copper tube, and I'm in business. Few minutes, the jug under the copper'll fill with the fieriest brandy in the county. I stir the coals. Add a chunk of dried cherry.

The lantern sputters. Something rustles leaves, maybe a squirrel.

All that with Ruth is ancient history. Now I got to think on Stipe's dog, what had his teeth in my neck. I got to figure out if I can win a war against Joe Stipe.

THIRTEEN

Mae packed Joseph into the car seat. The chest harness clasp was tiny and stiff and the belt safety clip chafed his thigh. She cushioned his leg with a Tempur-Pedic mattress sample she'd received in the mail.

She wouldn't have needed to make the trip if landlady Smotherman had ever answered her phone. The check came in the mail and as long as it did, the house was fine.

But the house would collapse sooner rather than later, perhaps with Mae and the kids inside. It was a rattrap. Figuratively—it had mice, not rats, and plumbing issues. The shower drain took Liquid Plumr the way Cory took Coors. The kitchen sink burped like a baby after a bottle. And Mrs. Smotherman—who had no husband but had to make a living, and found her calling as a slumlord—had apparently put her money into bribing inspectors instead of fixing the home.

Mae had delayed paying once, in protest. She'd stationed pen and paper beside the telephone and for two weeks, every time she remembered an item in disrepair, jotted it down. You want your rent? Fix the roof. A leak soaked the statistics text on my nightstand. I left the book open and didn't wake until water had been dripping on it so long that even after I dried it page by page with a blow dryer, the print looked like an Escher watercolor. So fix the damn roof and replace my statistics textbook. And the shower drain—Liquid Plumr won't touch it. I step into a shower and climb out of a bath. Disgusting. Especially three days a month. And I'm sick of that buzzing in the walls when I flip on the living room light. The wires are going to short and burn the house to the ground with my babies and me inside. Have you no conscience?

The phone call never came.

She received a letter from Smotherman stating Experian and TransUnion had been notified. Further delay in payment risked legal action. Mae responded that further delay in fixing the house risked legal action, too. Days later she worried about her credit score and the future launch of her as-yet-undecided business, and double-stapled a check to a polite fuck-you letter.

"Heading out?"

Mae rapped her head on the car ceiling. Baer stood behind her.

"Hi, Uncle Baer." Mae hugged him, smelled whiskey. His brow was wrinkled and his eyes had a perpetual squint, as if their job was to categorize and they were skeptical from the outset.

"I was going to the grocery," she said.

"More groceries?"

"For greens. And I was going to see the landlady."

"You ought to. This place needs tore down and put up new."

"That would disrupt her cash flow."

"Something particular need fixing?"

Mae extracted the list from her purse. "Items one and four."

"Says here the drain and the roof."

"The shower drain is clogged. Liquid Plumr won't touch it. And the roof over the bedroom. I get splashed with cold rain one more time I'm liable to find a gun and shoot her."

"You don't have a gun?"

"No, I don't have a gun."

"Kids in the house? Single woman, don't have a gun?"

"What would I do with a gun but shoot somebody?"

"That's exactly what I'm saying. What'll you do, comes time to shoot somebody and you don't have a gun?"

Mae watched his eyes shift to her cheek. The swelling was mostly gone and her makeup covered the bruise.

"You had a gun yesterday, he wouldn't have done that."

"He would've taken the gun, just like the money."

"Nah. See? You can't shoot somebody with money."

"Uncle Baer... "

"Tell you what. You want me to walk over and see Smother-man, get this shit straight, or you want me to take an hour and fix the roof and the drain myself."

"An hour?"

"'Bout that. After I get a couple supplies."

Mae hugged him. "Oh wait. I still have to go to the grocery. You want me to take you into town? What kind of supplies?"

"No, no. I'll walk. Keeps me young. I'm just headed to the hardware. And the grocery. You going to the grocery?"

"For greens."

"You got baking soda and vinegar?"

She nodded.

"I'll get everything I need and be back in a half-hour. I'll visit Roy Maple, and he'll hook me up fine."

"Roy Maple?"

"Main Street hardware. You young'uns go to the Home Depot. Us old'uns go where we know people." Baer turned, and stopped after a few paces. "Back in a half-hour, so."

"Thank you, Uncle Baer."

Mae returned from the grocery. She opened the car door and the sound of a hammer greeted her. Baer hunched on the roof, his back to her. She looked for his ladder—he must have placed it against the back wall.

Mae worked Joseph free of the seat clasp. She led Morgan and Bree inside carrying a bag of greens and other produce. Merle had been sweet—other than his entire conversation between "Hello, Mae" and "See you later, Mae" being a parenthetical grilling on how strange Baer had been acting. That his dog had been almost killed and he'd given Merle money for her groceries. And Baer was quiet. And clearly a fight was brewing, because Merle saw Stipe and his boys talking with Baer, and you can see when Stipe's boys are looking for trouble. Basically every time you saw them.

What the hell was Baer into? That's what Merle wanted to know.

"I haven't noticed anything strange," Mae said. She glanced out the window. Studied her wristwatch for a prolonged ten seconds. "But I was wondering if you'd let me interview you and look at your income statement for an MBA class I'm taking?"

"Income statement? I file a ten nine nine and a schedule C, same as anybody."

"Oh—okay." Although running the store's expenses through a Schedule C was like asking Richard Petty to do Talladega in a Model T. He'd win, of course, but it would be a marvel.

Merle took the hint. He gave Mae the original slip with seventeen dollars and a handful of change deducted, and she left—stepping past sweet old yammermouth Cora Winetraub, whose furtive brow hinted the delight she'd experience gossiping to all of Gleason that Mae had a line of prepaid credit at the grocer. Funny how the bluehairs clutching their Bibles and judging people like they were taking notes for the Big Guy never read the section on gossip. *Wives be not slanderers.*

Cora was a spinster; that was it.

And, lest Mae parry with spirituality and escape guilt-free, she reminded herself of the scripture against prejudging bluehaired women, though the exact verse didn't come immediately to mind.

But what the hell *was* Baer into?

Merle's observations about Baer's dog and the fight brewing with Stipe were enlightening.

Cory attended those dog fights. He'd told her it was sport and the dogs were like men. They loved fighting, if only for the glory of battle. Barbaric, she'd said, one more link to our caveman past. And Cory said, well, then your daddy's a caveman, and that makes you a cavegirl. He'd flashed his dimples. It was time to get laid.

The steady thunk of Baer's hammer on the roof reminded her she'd had a headache all morning stemming from an acute coffee deficiency. She opened the front door and led her tribe inside. Put away the groceries and five minutes later stood below Baer, back far enough from the wall to see beyond the eaves.

She called up to the roof, "I'm putting on a pot of coffee. You want to stay for supper? I'll cook something special."

"'Preciate you," Baer said. He continued hammering. "But I got to look on Fred."

Who would name a dog Fred?

"You sure? I'll cook some of that chicken. With collards."

"Tempting." Baer laid the hammer on the roof. "All done."

"All done? That fast?"

"It was mostly a problem with the seam between the regular roof here and the gable. It was cracked, and I caulked it but good. Lifted up under where the shingles was loose, replaced a couple the worst. Only real concern's falling through."

"Where's your ladder?"

Baer nodded at an oak tree with a limb that hung close to the roof.

"You climbed the tree?"

"Well sure."

"How will you get down?"

"Same way I come up."

Mae shook her head. "This is crazy. You need any help?"

"Help? What for?"

"I don't know. You want me to call the ambulance?"

He waved her off. She waited on the porch, partly hidden by the eaves, where she could see him climb down the trunk, limb to limb, holding a caulk gun and a hammer in one hand and the tree in the other.

Cory would pee his pants if he had to climb that tree with both hands and a safety harness. That was the difference—one of the thousand—between Baer and Cory. Danger simmered in both men, but with Cory it was only likely to boil over onto a person or thing weaker than him. With Baer, Mae just sensed he was a handyman competent at any task he chose, including violence.

Maybe she'd ask him about a gun.

She held the door open. He placed his tools on the porch.

"I'll have that chicken in twenty minutes. You can visit the girls. They've been through every room in the house looking for a window to see you on the roof."

Baer glanced at the driveway.

"They aren't going to be young forever," Mae said.

"You hope."

"Uncle Baer!" Morgan crashed past Mae's legs and into Baer's. He swept her up and stooped for Bree, immediately behind. He pulled them to his face and scruffed both with his cheeks at the same time.

Any other man only wanted to do that with tits. "Come in, Baer. Come on. Playtime."

"All right girls, Uncle Baer's going to teach you to fix a drain. Mae, you got that baking soda and vinegar?"

"Just a minute."

"Grab a plastic lid, like from a tub of butter." Baer deposited Morgan on the floor. "Run outside and find me a rock the size of your foot, okay?"

"Hunh?"

"Go on."

Morgan bolted. Mae presented Baer a lid from the drying rack by the sink.

"Upstairs bathroom," Mae said.

Baer tossed Bree over his shoulder like a sack of grain and carried the wriggling, giggling girl and the drain-cleaning supplies upstairs. Morgan raced inside with a rock.

Mae slapped a package of chicken breasts into a skillet. Washed collards. Laughter from above, then the rapid thud of footfalls as Baer bounded down the stairs. Only one set of feet, though. No doubt the girls rode his arms or shoulders.

If they weren't going to have a father in Cory, or a grandfather in Larry, at least they had a great-uncle in Baer. At least.

How long would it take him to check off every item on her list, if he set about fixing the house?

He stood in the kitchen entry bearing a conqueror's smile. Pioneer handsome. Rugged and focused. Appropriately smelly.

Virile.

"I was wondering," Mae said. "When's the last time you cleaned up for a formal supper?"

His face was still.

Shit.

"I mean, nothing against scruff and all… you're welcome to the bathroom. I could run your clothes through the wash real quick—I know you spend all that time in the woods. I… oh, shit. I don't mean anything by it. I'm just saying I'd like to do something nice for you and I don't have a hell of a lot I can do, unless you want me to look at your stilling operation's books and dig into your supply chain management. I'll do a Six Sigma on your moonshine operation. Don't look at me like that, Baer. I'm just trying to be nice because you've been so nice to me and I'm feeling about as dumb as I ever felt in my whole life."

He stared at her, judging her. Mae looked back at him as plainly as she could, skewered by his eyes. He saw straight into her soul and in a moment would decide if she was worthwhile. She waited for an expression she could read, a twitch.

Nothing.

"You're some kind of silly." He came across the kitchen. Took her close, and squeezed like she was… what? Lost for a thousand years and they'd been lovers. She felt his ache through his arms, his broken heart through his chest. "Something else. You got to put on a saucepan of water. Get 'er to a boil, and in precisely thirty minute, pour it down your shower drain." He was sized perfectly for her—his chest, shoulders, the spoon between, perfect for her head… he said, "Any clog you got'll be gone. If it don't drain quick, just have Morgan or Bree show you how I done it."

He pulled away. Held her at arm's length.

"You're one helluva good girl." He kissed her forehead. She smelled what? Sandalwood? Oats? She wrapped her arms around him and in that exact moment he withdrew. "You're welcome for all this... fixing stuff. I'll come by and work on your list, time to time. And you don't got to do no man's laundry, you hear?"

He stepped back. In a moment he'd announce he had to look after Fred.

"Baer!"

"Huh?"

"Don't go! Stay! Please? Fred'll be fine. I'll drive you home to make up for the time you stayed for supper. Stay?"

"Uh."

"It'll mean so much to the girls."

Baer grinned—almost a frown. He'd seen through her. It was barely a lie.

He pulled Morgan from the floor beside him. And then Bree. "Girls, you got to show your ma how we did that drain upstairs, okay?"

"Baer... you can't go now. I wanted to show you all about the degree I'm taking. At Penn State. Online."

He was still. My God! His eyes!

"I wanted to tell you about the program. The business program... it's the best in the country. I mean so good that companies offer jobs just because of the university's name. I get my MBA and all this... this house, these problems... go away. All that famous American opportunity is going to be mine. I want to show you the Internet. How I take classes from home. You have a couple of minutes, right?"

Somehow, he knew everything before she said it. She could see.

"You'll finish that school," he said. He kissed Bree on the cheek, then Morgan. Placed them on the floor and pushed them off toward the television.

"You prob'ly tops in class. I got to get back to Fred, 'fore all this… gets out of hand. You're a good woman. And as to this schooling, you jest remember… I don't know if it was the Bible or Darwin said it, but people is lower'n worm shit. They'll lie and take what's yours, and step all over you. And smile while they do it. So my advice is, you want to make a living in business, you own the business."

He closed the step between them and dropped another kiss on her brow.

She clutched him, pulled, threw her chin over his lapel.

"Whoa, now!" I scoot back. Drag my sleeve over my mouth like I'm afraid she give me cooties. "Whoa, Little Princess. Easy. This ain't what uncles do."

Her eyes is full and bright, and sometimes you see a woman's got something in her head so firm it'll take an oxcart full of no's to shake it loose. Mae comes after me again, without a hint of red or electric, and she's shameless. It's the most natural thing for her, and it don't make a lick of sense—but I'm half snookered any-how. She gets up close and instead of planting them pudding-soft lips on me buries her face in my jacket, and throws her arms around my back.

We've retreated, us two. Back to family-type salutations. This's the familiar goodbye hug. Or could pass for it.

This's wrong as two boys fucking.

"Mae, I got to go. That chicken needs flipped."

I got to run. They's people waiting in line to shoot me. Some-thing. Shit.

He was gone, like that. Mae checked the chicken and the collards. The chicken was fine.

FOURTEEN

Colder'n most October afternoons, but the walk to Bleau's has me hot. Pete Bleau cut my likker and said Henderson did it. Don't know why I think of Bleau... whoever stole Fred and fought him was a man goes to fights, and knew I got a dog of the breed Stipe cottons to. Only a handful men knows I got Fred but don't understand he's a puss.

Pete Bleau's one.

I've thought on the way he behaved, talking about cutting likker, and the signals he gave. Nothing unusual. I catch cheats all the time. Bleau knows Stipe, Larry and all them fight-circle jerkers. His cohorts make him liable to know something about what happen to Fred.

Bleau being Bleau, he won't volunteer information 'til I shake it out him. So we got to have a prayer meeting.

Bleau lives a mile out of town in a shack like the thirty beside it, tall skinny slum houses. I'm good and loose from a half-flask of my new apple brandy, and a little shook by Mae's kiss. Took a quarter mile to walk off the hardon. Pete Bleau's truck's in the drive. Paint is cowshit brown, but I peek at the tailgate anyway. Circle and glance at the undercarriage, and all along the drive. No oil.

Got last year's Christmas tree beside a row of trash cans agin the house. Stone steps up to a wide porch. Curled paint, wet-rotted boards underneath squeak like to snap. Wonder how Bleau ain't fell through. I beat the door. Dog barks inside.

Porch boards rumble. Pete's coming.

Lock slides. Chain dangles. Door swings open. Pete looks like he expected someone else. Behind, a German Shepherd growls hello.

"Shut up, Butch," Pete says. "What you doing?" He looks beyond me to the yard, houses opposite the street. He spits in a potted plant by the door.

Nothing yet, terms of red or electric. "Ran apple last night. Some of my best."

"I guess it's that time of year."

"High dollar." I shove a flask to him. "Can you move twenty gallon?"

"More'n last year, huh?"

"Stepping up production."

"I'll move sixty," he says. "Hell, a hundred and sixty."

"Then it's time to double the price."

"At double price I'll move half as much."

"There you go, Sparky. I got ten now. Another run in two week. Ten bucks. Oh, and you cut my apple brandy… I don't want to go there."

"Nah, shit. We got an understanding now."

"You know I got a dog?"

"Fred? Sure." Bleau drinks.

"Who stole him?"

His eyes glow from the sides and the color's hot. I get sparks between my fingers and if it gets worse I wouldn't believe him if he said I got a ten-inch pecker.

"What?" Pete says. He throws the flask back and swallows a couple gulps.

"What I said."

"That's potent shit." He wipes his mouth with his arm. "What's this 'bout your dog?"

"Someone fought him at Stipe's the other night. What you hear?"

"I don't go to them fights."

"You like that apple?"

"It's plenty good."

"I'll knock you on your ass and pour it in your eyes 'less you get straight with me. We both know you's fulla shit and I'm some-place you don't want me to be. So you better un-ass some truth. What you know 'bout Fred?"

The charge goes from my skin. His eyes cool into white-lie territory.

"Stipe run out of dogs. Hard to have a fight every week when you run out of dogs."

"How you know?"

"I talk to everyone."

"So who stole Fred?"

"Dunno. Just got word to keep Butch locked up."

"Who *give* you the word?"

"You wouldn't know him."

"Try me."

"Don't think I will. Don't matter who said it—truth's plain enough. Stipe fights ten dog a week, but only pits. Week in, week out. Even a dog that wins is licked for a while, and as many as five die each week. You got to have a lot of dogmen breeding them animals. And if you're stealing 'em, you got to have a broad sweep to stay flush. Only natural he'd run out."

"Step out on the porch with me, so your dog don't run out."

Bleau squints. Pokes his head outside and looks up and down the street. Steps to the porch in slippers and ragged jeans and closes the door. He takes another slam off my flask.

"Who give you the word, Bleau?"

"Don't—"

I swipe my flask out his hand and shove him to the jamb. Got him pinned with one arm, leaning with all my weight. I hold the potion over his face. "You want to flush your eyes in hundred-sixty proof brandy? Or you want to say who give you the word?"

I pour a little on his forehead like to baptize him.

"Ahhh! Don't blind me for chrissakes!"

He shoves hard and wipes his brow. We stand apart a few feet, me poised to throw punches and him trembling like a ten-year-old getting picked on by the big kids riding back of the bus. Likker won't blind him—leastways not this likker—but he's ignorant, confused with the wood alcohol.

Instead, I press my elbow to his throat and get him pinned again. Pour a handful of apple shine in my free hand and mash it into his eyes.

"Fuck, Baer!" Bleau heaves me back and twists into the house. That big dog slinks up. I trip Bleau and he drops. German Shepherd growls low and the teeth marks in my neck start to ache. I draw Smith and hold it on the dog, and he gets wise. Cants his head. The hair on his neck stands straight and he looks like a duffel bag of teeth.

"All right, Bleau. You going blind and your dog's getting buried in the back yard. Who the hell give you the scoop on them dog fights?"

He shakes. Moans. I got to ask again. He says, "Cory Smylie."

"Keep talking 'til I tell you to stop."

"Cory's been working for Stipe. Gets his bait."

"Bait?"

"Cats and dogs. Cory drives all over looking for strays or animals he can steal without any trouble."

"Bait."

"Yeah, bait. They throw em in with a bunch of fighting dogs. Keeps em edgy and looking to kill, I suppose."

"And Cory give you the heads up when he's doing the stealing?"

"Well, I don't think Butch'd make a good bait dog. Nah. Cory said Stipe paid money—called it a finder's fee—for anybody brought him a fighting dog. Cory didn't want anybody else to make off with Butch."

"How's come you and Cory Smylie's so tight?"

"Now that ain't got nothing—"

I kick his belly flab. Pull back the hammer.

Bleau groans. "We got other business arrangements."

My face is flat but I judge him with my eyes and he sees it. "You move his drugs to the shot houses."

"I'm not saying any more. Pour that whole flask down my face, I don't give a shit."

"Or is it the other way around? You bring Cory the drugs from cities?"

"You dig much more, you'll have men from all over hunting your ass." Bleau eyeballs me. "I heard you shot Stipe's dog."

"That so?"

"Shot him in the eyeball. That dog was Achilles—Stipe's latest, greatest champ. Stipe's planning biblical retribution on your ass. So you want to add every kingpin in three hundred miles, you keep digging."

"You hear something about Fred, better find me. Don't make me come pour shine in your eyes again."

Why not visit the Law?

"Chief Smylie, you know that fight the other night? That illegal fight you was at? Well, someone stole my dog and fought him... "

Don't think I'll talk at the police chief just yet.

Chief Smylie and me got an understanding—the only way a fella in my line of work can keep from being fined broke or thrown in jail. Want the freedom to do whatever work suits? Pay the thug. That's the way of things. Chief knows he can come by for a jug when he wants, and only swans over three times a year: first week of buck season, when he gathers his boys and they go to camp; July four; and his birthday in August.

Smylie joked one time he'd make Fred a law dog, what with the crooks smuggling dope through Gleason. "Our town is just a way station, a hotel and a party on the route from New York to nowhere. But since the drug men stop here, they sell here, and a dog like Fred has the demeanor and the nose for police work." Had. That was chief shooting the shit and making nice after extorting a jug. Well, chief don't have a white truck, and though he cozies up to Stipe, I can't see him bringing a dog to the show.

Difficulty with Smylie—he knows I got the still. I make trouble, he makes trouble. Time being, chief's out the picture.

Got to see about Larry's truck.

Don't know why Larry'd steal Fred and fight him, unless it was pure spite—and that's verydamn likely the case. If it was Larry.

Right this second, though, I'm thinking Cory Smylie.

Larry don't need money. After he stole back Ruth he put himself through night school and wound up cooking books for men like Stipe. Works for Big Ted Lombo, the restaurant man connected to other fine restaurantoors from the cities. Larry buys a car every two years, has a boy mows his lawn every week whether it rained or not. Even had the fashion to ditch Ruth and scrounge a second wife—some girl I remember from school, was a few years behind and had a personality like wet burlap.

Time I get to Larry's, the sun says midafternoon. He'll be at his office making numbers lie. His woman Eve'll prob'ly be in the house sucking a martini.

The house is plain vanilla with a row of daisies by the sidewalk. A tree out front, pruned round.

I come on the garage quiet.

Garage doors is glass at the top and I gander inside. Plenty dark, but I make his truck's outline. Light color; can't tell which. Truck is here because he drives a snappy sports car around town, looks like Snoopy's nose.

I try the big door. Locked. Side door's locked too.

"What you want, Baer?"

"Hello, Eve." I face her. "What, you stand at the window watching for people to swing by?"

"Something like that."

Her eyes is big and her stance is mousy. She's either got a clamshell under one eye, or Larry's corrected her. She holds a drinking glass looks like it's full of barbershop comb disinfectant.

"Larry at home?"

"He's at work. You oughta know that. Won't be home for a couple hours. If he wants."

Larry and me don't talk and it's been five year since I seen Eve. Downhill? Her looks fell off a cliff and left her standing on top. She wears shorts and even the fronts of her legs is pocked.

Her nipples poke agin her halter, force a fella to speculate on whether them tits make milk or sour cream.

"Why are you here?" she says. "Why are you looking in the garage?"

"Want to see that truck."

"I wish he'd sell it."

She takes a drink of blue juice and crosses her arms. Her glass sweats. I can't lie worth a shit. I got nothing to say, and she won't leave me hanging around gawking through the garage window. She shifts. Looks at the ground, then me.

"Why you want him to sell it?"

"It's junk. All the time either at the garage or the body shop. What people must think, seeing their accountant in a vehicle like that."

"He put it for sale?"

"You here because you want to buy his truck?"

"Nah. Wanted a word with my flesh and blood. I'll stop by later."

"Well, he won't sell it anyhow." She shifts her weight and throws one leg forward. Got her elbow tucked at her hip. Slut stance. "Why don't you come inside and have a drink?"

I'd ruther drink an oak keg fulla chicken shit than bounce in the sack with Eve. But a drink...

"What you got in the glass?"

"This?" She sips. "Blueberry Kool-Aid and Bacardi."

"I'll have the Bacardi."

"Come on in."

I follow her. Look across the lawn. The neighbors must be inside they houses. She walks with the swagger of a woman thinks a good wiggle erases thirty years. She holds the screen door open with her hip, and after I follow inside kicks off her sandals by the coat closet.

"Make yourself comfortable, Baer."

She stoops to a base cabinet and I get the distinct feeling she chose her angle to give me a straight view down her shirt. Comes up with a bottle and parks it on the counter. She opens a cabinet and I swipe the bottle from below her. Spin the lid on my flask and fill it.

"Help yourself," she says.

"Appreciate you."

A little spills on the counter. The bottle got just enough to top me off. "You got a rag?"

"I'll get it."

I sip from the flask. She looks at the empty bottle. Forces her face into a smile.

"Why don't we go in the other room?"

I pull the curtain on the front door and nod at a neighbor across the street, standing with crossed arms behind a picture window. "I did that, people'd think we fucked."

A quarter mile gone, I turn and look back. Woman gives me the willies.

FIFTEEN

It's dusk. I sit on a stump and watch the fire under the boiler. This ain't a pickup night; don't expect business, and I ain't had company since God shat the town of Gleason. With all that's gone between Stipe and me I got to suspect something's coming. Only thing keeps dread away is knowing if I see bad news first, somebody else gets the surprise. And I got an advantage.

Just same, I keep my head hunkered into my shoulders. The hair on my neck stands anyway, on account of that cussed sniper out there, somewhere, watching. Or maybe Stipe's got something else up his sleeve.

Mae tried to kiss me like I wasn't family—and her ex, Cory Smylie, been getting his drugs off the same fella buys most my likker.

Interestinger and interestinger.

Every girl I ever knew had a screwed-up head; Mae's no different. Got to wonder how she'll feel getting grocery money from me, now that I turned away such a bold invitation. She ought to feel like a dolt, but I hope she don't feel so stupid she lets the kids go hungry.

The steam-rattle's a few notes shy of perfect. Inside the boiler, corn mash bumbles around excited and alcohol busts into steam. The water part's a little more lackadaisical, and that's stillin. They's pure magic about to drop from the copper tube.

I had any sense I'd fetch Smith off the sleeping bag and reassemble it. Don't do no good in clean pieces. Fred wanted to come out the tarp and I got sidetracked.

I drug him out, crate and all. He got good ears, and if Stipe's boys is in the woods, Fred'll make sure I know. He keeps his face after the heat like he appreciates the smell of fire or the orange glow teases through his scabbed eyes. He sighs a lot and I sigh with him. No such friend like a loyal dog. Never in a foul mood, never holds things over my head, like it was my fault he got stole and fought in the pit. Though it was.

I busted my watch when I was a kid. A Mickey Mouse job, with big-gloved hands swinging around his body. I was tomfooling on my bicycle. Saw something coming up I didn't like and clamped the front brake, flipped the whole shebang. I wailed 'til Ma come running out to see how many bones I broke. Like any kid, I was made of rubber. I cried and cried and showed Ma my busted watch. She give me a good shake and when that didn't work, laughed at how silly I was. She said, "I seen some stupid fish but you're being a dumb bass." But I knew she'd saved up for that watch and it was special, her being able to give it to me.

A fella can't rely on a good person's grace to get him out of justful guilt. So when Fred grumbles as I rub between his ears, and beats his tail agin the crate, he's got a helluva lot of grace going to no good use. He was my responsibility to look after. It was my fault he was stole, and fought, and blinded, and left within an inch his life.

You got to own guilt. Even when it don't sit good.

The copper coil spits into the jug and the sound rattles me loose. The logs under the boiler glow red. I shove a couple chunks of split maple and nudge the last with my toe. Take the lantern to the jug and watch the shine drip out like a spigot has a bad leak— not a drop, not a stream, but a bunch of drops come out together, and stop 'til the pressure builds, and spurt some more.

Jug'll fill in fifteen minute. I'll strain it through charcoal to pull some of the oils. Looks like soapy water when you don't, iridescent and purple-tinged, and anybody don't know his likker'll have a case of the ass over you selling booze make him go blind. That's ignorance; them oils is nothing and sometimes I drink it that way out of pure happy laziness.

But get boys thinking they'll go blind, and you'll see how attached a man is to his eyes.

A horn bleats up at the house.

Shit.

I got the fire just right and the mash cooking. Likker dripping in the jug.

Horn sounds again, long steady blare gets louder 'til the whole woods is ready to come shut somebody up. I grab a stick, push the fresh logs off to the side.

"Guard the fort, Fred,"

Right, says Fred. I'll keep a lookout.

I head for the house with a dim flashlight. Prefer to do business in daylight but the universal signal says a man wants likker, he lays on his horn 'til the likkerman comes. I sneak inside from the basement, and climb upstairs.

It's a white truck.

I slap my hip. Left my Smith at the still site. House is dark. Don't keep anything in here but a rifle but that'll work. You don't handle likker business without something shoots bullets.

The horn bleats again. The door slams. I slip down the hall, pop the lock on the cabinet and pull out a three oh eight Winchester with a nine power scope set over open sights. Like I'll need either. Crack the bolt, check the brass.

Business calls.

I throw the front door open and from his shape it's flesh-and-blood Larry.

"Ah, big man with a gun. You son of a bitch," he says. "Come after Eve like you come after Ruth?"

"Nah. I fucked Ruth."

He steps toward me with fists like mallets. Stops. "What the hell do you want coming by my place?"

"Come by for you."

"But you went inside with Eve."

"You backslid, brother. I don't want a damn thing with her." I ease down the steps and he shifts sideways, like he'll jump one way or the other to keep me from scooting past.

"What you driving here?" I shine the flashlight to his truck.

"What?"

"What kind of truck you got?"

"You—what the hell? My truck?"

"I come by your place for a look. Eve said it's a piece of shit mostly in the shop."

He's quiet while I approach, and his eyes start to glow and I got a tickle all over my arms and the back of my neck. He come to raise hell and now he's playing defense. In so many years watching some of the goat-fuckinest liars you ever saw, they rarely do it cocky and strutting. I could count the times on one hand. The rifle set Larry back, and he's thinking deceit.

Or, I ask about the truck and he's all of a sudden leery?

Should've come right out with "You steal my dog?" But now he's red and sparking it don't matter what he says, it's all suspect.

I hold the flashlight to the truck bed. The grooves is wore to the metal and they shine. No blood.

"What the hell? Get away from my truck. Or are you going to try to fuck it, too?"

I get on my knees. Look up in under. Flashlight's dim enough I can't get a good read on the grime.

Footsteps, quick. Larry's boot finds my gut with a lot of pissed-off behind it. I'm sucking.

"Shit, Larry."

"You stay away from Eve! I'll bust every bone you got."

My fingers is twisted in the trigger guard—caught a rock and peeled skin. Get my hand out the metal and I'm on all fours, ready for the next. I'll bust off his leg and shove it so far up his ass his sac'll gag smelling his toes. He stands back.

"I mean it," he says. "You've been a snake your whole life. You come around my woman again and I'll kill you."

I get to my knees. I'd like to kick his ass from here to the lawn chair but I got another thought.

He climbs into the cab. The window's down. "You ain't going to shoot me, you fucking snake?"

"Nah, I won't shoot you."

He grinds the shifter.

"Larry?"

He looks.

"Turn in the yard there, so you don't back blind on the road. The turnabout's there like it used to be... just grown up in weeds."

He holds my look, and if ever there was a time I was spewing red and shooting enough juice to spark a powder keg from twenty feet...

Larry finds reverse, pops the clutch, and swings the truck over the weeds. Blows rocks out his back tires and spins to the road. It's been enough weeks the moon's near full again, but the damn thing ain't up yet. Tailgate's all the same color, but without the moon, the angle, who knows?

But at the turnaround I shine the flashlight close to the weeds, and sure as shit, oil.

Back at the still, Fred says, I worry.

"I do too."

Yeah, he says, but you can see em coming.

I settle on the stump and his words sit on my shoulders. Kick logs back deep in the embers. Tap the boiler. Five, ten minute she'll make steam. But why wait on the fresh stuff when they's vintage under the tarp?

Wailing on a car horn, again. Larry? Nah—don't sound like a truck. Sounds like a rabbit feeling a wolf's teeth; blares and don't stop. Fred perks.

"I'll go see. Don't trouble yourself."

He rests his head. One day I'll fix a leash so he does more'n lay around all day. Once he heals.

Put Smith back together in four seconds and slip it to my hip. Grab a gurgle a shine. Head for the house. Inside, I look through the window. Headlights is off—beat-up Tercel.

Mae.

The vehicle backs away. I step outside, down off the step and she don't see me 'til she's clear back to the road. The car sits. She's going to make me walk all the way. Never know what a girl's got on her mind. Not after she tries to plant a smooch and you back away.

She rolls down her window and I stoop. She looks ahead but the angle don't hide a fresh beating.

"Cory do that?"

She nods. Stares.

I look. All three kids is in the back seat. "Pull in the drive here and let the kids out and play. Then you can tell me exactly why Cory Smylie needs murdered."

"Don't say that."

"Yeah, he'll stop on his own, will he? You expect something different, but I been telling you five years."

"So now you get to say you told me so?"

"Come on back to the house."

She reverses to the step and parks. Kids tumble out rattled. Not in the mood for play. I sit on the step and hold my arms out to Bree and Morgan. Mae has Joseph.

"C'mere, girls. C'mere."

I coax em in my arms. Plop em on my lap. Nuzzle each.

"Guess you two saw some ugly today."

They's silent. Heads press to my shoulders.

"You prob'ly know by now, the world ain't made of candy. But this's what you got to understand. Bree, Morgan—look at me, now. Look in my eyes." Reluctant. "C'mon girls. You need to know."

They look, eyes big unblinking moons.

"Your momma'll be safe from here on out. And so'll you. Cory won't do this no more."

They bury they heads again and I rub they backs. Mae leans on her trunk.

"Tell you what, girls. It's about time for the fireflies to come out. I'll give you a dollar each if you can catch me one."

Neither stirs.

I lift the girls off my lap. "Catch me one them firebugs, girls. Catch me two. They's a Ball jar in the shed, bottom shelf. Run along."

They wander away.

"It's too late in the fall for fireflies," Mae says.

"Prob'ly. But it won't hurt the girls to look and I'll give each a dollar anyway."

Mae pulls her skirt closer to her knees. "I wish I knew where all the men like you hide."

"Woods. Stills. You call the police?"

"Gleason police don't want anything to do with the police chief's son."

"Yeah. You got a gun?"

"I've said enough about guns. Not with kids in the house."

"And you won't let me go string him by his nuts from a tree? That's out, right?"

She smiles, coughs, and that presses out a fresh batch of tears. "Violence doesn't solve anything."

"Enough of it sure as hell does. Every time."

The air is still and the girls straggle across the yard, stumped. At least the pursuit takes they minds off what they saw.

"What you want me to do? I'm no good at doing nothing."

"I don't know," she says.

"S'pose you could haul the kids to Mars Hill a couple days. Give things time to shake out with Cory."

"You're going to go after him, aren't you?"

"That's why you came, Mae. Don't tell me different."

"It's why I came."

"Uh-huh. Visit your mother a couple days. You come back, you won't have problems with Cory Smylie."

SIXTEEN

Been a week since I fell out the tree watching Stipe's dog fight. All this time I'm thinking if I had a sac the size of a three-week cabbage I'd have gone to work on that crew of dogfighters with Smith.

That's where my mind's at.

Naw, I won't go there and pull a six-shooter on twenty fellas rich with likker and surly from watching dogs rip each other to pieces.

Hell no. I'm going there to talk. See if I can't get a couple pieces of information that'll make the endgame clear.

Stipe won't kill me with all his boys around. I'm banking on it.

They ain't a trail between my camp and Stipe's fight circle. I follow the crick, turn off, and hoof a mile-two 'til their whoops and hollers guide me in. Gather my nerves with a healthy snurgle of shine, and sit on a boulder overlooking the lantern glow, and the men who come to see a few miserable dogs die. They dance around like leprechauns or gnomes or what's his name... Rumpelstiltskin. Evil sons of bitches.

I ease up to the edge of the lantern light. Fight just ended. I look over the faces. Half these men've bought my likker at one point or another. Lucky Jim Graves, Pastor Jenkins, Chief Smylie, Stipe—he didn't buy it, just took what I offered. George. I know most these men.

Henry Means carries a limp dog in his arms. Someone opens the pit gate, an oak shipping pallet. The man says, "He died game," and Henry nods, solemn like he truly gives a shit.

"What you doing here, Baer?"

It's Lou Buzzard, a regular buyer.

I swing a jug of shine. "Stipe here says I can come anytime, long as I fetch a jug."

"I said two," Stipe says. He tramps to me, clamps his jaws tight. All the men is silent. "But that was before you murdered Achilles."

"Brown dog? Bullet hole in his eyeball? I never seen that dog."

Stipe takes the jug from my hand. "You come for a dose of sledgehammer?" He looks around at the men, then meets my eyes again. "You got some gall, Creighton." He comes close and leans into me. His voice is a whisper. His eyes is red and I got the electric all through me. "We got business to settle, you and me. Fire and brimstone."

He smacks my shoulder like we's old friends, and though I'm braced I fly two feet. I was right. He'll kill me later. Not now.

I'm close enough to the pit I can smell it. It's a place of death, and the odors is everything happens when a body dies. Blood, from weeks and weeks of spilling. Piss and shit stamped into the mud so the circle stinks like a witch's kettle. Throw in a couple bat wings and chicken livers, fella could cast a spell.

"I want to know who stole my dog."

Stipe's face is flat, white like a can of Crisco what somebody drew a line across for a mouth and poked two fingers for eyes. "Make yourself at home, Creighton." He grins, backs away, and points. "Get Stinky Joe in the pit, Hank. He's up against Panzer."

Stipe gestures and a fella I know from way back steps beside him. Stipe leads him a few yards away, leans to him and says something. Stipe looks at me and the man looks at me. He crosses his arms and nods, and wanders toward me.

"How you doing, Burly?"

"Better'n you, I suspect."

Meanwhile, men shuffle at Stipe's orders. The one called Hank nods, but comes for a hit on the jug first. Stipe pulls the cork and holds the mouth to his lips. He sputters and passes it. Hank beats another set of grasping hands and I'm all but certain everything'll shape up the way I want. For Fred.

I move a few feet and Burly Worley stays beside me, half watching me, half the goings-on.

A truck engine starts and reverse lights flash. The vehicle stops shy of the pit and with the engine running and exhaust tumbling along the ground, the driver gets out and drags a big wood dog pen from the front of the bed to the tailgate. Inside, between the slats, a pair of feral eyes glows. It's the first time I ever detected a dog that was a liar.

"That Panzer?" I say.

Burly says, "That's him."

"I'll bet he's a tricky bastard."

"How'd you know?"

The dog's master pulls a long handle like fits a hoe from the truck bed. It's got rope looped at the end, comes all the way up the handle. Tool's purpose is evident—lasso the dog's head, cinch the rope tight, and maybe the handle will keep him far enough he can't chew off your nuts. The man bends to the crate door, unfixes a latch and cracks it ajar. He works the handle back and forth, muttering. I watch Panzer through the slats and shadows. Dog shifts sideways like a ghost, white and gone, there and no more, and finally his owner says, "All right, easy, boy. Easy now."

Panzer's every inch a fighter. His eyes glow like backlit blood and he keeps his head low. He shifts back and forth, like it's him agin the whole world and he'll keep us off guard by moving around. Muscle ripples under his coat, and his neck's bigger'n his ass. He's a brute.

Stinky Joe shrinks against the opposite side of the ring. His master stands beside him, not even bothering to put him on a rope. I wonder if that's how Fred looked—disoriented, scared at the smell of arena mud and the stench of booze coming out men's pores.

Panzer leaps from the bed of the truck and his master hops down with him. Men part as the dog approaches, eyes already fixed through the dog ring pallet slats on the quivering beast at the far side.

"Five to one against Stinky Joe," Stipe barks.

I wonder who'd name a fighting dog that. Call him Artillery, or Bullets, or Bone Crusher. Or Achilles, like that devil I killed. Stinky faces Panzer and drops his head low. The men hush and Stinky Joe's growl trips across the ground.

He's backed agin a wall and his enemy comes.

I think of Fred, mauled and blind, and the Smith on my hip feels like the better way to go. But if I can be patient, I got something in mind that'll make these fellas feel like God dropped em deep in the Old Testament.

I scan faces one by one, curious that Cory Smylie ain't here, nor flesh-and-blood Larry. Stipe tell em to lay low? These boys got something more planned for old Baer? Was stealing my dog the beginning of something a thousand times bigger, and do these boys think they's the ones delivering justice, now that Baer brought his bullets?

Good questions when surrounded by men packing pistols and knives, gulping a hundred-sixty proof shine. Burly watches the dogs, then me. He's been tasked with keeping track of me but he'd rather keep his eyes on the action in the pit.

Standing center pit, Stipe works mud off one boot with the toe of the other. "All right, five to one against Stinky. Last takers?"

The men is quiet.

"All right," Stipe says. He exits the circle and hovers at the edge with one arm raised. Panzer's owner has his forearm across the dog's breast—he's removed the pole and rope contraption. Since he's been in the pit, Panzer's been solely occupied spooking Stinky Joe. Stinky's searching for escape between gaps in the pallets.

Stipe drops his arm.

Panzer leaps across the ten-foot circle.

I turn. Burly has his gaze on the fight. I work away from the pen, unminded. Men jostle closer.

I can't see the fight but from the growls and yelps, low-tenored and breathy, I imagine what's going on. Back among the trucks I look at the tailgates for any seem brighter on the left than right. They's one with wide tires, but it's got dark paint.

A shout comes from the pit and I look back. The men boo and cuss and Stinky Joe flashes past me. He's jumped the wall and the little I know about these boys says Stinky better put a serious stretch between him and them. And never find his way home.

Burly figures out he lost sight of me and spins a full circle, looking. He shoots me an ugly look and starts working back to me.

Stipe pays money to the winners and says, "Time for King George and Gravy. Dogs to the ring! King George is a seven-time winner, undefeated. Never turned—not once in all his fights. King George is fighting in place of Achilles. You all know what happened there. Gravy… this is his first fight in this circle, but he's got two wins down outside of Charlotte. You can tell by his size he's going to give King George a mess of trouble. Three to one, King George. Who's in?"

Is Gravy like Fred? Like Stinky Joe? Some bullshit name and bullshit history in some bullshit town?

What bullshit name they give Fred?

I gulp shine from my flask and yank my Smith. Point at the moon and pull the trigger. Smith barks and flame flashes.

Men halt. Stipe stares. Burly's five feet away and I point at him. He steps back a half-dozen feet.

"You boys is a bunch of assholes."

Chuckles.

"Shut the hell up," Lucky Jim Graves says.

I point Smith at him. "Hey, unlucky. Want to play a game?"

Murmurs die. Eyes flash red like a pack of evil wolves in the dark. But they's no deceit yet, and the color fades.

"I don't know which of you recall a dog from last month. White pit didn't have the sense to hop the pen like Stinky Joe. But one you sons a bitches fought him." I point the Smith at Jenkins, the pastor. Then Lou Buzzard. Then George from the lumberyard. Come to a stop on Stipe. "Who was it?"

Stipe spits. "You sore 'bout a dog? A coward dog? You murder my champ and cost me real money, but I don't get stupid."

I keep Smith trained on Stipe's triple-chinned head. I didn't think before pulling it and I don't have an inkling of what to do. But if I put the gun away, these boys'll beat my ass silly.

George from the wood mill emerges from the group with his hands in the air and confusion on his face. "What's this about,

Baer?" His eyes is plain; wants to be the honest broker. He eases close. Reaches toward my left shoulder.

I shift aside.

"Don't think I can make it plainer. Who tossed my dog in this ring?"

"Put that piece away, 'fore someone takes you serious," Stipe says.

All this time and I ain't seen a bit of red anywhere, nor felt a single zap. I step back and listen to the sounds behind me. Leaves in a breeze.

I lift the barrel and squeeze off another above Stipe. He jumps, snarls.

"You're good as dead," Stipe says.

Eyes glow. All at once, every damn one of 'em, like I riled a nest of demons.

SEVENTEEN

Footsteps rush from behind. Something like a sledgehammer drops on my gun arm and my hand's empty. Arms around my shoulders; men wrestle me down. More boys rush up. Kicks to my legs and guts. A boot catches my shoulder blade. I reach on the ground and can't find Smith, and a heel stomps my hand. Boot in the mouth. I taste blood.

I got to get home.

Home's where I got a solution—but I relish the honesty in a groin kick, the alley tactics. They hate me and act with all the integrity they got, and their plain-dealing is nice for a change. I curl my knees tight to my chest but a couple kicks to by back have my muscles in a knot. These boys ain't letting up.

"Enough!"

The kicking stops. Men part. Stipe stands close.

"Get up, Baer."

Feels like every bone I got is busted, but it's the muscles doing the complaining. Burly bends over and yanks me upright.

"I brought you sons a bitches a jug."

"I don't got to tell you not to come back," Stipe says. "I don't got to mention next time you come prowling around here or my house or my dogs or anydamn thing associated with me—"

He censors himself. His eyes is hot and his brow tight. He looks across the watching men and something passes between him and Burly, who's taken three steps back and leans agin a black Suburban next to a table with a lantern. Bumper sticker says, *DEPENDS ON THE DEFINITION OF* TREASON.

I spot my Smith a couple feet away. Grab it and pull the hammer back with my thumb. They eyes is normal; just they faces is flushed. I point Smith toward 'em, wave it back and forth. But before I grabbed it they was already a dozen men with guns in they hands.

Burly Worley's gone.

"You already proved you're an idiot, Baer." Stipe says. "Put that away and don't ever come back."

"I come here to give you boys a chance. This shit ends tonight. No more fights around these parts. Or I'll murder every fucking one of you."

I point at the sky. Ease the hammer forward. The air's thick and humid and the breeze is cold. Moths around the lanterns have scampered off. I catch one man's eyes after another. Work to my feet and back away from the group. Snatch a quick look behind.

Every muscle I got screams but I don't have any new teeth marks in me and I got a clear conscience. I give these boys the chance to get right. I called out they evil, and delivered my message.

I'm a hundred yards out and it's darker now than when I set out a couple hours ago. One of them kicks to my noggin's messed with my vision. Each step reminds me next time I won't give a bunch of assholes the benefit of the doubt.

I keep a hand up deflecting branches from my eyes and feel along slow with my feet. The forest floor's irregular. I slip and catch myself on all fours. Pause a second with the silence. Look up to a moon perched on a beech limb.

A plodding noise comes along from behind. Crunches through leaves and twigs like it don't give a royal damn who hears. Black bear, like me, headed away from the fight circle. Had his fill of watching beasts and smelling blood. He ain't but a dozen yards off, and looks like a big black chunk of motion. He's like a tank bowling over scrub.

A stick snaps thirty, forty feet off, back the way I come.

I stay crouched and search the dark forms. Tree trunks is solid black voids and the space between is gray with silver frost on the moon side. They's a shape like another bear coming, few steps then pauses, few steps more.

But this one's upright.

He's homed on the bear, thinking it's me. It's Burly Worley. Has to be. He's got a pistol in his hand, but ain't got it aimed.

I reach back slow without rustling a single brittle leaf and pull Smith. I had time I'd dig a hole, fill it with spikes, slather em in people shit. Stretch a line across right in front, ankle high. Fix a knife to a sapling and bend it back like a two-hundred-pound bow, set with a figure-four catch. They's many ways to fuck with a man in a dark wood. But as he's coming now I got twenty second, and then it's plain old Smith.

Ten feet.

He stops, lifts his pistol arm and points. He sniffs. Ahead, the bear stumbles into a log and thrashes it, from the sound. I hear his sniffing nose pressed in the rotted wood. Maybe he's looking grubs for a midnight snack.

I can almost feel Burly's confusion.

Burly's so close I can smell him. He prob'ly lives in a house but don't bathe regular—a lot of folk don't.

Now that I look steady I see the bear again. He's a big son of a gun—you got the dog bears and the hog bears, some with high bellies and some with low bellies. This fella's a hog bear. Even still, black bear generally don't want nothing to do with people.

You want trouble with one, you got to make it.

Burly sidesteps like to circle the brute up ahead, and shifts two feet toward me. He's got his face pointed forward and ain't even looked my way. I make a noise he'll spook and shoot me, I know it. He's looking forward, but they's a red glow about his eyes.

I lighten the load on one foot and a leaf crinkles.

Burly faces me—swings his gun arm level and pointed at my head. He had me all along. "Hello, Baer."

"Hey, Burly. Doing all right tonight?"

"Better'n you." He steps closer. Places his pistol barrel to my temple.

I can feel the cold metal through my hair. "I don't think you'll miss. You want to give me just a fucking inch? A half-inch?"

He eases off. "Let's go. Nice and easy. Don't trip, don't jump. I might get scared and shoot you."

"I guess Stipe sent you out to put me down, huh? That it?"

"Nah, just to have a conversation. Let's both back away from that black bear, and maybe we'll talk a bit."

"Let me ask one thing."

"Move, dammit. Nice and easy."

"Do you feel the red coming out your eyes? Tingle like you drug your feet over carpet and you know you're going to give somebody a shock?"

"What the hell you talking about?"

"No? Because it gives you away."

I got my gun hand halfways aimed at the bear; it don't take but a subtle move to pull the nose higher. I point at his ass, best I can, and squeeze the trigger. The muzzle flashes orange and I spin away from Burly's barrel, knock his hand with my elbow. I jump to the closest tree and start scrambling. The bear grunts and swings our way. He's coming quick and Burly's standing still. I claw up a six-inch smoothbark tree, maybe elm. It's slippy and each time I gain a foot I slide back half. About ready to give out, I reach the lowest limb and get a hold.

And drop Smith.

That bear is right close. Burly faces him. Steps backward. He talks low-voiced and guttural like he's had run-ins with bears before. "You got a funny smell, baby," he says. It don't matter his words; bears don't speak English like dogs. It's all in the tone. Burly's playing it right.

I spot his gun on the ground. I must've knocked it from his hand.

Black bear stands on his hind legs, waving his head back and forth, only ten feet off. With the breeze agin him he can't smell worth a shit, and bears is halfways blind. So he steps closer.

Burly knows bears like any country boy knows bears. He can't turn his back, and he don't want to kneel for his gun. Holding a black bear at bay is a matter of not losing your cool.

"You stay back, you ignorant, overgrown hog," Burly says, low as he can. "Why don't you shoot him for me, Baer? Shoot him in the head this time."

"You best watch I don't call him in."

If that black bear wanted to charge, he'd have done it after I shot him.

I'm thinking I missed, and only startled him. He's mighty inquisitive—most would have run off after a surprise like that. He'll go on his way once he's satisfied Burly ain't a threat or food. And then it'll be Burly and me again. My gun sits not three feet from his.

That bear takes off, Burly's got two guns, I'm up a tree, and bullets climb trees faster'n bears.

Black bear lowers to all fours, begins a lumbering turn sideways.

I let go my tree limb, silent. Right arm high, coming down hard with my elbow. Burly swings his noggin at me and I catch his temple with my elbow. He's surprised dumb. I land on my feet. He staggers and grunts. The bear scoots away a few yards into the black night. I swing with my fist and clock Burly in the temple.

He drops to the ground and sighs from his throat long and slow. The noise has a groan of voice in it, like an animal been shot, or like his whole body froze up.

One of them sounds that make you think you gone too far.

I kick his boot.

Burly Worley ain't moved nor made a sound in five minute. Got one leg folded under the other, and his gun arm under his back. I stand shaking with I don't know what, adrenaline maybe, as I think through the logic of retribution. If a man does you ill, setting things right means giving back the same, and a little more for punishment. Burly's part of the group that left Fred for dead, and deserves to be dead. But him deserving it and me putting him in the ground? My mind ain't made the leap yet.

I point Smith at his head and get on my knees. Lean on one arm and stick the muzzle against his temple. He so much as twitch at me, his head'll meet that beech in pieces.

I park my ear above his nose and listen.

"Come on, Burly."

I smell whiskey. He looses a tiny sigh.

I ease back but I keep Smith ready to bark an order or two. Burly mumbles and I'm just about sure half of his problem is all the whiskey he drunk, not the popknot I put on his skull.

I don't think I been next to somebody sleeping since Ruth and me fell asleep in the back seat.

Burly Worley'll be fine, so long as he wakes before that bear gets hungry. But I never heard of a bear that eats asshole, so he'll be all right.

I wait ten more minute and Burly starts to snore. I'll be damned if I'm going to babysit any more of this. I set off slow so my feet don't rouse him.

I follow the crick bank, careful not to slip. The water's eaten away dirt and sometimes walking too close you get a squishy feel. But that's where the deer path goes, and I follow it because the brush gets thick elsewhere.

Ruth and me was a thing all right. While Larry was off at school we fooled around every night she could get away, but it got tougher as the weeks went on. Her daddy was hell bent on Ruth being a trophy wife, and nobody but some law-school boy set on ambulance chasing or politics was good enough. He must've had in the back of his head some greaser was boffing his daughter. She had to get clever to see me.

Well one day she came with a faceful of tears. Crazy like the world come to an end.

"What is it? Let's scrog. You'll feel better."

She turned her shoulder. "I'm pregnant."

I trip on a tree root and my knee catches a rock right where I landed on my binoculars a couple day back, but I'm hip-deep in memories. They wasn't a feeling in the world like Ruth telling me she was knocked up. That baby meant we'd end up together. Doing the right thing lined up pretty well with my life's ambition. I'd marry her and bust my ass to keep her happy.

But the right thing to her daddy was bound to be different, and that's what had her bollixed.

I come up with a plan to handle Preston Forsyth Jackson. This was deep in Larry's semester at college—November, memory serves. I'd been paying attention and learning at the garage. Wasn't anything with an engine and wheels I couldn't fix, and I was affable with anyone could talk gasoline and metal. Made a friend of a trucker passed through every week and I had an idea I could make a career move with his help.

I drove my Nova to the city and tracked down the company he worked for. Got a mechanic job and come home to tell Ruth.

The still site is quiet except Fred grumbles, I know it's you.

I cover Fred with a blanket, scratch his ribs. I'm as ready for the bedroll as I ever been, but I got one more errand. The river rocks I heat for the bathtub is cold as the ground. Fire's long dead. I start another. Time I come back, them stones'll be suitable.

I told Ruth I had a job. She looked at the floor.

"What is it, now?"

"Nothing."

"Well, shit. I'll tell you about my new job."

"I'm not pregnant."

It was all a scare, she said. A misunderstanding.

Fred says, You want to keep the mumbling to a minimum? Trying to sleep.

"I don't feel so good, Fred."

Know just how you feel, Fred says. Just one thing. Did you learn what you went to learn? Is the plan going to work?

I nod. "Think so."

Do you have the balls to do it?

I think of Burly, and not being ready to shoot him. "I don't have a single clue."

EIGHTEEN

I'm busted good and if I'd feel any better in the sleepsack that's where I'd be. But a fella don't rise to a lofty height such as mine without uncommon dedication. I stretch my bruised muscles and drink away the aches. Add a couple heavy logs to the fire.

So they liked your likker? Fred says.

"They surely did."

Didn't you know that from the last time they beat your ass?

"I get mad. And they didn't beat my ass. I fell out a tree."

If good men didn't get mad, it'd just be the bad ones, Fred says.

"You said a mouthful. I'll be back after bit."

Cory Smylie lives in a good part of town, up on Ketchum Street. I would've got in his face before going to the fight but them fights is only one night a week, and Cory's always a shithead. He ain't moved out his folks' house so I'll catch him somewhere else.

They's a black feller name of Harry runs a shot house on a hill in Swannanoa; serves booze all night. Used to buy my likker before Fletcher Rose sold his cheaper. I visited a couple times and Cory was there, on account the women, or maybe selling drugs. It's a long shot, but worth a walk. If not, I'll catch him when he comes home.

Every muscle I got's backsassing each step.

The shot house sits atop a wooded hill. Houses date to this being the rich neck of the wood, and they's practically mansions. But the yards ain't been tended in decades, and scrub trees grow right up next the houses. Feels like walking through the woods with a town dropped in the middle, and nary a tree cut to make room.

It's deep after midnight. A car moves slow up the hill, cigar cherry inside. People in the back seat got big hair. Giggles.

Men take women up the hill, get em sloshed and then go back down the hill. At two bucks a shot, these customers get a deal. You put my shine or someone like Fletcher Rose—that son of a bitch makes good shine—put his squeezins agin house likker at a regular bar, and ours is twice as potent for half the cost. Tastes like a gulp of bonfire; numbs pipes from smile to shithole.

Women say it goes straight to the gizzy.

Car parks outside a small cabin with an open door. The joint's packed, though they ain't four five cars outside. Smoke hangs at the ceiling and voices carry fifty feet. A pinball machine lets out a bunch of pings and zaps. Men bullshit on the step. They's a pinkish glow from every eye in the joint.

I wade in.

The men and women is black and white, all sitting ass-deep in deceit. Floor's wood. Walls got no paint. They's no windows, and barely enough room to wedge an elbow. I look over the faces but

Cory ain't here. His truck ain't outside and Cory Smylie ain't got the ambition to walk five mile.

I recognize a couple faces, no one I want to talk to. But Harry waves, and waves again, with vigor. The throng blocks me and Harry nods at the door. He slips out the back and meets me at the steps.

"Some kin'a sales call?" he says.

"Lookin' somebody."

"Whodat?"

"Cory Smylie. White kid. Ain't worth a can of owl shit."

"I know'im. Uh-huh."

"Well, I see he ain't here. Still getting your shit from Fletcher?"

"Thassaight."

"Had a couple yourself t'night... "

"Uh-huh." He slaps my arm and bends over, laughing, and his eyes glow on the white-lie setting. He pulls my arm with the strength of a mechanic. Takes me into darkness.

"You bes' watch your back."

He's suddenly sober.

"Yeah?"

"Stipe's boy Barrow been out twice, last two week. Fust was t' see if I bought from you. I says no. He leave. Week later, he come back and says, 'Okay, who *does* buy from 'im?' You know sometimes you can tell a puhson got they ill will going on? Get the sense he's looking t' get uuugly?"

"Know what you mean."

"Well, Barrow got his uuugly on. That mean Stipe do too."

"'Preciate you, Harry."

"All right. Let's have us a drink. You drink Fletch's shit?"

He leads me into the shot house from the back. Grabs a jug from twenty under the bar. Fills a glass and like the good people he is ignores my handful of money. I gulp the fire.

"Next you see Fletcher Rose, you shake his hand for me."

"One more," Harry says.

I oblige so I don't insult the man. While he ain't looking I drop my money on the floor behind the bar. Slap his shoulder and he winks. He does the drunk act good but he drinks like a stiller and I know he's fulla shit. I slip out.

If brains was leather I couldn't saddle a junebug. They's enough places Cory Smylie could be, I was foolish coming here. But they's one place a can of shit always winds up, and that's floating in the sewer he calls home. I reckon it's two more mile. Plenty of time to think on who stole Fred.

My flesh-and-blood brother and me's been right assholes about one thing or the other most our lives. But the dust settled twenty some year ago, last I talked with Ruth. No reason for Larry to strike up a feud now.

Cory Smylie? Been years since I wanted to shoot his window on account of the deer, and I don't ken he knew what I thought on the deal. Fred was gone before I dropped Cory to get the fifty-spot back for Mae, so anything he done was out the blue, a crime of opportunity. Just looking for a dog and saw mine. Maybe thought Fred was bait.

Stipe?

He's behind things all right. But it's the volition I'm after. I want to know the first man to conceive of Fred in a fight circle. That's the son of a bitch I want to say howdy to.

Years ago I come from the woods to a blaring horn to find three men in the drive. I never had nothing to do with Stipe. Knew he was a businessman, but not much more, and didn't learn these boys was working for him 'til later.

"We're buyin you out," one said. It was Huck Barrow, a fella with a neck as red as his eyes.

"You ain't buying shit." I walked away.

I heard the bang of a bitch pistol. Little fella on the side had a twenty-two caliber pointing at the sky, and wore a grin liable to split his head at the ears.

"Better work on your aim."

He pointed at my head, and Barrow said, "Not yet, Willie." His face glowed hot. I got the juice all through me and I figured, it's been a good ride, but it's over. One of them little bullets'll make clam soup outta brain. He said, "We got the money to make it square. We buy your inventory. The rig, the customers. You'll come work for us."

"Don't think so."

I headed away thinking I'd feel a bullet dance into me quick, and I hoped old lugnut was sharp enough to hit the back of my head in the middle. But I reached the house without dying and by the time I got a rifle through the window, they was gone.

Subsequent, I carried Smith walking to the edge of camp to take a piss.

Shot house Harry's story about Barrow asking questions don't surprise me in context. You make a good thing and somebody'll try and take it. But this going on the same time as Fred winding up in Stipe's fights challenges the way I understand coincidence.

Long-ass walk. Without the nourishment of those four shots of Fletcher's finest, I'd be out of likker and aching like a somebody. As it is, I got two flask to hold me.

Headlights splash like water from a bucket. First thought—I want to jump in the woods and haul ass. After Stipe's last promise, I'm maybe more jittery than a regular moonshiner ought to be. The vehicle passes. Ahead fifty yards the brake lights flash. White reverse lights, and a Cadillac truck revs back.

Stipe don't pay his boys that good, but I'm wary and the hair on my arms stands. Not the juice… just old-fashioned distrust. I don't generally associate with folks who ain't got the sense to buy a regular Chevy, or at minimum a Ford. I ease to the driver's side. Window zips down. Cigarette glows.

"That you, Baer?"

I exhale. "In the flesh come down from the mountain."

"Howya doon? Get in." He pops the door open and the dome light goes on.

I circle behind and climb in. Big Ted Lombo's across the seat. One of those fellas makes it his business to know everybody.

Larry does his books.

"How's the restaurant business, Big Ted?"

"People got to eat. How's your business?"

"People drink whether they eat or not. What brings you out, middle the night?" I fish my flask and offer it. "This's special stuff. Plum shine."

"Plum? Brandy?"

"Nah, shine. Corn, barley, and wheat. Double-stilled, then a touch of plum brandy. Tastes better'n plum gasoline."

"Never had neither."

"Take my word on both."

He grabs the flask. Spins the cap with his thumb.

"Keep both eyes on the road. You'll want to close em."

He gulps and the truck drifts to the white line. "Fuck."

"Ain't it good?"

He wheezes. "Coupla friends got a card game. You know Mickey, right? And Franky? I tell em every week I be there, but I got the rest'rant, yeah? So they start late for me."

"Appreciate the lift."

"Why ain't you got a car? I got a friend make you a deal. You know Guilio Salandra gots the Dodge dealership on Merrimon? I tell him 'Make my friend a deal,' you get anything you want at cost. I make the call tomorrow."

"Don't make it yet, Big Ted. Got to save up, you know."

He nods. I crack the window. I never seen a vehicle with so many fucking lights and dials. The air's a helluva lot cooler now that I'm moving fast through it.

"So what's this crazy shit you doon?"

"Which crazy shit, Big Ted?"

"Fight the other night. An' that thing with Stipe's dog."

"Saw the lights. Truck come out the woods where they's nothing but scrub, and in my line o' work, a fella wants to know his competition."

"Uh-huh."

"You go them fights much?"

"Nah. Once, twice. Don't like violence."

He looks sideways. A white-lie rose color comes from his eyes. He laughs.

Got a question stuck in my mouth: You know who stole my white pit and fought him a couple weeks back? But Big Ted plays all sides. He'd sure as shit tell me, and before sunup he'd tell who he told on, like I had the info and slipped and told him what I was thinking. I'd be no farther ahead, but I'd be in debt.

My flask's in his hand resting on the shifter. Thinking I'll make a grab and he upends it again. We's a mile out of town, and past the turn for the quickest route to Cory Smylie.

Big Ted beats his chest and hands over the flask. I weigh it.

"You keep them eyes peeled to the road, Ted. Put as much likker in your gas tank as you put in your gullet, you'd roll into Hickory before you need a fill-up."

"That's good stuff. You know, I could move some. I got friends always lookin hooch like that."

We enter Gleason. "Where you going?"

I grab the handle. "Here's fine." He swings to the curb. I pop the door, and in the light his face is flat.

"You don't want to go back to them fights, Baer."

"No?"

"None of my business, getting mixed in family… situations. But that crew out there's heard bad things about you long enough, some's bound to've stuck."

"Larry?"

He shrugs.

"Thanks, Big Ted. You give em hell at that poker table."

I close the door like a pussy and it don't latch, and I got to do it again. Inside, Big Ted's got a cell phone in his hand. He pulls off as the dome light fades.

I tramp back the other way and mostly out of town cut right. The clock in the Cadillac truck said it was two thirty-eight. Normal bars've stopped serving, and I'm thinking I'd have had more luck waiting at Harry's shot house.

Cory Smylie'll come back to Mom and Dad's, though.

It ain't a mile. His F-150's gone from the drive. A minivan sits next a Blazer. Opposite the Kenny place the houses is none too thick, with maple windrows between. Not dense enough to hide a man in the day, but shadows is deep at night. I'm warmed up after the walk to the house, but sitting next a tree in the middle of the night, the cold presses in. I work flask number two 'til it's gone.

Lights.

The vehicle passes the Smylie drive and I think of me when I was Cory's age. Spent all them years wishing things was different with Ruth—wishing I didn't have my talent, my brother, my nature.

By and by I let my head droop.

A door clunks. The F-150's in the drive, nose to the road. I'm awake like I run a mile. From the man's shape it's Cory Smylie. Got that muscle-bound slump to his shoulders, and walks like a pimp. He makes it to the tailgate and parks an elbow on the side. He's messed up.

I come out the shadows. Pull Smith, come up on him from his back right, while he's hunched. Glide over dewy grass and he's gagging on puke. I'm right behind, but I wait 'til he's done yak-king on his tire.

He climbs back up the side of his truck and wipes his mouth with his sleeve. He coughs. I grab his right arm and lever it behind his back. Press Smith to his head.

"Whoa—whoa," he says. "Dude. What's going on?"

I smell his upchuck.

"I got your attention?"

"You got it." He coughs.

I cock the Smith. "You mark my words. You listening?"

"Easy now… I'm listening." He shakes, but he's learning so-briety.

"You touch Mae again. You see Mae again. You think of Mae again, I murder you. It's that simple. Savvy?"

"I get it."

I smash the butt to his head.

NINETEEN

Mae leaned toward her crummy sixteen-inch computer monitor, attached to a machine running Windows 98, connected to the Internet via a 56K modem, and reread the sentence she'd just penned.

Thick.

She glanced at Bree and Morgan sitting too close to the television. Or had they changed that whole thing about sitting too close to the television?

She'd made mistakes. This MBA program could give her a fresh start in a different town where every bachelor didn't already know she had three kids by a dope-peddling loser named Cory Smylie. Cory had been a freshman-year-of-community-college disaster that years later still hung around her life like a noose. He had dimples, was boyish and troubled, and only used his brooding smile to get laid. (But it always worked, damn him.) Sure, he'd reformed after being busted. But he still didn't have a job and he managed to make his truck payments.

How would it work when Morgan and Bree were twelve and ten? Would Cory make them push product at the playground?

The question opened an interesting supply chain management topic, maybe a parenthetical diversion for her Age Diversity in the Workforce paper, due in eleven hours—which she'd wing after having sleep-read the assignments and fudged sentience through most of the discussion forums, like usual, because she was always exhausted and the kids demanded perpetual attention.

Mae glanced at Bree and Morgan, on the floor, and at Joseph, asleep on the couch. He was like a dog, sort of, always asleep on the couch. Always. As if he had a problem.

She went to him, touched his back, felt his shallow breaths. They were always shallow.

Bree twisted from the television and smiled at her, silently. Adoringly. Mae slipped to her knees and pulled Bree in, then collapsed with her beside Morgan, and they snuggled on the floor while an offensively bland cartoon reviewed how to count from one to ten.

Bree buried her nose at Mae's side and giggled. Mae squeezed her. "Mommy has to get back to work," she said. "I love you."

She'd matriculated to the Penn State online MBA, shocked at having been accepted to one of the few programs that fetched starry-eyed recruiters. But looking at her two-hundred-dollar second-hand computer, set off beautifully by the water-stained wallpaper, she wondered if forty-seven thousand dollars of debt, right now, made sense. Would she graduate and be unable to find a job because she lived in shitty two-stoplight Gleason, North Carolina?

She wanted a fresh start, away from Cory Smylie. Sure, she could pack the Tercel and head into the sunset, spending all the money she saved by clothing her children at Goodwill and feeding them with food stamps and getting their medical care from the government. She'd reach Charlotte on the first tank of gas, and then Research Triangle Park with the second. And then she'd be broke.

But finding a new place to rent? Covering old debts that were due and perpetually threatening her carefully protected credit score, ruining the possibility of a business loan when she finished school? Was she going about everything wrong? Should she start a business now, without school? The only place was hiring was Cory's Pharmaceuticals.

She sat at the computer. Hold on, she thought, until everything comes together. Lots of moving parts.

Outside, a door slammed. Cory?

"God," she said. She looked at the clock. "Turn down the television. Turn it off!"

"What?" Morgan said.

"Do as I say! Turn it off now! Hush! Pretend we're not here. Let's play a game!"

At the door she peered through the fisheye lens.

"Who is it?" Morgan said.

"Uh, wow. It's your grandmother."

Mae studied her mother. Ruth had lived in Mars Hill since the divorce and though only thirty miles distant, Mae hadn't seen her in several years. The last time they were together was an awkward, man-less Christmas. Mae had taken the girls to Mars Hill for a supper of ham (roasted with a single clove pressed into each cube) and baked sweet potatoes. Sparse conversation flirted at the edge of meaningful, but never penetrated it.

"How's Dad? Do you talk to him? Do you like the ham? I wish I could afford better."

Mae held the front door open, mindful of blocking Bree from bolting outside. In a fractured moment she took in her mother's face: a countenance that had aged decades in mere years; hair that had turned gray; crow's feet that had morphed into dinosaur tracks.

"Hello," Ruth said. Her brow became pensive and her lips formed a tightly drawn smile.

"Come in, Mom… come in!" Mae backed away from the door, glanced at her computer table, the barely begun midterm paper. All that white. So few words. So much research.

"I didn't call," Ruth said. She stared across the living room, disconcertingly beyond Mae.

"You should have called. I'd have made something." Mae shifted her weight from one foot to the other. "I'll make coffee."

Ruth followed her into the kitchen. Mae glanced at the grime on the shield above the stove. Did her mother see it? Or was she looking at the jelly bonded to the kitchen table, underneath a scattering of salt.

"My, look at that."

Mae turned with a can of Folgers in hand.

Ruth studied the open cupboard. "You come into good fortune?" Ruth opened the refrigerator, the freezer. A cabinet. She closed one cupboard and opened the next. "Look at this. Canned chicken and turkey? Soup? There must be thirty cans of soup. Did WIC buy all this food? Or did Cory? You still with Cory?"

Mae filled a coffee pot with tap water. "No."

"Why? He turned out all right, didn't he?"

"Mom, why'd you come? What's wrong?"

Ruth dragged a chair from the table. Her eyes were focused on something a hundred feet beyond the wallpaper. "This table is like the one I had growing up, fifteen years after aluminum was the rage. It's Larry and me. We're having problems."

"You've been divorced eight years."

"I need to talk to you about your father."

The first scent of coffee sifted through the air. Mae leaned against the counter and crossed her arms. "You know he doesn't want anything to do with me."

"There are things you don't know. That I want to tell you, now."

"Was it the milkman?"

"Don't joke. This is hard enough."

"Have a cookie."

Joe Stipe drove a GM double-axle with a step side. He had a red, white, and blue bug deflector and a black POW-MIA bumper sticker. For his sixty-first birthday his wife had hired a local artist to airbrush an eagle on the tailgate. In her eyes, Stipe was a small businessman carrying the weight of the world on his tax-bearing shoulders. It was only right that the eagle proclaim his patriotic superiority to anyone following him. Hell, he probably paid their rightful share of taxes, along with half their neighbors.

Stipe felt no need to correct his wife for considering him a hero, but he did find the eagle a little ostentatious.

"Don't forget to pick up an apple pie at the grocery," she'd said this morning.

Stipe drove slowly, a little detached, unharried by the Honda Civic riding his bumper. The car swerved across the center line only to be stymied by an oncoming pickup. It veered to the other lane again but backed off in the face of a blind curve on a hill. Stipe checked his side mirror and his rearview. The Civic was completely hidden behind the GM's tailgate.

Stipe thought of the pistol tucked under the seat. He tramped the brake and waited for the thud. Tires squealed. The Civic squirted into the passing lane and with a zip-rattle sound raced ahead. The car sat too low to grant a view of the driver, but Stipe noted the plate. 2FST4U.

"Little shithead."

The car zoomed around a bend, and when the tinny exhaust faded Stipe was alone with his thoughts, elbow out the window.

He was going to see Chief Smylie and had a feeling he might have to lean on him. Smylie was fond of Baer Creighton's whiskey.

Of the half-dozen men in the county who stilled moonshine, Creighton was the acknowledged maestro. Stipe had been to Creighton's still six years before, after his man Huck Barrow had failed to convince Creighton to join Stipe's cartel. Stipe went to tell Creighton he would either join or be beaten out of the business.

Creighton wasn't there—only his dog. Stipe had sized up Creighton's operation in a single glance. It was a boiler and a copper tube.

Stipe got the feeling Creighton was like a pool hustler using a warped house cue against a yuppie with a five-hundred-dollar stick... and kicking his ass all over the table.

Stipe had pried information from tightlipped stillers as they folded their operations into his. Creighton's expertise resulted from his indenture to an old master. Gunter Stroh had worked for the German government in World War I as a chemist refining the manufacture of wood alcohol. He had immigrated to the United States in the sixties and had taken Creighton as an apprentice in the early seventies, while Stipe was off fighting a war. Stroh had taught Creighton well, and when the old master died, Creighton took his place.

Creighton was known to dump imperfect shine into the dirt rather than sell it and despoil his name.

Topping Creighton's quality was out of the question. The only option was to help him arrive at a new understanding of his best interest. Through his proxy, Stipe had made Creighton the same offer as he had all the other local stillers. They'd enjoy ostensible autonomy, distribute through him, and receive monopolistic price controls. Stipe would skim a portion of the enhanced revenue and everyone would be happy.

When Stipe went to visit Creighton he had anticipated offering two stark alternatives: join, or be priced out of business. Though he failed to meet Creighton he decided to fire a warning shot. He lowered the cartel's prices, and quickly learned that most of Creighton's buyers were as happy with what he charged as they were with what he produced. Creighton had the better monopoly: brand loyalty.

Years passed and Creighton enjoyed prosperity at Stipe's expense. Whenever Stipe upped the cartel's prices, the overflow went to Creighton, which forced Stipe to continually lowball. He was not gaining the riches his scheme rightfully promised. This last round of manipulation was designed to bend Creighton until bones snapped, and if he didn't relent, break him in two.

From Creighton's behavior with the dogs, Stipe suspected Creighton would end up dead. He all but sealed that fate when he killed Achilles.

Men grew attached to dogs. Stipe had been fond of Achilles; the way he moved across a fight ring was something to behold. Whirling, flipping—he was an acrobat. The dog was wily from experience. Achilles was a brute, and sure to be the founding stone of a new line of champions. Stipe loved him. But what the hell was lovable about Creighton's wretched coward? Dog turned tail. No gameness at all. In fact, the fight was so lame the men lost interest. It would have been an embarrassment to any organizer. Stipe had ended the match early so the men wouldn't leave. There was no way to compare a dog as miserable as Creighton's to a warrior like Achilles.

Stipe had passed over Achilles when the bitch Medusa had gone into heat, waiting to afford Achilles more time to pile up exploits. The more he accumulated, the greater the value of his eventual progeny. Besides, Achilles was in no real danger. Stipe organized the fights. There were only a handful of animals of Achilles's ability, and Stipe could easily ensure they never met.

But Stipe had never considered the possibility that Creighton would sneak into the compound some night and put a bullet in Achilles's head. There would be costs associated with muscling Creighton, but his retribution had decimated Stipe's plans, and it was an affront.

In having Creighton's dog stolen, fought, and abandoned almost dead, Stipe had a singular purpose: convince Creighton that the only alternative to absolute destruction was to join the cartel. To convince a man like Creighton, Stipe knew he had to be willing to go all the way.

He just didn't anticipate Creighton would make him equally pleased with either outcome.

In visiting Chief Smylie, Stipe would set the conclusion in motion.

Creighton's habits were his weakness.

Stipe pulled into an empty space beside Chief Smylie's Suburban.

If Smylie had a problem accommodating Stipe's request, well, he'd throw in a choice pick from Medusa's next litter. Stipe shook his head. He wouldn't be losing much. And if that didn't work, maybe it was time for Smylie to learn of his son's connections in Baltimore and Washington, and the risks he was taking.

So often, good business was just a matter of reminding men what they had to lose.

Mae wondered if she could complete her midterm paper in her mind so when Ruth left she could type it out and be done.

Ruth huddled over the table's edge, picking at a nub of dried jelly. "Imagine you were the prettiest girl in school. Everyone wanted to talk to you and every boy wanted to hold your hand. Teachers expected you to be as smart as you were beautiful. Imagine not having the IQ to go with your looks."

Mae stroked her index fingernail, picked a skin tag below the cuticle. "I thought you came to talk about Dad."

"Your grandfather wanted me to marry rich. You know the thing about boys destined to become rich? They carried slide rules and never had the nerve to ask a girl out."

"What about Dad?"

"So I was at the dance one night and George asked me to the floor. He took my hand and it was like... you know how you get when your stomach just ripples, and you... the song changed to a slow one right as we were walking out on the floor."

Mae nodded.

"George put his hands on my waist. Back then they said you had to have enough space for a cat between you. I pulled him to me and he had a stiffy. I was in love."

"With George?"

"Uh-huh. But only until Bobby... but it was Mickey that got me in trouble. Every class has a Mickey."

"Pregnant?"

"Oh, no. Not at sixteen. Miss Lockwood and Mister Phelps—chaperones—saw me walk off the dance floor with Mickey an hour before the dance ended. We made out in the band room—be patient, Mae; I'm trying to give you the whole picture. So like I said, I was dumb. I never understood the things some boys wanted to talk about. Larry was a halfway point—barely acceptable to my father, and not as terrible as the ones he really wanted me to end up with."

"Did you know Baer then?"

"Baer… "

"There's a nerve."

Ruth glanced at the coffee pot. "That's been done five minutes."

Mae filled two mugs and placed one before Ruth.

"Sugar, dear."

"What about Baer? Why the nerve?" Mae opened two cupboards.

"Baer… we were mixed up at the same time as Larry and me."

"How does that happen?"

"It's what I was saying. After catching me in the band room, Dad wrote a list of boys I was allowed to date."

"How did he know which boys to choose?"

"Anybody from the country club who had a son, clean down to seventh grade. He told their fathers I was available. Every one ugly as a toad's ass. Imagine, forced to pick and choose from the slide-rule boys."

"So how far did it go with Baer?"

Ruth held her mug in both hands as if warming them. "Baer comes later in the story. My father was hell bent on matching me with the right young Republican. There was R-R-R-Ro-Rodger. Even knowing he was supposed to ask me out, and I was supposed to say yes, he couldn't get the words from his mouth in one piece.

I said, 'N-n-n-no.' John took me parking and I was riding the cotton pony. I got him all hot and bothered and told him to take me home or I'd scream rape."

"Jeez, Mom."

"Was I supposed to let him have his way?"

"Never mind."

"So Larry asked me out. He was a jock with a brain. He played every sport but was best at football. He was the quarterback. He took the academic classes so he could go to college. And when I had to sell my father on him, that's what I told him."

Mae took her mug to the sink and dumped the remainder. She leaned against the counter, glanced into the other room at her computer monitor.

"What's that look?" Ruth said. "I didn't come here to have you judge me. You need to know all this, and I'm being honest. Even when it hurts. So don't you dare judge me." Ruth wiped salt from the table into her hand.

"The sink," Mae said. "What are you doing here, Mom?"

"Can I go on?" Ruth stood. "I could tell Larry was attached to me right away. It wasn't our fourth date at the lookout until he blurted he intended to marry me. I wanted to go to college, where Dad couldn't dictate the clothes I wore, the people I saw, the dances I went to. Of course, Dad knew all that and made me volunteer for the district attorney at nights, so I'd be around the young attorneys. He said it would teach me to recognize industry in a man. That's what a girl wants."

"Yeah, I know."

Ruth wrinkled her brow. "I went with Larry all my senior year."

"Exclusively?"

"Sure. Mostly."

"Who'd you cheat on Dad with?"

"Oh, I don't know. They didn't mean anything."

"Neither did Dad. Is that it?"

"Of course he did. Don't you understand? I needed to be wild. Larry went to college at Chapel Hill. We were engaged, but Dad was after me to date the country club boys, and he only put up with Larry because he was the quarterback and wore glasses."

"Was Baer the one you… one of the ones?"

"Baer. I didn't even know him until Larry went away to school. I mean, I'd seen him, but he was booted out of school for being a tough guy. He was built like a wire nail. All taut when he walked, like he had pistols on his hips and a horse under his ass." Ruth grinned. "Wait." She jumped from her chair and trotted from the kitchen, out the front door.

Mae looked at the empty chair. All these years with nothing but a phone call here and there, and then this information dump right when she had no time.

Outside, a car door slammed. Mae watched the entrance to the living room. Ruth entered with one hand on her chest and the other holding a pocketbook.

"Look at this." Ruth opened the flap, dug out a plastic photo book, and flipped to a black-and-white of a smirking kid with defiant eyes and slicked hair.

Mae gazed into Baer's eyes in that single, camera-frozen moment. She understood his mind from the wrinkle on his brow. School was rotten. The next kid in line, flipping him off, was a shithead. The teacher in the classroom to which he'd return was an idiot.

"Do you have a picture of Dad?"

"That photo's from the year they expelled Baer. It was the only picture he had of himself when I asked, maybe four years later."

Mae lifted her gaze from Baer. "Are you saying you cheated on Dad with Baer? Is that what all this truth is about? I'm supposed to understand because he was cute?"

"I'm trying to give you a whole lot more than 'he was cute.' When Larry went to college, I was kind of promised to him—"

"Did Dad think you were waiting for him?"

"Yes."

"Did you wear an engagement ring?"

"It's not that simple."

"I'll bet Dad thought it was."

"You use words and you have no idea what they mean. Listen to me. Please?"

Mae looked at the photo again. The smirk. "If I'd have gone to school with Baer, I'd have been kicking asses right beside him."

"I always saw that. About you."

Mae remembered a night a decade before, when her mother and father's marriage ended. Mae had crept out of her room to eavesdrop on the accusations and denials. Larry knew Ruth's heart had always been elsewhere. Ruth denied everything. Larry had waited until Mae was almost independent and he no longer had to abide his wife.

Mae bit her tongue.

"I can see it on your face. If I was so crafty with men back then, how did I ever get on with Baer? That's the point. I wasn't dishonest. I was a flirt. I was outrageous. I saw a boy I wanted and I went after him. I let it all hang out. I was the one that was honest through all of this—with Larry, with Baer, with every guy I ever went with. I belonged to nobody, and they should have known. I was true."

"So you did whatever you wanted, and if they didn't figure out they couldn't trust you, it was their fault."

"I want you to understand because when Larry comes, he's going to say things to hurt you. He's been cra—"

"Say it! Would you? You had affairs when I was growing up? You cheated? He cheated? He beat you? What?"

"Baer is your father. I think I still love him."

Mae was still. Her ears rang. Her vision narrowed. She thought of the kiss, and Baer's revulsion. "So that's why he's been buying groceries. Spending time with the kids."

Ruth shook her head. "No."

"Baer doesn't know?"

"No."

Mae lifted her hand to block her mother's words and backed from the kitchen. Her legs were lead. She had the paper to finish. To start. Bree screamed and Morgan giggled and Joseph wailed. Mae's head swam. Baer was her father? She crossed into the living room and turned to the steps. She looked at her mother's eye and said, "Let yourself out."

"Mae, please."

"Does Dad—does Larry know?"

"He was going to come here to tell you."

"Why? Why now?"

"He's snapped," Ruth said. "He's been stalking me."

"How long has he known?"

"The beginning."

"You're sure?"

"There is no way Larry ever thought he was your father."

"I need to throw up. Please go."

TWENTY

It's morning and I'm late to rise. Took a piss at sunup, gandered through the woods for an early-morning sniper. Made me wonder if I oughtta check them traps I set out by the Hun blind.

Fred snores. While I was up I snuck a hand under the wool blanket and he was plenty warm. Besides the blanket he sleeps on, he's got another around the whole box, and then another folded on top of that. Not taking any chances with his condition making him weak, though truth told, he gets up as much as he wants. What's it been? Three week? He breathes natural, and soon I'll pull the stitches out his chest. Rest of him, save his eyes, looks normal. He's got emotional problems, but his body's come along.

Fred can sleep much as he wants. Me, no matter how I twist they's a gap in the sleeping bag lets the sun creep through, and once I wake I can't lay more'n a few minute.

That beating the other night didn't break me. Hell no. Anything but. Them boys thought they'd teach me something about my place in the world, and they sure as hell did.

They beat the shit out of me and they think I'm broke. All they did was steel my mind. My place according to them is eking out a living selling shine, and one day I'll die in the woods and no one'll be the wiser. But I live in the woods because it beats what the world's got to offer. I come and go as I want. Answer to nobody.

I'm thinking all this from the warmth of my bag, pissed off at sunlight.

A horn lets out at the house.

It ain't 'til I climb out the bag and set about getting my clothes that I feel the full measure of the work Stipe's friends did. My chest and back is hammered and my kidneys push a sick feeling through me. Sitting up, all my blood sluices to my feet and I'm dizzy. I brace my hands on my knees. Once my heart realizes I mean to see about the house, everything steadies out.

I take the Smith from where I left it when I bedded down, beside the old boot I use for a pillow, and strap it on.

Each step brings out another grumble or deepens one I thought I had a handle on. Time I come upon the house, I wonder if they's a single stretch of me ain't bruised or busted.

From inside I look out the window. It's Pete Bleau. They's a passenger in the truck, hid in cigar smoke. No red comes from either. No juice.

Must be after the apple.

Pete rolls his window and cigar smoke billows out. His passenger is Butch, his dog.

"You got to know I don't appreciate you dumping that brandy in my face—but as it turns out moonshine don't make you blind, even straight in the eyes."

"Uh-huh."

"Come after that brandy," Pete says. He looks me over head to toe. "You look like pan-fried chicken shit."

"How many gallon?"

"Of chicken shit? Twenty, minimum."

"Of brandy."

"Six for starters. Left your humor inside?"

"Got it beat out of me. Maybe that's why you're in such damnable good spirits." I hold out my hand. "Money first."

His eyebrows dip. He squirms his arm behind his back. Comes out with a wallet and fishes bills. Counts thirty-six. Butch twists away from looking out the side window. His eyeballs is bloodshot.

"You said six gallon," I say. "That's sixty."

He pulls more bills and hands em through the window. "What the hell happened to you?"

"Roll down the other window. Your dog's stoned."

Inside the house I grab jugs from a downstairs rack agin the cement-block wall. If they knew how easy it'd be to rob me a lot of these fellas would. Never lock the doors and I spend ten month a year in the woods. Make a point of always coming out the house, but the chain of thoughts gets me thinking.

Two jugs in each hand and it's as much as I can stand to haul.

"You get lost in there?" Pete says.

"Fuck you, Pete."

I tuck the jugs in the hay lining the truck bed. Pete's rolled down the side window for Butch. I return for the last two jugs. When I come out with em Pete's got a thought taking shape on his lips.

"What?"

"This ass-beating you took… anything to do with that dog of yours? And Stipe?"

I tuck the last two jugs under straw. "You talk to Stipe? That it?"

"Ain't seen him."

His eyes say he's playing it straight. "Why you bring Butch today?"

"It ain't that I think anybody'd take him. But why take the chance?"

"They bust in people's houses?"

"Why not? Stipe's got the police chief at the fights most every week."

"You'd think they'd have enough sense to steal dogs from some other town."

"Nah. This is the town they got sewed up."

"Yeah." I push off the truck. "Something else on your mind?"

"They beat you other night, didn't they?"

I don't got to answer.

"I was at the barber shop this morning. Heard bits and pieces."

"From?"

"Frank."

"Frank?"

"Murdoch."

"Ah."

"They got more in store, Baer. They plan on hurting you but good."

"How's that?"

"Dunno. But it's big. Murdoch made it sound like the end times for one man only. You do something special, set em off?"

"I ask myself why some shithead would want to steal my dog in particular, and all I come up with is some folks enjoy evil. Some men slap around they women. Some start wars. Anywhere you go they's men ain't happy 'less they got a foot on some slob's neck. But I ain't done anything special. Been minding my own business thirty—"

"What?"

"Nothing."

"Yeah. Well keep your eyes open." Pete starts the truck engine. "You got them boys riled."

"Thanks, Pete."

He nods, and backs the truck. His grimace says he thinks this's the last he'll see of me.

TWENTY ONE

Walking helps my bones. They's no particular ache worse than the rest; I got an overall ass-whoopin that'll take considerable spiritual intervention to rectify. So I brought two flask of the spirit and the first is already empty.

Brisk day. I keep my hands in my pockets and my eyes on my feet. Lots to think about on the way to see Mae. Make sure Cory Smylie ain't retaliated.

She always had the brightest hair. That's the first I thought when I saw Ruth with her—that and the shock that Ruth was at me and Larry's house, and had a baby… and was thick in the neck and arms, everywhere.

I'd gone to the city and found work rebuilding diesel engines on the big rigs. They put me in a bay with a set of tools and a 1962 F-model Mack, told me to tear it down and by the time I'd put it back together I'd have my schooling. Boss was a crusty jarhead served in Korea, liked to get to the point of things. I didn't have nothing better'n work to do and I was there all day, every day, close to two years. Found a bunkhouse nearby and saved every penny.

I stood looking at Ruth and Mae and my fingers tingled. I thought about a score of letters Ruth'd writ asking me to come home, declaring her loyalty. She stood with Mae in her arms and her eyes was clear, and sparkled with tears.

They was no red at all.

A truck rolls by, slows as the driver takes a long look at me. It's a chubby girl in a Nissan; she's got a chin puts me in mind of those flat-faced Macks I worked on, with a chrome bumper all the way to the ground. I don't know her and she keeps moving—but even just seeing me on the road shoulder, she's brewing deceit.

The world's a thundercloud moves as fast as a man walks, and no faster.

Larry stood beside Ruth and he glowed red. Sparks shot from my fingers; my joints had an extra jolt, like the juice made me stronger. Don't remember crossing the dirt. Only got off one punch before Ruth cut between us, with Mae in her arms. Mae screamed and Ruth sobbed, and Larry bounced off the wall.

Ruth stood her ground.

I shook, so befuddled I couldn't ask a question. No one said anything, but the electric was all the communication I needed. I stepped back from the porch and missed the plank. Landed on my ass and it rattled me loose from wanting to murder my brother. He came around Ruth and stood above me, shaking. Blood on his lip. Ruth ran in the house.

I was on my elbows. I fished all the money I'd saved in two years from my pocket, peeled off two twenties and threw the rest at Larry. Money roll bounced off'n his chest and landed in the dirt.

"This's my house now," I said. I could've kicked his ass or I could've gone after Ruth to win her back. But doing either would've given him the power over me. In that moment and every sober second since—most of the drunk ones too—all I wanted was to get out from under that storm cloud.

"You can't have the house," Larry said.

"If I get off the ground before that money does, one us is dead inside a minute."

Larry studied me. Ruth stood behind the screen. Larry wasn't moving, and my blood was boiling. I pulled my legs back and shifted to my side.

Ruth came out the door, jostled around Larry, and swooped to the money. A small diamond gleamed on her finger. She pulled Larry by the arm. I sat and listened to em argue inside the house, and tried to add facts that couldn't no-how go together.

All those letters. Lovey-dovey words. Faith-filled poems. Stories of recent small-town events that meant nothing save the beauty of being writ in her hand. Updates on the weather. She'd never once said, "I went back to Larry and had a baby. So fuck you and get the hell out my life."

Eventually I got in the Nova and backed into the turnaround. I sat on the hood and smoked a cigarette. Larry come out with a box and Ruth followed. Back and forth, they loaded the truck.

Pulling out the drive, Larry slowed beside me. Without meeting my eye he said, "We got more stuff to move. So don't you go in yet."

He was gone. She was gone. But I had the house. Spent that night in the woods at the very spot the still sits now.

I'm at Mae's. The drive's empty. I rap the door and Morgan pulls it open. She's in my arms, twisting my hair and nuzzling my neck. Now Bree's here—got purple jelly on the sides her mouth. She puts a finger to her lips and shushes me. Throws a bear hug around my knee, steps on my feet and I walk her inside.

Mae's doing dishes. Joseph sleeps in the other room on the sofa, snugged agin the back pillow. They's two glasses at the table and two plates with the remains of a PBJ-and-milk lunch. Mae finally brings her eyes to me. I don't expect she's too comfortable after planting that smooch.

"What happened to you?" She dries her hands in a dishtowel and comes closer. She hesitates.

"You got a little time?"

She takes my hand.

I say, "You keep up with your mother?"

"Why? Did she do this to you?"

"What to me?"

She touches my cheek with her open hand; eases her thumb across my cheekbone. Aches like hell.

"That's nothing." I ease her hand away.

She squints like a mother.

"Wanted to ask about Ruth."

"What are the odds?" She shakes her head, gives a smile reads like a wince. "Mom's been by."

"Been here? I don't reckon I come up in the conversation?"

Mae takes Morgan from my arm and stands her on the floor. Leads me outside.

"She say something bad?"

Mae sits on a lawn chair with frayed nylon straps. I take the other.

"She hasn't known what to make of you for years. Why are you asking now?"

Why am I asking? I want to know if they's any hope of redeeming a love affair died the day I saw Mae in her mother's arms. I'm getting old. Had the shit beat out of me. Considering action that'll land me in hell or heaven, one. Reached my breaking point and ready to holler so loud they hear me in Idaho.

"Nothing special. I think on her now and again."

"You two were an item, back in the day."

"You heard 'bout the day?"

"A little." Mae gleams pink, and it's unusual enough I got to study her in the eye. "What, Uncle Baer?"

"Nothing." The pink is faint like mother-a-pearl, and kind of pulses like a heartbeat. "You can tell me the truth," I say.

The pink vanishes.

TWENTY TWO

"She thinks she still loves you."

I stand and my knee pops and the lawn chair falls over. Mae ain't one to lie much but I won't believe it. Should've braced myself for some such stupidity, on account of seeing the pink. Maybe they's both liars—something in the blood, come from her mother, that makes a full-throated lie look like a whisper.

If that was true maybe one damn time she'd have writ a letter. Maybe when I walked all the way to Mars Hill and watched her three days, and finally struck the nerve to say hello, she'd have done more than run away. Maybe she'd have said, "Hello, Baer, I love you."

If she was in love all this time, she wouldn't have bedded my pencil-pushing pencil-necked gets-his-stones-off-in-the-woods-watching-animals-die brother.

"What's gotten into you?" Mae says.

I go into the house and check the cupboards because that's all I can think to do. Make sure she has enough food, then she can go to hell. Bree's got wide eyes and Morgan looks caught doing something wrong. They study me keen.

"You two got enough food?"

Course they do. Never ate better. Every cupboard's like I left it. Only been a few days... Ruth's in love with me my royal English ass.

Footsteps. Mae's at the kitchen.

"Baer!"

"I come to make sure you had plenty of food. Cory Smylie been here?"

"No."

"Good."

I shoulder past. Leave the front door open because if I closed it I'd throw it off its hinges.

I'm a mile down the road and her words still play. "She loves you."

Well who the hell are you to know?

Don't recall asking.

So I guess I ain't the only one can't see when she's lying.

Well shit, what if I don't love her no more?

What if I never loved her, and all we had was a bunch of car sex? Hell, I can't remember anything else. What if I hang onto her memory so I don't have to write off the whole human race, and I don't want her to love me back? Did you ever think of that? Stupid-assed meddling woman.

I'm three hundred yards from the house and the still, and a windshield glints through the trees. Somebody's parked in the drive, and another truck is alongside the road.

A rifle echoes. I pick up the pace. Another shot.

Fred.

Somebody come back for Fred.

Smith flaps on my hip. I yank it out and squeeze the grip. Move fast as I can without stretching a run. Back of my heart I know I'm late. Someone got two shots at a blind dog. Ain't likely he missed.

No, my hurry's to make sure he don't get away with it. That's what I tell myself so I can ease off my pace and lighten the strain on the pounder in my chest.

The truck on the side of the road is white.

I duck into the woods. Weave through brush. Metal clashes on metal and two more gunshots echo. First noise was an ax, someone having a good time with my still. Second blast was a shotgun.

I'm fifty yards out, coming from behind. Three fellas—two with long guns and one with an ax. The ax man's knocked the cooker from its blocks and he's going to town on the sides.

I stop at a tree. Aim with both hands, shaking so bad I rest my left wrist agin the bark.

Shit. That ain't Stipe's crew.

That's Mercer, agent works between the revenue service and the state force for likker law enforcement. Don't know the other two. Mercer maybe borrowed em from some other jurisdiction.

These men might not know Fred's at home. He's more'n likely tucked in a puddle a piss, shivering quiet inside his box under the tarp. Surely to God these revenuers didn't come to whack a dog?

I point Smith at the ground. Ease the hammer forward and slip Smith in my holster. Anything wrong with Fred, they'll be teeth in the dirt. Hands up, I step out from the tree. "Hey, boys."

The two gunmen draw stocks to shoulders.

"Easy, Mercer," I call. "Easy."

I cover the distance slow, let em gather they minds. They got the power and they know it, so I don't see any red.

"Hey, Mister Creighton… " Mercer says. "Thought you'd have run."

I come within they circle. The still's fulla shotgun and ax-holes. The copper tube's hacked in pieces, nice clean cuts, like he sit it on a log for support. Doubler's split. They's four barrel of mash with holes through the sides, and fermented corn and apple soup spills out and soaks the ground. The air stinks of rot, sweet with sugar and heady with undistilled shine.

I meet Mercer's eyes. He's a young feller, stocky like a log of firewood, and his small bald head sits atop like a bead of bird shit. I let my arms drift to my sides and check inside the tarp. "Mister Mercer, I hope to hell you didn't shoot my dog."

Fred's head lifts above the diesel turbine crate. His ears is up.

One of Mercer's boys points his rifle at Fred.

"Mister, that dog's half dead as it is. Blind as a bat and can't walk for shit. If you got to be afraid of somebody, point the damn rifle at me."

He obliges.

I tromp to Fred and whisper as I come. His tail beats the crate.

"You're under arrest, Mister Creighton. You know how this goes. You're coming with us."

I kneel at Fred. "You all right, stud? These knotheads shoot you?"

I run my hands over his coat. Look at the crate for BB holes. Fred makes a couple throat sounds and I'm so damn happy I kiss him.

I face the men. "Guess you prob'ly don't like me wearing this."

With my index finger and thumb, I dangle the Smith from my hip and step it to the closest fella. He takes it without changing his law enforcement scowl.

"Mercer—this the standard deal, right?"

"You work with us? We book you today. Judge fines you to-morrow, you rebuild this copper contraption tomorrow night."

"Fair enough. Let me feed Fred and get him covered. Don't want him to freeze."

Mercer nods.

Under the tarp I figure I may as well plan on nothing he said coming true. I fill Fred's dish with three eggs, and use my saucepan for another bowl, and fill it with dry dog food.

"One more thing," I say.

"Huh?"

"Lemme run over the house."

"Looks like you got everything you own here."

"Look here, Mister Mercer. I didn't run. Give you my gun. Just asking a little help."

"Roy—you done with the still?"

"Yup."

"C'mon, Mister Creighton. Lessgo."

I lead through the wood to the back of my house. "I got to go inside."

Mercer follows, alone. I stand before the rack. All total, they's a hundred gallon or more, and some is special blends, corn, wheat, barley, but flavored with fruit. Makes fruit whiskey, if you can noodle that. Mercer's eyes shift along the rows and he looks thirsty as hell.

"What the shit?" I say.

"We had to hit you," Mercer says.

"Hadta?"

"When Chief Smylie hisself phones in the tip, it trumps."

"Chief Smylie, huh?" I grab a jug and wipe the dust from the shoulder.

"What you doing?" he says. "You can't have likker in jail."

I shake my head. "Later on, why don't you come back and help yourself to a couple jugs? Special stuff's on the end. See this 'G'—that's grape. You got plum here, strawberry, apple, pear."

"I'da thought 'P' woulda been for peaches."

"Don't do peaches."

"Peach'd be nice."

"Fuck peaches. We good?"

"We good."

Jail cell's down a hall, not like the Western movies where you sit and jaw at your jailer.

Chuck Preston (I knew his daddy but shit if I knew Chuck got this old this fast) leads me down the hall in cuffs, for show, though they's nobody around and if I could brain him I'd walk clean across the county 'fore anyone figured they was a jailbreak. But that ain't how we do things. The code is simple. They come on a stiller and he sees 'em, he got the right to run. They make mincemeat of his operation and don't come back for a while. But they bust him and he don't fight. They's no sense shooting the lawman when all he'll do is put you in jail a night or two. The biggest pain in the ass, either way, is they smash the still beyond the restorative skills of even the handiest hillbilly.

Well, I don't got to explain turning myself in. I let em keep shooting, they was liable to poke a hole in Fred.

Mercer took the jug I carried out the house. I chose plum—the only jug in the whole basement with the liquor stamp on it. They's a lot of stillers in these parts and the judge is liable to've run across all sorts of bribes, but plum is an unusual fruit and not many stillers have the patience to tinge a gallon with it. In all I'd say apples is the most common. You get to strawberries or plums and you're dealing with high-dollar shit.

Any judge'd know that.

Also picked plum because it has a little something else in it—and how that something else come to be is a story any Carolina judge'd appreciate.

Chuck Preston slams the door behind me and I think I'd prefer one of the old-style jails with bars where you can see the hall outside. With bars, they's a border and you can see freedom on the other side and keep it fresh in mind. But nowadays they don't want men remembering liberty; the jail's made out of blocks, and instead of bars and a hallway where free men walk, they's a cement wall and a thick metal door painted light brown like a rich woman's pants. Can't see through it, and they's no independence to think about.

I sit on the bunk sixty, seventy years, and they finally shut the light off. I think of Fred, and wonder if some animal smells him and knows he can't hardly defend himself. We got coyotes now, and a pack'd give a blind dog trouble, pit bull or not.

I think on Mae and her crazy-ass words. If she believed what she said, that Ruth was in love with me, she don't know her mother. But she didn't believe them words. She was pink before she said em.

What would I do if it was true?

Sitting in a jail cell, I ain't doing a helluva lot about anything. I can ponder the future, but without a blade or spoon or chisel or hacksaw, I ain't in control. Least I got the sense to close my eyes and wander a bit. Sitting in the cell, stretching out on the bench and folding my hands into a pillow, I got to let go of the whole world, just for tonight. I can't save Fred from here. I can't make sure them dogfighting sons a bitches don't steal some other dog and fight him into hamburger. In this cell, most I can do is get my mind right.

I think on Ruth and ask what I'd do if she was in love with me. Real love, like neither of us ever knew.

I'd prob'ly take her hand. I'd put it in both of mine for a long while, and I'd try to smell her hair without her knowing what I was up to. Wait for the air to carry the scent. And once I got that perfume and I had her hands all warm and used to mine, why that's when I'd slip to her elbow and bury my face in her hair and breathe it in so deep—

But that's a bunch of shit. Mae's out her mind. And the rock-bottom truth is, I don't know what the hell I feel for Ruth. All I been doing is writing letters and wishing I was still young enough to enjoy getting laid in the back of a Nova.

Stretched on the jailhouse bunk, without the stars or the trees whispering back and forth or the crick keeping somber time, I get sleepy quick. All the stuff that'd make my heart beat fast and fill me with worry is gone, stuck on the other side the wall.

Yeah, this is Stipe's doing. Back and forth, each time worse.

TWENTY THREE

They've trucked me to the courthouse in Asheville and brung me through the back, where the court connects the jail. My nose runs with the morning nip. I ain't dressed for cold weather any better'n I was yesterday afternoon. I wipe my schnoz on my sleeve and it leaves a streak, and that's all I need, having the judge see that streak turned into a silver crust flashing sunlight at him.

Us criminals sit on a wood bench. We six is a surly lot. More whiskers and hair than all the rest of Asheville, now it's booming yuppies. I know Buck Hedgecock, down on the end, last in line, but he ain't sober enough to recognize me. The fella between us folds and unfolds an Allis-Chalmers cap. His first time in court, I can tell.

Worst thing about sitting next these boys is I know soon as they get close to talking—soon as they start formulating all they damned lies, it'll feel like they slapped me in the electric chair. Soon as they start thinking their horseshit stories.

And the body stink's like being dipped in mash.

A man in a crumpled suit—a pudgy pecker of a man—shuffles to the man on the other end of the bench and says, "Charlie Crystal?"

"Thass right."

"You guilty or not?"

"Who the hell're you?"

"Public defender."

"I ain't done nothing."

"Right. Okay. Not guilty. You got any proof?"

"That the way it works these days?"

"Well, that's the county attorney over there, and he's got nine witnesses ready to swear you were drunk and smashed six windows on Merrimon last night. You want to say you didn't, you might have some evidence that goes against his."

"I got my rights. I want a trial. Jury and all, like the Constitution says."

"You see that bench? In a minute, Judge Omar Bradley Hickory's going to climb up there, and you'll think you're looking at God. You'll want to piss yourself. My advice? Say you did it and you're consumed with remorse. Judge Hickory will give you a fine, order restitution, and send you home."

"I could use a dose o' restitution."

Ruth.

Mae said Ruth was still hung up on me. Wouldn't that be a barrel a titties?

Don't feel good leaving Fred like I did, but circumstances in this world is rough, no matter intentions. I don't begrudge folk doing they jobs, and if I can't get out of this on account of men of sublime integrity, then that's the way it goes. But I got a considerable problem with the sons a bitches made it agin the law for a man to sell homemade hooch. If I take apples and make em drinkable, and other folk is thirsty for apples, I oughta make money.

It's crystal fuckin' clear. Don't see how it's different from a man cuts a tree into boards, or another digs coal out the ground, or oil. They act like rednecks is ignorant and likker's evil, but if that was the case, I wouldn't be able to sell a hundred gallon a week, peak season.

Naw. Bottom line, they decided long ago to pick one thing a lot of people want and won't ever do without, and tax the living shit out of it. Comes to it, Judge Omar Bradley Hickory'll get an earful. It'll be the first unvarnished truth he hears all day.

If it comes to it. But I'll stick with the plan, until.

Cueball Mercer comes in. I can't see his hand from my angle. He damnwell better've brought that jug. He meets my look and dips his head.

Defender stands above me with empty eyes, as if the real courtroom work's lofty and beyond. He's got the look of a man wouldn't notice a red ant chewing his ear at a picnic; he's just looking at the sky thinking on the sanctity of the law.

"Baer Creighton."

"I surely done it, but the law's fulla shit. How I plead that?"

"That falls under 'guilty.'"

"Fair enough. Can I go first?"

"Judge Hickory will follow the docket."

"You sure he's gone?" Burly said.

"I watched Mercer haul him away." Ernie shifted sideways in the Suburban seat. Burly was behind the wheel. They were approaching Baer's house. Ernie's gaze dipped to the knife on Burly's hip. He'd been uncomfortable since he'd climbed into the

Suburban. If he'd seen the Bowie knife, he wouldn't have gotten in.

"Good," Burly said. "You look at the still? Cut up pretty nice?"

"More than that. Lot more."

Burly slowed as Baer Creighton's house came up on the left. He looked out the window and Ernie noted the corded muscles in Burly's neck. The house was unchanged.

"We ought to burn it down," Ernie said.

"Don't get ahead of yourself. Stipe don't like freelancers. You've already made him uncomfortable."

Ernie thought of Creighton's still site, which he'd visited right after the revenue boys hauled Creighton away. "Didn't I give him good information? Isn't that what friendship is all about?"

"Yeah." Burly swung the wheel to the right and the Suburban plowed over the grassy drive of the Brown farm. He parked. They sat a moment, both leaning forward, studying the house. "Thing of it is, Stipe don't trust nobody. So you come and say you been following his enemy and got an idea, and suggest bad things… how does he know you're not setting him up?"

"Come on, Burly. You know me. Didn't you tell him I'm okay?"

"Yeah, well, I don't know you too well either."

Burly opened the door and stepped outside. Ernie followed and they walked toward the house together.

Stipe being suspicious was bad news. Ernie had been too excited, maybe too aggressive in his approach. He said, "Then why are you even here?"

"How do you know Stipe didn't already have things in motion?"

Ernie stopped and Burly kept walking. The Bowie knife slapped his thigh with each stride. Ernie hurried to catch up. "I'm just trying to help the guy out. Man in his shoes needs information, and I wanted him to see I can get it for him."

"Everybody knows Creighton's been robbing the Brown farm since the old man died."

"Well, I got to ask again. Why are we here?"

"What do you think?"

"I'm in trouble."

"Maybe. You didn't think you'd make the man wonder? Show up at his house and tell him how to kill his enemy? You got to be real close to a man 'fore you suggest murder."

"And you're supposed to keep an eye on me? That it?"

"Maybe."

Ernie considered the ramifications. He imagined what the Bowie knife might feel like dragged across his throat. "Does he like my plan? Because I'll do it. That way it was all my idea and everything. He didn't know anything. I'll cover my own tracks and that's that."

Burly faced Ernie. He rested his palm on his knife. "What's your angle?"

Ernie stepped back. "No angle." His mind raced. Burly was a big man. If he lunged and managed to grab him, Ernie was as good as dead. But if he could keep a few feet away until he could think things through...

There was the gold in the tree, but he didn't want to dangle that in front of Burly just yet. Not now, when he could no longer trust him. He decided on the truth.

"No angle," Ernie said. "Shit, Burly. I want what you got. You rub elbows with the man who controls everything worthwhile in the county. He runs the dogs, and he's bought about every still. Stipe's the swingin' dick and I didn't think it would do any harm to do him a favor."

Burly pulled his knife.

Ernie took another step backward.

Burly pressed the blade into a house wallboard and angled the blade downward, popping free a wood chip. He snapped it off and turned it over in his hand, then tossed it to Ernie.

"Awful dry."

Burly kicked yellow grass growing close to the house, then walked along the side and turned the corner. Ernie trailed him, but stopped before rounding. He listened until the sound of Burly's feet rustling the grass grew distant, then eased past the edge.

"So how long's it going to take for Creighton to come over and steal every piece of copper out this house?" Burly said.

"He's got to get out of jail first."

"He'll get three days."

"Then he'll be here that night."

"You know Creighton's ways that well, huh?" Burly said.

"He'll be here that night. He's as cheap as they come. He won't spend a penny if he can help it. You wouldn't believe what he does with—"

Burly stopped at the next corner, peered for a long while at the other side, and drew his hand across the baked and splintered wood. "You come get me when he shows up. And here on out, you got information for Stipe, run it through me first."

Judge Omar Bradley Hickory's no slouch. Been up there fifteen minute and found two men guilty. Another's back in jail, pending word on his sanity, and the other two's out a thousand bucks each, and got to go to the anonymous alcoholics, and do a hundred hours community service. Hickory looks like a grade-school text-book picture of the abolitionist John Brown—white hair and a scowl built into his forehead. I heard cowboy boots clonk when he come in.

Only thing is, when these other fellas stood and lied to the judge, I didn't feel hardly a thing. Couldn't scope they eyes on account they heads was turned, but I'd have thought me being sober as a skunk and sitting right next em, I'd have felt sparks.

Bailiff says my name and the defender says, "Guilty, Judge."

"Creighton. Says here you run a still out of Gleason."

"That's right. Say, Judge? You remember Lou Creighton?"

"No. He kin of yours?"

"Uncle."

"He a stiller, too?"

"If he was, he'd be a good one. Mostly he just tells stories."

"Stories, huh?"

"You ever hear the one 'bout Mabel Kinney? Down Old Fort?"

"Doesn't sound familiar."

"Well this old girl could still. Had her an operation size of the Daniel Distillery, all in her tobacco barn. Everyone drank likker here to Boston preferred the Kinney label—and she charged double."

"I've heard of Kinney."

"She was in the barn bossing orders—and I can tell all this because you law fellers put her in jail and she died there, so I ain't breaking the code—well she was in the barn snapping orders and she was supposed to be a right bitch about t'bakka."

"This is pertinent to the proceedings, of course?"

"If you like your likker stories, it sure as hell is."

"Do I look bemused, Mister Creighton?"

"Well, I don't know. If you look that way all the time, I'd say no."

Hickory smiles flat. "You were saying she was a right bitch."

"So one of her boys has a mouth of chaw and he don't think she's looking. He lets a spit loose on a floorboard knothole, in the corner where he always does. Mabel Kinney sees this big ol' string of goop out his mouth, and comes stomping over. Says the habit's disgusting and foul and if any of that spit ever got in the whiskey mash, it'd be the end of her."

"This a true story?"

"Well I don't got to say that fella with the chaw was Uncle Lou. Surprised he didn't mention it hisself."

"Go on. Lou spat on the floor."

"Mabel lit into him—beating, pulling hair, pushing and shoving. Lou was a firecracker 'bout my size. Way he tells it, he's about to lay into her, since she was more man'n woman anyway, and he blurted out, 'I'll spit my whole chaw in that whiskey mash, and you won't do a damn thing 'bout it.' He shoves loose, starts edging to the vat. Mabel looks at the rafters like for God to intervene, and sees old t'bakka leaves hanging from the beams. She goes pale as piss and hollers, 'Eu-fucking-reka!' She bosses Lou and some other kid up there to fetch down them t'bakka leaves. She throws the t'bakka in the mash and that's how come, soon as a feller tries Kinney Shine, he's stuck on it like he smoked a pack of Camels."

Hickory shakes his head. "Addictive, huh?"

"Judge, I don't mean to be impertinent, but I thought you might like a jug of them squeezins. Mercer, you got that jug?"

Hickory shifts. Eyebrows float.

"Now judge, this ain't illegal shine at all. You can see the stamp from the likker board. They only sold fifty-seven them stamps since they been out, and I bought the first twenty. I'd surely appreciate if you'd take that jug as a token of my appreciation of the court, and the fine job y'all do."

"Bailiff, bring me that jug."

Bailiff takes the jug from Mercer and carries it. Judge Hickory bites the cork and pries it loose. He sniffs.

"This tastes bad, I'm holding you in contempt."

"I hope you're a rye man, Judge, because that's rye whiskey with a touch a t'bakka."

Hickory upends the jug. Adam's apple rises and falls one solitary time. The jug hits the bench top with a thud. Hickory beats his chest. Coughs like his voice is gone. Waits. Coughs again.

"Creighton, you innocent or guilty of the charges today?"

"Guilty, but the law's fulla shit, Judge."

"Well, it's our law, and we stick to it. Stand up, Creighton."

I stand. He's a stern old shit, and like the public defender said, I want to piss myself.

"I'm finding you guilty, Creighton. Sentence is a three-thousand-dollar fine. One year imprisonment."

His hand moves to the jug. I can't breathe.

"You have any more of this?"

"What I don't got, I can make."

"Sentence reduced to three days minus time served. But you still owe me three grand. Bailiff—"

TWENTY FOUR

Cory Smylie was forty-five minutes away from Gleason in the sticks outside of Hendersonville. He drove his F-150 slowly past a house. His lights were off. His windows were down. A large black dog bayed and strained at the end of a chain attached to a doghouse. Probably a Labrador; it was at the edge of the yard about thirty feet from the house. Closer than Cory liked, but doable. He drove until a wedge of woods blocked his view, coasted to a stop, and turned off the engine.

Cory lit a joint and sucked in the smoke while the dog barked.

The routine was predictable. In a minute, the porch light would flash on. The door would open. A man would curse in his underwear, scream the dog's name, and slam the door. The light would go off and maybe the dog would shut up. It wouldn't matter, because the man wouldn't come back within two minutes. That was all the time Cory needed.

He gripped a Taser he'd stolen from his father. The inept clown had actually asked Cory if he'd seen it. Gee, Pop, what would I want with a Taser? His mother, always quick to mount Cory's defense, suggested a few deputies had probably absconded with it and took turns shooting each other while they were drinking beer at the hunting lodge.

The Taser was comfortable in his hand. He'd come to know the weapon intimately.

This was his first stop of the night. He reached for the door handle and paused. Yeah. He was forgetting something. He switched his dome light to the middle position so the light wouldn't turn on, and then stepped outside.

The Labrador still barked, although being cursed by his master had stifled his enthusiasm. Cory crept along the road, still sheltered by the woods. He sucked a final hit from the joint and tossed it to the pavement.

Cory turned along the lawn's edge. The dog let out a volley of sharp barks.

Dogs were tricky. They moved fast. Cory had learned to wait until he was right on them before firing. This Lab was big and ornery. Cory grinned. He could do anything.

The Lab went silent. Cory walked closer. He was twenty feet away, too far for the Taser. The dog dropped his head. He growled and stepped toward Cory.

"That's right, fuckhead. You come to me."

Cory raised the Taser and sighted along the top. It was always easier to shoot a dog broadside, but they rarely afforded the opportunity. Dogs liked to face danger head-on.

Cory continued walking. "Hey, fuckhead. That's right. It's all good."

The distance was right.

The Lab launched. The chain jangled and the dog sailed toward him. Whoa, Cory thought. Teeth glinted. Cory adjusted his aim and jerked the trigger.

The dog kept flying.

Cory missed. The dog bowled him to the ground. Cory raised his arms to shield his throat and the Lab bit his wrist, then darted past his arms and snapped just shy of his face. Cory pushed back. Swung his arm to his side and with all his might shoved the Taser into the Lab's side.

The contact points blasted fifty thousand volts.

The Labrador grunted and shuddered and collapsed. Cory rolled to his feet and when he had his balance he kicked the quivering dog in the ribs.

"Don't die, Fuckhead. You ain't worth shit dead."

Cory put away the Taser and rushed the dog in his arms to his truck.

Fucking animals. Cory slammed the window in the back of the cab and turned on the radio to drown the growls and whimpers coming from the crates in the bed of his F-150. He'd been prowling the outskirts of Hendersonville half the night. There had to be a better way.

He'd "adopted" several dogs from each shelter in Buncombe and Henderson Counties. Each facility was more than eager to have him take the animals, but they wanted seventy bucks apiece. "To spay or neuter."

"Well, these two won't need neutered. I'll do it."

That didn't go over.

At seventy bucks a dog, with Stipe paying anywhere from twenty to a hundred depending on the animal, Cory would do better working at McDonald's.

Plus, how many times could he go back to the same shelter? He'd already taken two, sometimes three dogs from each. Any more and they'd grow suspicious. He'd surfed the Internet and found a woman operating a nonprofit called Adopt-A-Friend, and had taken two Rottweilers off her hands. Stipe had payed two hundred for the pair, leaving Cory a profit of sixty dollars. Cory scoured the web but hadn't found any other organizations like Adopt-A-Friend.

Afterward he'd staked out a couple kennels. There were hundreds listed in the phone directory. The problem was they were all surrounded by chain-link fences and had scores of maddened and desperate dogs inside. Stealing one would raise such a ruckus he'd end up in a shootout.

The only option left was cruising the streets at night listening for barking dogs, and tazing them.

What he needed was a contact inside a shelter, someone to slip him animals out the back. Unless he came up with a story. Maybe if he paid some college geek to set up a website, and posted photos of animals up for adoption, he could make it look like that Adopt-A-Friend site. He'd splatter rainbows and hearts all over it and the shelters would give him all the animals he needed.

Cory shook his head. What was he wasting his time for? The real money was in drugs, not stealing dogs for Joe Stipe. His plan had been to use the work as a stepping stone, like starting out in the mail room. Eventually he'd prove himself and advance deeper into Stipe's organization.

Drugs, he thought. He'd make a hundred bucks an hour, not a night.

But if the drug world offered real money, it also exposed him to real risk. He'd already served time, and another strike would mean he didn't get out of prison until he was forty. Asshole judges were cracking down. Plus, you never knew when some city kingpin would go batshit and whack you. You wanted to play in the underworld, you had to be comfortable living on a razor's edge.

Stipe offered a different path. Cory would enjoy the powerful man's protection and rise through the ranks while Stipe took the risks. Cory only had to be the muscle. He'd take what he knew of how city operators handled business and surprise the shit out of the sleepy bumpkins in Gleason.

Cory imagined himself as one of Stipe's lieutenants. Stipe asking his opinion on a difficult matter, nodding gravely at Cory's advice, and saying, "Are you sure?"

"I don't see any way out of it."

"You're the best I got. You handle it, son."

That's what he'd say. Cory would nod. "It's going to cost money."

That beat the hell out of some Columbian slitting his throat with a machete.

Approaching Stipe's trucking compound, Cory slowed. Stipe had hired a crew to build a chain-link fence around the entire place. Fresh dirt piles were tamped around the posts, and a pickup with tools was parked where work had ceased for the evening, just beyond a newly installed gate across the drive. Cory stopped.

"How the fuck do I get in?"

Cory jumped out of the cab, leaving the engine running and the headlights on. He looked inside the compound to the mechanic's garage, and to the house, set back off to the right side. Though it was after two a.m., lights were still on inside both.

Stipe had never given him a phone number, insisting that face-to-face communication was all they'd ever need.

A dog growled from inside one of the wooden crates in the bed of his truck. Cory slammed his palm on the top of the crate. "Shut up, Meat!"

"You there!"

Cory raised his hands. He turned his head and saw a man on the other side of the cab, on the inside of the fence, with a rifle aimed from his shoulder. Security?

"Who are you?" the man said.

"Cory. Here to see Mr. Stipe." The man's build looked familiar. He was big, with a belly. "That you, Worley?"

The man slung his rifle over his shoulder and swaggered in front of the headlights. It was Burly Worley after all—the man who'd asked Stipe for a job that night at the fight. Sourcing bait dogs wasn't Hollywood, but it sure as fuck beat rent-a-cop security.

Worley produced a key and opened a padlock. He swung the gate open. "You know where to take them?"

"Yeah." Cory snorted. He hopped into the truck and drove inside.

"Let's see what you got," Stipe said. His eyes were watery and he smelled of alcohol, though he hadn't brought a drink outside. He'd come out of the house as Cory pulled in, as if he'd been up waiting. Cory stopped the vehicle and met Stipe at the front porch steps. Stipe was a huge man and walked slowly. Cory followed a pace behind.

"Got a big-ass Labrador, a boxer, a pit, and two of them little wiener dogs."

"Two chewtoys—and did you say a pit?"

"A bitch."

"Which crate? Let me see her."

Cory opened the cab and withdrew a long flashlight, also courtesy of the Gleason police, and directed the light beam at the crate closest to the cab. The white-and-brown dog snarled, though she remained mostly hidden by the crate slats.

"You put her in a pen by herself," Stipe said.

"You ought to see her. She's a blockhead. Beefy as hell. Top-dollar dog."

Stipe grunted, moved sideways and leaned closer. "No blood-line, boy. What, you thought I'd breed her?"

Cory shrugged. "Yeah."

"The breed is just the starting point. You need years of pairing only the gamest champions. You have to cull weakness from the line for twenty generations before you arrive at a dog that'll never turn *and* have the physical traits. The big lungs, the thick neck, the speed. You don't just start off with some mutt."

Cory allowed the light beam to drift.

"Give me that light." Stipe snatched the flashlight from Cory's hand.

"What?"

Stipe pressed against the bed and placed the flashlight between the slats.

"That's your pit, huh?"

Cory looked. "That's her."

"That's an American Bulldog, you dumb shit."

"Looks the same."

"Dumb shit." Stipe shined the light into the other crates one by one, grunting at each. Finally he handed the light to Cory and drew out his wallet. "I'll give you a hundred for the whole lot."

A hundred. Cory thought of taking the money, wadding it, and shoving it down Stipe's fat throat. Instead he leaned against the F-150. No, he'd take the money. He'd haul ass tonight to Balti-more and connect with some people he knew, and in two days he turn that hundred into a thousand.

"What?" Stipe said. "You got a different opinion?"

"I have to do better than that."

"Maybe you do, but a hundred dollars is a favor. You don't like it, take them back where you got them."

"I got bills. I got kids."

"I know you do. Funny time for you to tell me about that."

"What?"

"Come here smellin' of reefer, eyes like two mud puddles. Kids at their mother's, and you don't have a clue what she's doing, do you?"

"This time of night she's in bed."

"Yeah, Cory. But with who?"

"Who?"

"Like you give a shit. Mother of your children involved in the worst kind of sin. Your kids growing up in a house with pure evil. Very hand of Satan rules that house, and you'd rather smoke dope and steal dogs for a living. And you don't even take that serious enough to learn the difference between a Bulldog and a pit bull. Only thing the same is half the fucking name."

Stipe offered a hundred-dollar bill. Cory grabbed it.

"Pull these brutes to the back and get them unloaded. Pick up another set of crates—"

"Who's Mae with?"

Stipe stared. "You don't want to know. Just give you another thing to snivel about when you go home."

"Who?"

"A man wants to make sure a woman stays his, he got to put a chunk of metal and a rock on her hand. He got to get a job, Cory. He wants to raise a nest of children he's got to work from sunup to sundown. That don't sound like you. That's hard work. Fact is, you turned your back on your responsibilities and it don't matter who she's with."

Cory withered. Stipe was watching him through narrow, appraising eyes.

"It's her uncle nailing her, you dumb shit. Her uncle."

"Baer?"

"Same man knocked you cold that night in your driveway. But you was too drunk to notice. Tell you anything about her feelings for you?"

Blood rushed in Cory's brain.

"Take these animals to the back."

Cory remained leaning against the vehicle and lifted his head enough to watch the big man amble away. He sensed a crisis— that this moment was meant to be something more. He'd always thought of himself as a kid, a boy. He'd never wanted to be a man, never wanted to take the title and all that came with it. But this moment of truth was more important than standing before a judge being sentenced to three years. This was more important than the first phone call he made on the day of his release, or the first joint he smoked that afternoon.

Cory stepped uncertainly from the truck and it felt good. It was a departure. He felt radical. He would either shrivel from life or he would seize it.

"Stipe!"

Cory hurried after him. Stipe stopped.

"You got to bring me in. I'll get these dogs if that's what you want. I'll get on my belly and low-crawl across that lot if that's what you tell me. I'll go put a bullet in Baer Creighton's head. But you got to tell me what to do. You got to help me get all this shit right."

Stipe exhaled. He studied Cory, then resumed toward the house.

Cory jumped into his path. "I'm serious. I'll do whatever I have to do."

Stipe latched onto a handrail and swung his ass onto the steps. "Sit down."

Cory sat and placed his elbows on his knees. His head drooped. He closed his eyes and his mind swam. It was like being ten years old and being in church, surrounded by God, and defenseless.

"I got a spy," Stipe said. "He watches Creighton all the time. He was there when you got stoned and shot all over the woods, and damn near got yourself killed."

"I got a bad habit. A real bad habit."

"It's who you are, deep down. You're a coward."

Cory nodded. He brushed his forearm to his eyes.

"Being a coward means you only fight somebody when you can sneak up behind him, and you never fight yourself or your worst demons because you can never get the drop on them. You think I'd have the truck company, a wife, grandkids, a few million in the bank, if I'd followed every foul instinct? If I never met my own weak heart head-on?"

"No, sir."

"Hell no. Self-discipline is how you get somewhere. It's the first law. It's like starting with the right kind of dog. There's a lot of work afterward, but discipline is where you start."

"What do I do?"

Stipe shook his head. He rested his hand on Cory's shoulder. "Get off the drugs. Get your mind right. Take them kids out of that house of sin, and let me see you three times in a row without bloodshot eyes. Show me you're serious, and we'll figure out where you go from there."

TWENTY FIVE

Got my thumb out. Not too awful damn safe, hitching, but I got my Smith back when they cut me free this morning, and now that Stipe and Smylie smashed my still I figure we're even. Time being.

Fred'll need a half-hour of story-telling and lie-swapping to get his mind straight after all that shooting. I been thinking on Fred, and Stipe too. Chief Smylie called in the tip that got my still busted. What'd motivate Smylie now, other'n Stipe?

What I don't know is where things sit, morals and all. Mae said violence don't solve anything. One man do something wicked and the other comes back with something wickeder. Back and forth. It don't stop 'til one man gets hurt so bad he quits. Or can do nothing more. As things sit, Stipe and me is about square. If I called it quits and got on about my life, maybe he'd call it quits too. I don't like what he done to Fred, but I guarundamntee he don't like what I done to his champ.

Just thoughts.

Two days looking at a wall. Lot of time with no likker. Things that was clear in one light look sketchy under a sixty-watt bulb. I come after Stipe 'cause he's pure-ass evil, and had a hand in Fred's situation. But I'm no closer to knowing who tossed Fred in the weeds. Other thing's got me is how I can be ratshit sober and hardly tell when a couple crooks tell a judge they's innocent. I got a little juice, but wasn't as strong as even the other night, when I fell out the tree.

The feeling is strong only when I remember what it used to be. At this rate it might be gone in a week, and I still don't have the truth on Fred or Ruth.

They's always been a connection with the likker. I kept myself sloshed mostly to hold the curse at bay. Now the likker's just about got my skill stamped out right when I need to know who the hell has it in for me. Often thought I wouldn't miss the curse at all. I'd rather not know everyone around me was a liar—it might be good enough just to suspect it. But the liars I'm up agin is more than mere liars. They's evil, and I almost think it makes sense to quit the likker and see if I can't hang onto my talent.

How'll it be, first time I see a man and don't know if he's fulla shit?

Sunshine looks good but I bet Fred ain't too happy. I hope he got in my foodsack but he never been one to neb. I get home I'll cook him some eggs and Alpo; he likes that. Maybe get on his good side again.

My feet is about peeking through my shoe leather, and if they was any cornfields 'long the road I'd raid one of em. Gleason coming up and I'm hungry enough to eat the grime out a muffler and wash it down with antifreeze. Course a nip of shine'd taste better.

I shortcut town on the north side. I don't need to run into no one. All this walking after that beating I took, and that festering slice out my shoulder, and sleeping on a cold jail bunk—I'm like a clock losing ten second a minute.

Less'n a mile from home. Old Fred—I can see him now, sorta, head above the crate and perking an ear. He got a gift, lets him know long before he hears feet crushing through the leaves or smells a man's armpits.

Come up on the still site from the woods and things is disorienting. Everything chopped and hacked, mash barrels tipped. Flies everywhere buzzing. Air is still and quiet, and smells like stale fire. Big stale fire. Old fire.

"Hey, stud. Guess who's home? I got some lies to swap. That's for damn—"

Fred?

Step into a cloud of flies under the tarp. He's in his crate, covered in rolling black shiny wings. I swat 'em, smack 'em, shout at em. Run my fingers over Fred's coat.

He couldn't have starved in three days. No way.

"Fred?"

They's blood matted under his head and now I see a bullet hole done it.

"Fred!"

Somebody shot Fred through the scab was his eye.

I toss up my guts. Fall over in it and lay on the ground. I listen to the woods and every critter knows disaster's come. Every critter's silent, holed up, spooked off. Nary a bird's got the stones to chirp.

TWENTY SIX

Ernie and Burly had been waiting for hours in a copse of apple trees, parked between dead blackberry brambles. They sat in Burly's Suburban on a hill overlooking plowed-over fields that stretched like a rolling, mile-wide lake, Brown's decrepit farm an isthmus halfway across. Adjacent a tiny recess across the road was Baer Creighton's burned house.

Like Ernie had promised, he'd sought Burly as soon as he'd seen Baer return from jail. The two hauled ass back to stake out the Brown farm in case Baer made his move. So far, he hadn't.

After an hour of waiting in near silence, Burly said, "I thought you said he was ready to go to Brown's."

"He might have gone while I came to get you."

"Or he might not go at all. I've got work to do. You see him getting ready to redo his still, come get me. If not, neither me nor Stipe has the patience for games. It'll be Plan B—a bullet in the head."

Burly had left and now just Ernie remained, waiting in his own car. How was he to know when a man was getting ready to redo his still? It wasn't like a light bulb went off over his head that could be spotted from a half mile away through a hundred yards of forest. But Burly was agitated, and had made clear that the plan Ernie had pitched to Stipe was too elaborate for Burly's taste. He would rather sneak to Creighton's camp, pop him in the head, carry him across the road, and dispose of him that way. The only thing gained by waiting on Creighton was that Burly wouldn't have to get blood on his clothes.

Ernie watched through binoculars. Hours passed and he dared himself to sneak closer. He walked the dirt road toward Creighton's house and then eased into the woods. Creighton was distraught. His dog was dead—a little freelance work Ernie knew Stipe would appreciate, even if Burly couldn't see the poetry of it.

Creighton would be off his guard.

Ernie had his binoculars and could safely watch from a distance. He approached a little at a time and when Creighton's camp was barely visible between trunks, Ernie found a hidden spot to recline against a tree and watch.

Ernie considered Burly's distaste for the operation. It was the best evidence that Stipe liked it. There was nothing else strong enough to compel Burly to do anything.

Plan A was much more poetic than Plan B, but it wouldn't matter in the end. Ernie would watch Creighton until he made his move. If he wandered off, Ernie would follow. If he had loose stools, Ernie would know.

Whether Creighton walked to Brown's or was carried there, he would go and not return.

The stench of burned wood and metal lies heavy on the ground.

My house is a charred shipwreck shoved into a basement. Ashes. Burned two day ago at least, judging by the trickles of smoke and the black jutting boards. Burned shortly after my still was busted and I was hauled to jail. Maybe burned the same time Fred died.

October leaves flutter yellow and red, lazy, and when they land it's just me amid all this ruin.

I'm going to burn you down.

Stipe let the shed stand. I grab a shovel. Head back to the still site. I look in on Fred almost like I'll find it was all a bad dream, but as soon as I see him I recognize part of the smell of rotted mash and stale wood ashes is dead Fred.

My knees go weak and I steady myself agin the shovel, dry-eyed but so godawful broke inside I could die.

Only been three day but it looks I been gone a year, and the woods is taking over. Hundred years, none of this'll matter. But it'll take every fucking minute to wear off.

I meditate on my knees by the crate, hands on wood wore round by four generations of man's best friend. I look to the dirt beside the diesel turbine crate as if any tracks might help me cipher how Fred spent his time. They's enough paw prints I'll never know which was last. Down by the crick, they's prints at the edge. He was comfortable getting his own water, and I been letting him build his confidence. Don't know which boot prints belong to Cueball Mercer and his boys, or which go with whoever finished Fred. They's one set of prints looks like they belong to a kid, they's so small.

A few feet from the fire circle I plunge the shovel into the dirt. This is where Fred'll rest, right in the middle of everything he loved. I jump on the back of the shovel and work it back and forth, and pull out the first big clump of black dirt. I stab the ground again and hit a root. I stab and stab and find the root's cut and I'm still stabbing.

Tearing out dirt is violent, satisfying work but I got to reel in the anger and make it work for me. I got to set that shovelful down in a pile, not fling it off through the wood.

Three feet long and two wide. Four deep. I wrap Fred in his wool blanket. Climb down the hole. Kiss his cold nose and squeeze him like to bring him back. They's a scream in my head but my throat's silent. They's rage in my eyes but they's closed. I'm calm and slow but my soul's jumpin up and down like to go to war.

Goodbye you old son of a bitch. I love ya.

Fred don't say anything back.

I lower him to the bottom. Backfill, and tamp the ground.

I talk to the congregated woods. "Fred was good people. Some dogs is like cats, all prissy and fuck you all the time. But Fred was the kind of fella who'd give you a smooch just for the hell of it. He'd say the damnedest things, just as you was thinking the same. And he never begged. He was as self-respecting a dog as ever was."

I got to fight hard not to dig him up and hug the son of a bitch one more time.

I'm going to burn you down.

I shake the voice out my head.

I got my Smith. Even checked to make sure they gimme back my bullets. I trek into the woods.

Head up a hollow that curves into the side of a no-name mountain. In twenty minute I'm two mile from Gleason. Every step carries me someplace more remote'n the last. No one comes this way. Used to think if I ever got totally fed up and had to disappear ten years, I'd hide out here. Following the crick back to a trickle over a couple flat rocks, a cave sets two-thirds up the mountain, looking over a grade. Man could sit and shoot squirrel all day. Maybe buck or bear, if he had a mind.

Or anything else wanders by.

They's maple trees all over; a man'd have all the sugar he'd need.

Oaks drop acorns like rain. Hickory and walnut, too. They's fish down the stream and a glade where the sunlight pokes through and a man could grow potatoes and leeks.

Out front the cave, they's a chunk of metal all busted to hell and rusted.

This is where Gunter Stroh taught me to make shine.

He used to brood on his fire, rifle in reach. He'd lean and pitch wood under the boiler and his mouth'd water soon's he heard the tinkle-rattle, the hiss coming out the copper. He'd smack his lips and spit, and his shaking hands would steady.

Long gone.

I used to come back this way with Fred.

I wander inside the cave and poke around. They's a mess of rotted blankets, moldy threads. Bones from some animal, likely not a man. Maybe a cougar called this place home, though I ain't seen cougar in thirty years.

With the house a pit of embers and the still cut up, and Fred… this cave has all the solitude a man could want.

I stumble down the hill.

Time I hit the flat ground, the stream's a bona fide crick, with pools deep enough for trout. I circle east, sweep the woods.

I call "Fred!" and listen. My voice just goes off to nowhere, and I half-expect Fred hears me on the other side.

Time to put the plan back on rails. The plan I thought of that very first night, when I set one mash barrel aside from the rest.

I got that tree fulla gold. They's the one bucket hanging from the nylon cord, but they's two more dropped inside, full. I set that money aside and if this ain't a rainy day I don't know what is. Time to fetch an ax.

I ease off my pace coming up on the still site. I stand in the middle next to Fred's grave. Thirsty. Kind of blank in the head. I set for the house.

Come up from the backside, like always, except now they's nothing between me and the road. House is level, collapsed in the basement. Smoke wanders across the ground, looking for answers. Roof's fell in. Shingles burned clean away. Only thing left is pieces of timber look like chunks of firewood at the campfire edge. Wood juts up, sides black and white with ash.

At the back foundation corner I circle to the basement. The door's burned away. This must've been the hottest part by a long stretch. All them jugs of hundred-sixty proof likker is puddles of glass on the cement floor. This's prob'ly where they started the fire. Loaded the pickup—they white pickup—with likker and busted the rest open, and tossed a match, and skedaddled quick.

I hoped maybe a jug survived the heat.

Back at the still site, I strip to my skivvies and grab a towel and soap.

Brook water's liquid ice. At the edge I kneel naked on a rock and scrub my pants and shirt and skivvies and socks like they did in the Bible. I hang drippy clothes from a dead hemlock branch and tiptoe into the water, careful on slippery rocks.

Fuck the tub. I got to feel something.

At the middle the water's only a foot or so deep; I sit on a smooth, flat rock and soap up, and splash my pits, and get my privates. Dick's shrunk like the cap on a ballpoint pen. Nads all up inside, huddled tight with my ribs, saying he's lost his fucking mind. Again.

Ribs say, Naw, I got word from his heart. That's rage.

Can't stand but three minute and it feels like three years. I dry off so cold my guts rattle. I climb in my sleeping bag and zip it over my head.

Peek at all that busted metal, and the empty turbine crate.

I don't think I ever been quite so licked.

I wake at night. Late enough they's no crickets from the house, echoing through. No fireflies wandering in—but it's been weeks since they had the run of the place.

They's no sound in the crate, no Fred snoring.

Climb out the bag naked and cold and drag the diesel turbine crate on top the fresh dirt mound off the side a camp. Grab a lighter from the tarp and set them blankets aflame. Huddle on the ground and watch the orange and blue.

I'm going to burn you down.

Yeah? I'm going to fucking *kill* you.

TWENTY SEVEN

I got to piss and my arm pressed groundside's asleep and tingly. Sun's out and the birds've come back. Got a little food here but most was in the house. Got some eggs. I cook em.

It's quiet without Fred.

Time's getting on for ending all this. Fight's in a week and I think it's divine providence the Lord made me a stiller.

I got a powerful thirst and water don't touch it.

Pete Bleau's in his truck.

Once in a bleau moon someone comes up while I'm at the house anyway. Just so happens I ain't got a house now. I'm looking at ashes.

This ain't Pete's day for likker.

Meet him at the truck. His look says he ain't trustworthy but they's no red, no juice, and some folks just look shifty.

"Had a visit this morning," he says.

"That so."

"Huck Barrow."

"Why don't that surprise me?"

"Said they busted the still."

"They?"

"Revenue."

"Uh-huh."

"And Barrow said I'd want to run my business through him. They was willing to sell for six a jug."

"What a deal."

"This ain't the first Barrow's been after me."

"I know."

"Thought I ought to tell you. When you be back in operation?"

"Ain't thought 'bout it."

"You know I got to find a supply."

"I know it."

"I been saying for years I'd move twice as much, if you'd make it. Maybe this is an opportunity, Baer. You put in a modern operation. Double the size your boiler and run it twice as much. Shit, I got people clear to Philly buy whatever you make. Them shot houses is rip-roaring, what with the economics in the shitter for good."

"All that's true."

"You want me to wait on you to get your operation up again?"

I think of the decision I made when I first found Fred, and rededicated myself to last night. Park a pile of hell on Stipe's front porch, then drive 'til I find someplace nice, and stop there. I can see the road. Dotted line flashes under the hood. Trees zing by. Wind blows through open windows—maybe even with snow outside.

"Don't think I'll set up anytime soon, Pete. But I appreciate you stopping by. They steal your dog yet?"

"He's laying on the seat. Hey boy." The Shepherd stands. Bleau says, "He don't go out the house except to shit, and that's with me watching."

"Bet he likes that."

"Take care, Baer."

He leaves and I'm stuck with a bunch of ashes.

I sit beside chunks of still and copper. Part of me wants to red things up.

I made a living with that still for years and years; all the time avoided the revenuers by working with a select group of men, a dozen drinkers and a couple wholesalers who moved my stuff to shot houses. They always said they'd take whatever I made, they was such demand from migrant labor down south, and continual opportunities in D.C. and Philly. I never did it to get rich, just to live the way I wanted.

Now they's no way in particular I want to live.

Can't go back to them days, and even if I fixed up a new still and found a new pit bull pup, it'd never measure up. I got a sick feeling like a traitor even thinking it. All these chunks of copper is an affront to the eyes, but the rest of me wants this place to stay like this 'til kingdom come. Let the woods reclaim it, like that busted still at the cave.

And Ruth?

They's only one thing left, regarding Ruth.

I kick off my boots. Crinkle my toes and kind of work em back and forth with my fingers. The little one pops. Back in school, 'fore I quit, Mister Ping told us them bones ossified like the skull bones and the tailbones. I set 'bout making sure my piggy toe bones never ossified. I've cracked em every single night of my life since.

I pop my toes and when I got my mind where I want it, grab a pen and sheet of paper.

Dear Ruth—
On account of you never writing back, I'm done.

I scrunch the paper into a ball and chuck it at the fire. Go to the crick with a brick of soap and get the toe funk off my hands.

Dear Ruth—
I hoped one day you'd send a letter and tell me why our lives didn't turn out the way we thought they would, back at the start.

You know by now I've stayed stuck on you. But I don't even know what I'd do if you showed up. It's too late. Things is going to happen that change the rest of my life, and I don't know which way it'll change.

But I like to think if you showed up, we'd just take a car and drive all day and all night, and not stop until we got somewhere nice. I'll say bye with that.
—Baer

I read it over and the words don't say half of what I want her to know, but if I ain't said it in all these years, too bad. Part of the responsibility's on her; she ought to carry some of the water if she wants a drink.

She don't want a drink, though, and that's why I'm through writing. After this's over, I may be dead and gone, I may be living in a cave, but either way I won't write letters to Ruth.

TWENTY EIGHT

Mae's heart jumped. Cory stood in the open doorway, gun dangling in his hand. He was stoned.

Don't take the fight to him. Don't challenge him now—he doesn't have the sense to think. But don't take his shit. Don't be one of those women who wind up on Oprah, explaining how it was rational to submit while her babies watched her get beaten into the ground.

"You got things to explain," Cory said.

Cory was here to fight.

"Just a minute." Mae twisted to her computer and hit "save." She should have planted a knife in the desk drawer. She closed the document. Spun on her chair.

Should have asked Baer for a gun.

"Getting a little uppity, all this college." Cory stumbled on the rug. He waved the pistol and recaptured his swagger three steps into the room. "But you're a real smart girl. Real smart. Got all the men you want, and none the wiser."

"Girls, go upstairs. Go to your room and play for a little while."

"No! Stay here. You two want to see this. So you know the difference between right and wrong."

"Girls, upstairs. Now."

Morgan took Bree's hand. They backed away. Their eyes moved from Cory to Mae and back to Cory, until they turned at the stairs.

Cory lunged, trapped Bree under his arm like a satchel of books. Bree screamed.

Mae jumped across half the living room, and trembled two feet shy of Cory. "Put her down! Cory, don't do this. Morgan! Upstairs now! Cory, listen to me. Put her down. Let's talk."

Cory strode past Mae. He swung Bree upright as he dropped into the couch, and plopped her beside him. Bree's face was terror. Morgan stayed on the steps, three high, shrunk against the wall.

"I want my baby girl to understand what happens to whores."

"What are you talking about?"

"I know what you been doing behind my back."

"Cory—you're not… " Don't tell a man he isn't sober. "Cory, not now. Let Bree go. We can talk all you want."

"Talk. You're good at talking. Never shut the fuck up. So why don't you start running that trap of yours and explain all that food in the kitchen. You got to 'splain four hundred dollars waiting at the grocery." He smiled. Rubbed his cheek with the pistol barrel. "You got to 'splain making out with your uncle." Cory pulled Bree closer. She wriggled. "Honey, I'm going to take you away tonight. In a minute we'll go upstairs and get your things. You won't have to grow up watching your momma be a whore."

"What are you doing? She doesn't even know those words! Let her go."

"You see, Bree—and I see you over there, Morgan. It's good for you to listen when your daddy's talking. You see, girls, your momma's been a bad, bad girl."

"Why are you here, Cory? I don't have any money."

"I wonder. I bet your daddy'll be real interested in you fucking his brother."

Mae forced her mouth closed. With her eyes she urged Morgan to climb the stairs but her daughter stood transfixed. Bree's horror had become shock. Things were quickly unwinding.

Mae wiped her eyes. "Cory, don't do this... please?"

"You never once said it wasn't true, Mae."

"It isn't true. He's my... uncle!"

"What was you going to say? You can't lie your way out of whoring. Guess it's in your blood. Yeah, I know about that too."

The gun barrel reflected light from the bulb overhead—it was like a star. Mae looked away. "I kissed him. Baer backed away and left five minutes later. You saw that too, right?"

"Fuck you."

"Yeah, you saw it. So what are you up to, Cory? Or did you take off so fast you didn't see what you thought? Put the gun down."

"Listen to you. Put the gun down. How about I use it instead? Use it on you." His voice cracked. "But you got to answer one thing."

Bree wriggled. "Mommy?"

"Hush!" He clamped her closer. His eyes pointed across the room, to the floor, to the kitchen.

"What is it, Cory?"

He nudged Bree. "Look at your mother." He leveled the pistol at Mae.

Oh God!

"You still love me, Mae?"

"You don't want your babies to see this, Cory. Send them upstairs!"

"I want them to see you lie to me. Do you love me, Mae?"

"Bree—I love you! Morgan—I love you!"

Mae stared into the end of the gun. The pistol wavered. Cory lifted it until he met her eyes over the sights.

"I don't love you, Cory."

"You're one dumb cunt, you know that?" He closed his eyes. Inhaled deep. Opened his eyes and said, "Wasn't too bright, sending Baer out to jump me at the house." Cory released his grip and swiveled the pistol barrel toward the ceiling. "You haven't loved me for a long time. That's the truth. Now we're going upstairs, all of us. Pack some things."

"This is kidnapping, Cory."

"I'm not taking you."

"That's what I mean. You take them with a gun, there isn't a court in the state that'll let you keep them. Listen to me. Listen. You think you'll do better bringing them up, do it the right way. Not with a gun."

"Upstairs." He gestured with the pistol and stood between the door and Mae. "Upstairs, everybody."

Mae was still. Cory stepped to her.

His hand flashed. She saw it coming and heard the butt crash against her brow. She felt blood in her eye, carpet on her cheek. Morgan punched Cory's legs with fists light as clover bundles.

"Come on, girls. Upstairs."

Last I went to the Gleason post office I carried two flasks. Now I ain't had a drink in four day. I wait in line and avoid looking at anyone. My turn comes and I slap the letter on the counter.

"You can't carry a rifle inside a post office," Harry says.

"What? I'm gonna steal a letter? Here."

"Letter to Mars Hill," Harry says.

"Last one."

"That so?" He looks at me like I said a dragon shit in my scrambled eggs.

I turn.

"So don't you want to know how long it'll take to get there?"

"So long, Harry."

I swing by the grocery. Merle's parked on the stool behind the register. I slap a gold coin on the counter.

"What's that?"

"What's it look like? Real money. By weight, that's eight hundred fifty dollars."

He lifts it. "A maple leaf."

"It's from Canada. They's fond of maple."

"What you want me to do with it?"

"Write eight hundred dollars in that book of yours for Mae."

"She hasn't used twenty dollars of the other you left."

"She will. She's got them kids."

"Why don't you take that down to Millany and turn it into money, 'fore you bring it here?"

"You don't know what the hell money is. And I'm lazy, like you. Put down eight hundred on a slip for Mae, and I'll take a ten-dollar jug of bourbon here, and maybe five dollars of that cheddar-type cheese. So you get a commission for working with me, this one time. Right, Merle? Good with you?"

He nods and I go to the cooler. I stop by the register and he hands me a pint of Wild Turkey. He shoos me away.

That Kentucky shit washes cheddar better'n water. After a few drinks I realize how dried out I been since the house fire cooked all my jugs. Now my brain's starting to work.

I head for Mae's, already thinking ahead to what I'll do if I see Cory Smylie there.

I've recounted the facts as I know em. I've replayed that night I found Fred, matching the shape of the shadowy man that dumped him in the dirt to Cory Smylie and to flesh-and-blood Larry. I've thought of Cory's truck, that day he was at Mae's, and how it maybe was or wasn't the truck I saw that night. How Cory washed his truck and there'll never be any telling if the tailgate was dirty on one side. I've thought on Pete Bleau 'fessing that Stipe pays Cory to steal dogs.

But you can't know a man done evil 'less you know he's got evil in his heart.

With Cory it's about as sure as venom in a rattler. It was five year ago, after him and Mae started popping out kids. I didn't have nothing to say about the way they wanted to work they affairs. I tried to get on, and be civil.

I was at the still one day and heard a horn. Went to the house and found Cory with his new F-150. The grill was smashed, the hood crinkled. Spider web on the windshield. He had a dope-headed grin and hung to the mirror for balance.

"You got a ball bat?" he says.

"I dunno. What for?"

"Hit a deer."

"You say you hit a deer?"

"That too. He's still alive and I want to club him."

"I'll get a gun."

"Look how he dicked my truck. I'm going to club him."

"I'll club you. Where is he?"

Cory pointed across the drive to a bend where deer cross from the wood to the field at dusk.

"Go on home, Cory. I'll handle it."

He studied me like a punk taking my measure. I watched him do the math. Add a little for experience, subtract a lot for age. The math always puts a punk on top. The longer he looked at me, the sharper the electric got, and his eyes glowed in the dusk.

"Yeah," he said. "Guess I'll head home."

I went in the house and come out with a thirty-thirty. Cory's truck was gone and time I reached the road, I saw him driving back and forth over the deer. Each time he hit the gas hard, the truck bounced and the body flopped. I swung the rifle to my eye and lined the sights to put a chunk of lead through his cab, but before I pulled the trigger, I figured it would end in me putting a chunk of lead through him.

I set off down the road and he was long gone. It was a doe and she was smashed good, and dead maybe from the second time he hit her. I fired six times into the dirt just to blow steam, and dragged her to the woods.

In my book, Cory Smylie's a human septic tank. Only thing good that'll come out him is daisies in the cemetery. A man that'd treat one animal like that's about as likely to treat another. Maybe since he's hunted dogs for Stipe, he had the moxie to steal mine. Maybe Stipe put him to it, specific, because he was working some other angle. I dunno. But I know he's got the evil in his character, and adding everything else, I'm about certain Cory stole Fred.

I reach Mae's and rap the door, making sure not to knock it in. It's dusk, but they's lights on.

She opens the door in a bathrobe. Big old smile, even with half her titty hanging out. She covers it.

"Don't got but a minute," I say. "I wanted you to know I'm going away. Maybe a long bit, I dunno. Left another eight hundred down at the grocery."

She stares at the porch planks. I look closer. Her eyes is wet, and her big old smile changes—or my understanding changes—and all of a sudden she looks like she's been bawling an hour.

The bruises from before've progressed to a sick black yellow—but they's new swelling and a cut in her brow she's tried to cover with makeup. Bruises on her arms.

I turn away. Cory Smylie made a liar out of me to them girls—but I'm the fool promised what I couldn't deliver. "Was the kids here, this time?"

She nods. "He took them."

I punch the wall. "I did it your way. I shoulda cut off his fucking head."

"I just want my babies."

By Tercel it ain't ten minutes to Smylie's house. I'll take the police chief and all, he gets in my way. I got the rifle across the back floor and Smith on my hip. Mae sits on the passenger side. She says, "I'm ready to do what I have to do."

"You don't got to do nothing. First we see what's going on. We'll get the kids back."

"I called Mom and she didn't answer. It's been two days. And I drove to your place and the house was gone. Just burned. What was I supposed to think? Why didn't you say your house burned? I mean, what the hell? What the hell, Baer?" She faces the window. "Last I talked to Mom she said Larry was giving her problems. She was worried."

I look at her.

"Watch the road. You're speeding."

"Since when you call him Larry?"

"Since now. Since he started giving Mom problems and threatening her."

"What kind of problems?"

"Coming around, like a stalker. She caught him watching her at night a couple times."

"He's married again."

"When did that ever stop a man?"

"When was all this?"

"Last week. I told her to get a restraining order."

"That won't work."

"She hasn't called back in two days."

Seems like words is useless. Between the time for saying and the time for doing is silence. We drive through it.

The Smylie house lights is off, like the whole family's gone. The upstairs windows glow from a nightlight, or a lamp left on, but the rest is dark.

"Where'd he take them?" Mae says. "This is bullshit! I'm going to kill him!"

"Easy. You don't got to." I touch her shoulder then think better, and pull over beyond the Smylie house.

"What do we do?" Mae sniffles. "If there was ever a time I could break all the rules this is it. They're out with their high-price lawyers," Mae says. "They're stealing my babies."

"Quiet, now. I'm going to poke around. Stay put."

I leave the car without slamming the door. The minivan's in the drive. Cory's truck is gone. I slip alongside the house and the only noise comes from neighbors out back, with a fire pit and a circle of lawn chairs. A bug zapper. Old-fashioned marshmallow roast. The fire and bug light throw a glow on Smylie's back yard. I stop at a window. With no lights inside, anybody in there could see me—but they's nobody in that house. I flat-out know it.

Back in front of the house I stop to a sound—if them sons a bitches with the marshmallows would shut up for one minute I could hear it. Footsteps. Patter like raindrops so small it's like mist on leaves.

The knob's locked. I press my elbow to the glass pane—but the neighbors would hear it shatter. Other side of the house, I slit screens with my Leatherman tool and press windows 'til one budges. I pry the screen out and push up the window, all the way. I jump, ease through on my belly, and land on a nauseating sofa that smells like spice and flowers.

Feet patter upstairs. I stand in shadows and get my bearings. Smylie's got an organ agin the wall, a coffee table right where a man'd stumble on it. Maybe an alarm system tattle-telling the Gleason police.

"Morgan, Bree?"

Whispers. The stairwell's behind me.

"Uncle Baaaar?"

"That's right. I got your momma outside. I come to take you home. Anybody else here?"

"No sir," Morgan says, voice squeaky scared. "I don't think so."

"Where's Joseph?"

"In bed. Upstairs."

"Let's get him. Show me."

I come up the stairs and this whole setup don't feel right. Like I shoulda looked up and down the street for Cory Smylie's truck. Like I'm the man breaking and entering another man's house. I pass Bree on the stairs. She clings to the rail. "Go downstairs and wait by the door. I'll be right there."

She nods. I'm high enough now I can see they got a nightlight in a room down the hall. "Morgan—which room?"

My arm tingles real faint.

Morgan scampers ahead and stops. Points.

Any number of ways this could pan out. Cory's inside with a gun at the door, and Morgan's old enough to know Joseph's in trouble. But her eyes don't glow at all.

Or Cory's outside waiting on catching a burglar in the act. Or he's downstairs stowed under a desk, waiting the right moment to drop me.

My curse is weak and I feel damn near sightless.

The door's open. I swing inside, arms high enough to block a punch, but none comes. I twist around and the room's clear, save a closet. I grab Joseph—he lets out a cry and this's ten times worse'n having a bunch of dogfighters rush you in the woods. I'm about blind, all these walls. I pull Smith, then holster it.

"Come on, Morgan. Let's go outside. Your mommy's in the car up the street."

I lead the way and the tingle gets stronger—as much a signal as I've got in the last week.

"Where you at, Cory? I know damn well you's here."

I glance down the hall. Nothing. Shuffle along, fast. Outside comes a sharp red glow like four hundred liars. It's either the United States Congress come to order on the front lawn or police black and whites.

"Girls, c'mere! Out the window. Like I come in. Here we go."

I sit Joseph on the sofa. God's on my side; Joseph's quiet. I sit on the back of the sofa with Morgan. She wriggles through and I dangle her to the ground.

"Go the end of this wall and hunker down. Bree—c'mere!"

She steps up like a soldier. I get her out the window. "Go to the back and wait."

Now for Joseph. I'll prob'ly break my back, but they's no good way. I sit him on my lap and swing my legs through the window. Lean back 'til my spine's about to snap, and slip down the sill.

Vertebrae pop like Rice Crispies. My chin hits the window. I drop to the ground and freeze.

A flashlight cuts across the front lawn—a cop covering a lot of ground. I shrink behind a shrub and a man steps around the front corner. I got a baby in my arms and a cop twenty feet off looking something to shoot. The beam flashes me in the eyes but how the hell you know if they see you? Got to wait.

The light shifts away and I'm half-blind, and they's raised voices far off—man and woman. Mae.

Flashlight comes back, parks on the open window. "Hey Bob! I got an open window. Think we got someone inside!"

You jest go on thinking that.

"Keep it covered."

I'm pinned. I make a break for it, I got a baby liable to scream and two girls can't run in the dark. I got neighbors cooking marsh-mallows happy to holler, "He went thataway."

The cop with the light moves closer. The beam on the window gets tight. If I move, he sees me. He comes to the window. He's five feet away and only a bush between us. Then they's the girls. White, or light blue clothes. This cop's blind, not seeing em even through the hedges.

"Hey, John!"

The copper moves quick and the beam catches me full on and keeps moving. He's turned away.

"Yeah?"

"C'mon up front. It's Mae looking for Cory. She set off the alarm."

Cop John goes back around the front corner and I'm beside Morgan and Bree in three seconds. They huddle tight to the wall, arms around each other.

"You girls did a real good job," I whisper.

We're on the edge of the bug-light glow coming from the neighbor's.

"Follow me, girls. Real quiet. Your momma's out front but the police is talking with her. She's got to tell em a story, and then we'll go."

I lead along another neighbor's house. They's upstairs, judging from the lights. We walk a line, turn the corner. Up front, I get low and scope the goings-on. Two police cars got flashing lights. One's in front the Smylie house and the other's behind Mae's Tercel. She's talking to four cops by her back bumper.

I got electric on my arms. I'm surprised Joseph don't yell for being shocked. This is the best juice I got in a week.

Morgan gasps and they's a one-foot shuffle.

Got a gun agin my head.

"Hey, Cory."

"Hey, kidnapper. Put Joe down."

"What you want?"

"I want to paste your brain against that wall, but we got to wait a few minutes."

"You want to do that front of your kids?"

"Don't you start that shit too. Morgan, Bree—stay right there."

Joseph gurgles.

"Shhh," I say. I get him up close, feel the metal press hard to my head. "You go easy with that gun." I rub my nose on Joseph and he gurgles a little, something not quite as angry as a shout, but not altogether happy. "You want to ease up on that thing? I got your son in my arms, dipshit."

Cory backs off. He pulls another gun from his belt and I see right off it ain't normal. The front is big and square.

"Put Joseph on the ground."

"Cory, it's cold. This is your son—"

"Put the fucking kid down!"

He straightens his arm and points a Taser at my chest.

"Easy, Cory." I bend to the ground and sit Joseph down. I stand.

I hear a zip sound and feel two bee stings in my chest and I got electric coursing through me for three full seconds. Feel like I'm a battery got plugged into the wall. Feel like a tired man just ate a three-pound steak. My whole body shakes and damned if I never felt so good and strong and surly in my life. The juice ends and then another juice, the kind I'm familiar with starts and the hair on my forearms shoots straight out inside my sleeves and Cory's eyes flame red like I was sober, twenty-four years old and just saw Nixon say I ain't a crook.

Cory Smylie healed me.

He's still got his arm stretched. I knock the wires loose, step in close and bring my fist from low and smash it into his jaw. Cory's head pops back and he drops agin the neighbor's house wall, then crumples to a hedge.

Joseph cries and I grab him off the dirt and nuzzle him to my stubble. "Hey son, you're all right. Yessir. Whooeeee." But he keeps on. Maybe the cops'll think he's with the neighbor's kids, roasting weenies. Cory groans—the gun in his other hand points thisaway and that. I grab it. Bring the hammer forward, check the chamber. Dumb fuck was ready to shoot with his babies right here. I smash the grip to the back of his skull. He's stunned like a thumped rabbit.

The girls've run back the way we came.

I kiss Joseph's forehead and make a fart sound with my lips. Joseph giggles like he's on the edge of tears.

The neighbor's front light goes on. "Who's there?" comes the shout.

I tuck the gun in my pants while I run and stumble on the girls waiting at the back of the house. Again Joseph wails.

Mae gives the cops a hard time, or her voice carries better than cop voices. Joseph's liable to end this rescue if he don't stop his confused whimpering and giggling.

"Morgan, you got to settle Joseph."

I put him in her arms and it's a miracle. The little girl's already got the momma know-how. She coos and cuddles him, and it's just pure-ass crazy, this whole thing. Out here with only the hardiest crickets still chirping, and the moon out, and them marshmallow people, and the four cops sassing Mae, Mae talking shit back, and Cory knocked out cold—in the middle of all that they's six-year-old Morgan got an infant in her arms, making him believe he's the safest critter in the night. Just pure fucking uncanny.

"Now girls, you listen good. Them police think your mother maybe busted into the house to get you—and she'll prob'ly let em think that so's we got time to scoot. We find a place we can watch, maybe they let her go in a little bit, and we'll go find her."

Bree takes ahold my leg like I'm not getting away. Morgan looks up from Joseph.

"Okay, here we go. Now we got everybody in the neighborhood riled up, so we got to head straight to the woods—all the way through these people's back yards. We'll circle around and watch for your momma from up the road."

Safest bet's crossing well behind all the houses. Morgan passes Joseph back to me and we set off. These people got back yards used to be wheat fields, I guess. Goes on and on, and a hundred yards out, I cut right. Ain't no way they can see us. "You girls, if I say drop, you drop quick. I see a spotlight, they won't be no time to think, you hear?"

Police lights flash against trees opposite the road, and the houses between us. Bet the neighbors is happy, heading for bed with strobe lights making they bedrooms into discos.

After a hundred yards, I angle at Mae's car, then hunker with Morgan and Bree. "All right, girls, you see that police car up there? Right in front, that's your momma's car. She's talking with em. We'll get a little closer and wait on them coppers. They leave, we go up and surprise your momma. I'll tell her you deserve a vacation."

Bree seems to doubt vacations is good.

I stay low long enough my knees is about to bust and I plop back on the grass. Joseph's got these little snores going on.

Morgan pulls my collar. "Uncle Baer—they're taking Mommy."

"What?" I shift a little sideways, roll to my feet and take a few steps. They take Mae to the closest cop car. Put her in the back seat—do that number with the hand on the back of her head. Mae stares out the window at Cory's house. A streetlight shines in the back of the car, and Mae looks about unglued.

"They're taking Mommy," Bree says.

The police cars turn around in different driveways, and they's gone.

"Where they take Mommy?" Bree says.

"I'm cold," Morgan says.

"Me too," says Bree.

The sky's clear. Whatever heat's been sticking to the ground'll leave soon enough. By midnight, I'm thinking frost. These girls got they shirts and pants and jackets on.

"Morgan, I want you to take your brother a minute. I'm going to the car. Be right back. You okay? Can you watch Joseph?"

"You coming back?"

"I'll be right back. You'll see me the whole time—straight to the car and straight back."

She nods somber-like, and it's the first time in my life I wish someone had a wisp of my talent, enough to know they's one person won't ever lie to her.

I set off quick and low, Cory's pistol in hand. Everything's quiet. Don't know if Cory's had the sense to go back inside the house, or if he might be along the police station. I listen at the edge of the lawn.

Mae's driver-side door is locked. Passenger opens. I unlock the back and grab the blanket covering the back seat. Try to yank it but this baby seat's buckled on top, and now I'm thinking I walked square into another trap. Blind under the dome light, ass hanging out the door.

But the girls is cold.

I unclasp the buckle and that ain't enough. Another rig somewhere holds it down. I lean deep inside and see another buckle. Pop it loose, thread the strap through the hole, toss the car seat. Mae's cut holes for the seat belts but the blanket'll do. I poke around for anything useful and find my rifle on the floor agin the seat. Mae must've thought quick and tucked it under the blanket draped over the side.

I worm back out the car, lock the door, close it. Expect to hear "You're a dead man" or some Hollywood horseshit, but it's just me in the dark. Street's quiet and the houses is mostly dark. Ain't a dog anywhere got a problem with anything.

It's downright eerie, expecting to be caught, and not.

I find the girls where I left em. "I got a blanket, keep you warm tonight."

"Where we going, Uncle Baer?"

"Camping," I say. "Just a little ways. I know a place where we can get warm and snug with a fire, and you girls can bed down. Maybe I'll tell a ghost story, something."

Bree looks at me.

"Maybe not."

Mae sat in a straight-backed metal chair and squinted under fluorescent lights. She imagined her babies in Cory's parents' car, speeding to some distant state where she'd never find them.

Officer Randy James sat across the desk. They'd graduated from the same high school class—he'd asked her out six or eight times, and never acknowledged her disinterest.

He probed his incisors with a toothpick. "Mae, none of this makes sense." Randy removed his hat, spun it so she glimpsed the stained headband, and placed it on his desk.

The Gleason police headquarters was a narrow two-story sandwiched between a travel agency and a boutique picture-frame store that survived on tourist dollars. Mae looked around the station and listened to the deputies' voices coming from the hallway. Each member of the four-man force had been academy-trained and walked and talked with uniform rigidity. It was a good presentation. But Chief Smylie had recently groused in a newspaper article about not having the budget to hold suspects in the basement jail. While the deputies' crew cuts proclaimed they wanted every trespassing charge to lead to breaking and entering and the discovery of a moldering corpse, in reality, if a crime didn't involve a bucket of spilled human blood, or couldn't be handled with a ticket, the accused walked. Gleason hadn't had a murder since the fifties.

"The logic don't make sense," Randy continued. "You say you knocked on the front door and triggered the alarm. But we got the open window in the back that did it."

Baer made it inside! "What I have repeatedly said is that I knocked on the door and eventually the alarm went off. I didn't say that I triggered the alarm. I was never at the back of the house."

"The back side. It was on the side of the house. But you knew that, right?"

"No, I didn't know that. Was anything missing from the house?"

"If you don't mind, I'll ask the questions."

"I don't mind. Was anything missing from the house?"

"As you know, Chief Smylie and Mrs. Smylie are away all week at a conference. So we don't know what's missing just yet."

"I didn't know they were gone."

Randy paused. Studied her with a trick behind his eyes. He grinned. "We pulled fingerprints from the window. Big ol' prints, clear as can be."

"Why am I here?"

"You know that, don't you? Come on. We've got Asheville running those fingerprints through the database. Why don't you tell me your version of the events one more time?"

"I don't have a *version*, Randy. You got any coffee?"

He stared. "Sure. Lots of cream and sugar?"

"Black."

He disappeared to an anteroom.

Deputy Leroy Dupont entered from the hallway, trailed by Cory Smylie. By the addled cant of his gaze and the disgust on his lips, Cory had crashed from his high. He rubbed the back of his head. Leroy stood at the open anteroom and reported to Randy.

"Cory here says he was inside, asleep, and stumbled down the steps when the alarm went off. He likes to sleep at the top of the staircase. Knocked his head on an end table. He went through the house, and nothing appeared out of order."

Randy sighed. "All that work on his skull come from a night table?"

"I'll have my dad check the alarm," Cory said. "Maybe get a nightlight."

Randy snorted. Shoved the form he was writing on a few inches away. "All right, for now."

Leroy led between the desks and paused at the front. Cory stood behind him. "You want, I'll take Mae back to her car," Cory said.

"'Preciate you," Randy said. "But I'll take her back. I want to look things over one more time. You understand."

Cory grinned. Dimples. "See you later, honey."

Randy handed her a Styrofoam cup of coffee.

Mae placed the cup on the desk. "I guess this means we're through."

"Let's get another look at your car." He remained standing.

Mae stretched her back. Saw Randy appraise her chest.

"Don't forget your coffee," he said.

"Styrofoam emits xenoestrogens. But thanks."

She rode in the back of the Chevy Caprice cruiser and her thoughts returned to worry. An image flashed to mind: three terrified kids looking through the back window of a car speeding into darkness.

She'd kill Cory yet.

The rifle! She'd left it under the backseat blanket.

Could she challenge Randy? Didn't a search require probable cause? Or had the Supreme Court decided cops could do anything they wanted? She'd talk her way out of it. Wait—if Baer had the kids, wouldn't he have taken them home in the car? Unless he wiled himself out of the thought. The rifle—she'd use Baer's logic. She had kids, therefore she had a gun. Randy would understand. Besides, it wasn't concealed… yes it was. Under the blanket.

Cory had been willing to drop the issue at the station. Did he still have the kids, or did he fear an investigation might escalate beyond his father's protection? The window fingerprint had to belong to Baer, and Baer owned the damage on Cory's head. But what if the children hadn't been at the house at all?

And what about the rifle in her back seat?

"You know, Mae, times are tough for women, and all."

"What's that mean? And all?"

"You got that cut on your face. We got Cory Smylie, back of his noggin looks like someone took a sledge to it. How long you and him been an item?"

"An item?"

"You don't like a word I say." Randy turned onto the road that led to the Smylie house. "What happened? He knock you around, and you come back for him? Maybe talk? Maybe settle the score?"

"No."

"What happened to your eye?"

"I fell and hit it on an end table."

"No call to get smart."

"I don't appreciate harassment, Randy."

"Cory's folks are out of town. You ain't clear yet. Chief gets back and Cory gives him a different story, you might find yourself answering a new set of questions back at the station."

Mae looked through the windshield, saw her car beside the road. Randy slowed; Mae watched as they passed the Smylie house. Cory's truck was in the driveway, and he sat like a sleepy sentry on the front step, elbows braced on his knees. He watched.

"There's your boy right there," Randy said. "Waiting." Randy parked behind Mae's Tercel. "Anything you want to tell me before I search the vehicle?"

Yeah—that rifle in the back seat—Cory stole my kids, and if you hadn't shown up, I would've killed him. "I disapprove, on principle."

"Right." Randy got out and approached the Tercel like it was a slumbering beast. He approached the passenger side, cast the flashlight beam over the trunk, license plate. He knelt and shined the light on the tire tracks. Back to the car. The rust hole on the trunk probably revealed the spare tire inside. Randy leaned close to the hole, then continued to the back door.

He shined the light through the window and tilted his head toward Mae, revealing a cultivated, professional frown.

Randy inspected the front seat. He held the light steady, probably studying the console, the floor. Hoping to find drugs, if she had to guess. He stepped around the front, passed the driver's door, and again blasted the light into the back.

Mae wilted. I have the gun because I have kids. No. I have kids; I have a gun. Of course I have a gun. I have kids. God.

Randy returned to the Caprice and opened the door. "You want to hand me the keys?"

"I don't want to."

"Just give me the damn keys."

She dug in her purse. They were at the bottom of the center compartment, but she missed them three times. Pulled out a plastic packet of tissue. A maxi. Chapstick. He'd seen the rifle; why else come back?

"Randy, what are you doing? Don't you want to go home, go to sleep?"

"Night shift. The keys. Or are you finally coming around?"

She passed him the keys.

"Stay put," he said.

Randy left the door open and walked back to the Tercel. He opened the driver's door. Reached back and unlocked the rear, and opened it from outside. He waved her forward.

Mae approached.

"You been robbed."

Randy stepped aside and Mae looked through the open door.

"I distinctly recollect a blanket on the back seat. It had a bunch of ducks and whatnot. Daffy and that. I got powers of observation, you might say. This vehicle's the site of a crime, Mae. We're going back to the station—"

"Over a blanket? Who gives a shit about a blanket?" She snatched her keys from his hand and saw his grin. "That's bullshit, Randy. Asshole."

She slammed the rear door. Jumped into the driver's seat.

"You drive safe, sugar."

She screeched into the first driveway. Snapped the shifter to reverse. Calm. Now. The blanket gone—and the rifle with it. Baer had the kids—had to have the kids.

TWENTY NINE

Sunlight breaks through trees, leaves fussing like cornhusks rubbing in a breeze. I ain't slept but a couple winks; spent most the night keeping the fire hot enough to melt lead. The girls never been in the woods at night, didn't like it a bit. Every deer or fox or who knows what wandered by in the dark, they eyes got big and white. Every story they ever heard about bears eating kids come back to em. Bree stood and pointed into the black, gutsy but trembling.

"The Boogeyman!"

"What's the Boogeyman?" says me.

"He's made of boogers."

"Well, I'd be afraid of a monster made of boogers too."

Didn't calm her none, so I went to the Boogeyman, a clump of scrub oak. I give it a shake and she screamed. Next it was goblins and trolls and, good shit, it never ended. I'm bleary-eyed and sober, not the best combination.

We bust camp first light. I cut the blanket in two pieces and wrap each girl in half, like they's Arabian princesses. That's what I tell em. I got Joseph in one arm, Cory's pistol in my pants, my rifle in my hand, and Smith on my hip. A single flask of shine and I'd take all comers.

The kids follow. They's so beautiful it puts the woods and sunlight to shame.

On and on. They ain't used to trekking and the going's slow. We avoid roads, mostly follow trail cut by four-wheelers and dirt bikes.

"I'm tired," Bree says.

"I'm hungry," Morgan says.

Joseph sleeps. Now and again I feel along his neck, down into his chest. He stays warm tucked in my coat and arm, but the girls…

"I'm tired," Bree says.

"C'mere." I go down on my knees. "You see down there?" I point the rifle. "See them houses? That's yours on the end. See your car out front? That means your momma's home, waiting on you. We got another ten, fifteen minute and we'll be there, and you can raid the kitchen. I'm sure Mae'll cook some breakfast. Can you make it down the hill?"

Bree yawns. "My feet hurt."

"It's just a little farther," Morgan says.

"That's right. A little more."

I walk a few steps. Turn. She ain't moved. "This's the plan." I pass Joseph to Morgan. Take the rifle, eject the cartridge, and ease the lever closed with my finger in the breech. Pass the rifle to Bree. "It's empty," I say, and show her the cartridge. Slip it in my pocket. She takes the rifle. "All right, Bree. Climb on my back."

I get down on my knees and she boards me like a horse, holding the rifle in front of my neck, pressed agin my throat so I can't breathe. I got one her legs hooked in my right arm, and take Joseph back from Morgan with my left.

"We ready?"

"Giddyup," Bree says.

We get to the house and I'm ready for a stretch on the dirt with my eyes shut. I put Bree down on the front yard. Morgan's already run to the house and Mae throws the door open before she hits the steps.

"Oh baby." She sweeps up Morgan and races down the steps for Bree.

"Ought to get you out of town while matters settle."

"I can't reach Mom. I've been calling all night and morning and can't reach her."

"Uh."

"It's been three days now. I tried to call her yesterday, before all this. Something's happened, I know it."

"What's happened?"

"We talked the other day. Last week. About everything. About her, and you, and Larry. She said they'd been fighting and he'd threatened to come hurt me."

"Hurt you."

Mae puts Morgan and Bree on the ground. "Go inside. Hurry." She waits a second. "Mom's in trouble." Mae takes Joseph from me, checks his vitals. Temperature and heartbeat. Color. "I'm worried sick. I know he's done something to her. She doesn't stay out all night."

"You got your car keys?"

She tosses em. I chamber a round in Cory's nine. Hand it to her. "Pull the hammer back this way. Release the safe here. Squeeze the trigger and whatever you hit won't be there no more."

I'm in Mae's Tercel again—a chunk of highly fuel-efficient rust, spring-mounted on four bald tires. Shimmies like a fat girl's ass between forty-five and sixty, but smoothes out at seventy.

Mars Hill sits way north of Asheville. Got a little college, a bunch of houses, a few businesses. Only been here a few times—the last ten year ago after Ruth divorced Larry. I caught word from a fella I sold likker to, Job Harding. He did me a favor and dug into her address. Every likker drinker wants a stiller in his debt. Wasn't much digging, it turned out. Him and Ruth lived on the same block.

I couldn't believe Ruth and Larry parted, so I snuck to Mars Hill and scoped her house. Saw her once, purty as ever. I ducked behind a tree and made sure she never saw me.

Been sending letters ever since.

Memory serves, I follow the main drag to the end of town and watch for a left. It ain't the road on her address because they's a turn after that. I get mixed up and drive back and forth a half-dozen times, left and right a couple more, and see Tilson Drive. Must've writ "Tilson" two thousand times, front and center on two thousand envelopes.

There. I stand beside the Tercel and stare. Ragged and over-grown, shingles falling in rusted eaves. A lightning rod leans side-way at the roof apex.

"She's gone," a man says.

I didn't see him coming. His features is plain. Honest.

"Ain't seen her in a week," he says. "Say, you seen a Collie wander by? Dumb shit just up and disappeared last night."

"Nah, I ain't seen your dog."

THIRTY

One day years back Job Harding came after a bunch of jugs and said they'd be his last. He was giving up the life and these ten cases was for personal consumption, to last 'til the day he died. I said if he got to the final jug and still felt spry, he'd better drink it all at once.

He lived on the same block as Ruth, but looking from one home to the next, I don't know which. Houses is dense like most the town was done and the builders already tipped a few jugs, and the foreman scratched his nuts and said, "We need space for five more houses." All these towns is just houses wherever somebody bought a chunk of land and threw together some sticks. They's a testament to the freedom to screw things up. That's why they's so comfortable.

I scan the street back and forth and try to picture Job Harding's pickup. It was an American model... an S-10. He used to brag it had a Camaro engine. It was dark green and he had chrome mags on the stupid thing, and these psychedelic green plastic jiggies on his windshield wipers.

That's the whole nineties, right there.

I pass a house and another. No names on the mailboxes, just numbers. No vehicles in the drives. Comes to it I'll beat on every door.

End of the street I look back the way I come and the next road over, through a windrow of scrub and trees. Weather-beaten houses got one foot in the grave. Eaves coming loose, shingles in disrepair, paint cracked or mostly flaked off. Big old gaps between cement blocks. Some of these folks don't enjoy lawn work and I don't blame em. Big tufts of grass by the trees, along fences and foundations. They's grass all around a beat-up S-10…

I'm tromping straight for the door, realize it's the back of his house and he'll meet me with a gun. Circle up front.

"Job!" I beat the door with the side of my hand. "Job!"

The door rattles in its frame; I give it another pound. The door gaps open—

"—the sam hell's going on?"

"Job! Where's Ruth?"

He opens the door a bit more. "Hunh?"

He's thinking so hard his eyes is crossed.

"Job! It's Baer Creighton, out Gleason. You remember?"

"Baer."

"You remember. You bought the likker. Job?"

"Bought the likker. Right. Bought the likker."

He don't know whether to scratch his watch or wind his ass.

"How you doing?" Job says.

"You remember ten year back, you told me Ruth Jackson lived a couple houses down? I'm looking for her."

His brows tighten. "Poor girl."

"How's that? Where is she?"

"Prob'ly in the ground, halfway to Pisgah. Who knows?"

"Why… why you say that?"

His eyes widen. "Oh! You're Baer Creighton… out Gleason way!"

"That's right, Job. What happened to Ruth?"

He exhales a long breath. Slumps to the jamb. "Larry Creighton happened to her."

"He take her away?"

"He beat on her, is what he did. I saw through the back winda, here. His truck was in the drive, and since I know the history, I watched close. Cracked the winda, case I could hear anything."

"What do you mean, you know the history?"

"Oh, goin' way back when she moved out here. She told me all of it. Woman loved to talk. Loved it. And when Larry started coming around again a few weeks back, I paid attention. Hell, half the time he'd park down the street and never get out—just sit there in the truck smokin' cigarettes. This last time he went in the house. I sat on the commode all of twenty minute. Then he comes out, and she comes out, and she's hitting him all over. Just angry as a hive o' hornets. He's got his arms up and she's thumping him any which ways. She screaming gibberish and he's shouting back. Then he reaches one arm way back like this, I swear to you, Baer, just like this. He curls that hand into a fist, and comes around. Clocks her to the ground, and she just lays there."

I look behind me and to my side. Nowhere to sit, and my legs is about give out. I don't get a single shock and his eyes is plain white. "You saw all that?"

"Every bit of it. Larry looked all around, see if anyone was watching, and put her in his truck. You know how it is when a body's just a body and they ain't no person in it. Arms and feet dangling."

Cement comes up to my knees, then my hands. I swing my ass below me. My head tingles and my ears rush with noise. My mind steadies and I sit on the cold cement a minute. I think of Mae saying Ruth still had a thing for me after all these years. I should have gone and found her five years ago. Ten years ago. Hell, I did find her. I should have come out from behind that tree and said I'll take you now, and we'll never look back. We got twenty thirty years left—let's run out west and spend em together.

That letter I mailed her today—I don't think I ever before said we could go away like that.

I breathe and for a few seconds that's all I can do. "What kind of law you got around here? You tell 'em?"

"I told em."

"What'd they do?"

"They didn't believe me. They went over and knocked on her door, said she was out getting groceries. Walking her cat. I said she don't got a cat and they walked off while I was talking at em. One stayed in his car there at her house for a half-hour, then he left too. Ain't been back."

Ruth's door is locked. I beat on it and glass panes rattle. I wait on the step and think maybe she's coming to the door right now. If she answers… if she swings the door open right now, what'll I say?

I rap again with a little less gumption. Look at the lawn and imagine Larry walloping Ruth like Job said. See her fall, knocked out. Knocked dead. And him carrying her into his truck. This back-and-forth with Larry—all these pieces start to fit a little better. I come poking around and talk to Eve, and maybe Eve says I come on to her, like any scorned woman might. So he looks at his hand, decides to raise me. I'll take your dog and the only woman you ever give a shit for. This won't stop until Larry and me throw down the cards and go sideways out the window.

I try the doorknob again. Job's on his front step, shaking his head, talking.

My coat sleeve's good and stiff. I smash my elbow through the lower pane. Rips my jacket and pinches the skin. I reach through and feel for the lock and in a couple seconds I'm looking over Ruth's living room. Coffee table, sofa, small television with rabbit ears. Telephone on the end table… I can see her curled on the couch with the phone, talking with Mae about all the crazy shit women talk about, and it pisses me off. She was supposed to be my woman, and that was supposed to be my life—seeing her yammering all day and night, and me having to go to the other side of the house for a moment's peace. That was mine.

They's the kitchen beyond; I should've had the last thirty years of her banging pots and pans and roasting whole chickens. Thirty years of sneaking up behind her and giving her a squeeze.

"Ruth?"

My voice checks the rooms and echoes back empty-handed.

I breathe in deep and catch a cinnamon scent. I glance things over. If I don't get the full scope of this house, and miss something that might tell me what happened, I'll spend the rest of my years with another kind of guilt.

In her bedroom is a bureau with frilly things that smell nice. I pull each drawer and push it closed without molesting anything. They's a photo of Mae on the nightstand. One pillow on the bed. Closet with clothes, extra shoes at the bottom. 'Bout a thousand. I look at her desk, with a mirror and lights above. An antique-painted monstrosity with a box of makeup looks like a tackle box of fishing lures. All of it, everything, is stuff a woman would take if she was leaving for a while, and it's the best evidence old Job saw what he saw.

I check the bathroom. Toothbrush in a cup.

Kitchen's fulla food... not a lot, but assorted. She was partial to Spam.

I'm back to the living room and on the coffee table spot a letter I missed the first time through. It's one of the handful I sent last week, opened, letter partly out the envelope. They's a shoebox fulla letters under the sofa.

I lift the box and thumb across the tops. In order, by date.

Job's still on his stoop. I head at him and he says, "Find anything?"

"Where's the police, this town?"

"Twenty-eight Main. That'll be the north end."

Six minutes I'm there. Step inside and smell burnt coffee. By the look, the day shift is accustomed to nothing going on. College kids might keep the night crew busy, but this town walks like it's got a stick in its ass, so maybe not.

"Help you?" the man says. He's got a beard and no mustache. Eyes lidded like a frog's, and feet propped on the corner of his desk.

"Fella named Job Harding reported a woman missing a couple day back. Ruth Jackson."

"Yeah."

"Well, she's still missing."

He studies me. "Guess we can file a report."

"Thought maybe you'd get off your ass and look for her."

He drops his feet off the desk but don't trouble to rise. "Last I looked, there was no reason to suspect any foul play. She just up and went somewhere." He squints. "You got different information?"

"She ain't where she always is."

"You a member of the family?"

"No."

"Well then who are you?"

"Never mind." I back out the door.

"Hey!"

I get in the car and head out of town.

It was clear to Cory Smylie that Stipe had been correct. The foundation was self-control. He'd screwed up because he'd been intoxicated. He'd humiliated himself again. He hadn't been able to think, and a millisecond after a decision, he'd known it was wrong. Yet he pushed through reckless thinking and moment by moment his situation worsened. He should have known Baer Creighton would mount a rescue. Creighton was Mae's hero. He should have foreseen a police response—his father was the police chief. Instead of being guided by slow anger and being painstaking in his planning, Cory had been guided by rage and planned not at all. He'd been high. So much for invincibility.

The humiliation was real. He owned the respect of no man in the county. His kids feared him. His woman chose to screw her flesh and blood over him. Stipe had surely heard of the night's misadventures and by now had written him off as a failure. He'd done it to himself.

He would do things differently this time.

He'd awakened the following morning with a knot on his head that made his brain feel like it had been flattened by a steamroller. He looked around outside for his gun and couldn't find it, but the Taser was in the neighbor's hedges. He went inside the house and drank water and took four Tylenol, and went to sleep.

He woke at noon and lay in bed, staring at the ceiling. A dull ache filled him, the residual pain of a body continually fed poison. He wanted a joint to smooth things over. A cup of coffee and a joint and a beer. Between the three of them, his body would find the chemical it craved.

Then he thought of Stipe. How he'd placed his hand on Cory's shoulder. How his voice had softened. The most powerful man in Buncombe County had seen something in him worth saving, and the moment was like being in church. Guilt. Hope. Work. Stipe had told the truth. Cory was destroying himself, and if he didn't get a handle on his addictions, it didn't matter how hard he tried to do anything else. He was sabotaging himself.

Cory rose from bed. His head throbbed and he stood with his hand on the headboard for a full minute while his blood pressure evened out. He couldn't continue like this. He felt like an old man.

Shame washed through him. Disgust.

Discipline. Cory closed his eyes, embraced the pain. *I will beat you,* he said. He thought of Mae, saw her in her uncle's embrace. Cory needed discipline to right his life and save his kids. He owed it to them. He'd been a coward too long. He would face himself, and when he had control, he would face his enemy.

Cory swallowed two more Tylenol and three glasses of water. He was parched. He reached for a pack of Marlboros and withdrew one. Stuck it in his mouth and lit it.

He inhaled smoke.

This is the shit that is destroying me.

He stubbed the cigarette in an ashtray.

He needed to go away. He could go to Baltimore, where he had contacts…

He shook his head and the headache stabbed. *Wrong decision.*

"My troubles are right here."

He squeezed the pack of Marlboros in his hand. He crumpled the box and worked his fingers back and forth, grinding the cigarettes inside. When the box was a ball and the aroma of the tobacco rich, he dumped the contents in the toilet and flushed.

Cory returned to his room and pulled a shoebox from under the bed. He'd never had to find a crafty way to hide his drugs because his parents never looked. He opened the box, removed a plastic baggie of pot, and took it to the bathroom.

He was being rash, but he also knew from the silence of the little voice that this was right. Drugs were killing him, not just his body but his mind and his hope of ever amounting to anything. Drugs were his perennial retreat. Drugs were cowardice incarnate. He dumped the baggie into the toilet and flushed.

Still in his boxers, Cory grabbed his keys, walked down the steps, exited the house, and opened his truck. He pulled a leather satchel from under the seat and carried it to the bathroom.

He stopped. Wouldn't he be better off selling it, and then being done with it? At least get his investment back? He only had a few hundred dollars, and this bag was worth a couple thousand. The little voice said no. One by one, Cory emptied pill bottles and baggies into the toilet.

That was going to be one stoned septic system. He smiled.

He had faced himself. He was learning self-control. Once he reined in his mind, he would revisit Stipe's recommendations. He'd think things through, but one way or the other Mae and Baer Creighton were over.

He'd show Stipe he was serious. Cory had just the right idea.

THIRTY ONE

Them dogfighters got the law with em. No way Horace Smylie'll turn on his friends. That ain't how the bloodsport clique works. It's an invitation-only affair, and if you ain't got a ticket stamped by six of your daddy's cousins saying you're salt of the earth, death-lovin and blood-lovin and prone to keep mum, you won't ever be part of the club. They operate in secret because most folks—even being liars and cheats—recognize pure-ass evil. These dogfight men'll say dogs is born to fight, that they crave squaring off agin another dog and seeing who's best. They'll say it happens every day in the wild, and most wolves don't die from old age, but other wolves.

I've had a bellyful thinking about what Fred endured in the pit so these men could guffaw and place bets and see life destroyed. And that—whether the dogs want to fight or not—makes it evil.

I been thinking on Larry, and how my past with Ruth has got things mixed up. She was with both of us, back and forth. I did wrong by Larry, strictly speaking. But you can't turn your back on family like Larry did—you can't show disgust for where you come from without showing disgust for who you come with.

Ruth went back and forth. She had Mae and I took the house from her and Larry.

After, I went out and found the house they was renting. It was evening and Larry was at college. I give the door a knock. Stand there with a clump of lazy Susans wilting in my hand. Ruth answers the door but won't take the chain off, so I'm looking at her through a two-inch gap.

"I'm going to win you back," I say.

"You got to let things end."

"Hell I do. If it's money you and your daddy got to have, I'll get it."

"Don't matter if you do. I'm married. I'm a mother."

Sure as shit she was.

I had a hunch I could make money off my talent. Knew a fella from working the gas station. Lou Debenker. Drank beers and shot stick at the bar and he was working some insurance racket, said he drove around all day and collected money off people, and only thing he did was ask each one if it was time to buy more insurance, every week when he saw em. He'd get the neighbors' names and sell the insurance to them too. Product sold itself, Lou said, if a salesman had the knack. Company paid for miles and he got money off the sales, and best, they was no limit on the dough he could make. Lou gulped from his beer bottle and arched his eyebrows high to demonstrate the concept.

Only thing, they was electric all through me. Lou didn't have no red in him, so I let it go. I figured the juice was coming somewhere else.

I always thought they had to be a way to turn my curse into advantage, instead of being the dumbass that couldn't lie to save his life, and had to be shut in a room with nobody near just to keep a job.

Lou introduced his boss, a sideways guy playing pool the next table over. Permanent red coming outta him. He was the source of the juice. He didn't mean harm—some folks broadcast they's liars and cheats, and that almost makes em honest. Lou's boss was listening and said he'd give me a job on the spot if I'd ask every man in the bar if he needed life insurance.

Sounded easy enough. I go to the first five six guys and each either looks or says "piss off." Next says no, but his eyes flash red and I get a shock. In them days shocks was live-wire hot. I said, "I think you do need life insurance, and it's been eating at you. Come talk to my buddy over here and he'll set you up so you can sleep at night."

Day later boss shows me the ropes. Every time I ask if a man needs the insurance, and he says no but lights red, I push 'til he's honest, and that does the trick. The insurance didn't cost but a couple dollars a month, sometimes less. A man'd look at his wife and kids, and time his eyes got back to me they'd be red and he'd be done for. I'd trick him into taking care his family.

After a few months selling more insurance than the whole office, I had a pile of money and the kind of prospects Ruth's daddy could appreciate. I had snappy clothes and fields of green in my billfold. Went to see Ruth while Larry was gone again and she looked through the two-inch door gap.

"You can't come here," she said.

Her eyes glowed.

I about shit myself. Thought my curse failed—she was all the time honest and randy, and I didn't figure she was honest because our desires was congruent 'til I thought on it a decade. One time, one big-assed lie. But just because you know a person got deceit festering in they heart, you don't know which exact words is the lie. I didn't arrive at her real lie 'til long after.

"I got money," I said. "Look at this." I opened my wallet and stood there like a fool. Might as well have had a fedora with a flamingo feather. Boots with my pant legs tucked in.

"You rob a bank?"

"I sell life insurance. Setting records every day."

"You're a life insurance salesman?"

"Ruth, you ain't got no call flipping back to Larry. Don't you get it?"

She slammed the door. Locked it.

That was that. Didn't matter if I had money. Had to get it the right way—either inherit from somebody else or have a sit-on-your-ass job looking down on everybody. I quit my insurance job and went to see Gunter Stroh. After that I put my money into a still, and a few hundred pound of corn, wheat, barley, yeast, and sugar. I wrapped my tie around a spruce pole and made a torch, and used it to light the first fire under my boiler.

Thinking of Ruth in them days don't come close to taking the ache off her being dead. I give up on people, but I never give up on Ruth. If I'd done that, life would have been hopeless.

Now I lost Ruth I got to face the truth. Evil is everywhere. She had it too. She lied.

I know what I need to know to feel right about killing.

I hope to hell Larry's at the next fight. I'll kill him for watching Fred and countless other dogs slashed to ribbon—but he'll deserve it even more for what he done to Ruth.

It was Cory stole Fred. Got the right color truck, took it for a wash so the tailgate was all clean after that night. Stipe paid him to find bait dogs and somehow he knew about mine. He knew about the Hun blind—that musta been him smokin' dope in there and couldn't shoot for shit.

Cory's flat got it coming—him and every other man goes to them fights. The men who pay money to keep the institution alive. The men who bet on it. The men who hoot and holler. The man who staged the fights. The whole crew. The ugliness goes on and on. So I know what I know and I feel positively sanctified about the killing to come.

THIRTY TWO

Cory Smylie was sober.

The first day was easy. His ill feeling reinforced his commitment. He kept his goals foremost in his mind, and found that when he needed to focus his self-control he thought not of putting Mae in her place, but of Baer. Destroying Baer Creighton was the glue that kept Cory coherent.

With every decision from taking a leak to eating a hot dog, Cory asked, "Does this make me stronger?"

Without chemicals corrupting his thought process he felt grounded. The right path was easy to spot and simple to walk. Self-control was the ultimate thrill and revenge upon Baer Creighton was a compass point keeping his heading perfect.

But on the second day his thinking grew hazy. His thoughts were nebulous. He couldn't concentrate and every challenge left him frustrated. He tore the cereal box because the assholes at Post used too much fucking glue. His parents had been gone for days at his mother's business expo in Baltimore and no one had done the dishes, and he had to wash a cereal bowl and a spoon. The phone wouldn't stop ringing—probably deputies wanting to question him again, or worse, his lame-ass father wanting answers on an attempted break-in.

Man, could he use a joint.

But each time the little voice squeaked to his rescue, and every time he listened the voice grew stronger. More adamant.

In high school he'd wrestled. Long before he tried dope, he'd subjected himself to grueling practices and grew intoxicated on the heady achievement of producing sweat. Sitting with his mind spinning out of control, what he desired more than anything was to exert himself and feel blood rush. His lungs fill with air. His muscles respond with strength. He wanted to sweat.

Almost desperate, he threw on a pair of shorts and running shoes. He wrapped on a Velcro wristwatch.

He'd see how much he'd slipped. See how far he had to go.

Cory started out fast. His body hadn't felt this good for a long time. Adrenaline shot through him. His legs were pistons and his arms worked back and forth like locomotive rods.

Within a minute his lungs were on fire. His legs grew wobbly. He eased his stride and looked at his watch, gasping. Two minutes. He used to run for an hour at a time, fast. Way faster than this. He glanced at his watch again and looked up to see a cute girl jogging toward him. He grinned and his toe caught an uneven sidewalk slab. He urged his right leg way forward to stop his fall but his leg didn't hear. His muscles failed. Cory flew against a hedge and rolled back to the cement.

He sat on the sidewalk with his elbows on his knees. His eyes rimmed with tears. The cute girl trotted by and he was too ashamed to watch her wiggle.

And then he got up and smacked the dust from his ass. He picked a thorn from his palm and resumed his run. He wouldn't attempt a full hour, but he owed it to himself to try. What else was he going to do? Smoke a joint? His anger for Baer Creighton swelled.

Hell no.

Cory Smylie hadn't felt this kind of emotional stability, such cold blankness, for years. Every action resulted from thinking things through. He had time and commitment.

Cory crinkled the cash in his pants pocket. He'd taken every stashed dollar. He'd pored over every detail of his plan. He knew how to get close. He knew those woods almost as well as Creighton. He wouldn't make the same mistakes as last time.

He had been crazy to think that while he was high, drunk, and short on sleep he could outwit an animal like Creighton. He was lucky to have failed, for if he had been successful he would have returned home with the murder weapon. He'd seen *CSI*. Mae would have thrown the spotlight on him and the police would have matched the rifle.

But not this time.

He stood behind a glass counter at Frankenmuth's Big Sports studying a row of Cold War–era rifles. He'd driven to Charlotte. In case there were cameras in the store, Cory wore a stick-on mustache. He'd dyed his hair black and covered most of it with a Carolina Panthers baseball cap.

He scanned the racks back and forth but his gaze kept drifting to a 1953 Soviet-made AK-47. The rifle looked rugged, and from what Cory had heard, it was universally renowned for durability.

"It's a great rifle," the heavyset man in plaid said. He found a key from a ring of fifty and removed the rifle from the rack. He handed it across the glass counter. "What'll you use it for?"

"Targets."

"Any distance?"

"Two hundred yards."

"Well, it's a good gun."

Cory heard a subtle change in tone. "But?"

"AK's are known for standing up to abuse. That's because they're manufactured sloppy. You could charge it, shove a handful of dirt into the bolt housing, and it'd still cycle the next round, and the next. They're indestructible, but all that sloppiness costs you, especially on a fifty-year-old rifle. Hell, you could bolt this thing to an iron table and not shoot a ten-inch group at two hundred yards."

Cory nodded. "So what's better?"

"Damn near anything, if you want accuracy." He lifted the AK from Cory's hands, replaced it in the rack and removed another weathered rifle. This one was clearly older and had seen more use. The stock extended to the end of the barrel and the bolt handle stuck straight out the side. The man passed the rifle to Cory. "Take this Mauser. Fine German engineering. By the time they made this in 1898, they'd already had thirty-plus years to work out the bugs. Open the bolt."

Cory did.

"See how tight that is? No play at all. Smooth action. Now slam it home."

Cory slapped the bolt handle forward and down, a liquid action. The rifle balanced in his hands and the smell was rich like metal and oil. "This accurate?"

"Oh hell yeah. Two hundred yards is short-range. I hunt deer with one of these and bagged a ten-point at four hundred. They say they're accurate to a thousand yards. Way more than the average shooter'd know what to do with."

"Right," Cory said. "How much?"

"This one? We got a sale going on today. One ninety-nine. I'll make you a sweet deal on two."

"One will do the job."

Cory passed the Gleason interstate exit. He'd spent the two-hour drive from Charlotte dreaming of his Mauser's recoil and hoping it would be robust. He'd bought four boxes of ammunition and everything he'd need to sight in the rifle and become fluent with its mechanics. He had two hours before dark.

His ears rang. They'd been ringing all day, but he hadn't realized it until he slowed coming off the Old Fort exit. His body missed drugs, but his soul was greedy for the coherence of sobriety. The tightly-wound daftness of physical withdrawal would pass. Too bad. The heightened lucidity was really helping make his priorities clear.

Sykes Range was a dues-paying club located a few miles from a church-and-crossroads community north of Old Fort, ten winding miles down the mountain from Gleason. It consisted of a small cabin attached to a fifty-foot indoor pistol range. The range only permitted members to use the indoor facility. Outside, they'd removed a wide swath of trees from the mountain approach. Rough-sawn posts and fence rails were spaced fifty, one hundred, two hundred, and three hundred yards away. Each splintered and riddled with holes.

Locals used the outdoor range as they pleased, usually sighting in their rifles before each buck season. Cory had visited the range several times the year he graduated high school, and had a sense for its pace. With almost a month before regular deer season, he was unlikely to encounter other shooters.

But he had to be prudent. He motored over the gravel driveway and rehearsed the vernacular that would prevent him from arousing suspicion. "Coming in a little high last season. Thought I'd bring it in. What you shooting?"

Cory pressed down the sides of his fake mustache and threw on a ball cap. Trees along the drive obscured the parking area but so far he hadn't heard any gunfire. He slipped on dark sunglasses but the sun was already behind the mountain. Sunglasses at dusk looked queer, not country. He tossed the shades to the console.

The driveway opened into the parking area. Cory was alone.

He parked and filled his pockets with a marker, thumbtacks, and three boxes of cartridges, then carried the Mauser to the back of the Sykes building. A row of triangular shooting tables sat under a rusted sheet-metal roof, supported by weathered, salt-treated deck lumber. A cold gust made his eyes water. An unanchored piece of metal tapped a post. Cory chose a table with a serviceable chair and rested his rifle on the sandbags.

When he'd been here as a teenager, his friends had ridiculed him. He'd never shot seriously, for accuracy. But he listened to his friends' tips and watched their mechanics. He learned to control his breathing, assume the same posture every time, and find an identical sight picture before firing. He fused his friends' lessons with his innate sense and over a few weeks he became the best shot of the group. Cory looked downrange with trepidation and regret. How much skill had he lost? How much life had he pissed down the drain?

He emptied his pockets and carried the targets and tacks to the leftmost fence at two hundred yards. He affixed a black bulls-eye and returned to the rifle.

When he'd come to this place as a teenager, he'd been steady and his eye was clear. Now his mind was ringing. His nerves were sharp from the absence of drugs. He was kind of spacy, kind of focused. He'd hold a thought with relentless concentration and then realize after a moment that he'd been thinking of something entirely different, and couldn't remember what he'd thought before. At any moment he might penetrate some deep truth. He was conscious that he was conscious, and his self-awareness felt like an awakening. A turning point. He would choose what he wanted to be. He would be anything he chose.

He slipped a cartridge into the Mauser's open chamber. He would be lethal.

THIRTY THREE

Ernie Gadwal had felt a rush watching through binoculars as Baer Creighton buried his mutt. He'd shifted sideways a little and pressed his pants, shifting the erection below with the palm of his hand. Wished he could do something about it.

Misery drove Creighton's shovel into the dirt. Wrath pulled it out. Ernie had studied Creighton's motions and thrilled, musing how Creighton would react if he knew his dog's slayer was so close.

Like Nietzsche said, build your cities on the slope of Vesuvius.

Ernie followed Creighton's long forest trek to the cave bearing the remains of an old-timer's still. Ernie followed Creighton to his busty niece's house. Several times he'd thought Baer had spotted him, but his size and craft kept him safe. Ernie had never walked so much in his life, and when Creighton took off in his niece's car, Ernie had a use for the free time.

Burly scared him, but Ernie saw their eventual partnership as a détente between men who had more to gain by cooperating with each other than by destroying each other.

Requisite to détente was the ability to mount a strong defense, and Ernie had grown weary of fearing for his life every time Burly was around. If Burly was going to wear a Bowie knife, Ernie strapped a surprise to his ankle—a .25 caliber pistol he'd picked up at an Asheville pawn shop a year before. It wasn't accurate but Burly was big.

Ernie sat on the trunk of his car. He spent as much time glancing over his shoulder toward town watching for Burly as he did the other side for Creighton. Ernie had duplicated Burly's preparations in case Creighton crossed to Brown's farm while Burly was absent. There were four five-gallon jerry cans of gasoline in his trunk, right under him.

Two days ago Burly had led Ernie to believe he'd return the following morning. He hadn't. A day later, Ernie was certain Baer would make his move. Ernie had returned to the hillcrest after filling gas cans and grabbing his .25 caliber, and had spent every anxious moment reviewing his plan.

It had to work. Stipe would realize Ernie's value, and other elements would fall into place.

Overtaking Stipe would be a long, surreptitious operation. Ernie would be clever and endearing until Stipe was no longer useful. Then they would become competitors, and Stipe wouldn't know what hit him.

Ernie returned his thoughts to the present. He knew he could get Burly to imagine being more powerful than Stipe. But could he convince Burly success was only possible with Ernie as his partner?

Burly said Stipe wanted Creighton dead sooner rather than later. Burly would return, and when he arrived he would go to

Creighton's, shoot him, throw him over his shoulder, and carry him to his final resting pyre at Brown's.

Creighton would be equally dead whether Burly followed his troglodytic impulse or Ernie's nuanced plan. The method of execution only mattered insofar as Stipe knew Ernie had conceived it. Ernie drummed his fingers against the car trunk.

The money would make a stronger argument—money, and a challenge to Burly's courage.

It felt like madness, giving half the gold to Burly. But in exchange Ernie gained Burly's most fervent labor. Ernie had considered all this before. He could steal every dollar from the money tree, keep it and pay Burly by the hour, but a wage man wouldn't toil like a fifty-percent-equity man.

In the end, he would exchange half the fortune for Stipe's favor and Burly's labor. Wasn't that how empires were built? Strategic bets at opportune moments?

A distant, high-pitched sound came to Ernie and he glanced toward town. A dust plume chased a black sport utility vehicle up the hill. Ernie leaped from his trunk. He dashed across the fifty-yard stretch to the road and arrived as the Suburban crested the hill.

Ernie waved and watched for the Suburban's nose to dip. Instead it raced closer.

Ernie jumped to the center of the road and threw his arms wide. The Suburban swerved and skidded. Inside, Burly cursed and beat his fists to the dashboard. The window lowered and Burly craned his head out. "Get off the road, you stupid asshole! Move!"

Ernie looked downhill toward Creighton's place, a half-mile away. He motioned with his hands for Burly to keep his voice down.

"Move, shithead!"

Ernie put his hands on the bug deflector. Burly revved the engine. "You have to wait a minute. It won't be long 'til he goes to the Brown house and we can do it the right way."

"I want it done with. Get off the road. You think Stipe gives a shit how it happens?"

"I do, and if he don't he ought to. My way leaves no evidence. You can't just off a man and carry him two hundred yards in broad daylight dripping blood! Besides, there's no poetry to it. There's nothing to give it any class."

"Step aside or I'll throw your body in Brown's house too."

Ernie rushed around to Burly's side window. Burly reached for the shifter.

"You don't want to do that," Ernie said. "I know a million reasons you don't want to do that."

"What?"

"I know where Creighton's hid a million bucks. His life savings, all in gold."

"Bullshit."

"Think about it. What's he do with all that money he makes? He lives in a damned lean-to! You can kill me too, if it isn't true."

Burly wrinkled his brow. "So why don't you go get it?"

"I need your help. All I know, he's got booby traps all over. He's wily. If you go after Creighton right now, you'll be dead inside of five minutes. I've followed him twenty-four seven for the last two weeks, damn near. There's no way you can get the drop on him. He's got eyes in the back of his head. Closest I got was two hundred yards, and that's in the woods. But you wait for him to get inside the basement of that house, those eyes in the back of his head won't matter. He won't stand a chance. When that's done, then we get the money."

Burly frowned and stared down the hill. "You followed him everywhere?"

"I followed the night he got the drop on you after that dog fight, and left you for a black bear to maul."

Burly looked away and spit as if trying to remove a fleck of tobacco from his tongue. "A million dollars, huh? Don't make sense for you to tell me when you could have it all yourself."

"I need your help. Not just to get through all those booby traps. What to do with it. Think what you and me could do with a million bucks, you being so tight with Stipe. We'll go into business."

Burly grunted and removed his hand from the shifter. "What kind of business?"

"I've given it some thought. I can see from your face you think I'm batshit, but that money's real and I'll show you where it is once Creighton can't put a bullet in my back."

"What makes you think I won't?"

"That's a chance I'll take. Think about running your own business, with an operations guy like me handling the paper and gathering the intelligence. You in charge. Think of passing men on the street and their eyes light up with fear. Respect. Their voices shake when they talk, and by God they say 'Mister' if they say anything at all. You wearing a black suit, driving a new Lincoln truck. Tell me that wouldn't make you proud as shit. Let's get real. You'll be bigger than Stipe."

Ernie paused and lifted his hands from Burly's window.

"If I'm wrong, you just go on down the hill and get shot. I'll partner with someone else. But if I'm right, why don't we go back to the lookout? We've got business to talk. We got capital, we can do anything. There's going to be a shortage of top-notch moonshine in a week or two."

"Get in."

I sit for two days looking at Fred's grave before I make the absolute final decision.

Brown used to have a still. I seen it in the basement—little two-gallon can with five six feet of copper. Operation I have in mind, that's subpar. But they ain't a lot of places a fella can go for a twenty-gallon cooker.

I slip to the drive, look both ways before crossing. Feel hunted on my own land. Every time I pass where Fred bled in the dirt and grass it's like a fist inside my head and eggbeaters in my belly. The one makes me mad enough to kill; the other makes me want to bowl over and throw up.

I look from the blood-stained ground up to Brown's house, with its bowed porch looking like a dopey smile and the shattered upstairs windows like stoned eyes, and I'm reminded everything decays, and that's the way of it. And as soon as I murder every man that watched Fred get chewed, things'll be right as rain.

Brown never was a full-time operator. He made soap and he made likker and sometimes the one tasted like the other. I study the device he left. A little professional attention and Brown's booze machine'll find its voice.

I glance over tools on the workbench, hanging on the wall, stuffed on shelves. Coffee cans of rusted screws. A carpenter's level. A square. A plumb bob. Trowel. Fishing poles between the joists, tucked above white electric lines. How long it been since I had a batch of leeks and trout?

I carry a hacksaw to the water heater on the opposite corner.

The inch-thick copper out the top is too fat and won't bend. But I already took all the thin, flexible stuff, and the goons hacked it to pieces. I cut close to the water heater until the pipe dangles. Fetch a rickety stool and saw again, fifteen feet from the water heater, where the pipe hangs below a two-by-six.

With a claw hammer from the bench I pry the U-shaped supports and then cart a long, bowed pipe and the two-gallon still from the house. I rest em on the ground out front. Down the road a ways on the Gleason side, a big old rooster plume of dust billows up. Somebody's making good time.

I head back to the basement. Boiler that small, it'll be twice the work unless I get a doubler. Water collects as the sqeezins pass through. I shake a turpentine can and find it empty. I'll drill the sides, slap on a couple fixtures. Good thing Stipe didn't burn my toolshed.

They's a motor outside. Door clunks shut. Somebody got a dog to get rid of? That vehicle was coming from town, not the other way.

I think on it.

A long-lost heir come to claim the rust and rot? Or somebody looking to settle a score with Baer Creighton? Turpentine can in one hand, Smith in the other, I take the steps sideways, each foot slow. I listen. No more sounds. I got electric on my arms and neck. Electric on my nads. Evil come to town. They stay outside. I hear metal tinkle with the timpani sound of a jug of liquid. Jerry cans, maybe. Voices mumble.

I climb the steps and stay within the shadows at the top, looking into the kitchen. Through a busted window I see a black Suburban got a shiny white bumper sticker on the front left side.

I bet a bucket a gold it says *DEPENDS ON THE DEFINITION OF* TREASON.

Just like at the fight when I got my ass beat. Burly Worley's Suburban.

Short man crosses front of the window, got his eyes pointed at the base of the house like he's looking bugs. He's gone. Says something to another somebody, out of eyeshot.

Glass shatters and metal clangs.

I smell gasoline. They laugh.

"Go ahead. Stand back."

That'd be Burly.

I creep down a stair and ready myself for a kamikaze run. Whole house is a tinderbox.

They's a whoosh and a roar! Wood crackles. Sound rushes around the house; flames shoot past the window and dance inside. Them boys lit the fire; Burly Worley and some short gidgit is walking back to they vehicle.

Let's think a minute, before all I got time for is raw-assed panic. Them boys won't stay outside forever, smoke headed high and calling attention miles around. They'll scoot.

Black smoke already hangs at the ceiling. Flames flash and glow in each room.

Years and years ago I sat with Brown in this kitchen. He liked to play solitaire while he talked, whether he was telling lies about an eight-point buck he saw eating apples or how he was going under the knife to cut out the cancer. I bet he never foreseen this.

Burly Worley's little sidekick puts me in the mind of a taco dog always hopped up on drugs. Each carries a shotgun like he thinks a bird'll flush. I'm the bird. Burly points to the right while he steps to the left, and they split to cover all four sides of the house from opposite corners.

Flames jitterbug through the kitchen. Walls is orange and the ceiling black. Getting right hot. I back down a step as I got nothing needs cauterized just yet.

I rumble down the stairs and get my mind right in the basement. Above is pure hell, no way out but through it. If the fire don't get me the shotguns stand a chance. They's a door out the basement, one of them slope-roofed jobs—but Burly and the taco dog would see it pop open, and if they knew I was here and was hoping I'd end up a charred corpse, it wouldn't be too damn hard to put a cap in my ass coming out and toss me back in. That electric jolt that upended the hair on my nuts—that wasn't 'cause they come to throw a party.

I wonder if one of them fired my house, went to the still site and put a hole in Fred? Maybe the taco dog left the child's footprint.

The upstairs roar sucks air out the basement. I see flames between floorboards. Glass shatters. I step half across the basement. Stop, jog back to the stairs. I got that boiler outside.

Shit. I don't think good sober.

Two windows let in outside light, but they ain't twelve inches tall, and they bottoms is seven feet up.

I climb in the slope-door cubby. Dank and spider-webby, and the whole damn joint's getting hot. Smoke even down here, lower and lower. Some point, shit'll start falling through. A cast iron tub on the head'd do the trick.

Stone blocks is cool. I press agin em and keep my head low.

A rattle sets me back.

Snake!

I ease back. Where the hell is he? I check my parts and step back again. He didn't strike, yet. You'd think I could see his eyes or something. Shoot him? Not exactly easy to see down here, but he's coiled back in the cubby.

They's an old shovel handle with no blade, other side the basement. Ducking smoke, I run over and grab it. Head back to the snake. He ain't happy, got that tail-rattle snapping. I toss him across the floor and probe with the handle along the steps.

I'm off the side now; whole house could fall in and it wouldn't hit me. Can't get air from the door—can't open it for fear of two wandering shotguns.

I freeze, all but my heart. Scales and slithering on my leg, where the pant's pulled over the boot. Snake crosses my ankle, give me a shiver up the spine. I got something on my neck feels like a big old freaked-out spider. Every inch of my body tingles and I never knowed fear my whole life until now. I'm resolute on that. That rattler's a long somebody, seems like fifteen minute 'til the last of him crosses.

I smash some bug was on my neck, wipe my hand on the cement.

"Look'it that!" Voice outside the slope door.

"Shoot the damn thing!"

I roll down the cement steps and a shotgun barks. Part of the door blasts inward and I'm looking out a hole. Sunlight sheets in through the smoke, and I see Burly Worley's got his shotgun pointed. He grins at the dead snake and don't see me.

I just about can't breathe. Upstairs is howling. Smoke burns my lungs. I'm low as I can get but the smoke goes to the cement floor. I hold my breath.

They must've seen the still and pipe out front. They wait.

I'm ready to come out shooting. Move forward on my belly, Smith up front. Upstairs is all whooshing and roaring. Them boys got to be back ten fifteen feet else they'll get suntans off the house. I blink away the burn in my eyes but it comes right back. Try to breathe with my sleeve over my mouth, but it don't cut shit.

Something upstairs drops. Sounds like the whole damn place is falling in. Back in the cubby. If they's more snakes in here they ain't worried about me. Shaft of light comes through the shotgun hole; the smoke looks heavenly.

That short devil outside shot Fred.

I can't breathe. My eyes is on fire.

I push up on the slope door. Rock solid. I gag out a breath and suck in a new lungful but it's hot and burns like acid.

If I stick my face in the shotgun hole, it's liable to get blowed off.

I go flat against the floor and slither with my nose agin the cement. I got spit coming out my eyes, grime in my teeth. That beam of light from the shotgun hole cuts through the smoke and halts at the center of the cement floor, at a drain hole.

Clear air eddies up through.

I crawl. Blink. Scrape, and I'm there. I stick my mouth on the drain and suck in the sweetest outside air, cool like five feet underground. I pant. The inferno is above me. I'm dead center in the basement, where the whole shebang'll drop in a couple minute.

I breathe while the clean air lasts.

THIRTY FOUR

Ernie and Burly stood with their shotguns at the slope-doored basement exit. The upper house was flames through and through. If Creighton was alive, he was in the basement, and if he tried to escape, it would be through this door.

"Point there," Burly said. "Don't wave that damn thing around all the time. Or put it in the Suburban if you don't know what to do with it. He's dead by now anyway."

Ernie aimed at the basement door. "He's not dead yet. Wait until the whole house falls in, then he's dead."

"Look at the smoke pouring out that hole. He's dead."

"It doesn't hurt to be cautious."

Burly stared a long while across the road at Creighton's woods.

Ernie had watched the idea take hold of Burly as they discussed setting up a stilling operation. Stipe would gladly include them in his distribution scheme. The only tense moment came when Ernie suggested they would need to keep their wealth and ambitions secret. Stipe's success resulted from exploiting the little guys, keeping them locked in meager stations. As far as Stipe needed to know, scraping together enough money to rebuild Creighton's business would almost bankrupt them. They would secretly use their windfall to expand, develop their own distribution channels, enter new territories and buy out existing operators—or take them out the old-fashioned way. Once they'd grown to a position of strength, they'd dictate terms to Stipe.

Burly's caveman brow had crumpled at the thought. "If I'm anything, it's loyal," he said.

"You think Stipe was loyal to the people he shoved aside or outright killed to get where he is now? You can't build something big without being loyal to yourself first. And if that's a problem, we better rethink this partnership."

Burly had frowned at Ernie's brazenness, but coming to accord on the long-term vision was paramount. They had to want the same end.

They would not merely do business with Stipe. They would exploit him and then supplant him. Burly's brow did overtime, but by the time they stood beside the basement exit, watching smoke pour from the shotgun blast hole, Burly was unambiguously on board.

"Two minutes. It's enough smoke that he can't breathe. So we give him two more minutes," Ernie said. "Then we'll get the gold."

Burly looked at his watch.

⁂

I gulp one big final lungful of air and I'm ready for battle. Strength's back in my arms and legs and Smith's ready to bark. I lead with my shoulder. Hold my breath and hit that door with all I got. It flies open.

I'm in daylight, looking, spinning, gagging in smoke and the heat's a furnace door. Damn grass on fire! My legs.

I scoot. Run and dive and roll. The ground twists Smith out my hand. I come up on my feet and Burly and his taco dog is gone. The Suburban's gone.

I grab Smith and point. Turn a full circle. A blast of flame lashes out like a fist and it's gone before I can duck. This whole place is going to come down, and maybe the barn off'n the side. It ain't lit, but they's nothing but dry grass 'tween here and there.

Sirens come from down the road, big-assed fire trucks leaving a half-mile plume. I beat the flames off my legs. No way I can get across the road to my side before they get here. They'll want water from the crick, maybe? Nah, they'll watch this place burn; try and make sure the fields don't catch, or the woods across the road.

I trot back into the orchard and hunker in the brush. I'm fifty yards off and when the wind comes this way it carries the heat.

Lot of supplies going up in smoke.

I got to get my mind around all this.

It wasn't no accident, me being inside. Stipe knows I pick apples and whatnot out of Brown's place. Stipe burned my place to the ground; sicced the law on me, destroyed my still; went after my customers, and just so I couldn't get em back, he burned the Brown place. Maybe me being inside was just his good luck, but it seems Stipe wants me out the picture, and he's got a wagonload of assholes dying to help.

Cory stepped three paces and stopped. The Mauser in his hands was an extension of his body, of his mind.

He had shot three full boxes of ammunition the night before. He'd placed a single cartridge in the chamber, assumed a supported position with the barrel wedged between sandbags, similar to what he would experience at the blind—took aim, and fired. Then he ejected the shell and went through the entire process again, loading each shell individually so he would learn to find the same posture and sight picture every time.

After every third shot he checked his target and adjusted his sights. His groups had started out scattered all over the target. Some didn't hit at all. With sober precision he relearned what he had forgotten. He held his breathing steady and fired on an exhalation. He kept his eyes open. He squeezed the trigger slowly. But he also reawakened the talent side of the skill. As he became comfortable with the rifle he developed an intuition for how it would fire. He knew beforehand whether a shot would be good or bad. He learned to hold off on a bad, reacquire the target, and wait until the mechanical orchestration was perfect. After shooting three boxes of ammunition, he hit a three-inch group every time.

He was lethal.

He disassembled the weapon that night, staying up late to punch the tube and make it shine. Using a section of coat hanger hammered flat on one end, a device he found in his father's old Army rifle cleaning kit, he picked carbon from the bolt. He scrubbed the innards with a toothbrush and coated everything that moved with a light layer of oil. He relished the bolt's crisp action. When he was done the weapon was mesmerizing.

He slept with the Mauser in his bed, under the covers, and when he got up, he held the Mauser in one hand while the other aimed his morning whiz into the toilet. He scrambled eggs with it slung over his shoulder. He drove with the rifle across his lap.

Nothing was more comfortable than the worn stock or the metal-oil smell. He understood why soldiers gave their rifles women's names.

After all this was done he'd find another woman.

Wearing camouflage and hunting boots, with a camo net over his face, he approached the rocky lair two hundred yards removed from Baer Creighton's camp. He stopped and scanned the trees for movement, colors, anything. But the trees were motionless and the silence replete. He stepped forward again and waited. Again and waited. Nothing could break his concentration. He'd learned the first lesson: that remaining meditatively in control of every desire, every thought, every action, was the highest high. It unlocked his unlimited potential.

Cory considered sneaking across the top of the rock for a better vantage, but decided he couldn't afford such a careless risk. Baer was wily and might detect movement, and certainly he would be on his guard.

Cory halted. Implications…

Baer lived and breathed in the forest, maybe with an animal-like sixth sense for the movements and pulse of his environment. Would Baer be waiting for him, perhaps in that copse off to the left, decked out in camouflage and hidden behind a fallen log?

In practice, Cory had assumed he'd be shooting at a fully ex-posed body. He squeezed the Mauser stock. If presented with a concealed target, would he be capable of a head shot? What if only the top half of Creighton's head was exposed?

Would he take the shot?

He should anticipate every potential situation and know the appropriate response beforehand. Standing motionless, Cory evaluated the risk. He was excited, nervous. Facing a skilled ad-versary and presented with only a head shot, Cory had to admit the possibility that he could miss. It would be a game changer, turning a simple murder into a shootout for which he was unprepared. Disabling his quarry on the first trigger pull was imperative.

Given a less-than-perfect target, Cory would not take the shot. He would wait all day and night if he had to.

He scanned the terrain again and approaching the rock from the rear, took three steps at a rightward angle. He waited. Stepped. Waited. He proceeded at a glacial pace for a half-hour until he saw movement ahead.

Cory stopped midstride and eased the Mauser stock to his cheek.

Two fire trucks in the drive and six men standing around spitting and jawing. They've hosed the grass but the house and barn is doomed.

I've low-crawled through tall golden grass. I slip across the road and duck in the woods a hundred yards closer to town than I usually do. My nerves is in a jamble. I trek slow, like I'm stalking deer. Normal man'd go inside his house and trust the walls to keep the world where it belongs. Me? I'd have to crawl into the back seat of the Nova on blocks. They didn't burn that.

I got a chill on my arms though I'm plenty warm and realize I been hearing voices a second or two. I ease behind an oak and peer out.

Ahead is Burly Worley and his friend. Jawing and jabbering all excited.

Nothing down that way but a tree fulla gold.

I pull Smith. Knock out a chunk of dirt wedged in the hammer. I got a lot of wrath inside, a lot of burned-lung, busted-shoulder, fear-in-my-soul anger. I got a dead dog, a burned house, a smashed livelihood.

They won't pass me by fifty yards. Too far for pistol work. I wait a second for a good line of sight. Burly's got a bucket in his hand and he tips to the right on account the weight.

One bucket.

I let Smith hand hang at my side but my trigger finger twitches like the tail on a cat stalking a bird. I could leave Burly go. I could give up one bucket of gold. What's that? Fifty pound? Six, seven hundred grand? They's double that left in the tree.

But that short fuck killed Fred. I know it.

My heart thuds. They walk toward my burned house. Prob'ly walk right over Fred's grave.

That night I found Fred I thought on impunity, on men doing as they please to other men, no compass save they own wants and wishes, and no victim ever coming back to say you can't do shit like that so long as I'm around. All this back and forth with Stipe—him fighting Fred, and one of his cronies leaving him for dead; me shooting Stipe's champion in the eyeball on accident; him burning my house, calling the law on my stilling operation, killing Fred. Landing me in jail. And now burning Brown's house on top of me. All that's him fighting back, saying, "I'll fight dirtier to take what I want than you will to keep it."

Men like that got no law. Society got no hold on 'em, and seems like even God turned his back and said it ain't worth the fight. Only thing ever make em quit is some sorry bastard like me finally meets em at the edge and says, "No matter how far you go, you'll find me one step farther. And if we both fall off the cliff, then so fucking be it."

I swallow. So fucking be it.

I skitter across the ground. I'm stooped, got my arms out like a hawk gliding low. Rapid as I can. My eyes feel like crystals seeing everything in harsh lines and sharp colors. Fingers tingle.

Burly holds both shotguns in his left hand for balance. I come in from his back right. Thirty yards out, he pauses. I cover ten yards quick. He turns. That short man spins, got a fighting stance. Burly's eyes flash wide.

Ten yards out I swing Smith up and parallel. Squeeze off a shot. Burly drops the bucket and the guns. Mouth wide, he slaps his hand to his chest. I'm five yards out and point at the taco dog man. He's stooped to his ankle. I pull the trigger and the shot catches him in the low neck. Sets him back a foot. He starts to stand and I put another in his chest. Burly's on his knees, reaching for a shotgun. He falls on top of both, and his buddy collapses across his legs like to keep him in place.

I grab my bucket and take the shotguns too.

THIRTY FIVE

Cory watched the forest beyond his front sight post. He'd seen motion just seconds before but now was unable to detect anything other than subtle changes in the autumn forest colors. The Mauser grew heavy and he eased it downward. He stared at the exact place where he'd seen motion but the longer he looked the less certain he was that he'd seen anything.

He could have imagined it.

Movement again.

Cory shifted behind a tree. His hands were sweaty and he exhaled in bursts. He leaned until he could see around the tree into the thick forest ahead.

A whitetail deer bounded away, flashing its tail high in the air. Two more deer followed. Cory fell against the tree and inhaled deep; he held the breath in his lungs as if it was marijuana smoke and when he released it his nerves had settled. The deer hadn't seen him—so what had spooked them?

About to step forward, Cory heard a pistol shot. In the quiet of the woods it was abrupt and loud. Cory scanned the trees but couldn't tell where the sound originated. Another shot followed, and another. He guessed the distance to be at least a hundred yards. Cory locked his gaze on a narrow aperture of forest, a slight angle from Baer Creighton's camp.

As abruptly as it started the shooting ended. It had to be Creighton. Warning shots? Cory looked across his shoulder at the openness of the forest and longed for the protection of the cave.

His next steps would reveal the crag's face. Cory hesitated. Everything to this point had been preparation. Moving forward would carry him deep into the execution stage of his operation. The risk grew higher and his performance had to be flawless.

Cory inhaled. Exhaled.

He stepped forward and stopped. He leaned until he saw the rock face. That shooting he'd just heard—it could have been anyone. Cory's heart raced and the sweat was cool on his brow. Was Baer in the cavern? Behind the hemlock next to the trail? Something was out of place.

He surveyed the terrain again. He lifted his leg to step forward. The nagging unknown gave him pause. He planted both feet side by side. He would wait until he knew what was wrong. He would ignore the creepy feeling at the back of his neck, the feeling that another man with a gun lurked somewhere behind him. He had no margin for error. He had to master his fear and identify what had changed since the last time he was here.

Cory studied every protuberance of the timeless rock. A rope hung over the edge, but he remembered it from before. His gaze drifted to the right. He studied the trail in front of the rock, rustled leaves that could have been disturbed by deer as easily as a man. He squinted at the hemlock to the right of the path, and after a moment he grinned. It was different. The shape was wrong—a branch had fallen across the path.

Cory exhaled. It was good to have been cautious. He did one more visual sweep, pausing to stare in the direction of the recent pistol shots, and stepped forward.

The discovery of the fallen tree branch confirmed Cory's new-found powers. His confidence surged. He stepped five paces, twisted right and searched the forest. He stepped another four. He would avoid the fallen branch and leave no evidence of his passing. He'd already thought through that aspect of the operation. No note, like Stipe had made him leave; no brass abandoned on the cave floor. He'd considered the ramifications of having left brass the last time and had concluded that using a different rifle and picking up spent shell casings would sever any link between this shooting and the last.

Besides, they would have a hard time proving a murder without a body.

Cory pressed close to the rock wall. He looked to the cave entrance ten feet above and then, partly supported by the rock, lunged for the trail cutting back up the rock face. His boot struck off the edge. Teetering, Cory saw on the trail below a rusted strand of barbed wire that he hadn't noticed before—but he'd been stoned and the rust color didn't stand out—

Cory swiped at the rope strung from above. He barely reached it with his fingertips. He bucked out his ass and clutched the rope.

It held a brief moment—enough to restore Cory's balance. Then it went limp in his hand. From above he heard a rumble that reverberated through the air and the rock face he clung to. He looked upward to the sound and a cascade of round rocks dropped upon him. Cory looked to the side and back to the ledge. He raised an arm above his head and stones smashed against his elbow and shoulder. He batted one aside and another glanced his head. His rifle clanged against the rock wall. Another rock struck his shoulder and another his head, then his forehead, leaving him dazed. He leaned into he wall but still the rocks fell, now striking his shoulders and glancing his back. Finally, when the noise ceased he leaned out and looked skyward—and the last crashed into his forehead.

Cory fell. He regained awareness mid-fall and saw the strand of barbed wire and the out-of-place hemlock branch. He twisted, threw his free arm to cushion his landing. He saw pegs hammered into the side of the tree holding the branch in place.

He hit the branch full on. It popped from the tree, loosing a great whooshing sound. Ahead, a bent-over tree snapped from the ground. The barbed wire tossed leaves into the air. The barbs shredded his pants and Cory felt the wire teeth rip through the muscle next to his groin, each metal tooth seeming to tear a completely new path, deeper and deeper.

Cory gasped. He struck his elbow on a root as the last stone hurtled from the ledge and gouged his ankle.

The bowed tree stopped its ascent and the wire ceased ripping his groin.

Cory straightened his arm and finding it functional, slipped his hand into his pants. His balls were intact. He exhaled.

He'd fallen into a trap, but he'd survive. He was wet and sticky and bleeding, but he hadn't lost the family jewels. This wasn't a disaster. He rested, gathering his thoughts. He was hurt bad. He tried to calm his racing heart. He'd think it through.

He'd stepped into a trap. Where was the next? He glanced above and saw only tree limbs. He felt woozy. His leg was warm, and his groin, and as he rested the blood soaked into his shirt.

He tried to drag himself forward and then rested. Where was he going?

He would wait a moment and get his bearings. But it was growing difficult to think. As his mind succumbed to blackness, he considered the great artery in his thigh that ran close to his groin. He couldn't remember the name.

THIRTY SIX

Burly left his Suburban parked on my drive with the keys in the ignition. I grab a pair of leather gloves from the shed and plow the vehicle through a mess of briars down into the wood.

I need supplies.

I stuff a handful of coins in my pocket. I leave the bucket of gold in the trunk of the Nova on blocks. It don't close, but who the hell'd look?

I take the lantern from the still site, roll my bag and gather a few things into a duffel and bring everything to the shed.

The lantern is empty. Mostly I burn a homemade blend of gasoline and triple-stilled shine. I land the lantern on the workbench and grab a fuel can from the dirt floor. An ax hangs on the wall. The blade gleams. A tool like that would hack a dog-fighting man into pieces so small the worms and flies wouldn't have any work at all, just a big-assed country buffet.

I run my fingers across the ax head's edge and then look at that jug of special lantern fuel. The idea that's nagged me since the night I found Fred comes back, and I got no other path.

Reckon I walk like somebody feels guilty, continual looking back over a slumped shoulder. But they ain't no other way when you just capped two men and know society ain't likely to see things your way. I head for Millany's. By the sun, I got plenty of time. I cut through the woods and avoid the road most the way. Project'll take days, weeks maybe—but I got to start while the anger's hot, and before the law shows up asking about that fire and finds a couple men died of bullet holes. I take the long way around each field. In town I keep to second streets.

Millany's door says *CLOSED*. I beat on it. He lives upstairs. "Come on down, you old goat." I rap 'til a light goes on inside the shop.

He arrives behind the glass, shaking his head. Opens the door. "Can't you read? I'm closed."

"I can read. I just got business, and since you ass rape me each time we trade, I figured you'd be game."

"How much business?"

I follow him inside and drop a handful of coins on his counter. Pull two more out the bottom my pocket.

"Nine? Shit, Baer; I don't keep that kind of cash in here."

"Let's go the bank."

"What the hell kind of 'business' you into?"

"Guess maybe you heard they hit my still?"

"It don't take eight grand to build a still, Baer."

"No. No it don't, at that."

He looks at me. "You ain't saying any more than that, are you?"

"Let's go to the bank."

I got eight thousand, three hundred and twenty-five dollar in my pocket. I leave Millany shaking his head. Slap him on the shoulder. I got a Ted Nugent song playin' in my mind. Don't recall a single damn word but the guitar is like swordplay and keeps me focused.

The sign says Big Ted Lombo's restaurant has a brick oven. They serve pizza and red wine. Family-type folks clear out at night and the goons get together. I ain't had pizza in a long damn time.

"Can I help you?"

"I want pizza. Onions and pepperoni."

"Small pizza?"

"Biggest you got. Extra cheese."

"Eighteen bucks."

"Go ahead and cook one up. And I want to talk to Big Ted."

"What for?"

"If telling you'd do the trick I wouldn't ask for Big Ted."

The kid looks to a goon posted by an arched door. The goon nods.

"Big Ted's in back."

"Baer, how you doon?"

"You said you got a friend up Merrimon sells cars."

"Yeah—I call him right now. What you looking for?"

"Get him on the phone. You do me a favor and I won't forget it. Tell him to bring the best three-thousand-dollar one-ton truck he's got. Tell him to bring it to you—like it's you that's buying it. You do that for me, Big Ted?"

His smile falters. One eye narrows. He chews the end of his cigar. "Yeah. Fuck yeah." He lifts his phone and drives fat fingers to the keys.

"Guilio, dis what I need. It's Ted, motherfucker. Lissen…"

Left Big Ted thirty-one C-notes, one for the favor. In an hour I'll have a truck that runs decent. Meantime I need tools. They's a body shop a half-mile east of town. I walk. Cheese in my belly's like a bucket of river mud.

Garage sits between 70 and Old Highway 70, thirty yards behind. Everything between is blacktop, and covered in beat-up Volkswagen buses abandoned after a hundred round trips to San Francisco.

Some wrench-monkey with a pierced lip and three-tone hair looks from under the hood of a Dodge Intrepid. "Help you?"

"I'm looking Gatchell."

"Who?"

"The owner."

"I own this place."

"What happened to Gatchell?"

"I bought it from Norton."

"Guess it's been a while since I paid attention."

"I do good work. What are you driving?"

"That ain't why I'm here. I'm looking for an acetylene torch and a box of tools. Got cash right now."

"Yeah, well… I use what I got. Sorry, mister."

"You can buy new."

"So can you."

I look at him and he looks at me. "Ahggh." Piss on him.

"Mister?"

I turn. "What?"

"Why don't you check Craigslist?"

"Don't know him."

He smiles. The fucker smiles like we's friends. He knows me, wants to help. Dips his hands in a tub of orange lava at the sink. "I take it you're not connected to the Internet."

"That's mighty astute."

"Why don't you pull the pipe wrench out of your ass? Check this out."

He grins. I grin. He eyes my Smith. He sure as hell whacked my buttons but I don't got any electric or red and I kinda got soft spot for a smartass in a grease garage. Shit if I don't think I'm looking at an honest man. He steps into an office space, got a computer facing the door. "Come on in. Don't mind the mess. I spend my energy fixing cars, not cleaning up."

I step inside. Check behind the door for the boogeyman, something.

"See?" he says. He taps some buttons and the screen flashes a white page.

"See what?"

He points. "This is Craigslist. This is an ad from someone in Swannanoa with a torch for sale. That's the picture. Two fifty, condition like new. Call the number." He dials the phone.

I take the receiver. "Yeah. I want that torch you got."

"Two fifty."

"Does it work?"

"Like new."

"Hey, who is this?"

"Frank."

"Buzzard?"

"That's right. Who's this?"

"Baer Creighton."

"No shit? Creighton?"

THIRTY SEVEN

Joe Stipe wiped sweat from his brow. He leaned on the hood of Burly Worley's Suburban, which had been driven into the weeds and over a steep bank. If not for the tracks through the grass the vehicle would have remained hidden.

Close to the driver-side door a deputy held a flannel shirt to a bloodhound's nose.

A car door slammed. Stipe looked over the slope toward Creighton's driveway. Chief Smylie approached from his car. He strode with a scowl on his face. Stipe spat and looked back to the dog.

The deputy pulled away the flannel shirt and said, "Let's go find 'im!"

The bloodhound bounded away, baying. Stipe wiped the side of his mouth.

Smylie stopped at the edge of the yard. "You mind telling me what the hell's going on?"

Stipe regarded him. "Lots going on, Horace."

"I come home and right off there's a message you've taken over the Gleason police. I don't appreciate that."

"Somebody had to get them off their asses."

"My deputies dream of working a big case, so there wasn't anybody sitting on his ass."

"I needed a man with a dog. I got one."

"All right. That's that. So what the hell is going on? What's this?"

"Burly's truck."

"What's it doing here?"

"Don't know. Maybe your man with the dog can show us."

"Since I been gone, Brown's house burned. Creighton's place burned. I hear Burly and Ernie Gadwal are missing. And where the hell's Creighton?"

Stipe pushed off from the Suburban's hood and walked downhill in the direction of the baying dog. The deputy had already passed from view. "Come on. Let's see about Burly first."

Stipe had a bad feeling. Burly wouldn't likely drive his truck across Creighton's yard, wreck it halfways in the woods and abandon it. Nor would a crafty bastard like Ernie go into hiding. Even if he'd screwed up, he'd be around trying to turn it into a new advantage.

And Creighton—he'd never gotten around to declaring war like he promised, but this looked like it might be a beginning.

Stipe weighed the possibilities. If all three were dead, a host of problems would disappear, and the less he told Smylie the better. Men settle scores all the time. Things tie up neat. But if there were any loose strings, if any of the three was unaccounted for, Stipe would have to manage the situation. It wouldn't do to have investigators outside his influence digging into who had threatened to have someone killed in front of a dozen men. Nor would it do to have a chickenshit police chief concluding he knew enough to bend Stipe to his chickenshit will.

The situation was on the verge of becoming tenuous.

The easiest way to keep the problem local was to account for each man quickly and ensure that only men within Stipe's sphere knew anything at all.

Stipe heard Smylie's feet strike dry leaves behind him.

"What's going on with the Brown place? You part of that?"

Stipe turned. "How the hell can a man be part of a lightning strike?"

"We haven't had a storm in a month. What about Creighton? Kind of funny, him not being around."

"How's it funny?"

"Makes a man—an officer of the law—wonder."

Stipe stopped walking and faced Smylie. "Since when do you give a shit about Creighton? Or anything else until I tell you to give a shit about it?"

Smylie was silent.

The hound stopped baying and a shout carried through the forest. Stipe headed for the sound. The up-and-down slippery terrain taxed his lungs. After a few dozen yards Stipe braced his palm to a tree and stooped while his lungs heaved. Smylie went ahead. When Stipe's strength returned he started off again. Minutes later he reached the deputy, Smylie, and the bloodhound.

At their feet were two bodies. Only two.

No one spoke. The cause of death was apparent. Blood had solidified and the afternoon sun had brought out black flies. The two men's tangled legs looked like the supports of a collapsed building.

Neither man was armed.

Stipe shook his head. Burly had been a decent man. Followed orders. In the short time he'd been in Stipe's employ he'd demonstrated loyalty. He'd had a lot of potential uses. Ernie—he hadn't been trustworthy at all, but he'd had his uses too. Stipe felt robbed.

The deputy glanced at Smylie, then fixed on Stipe. "Who do you suppose did it?"

"I'd bet it's the man who's missing and we ain't found a body for. Just my two cents."

Smylie nodded. "That's right. Creighton."

Stipe squatted beside the hound. His knees dropped to the leaves and he scratched between the dog's ears. "You ready to work? I got a big-ass job for you."

The dog wagged his tail.

Stipe said, "Travis, I want you to head over to that tarp by the busted-up still we passed, back by the house. Get this hound after Creighton and don't stop 'til you have a prisoner or a body. I'd prefer the latter."

Travis glanced at Smylie as he turned to comply. Smylie shook his head. "Hold on a minute."

Travis bent to the hound and leashed him. He looked again to Stipe and was waved away.

"Walk with me a minute, Horace." Stipe rocked to his feet, took a half-minute extending his knees. "You and me need to come to an understanding."

"You're damn right we do. You can't—"

"I've never gotten on with men who tell me what I can't do. Keep your mouth closed for the next two minutes while I set the table. I got your balls in a vise, and I'm going to squeeze 'til they pop or you tell me what I need to hear."

"How you figure?"

"This is about that stupid-assed boy of yours."

"What's he got to do with Creighton, or any of this?"

"I don't know. Nothing. But there's a heap you don't know about what he *is* involved with that I'm sure you don't want making its way to various law enforcement organizations. We're talking Feds. DEA. FBI. He's earned ten years in prison just with what I know right now. I ain't even dug. Yet."

Smylie was silent.

"All that comes out, I don't see how you keep your job enforcing Gleason's laws. Not when you can't run your own damn house."

"He's lazy is all. He's at school right now."

"My money's on him being in Baltimore the same time as you, right under your nose, picking up a truckload of dope."

"You don't know that."

"After the DEA shoves a microscope up your ass, we'll talk about what I know and don't know."

"You're the one got him into all that."

Stipe lurched into Smylie, grabbed his shoulders, shoved him against a hemlock. "I tried to talk him out of it. I busted him over the head with a two-by-four to get his attention. You know what else he did while you was gone? Kidnapped his kids with a gun! Father needs a gun to get his kids, he ain't a father. You ought to be quiet as a church mouse and instead you run your mouth like you got an opinion means something. Shut the fuck up and think for ten seconds. I get what I want or you and your high self-esteem family goes straight the fuck down."

The police chief drew his hands into fists. He glared. Stepped back from Stipe and wiped spittle from his cheek. "All right. What you after?"

Stipe lifted his arm, closed with Smylie and draped his arm across his shoulder. "I'm glad you come around. We work this together, we both come out smelling like a rose. Now, you're in charge of your operation. Not me. You'll have to call me with updates so our men don't overlap and waste effort. And I want you to handle this in-house. Deploy every man on tracking Baer Creighton, and when you find him, you turn him over to me."

THIRTY EIGHT

It's darker'n shit. Guess it's late enough to head out.

I let the fire die to a wick of orange and sit on a big rock don't get warm no matter how long my ass incubates it. Cave at my back, I look downslope. Nothing sounds right but it's my first night here in thirty year. I been seeing ravens in the trees, shadows moving about like werewolves. Ghosts in my head, already. Burly and his taco dog friend. I think on Fred being dead, and Ruth most likely dead too. I think on Larry and Stipe, and Cory Smylie.

This is my new homestead, time being. Got a bucket of gold in the back of the cave, in a little hole off the side. Cleaned away all them bones and rotted blankets. Made a bed of spruce for shits and giggles.

But I ain't shit or giggled.

I don't like being in a cave. Plug one hole, you got yourself a grave.

I camped here for weeks with Gunter Stroh back after I quit life insurance. He let me have the front of the cave where it was cold and he slept in back. Told me about a situation called the Weimar Republic—then he was a Nazi, then he was a new socialist, then he jumped a ship and came here and was an old man just wanted left alone. All he knew was the work he did in the Kraut army. He had a knack for chemistry.

He worked hard and built a reputation as the finest stiller in the state, and I come along right when he was afraid all his ways would die with him. I didn't tell nobody but word got out after Gunter died. People said my shine was like his. Wasn't long 'til I couldn't make enough.

Gunter liked to sit nights and sip from different jugs and comment on what made each distinct. Some you could taste dirt, if you tried. Apples bought from Brown was growed out of red dirt, and tasted like iron, whereas you buy from down Henderson you're liable to get wine so clayed up you got to chew it.

He was old as Lincoln's grandmum and walked with a hickory stick, and his joints give him trouble 'til he likkered em up. Sometimes he lost track of years. Right before the end he'd ramble about the art of stillin and call me Heinrich. I'd know he was seeing his earliest days. He talked about how to shave the wood and cook it, and bust out them chemicals with acid. Then he'd kind of wake up and his eyes narrowed like he come out of a dream and didn't know what he'd said. That was right before the end.

Truck's parked a half-mile off—I followed a log road 'til it give out. Ain't no particular trail leads there. I get turned around and got to reorient by the stars and a crick that winds back and forth, more confused than I am.

Finally I'm sitting in the seat of a 1998 F-150 that stinks like they emptied a bottle of new smell on the seats. I twist the ignition and sit with the lights off. Swing through a few radio stations. Listen to the jabbermouths yammer about some war or other and turn the thing off.

I surely wish I'd turned around this truck in the daylight.

I get out and scout behind me. Rocks and logs and trees. But down a ways is a space between the hemlock. Back inside I put her in reverse. Tranny grinds like somebody pitched a chunk of metal inside a turbine. I jiggle the shifter and she seats.

Back, back. Swing her around. Do-si-do.

I stumbled on an odd place years back. Take North Fork Road and eventually a turnoff leads to a thirty-acre stretch of strip-mined land where they backfilled the deep dirt over the topsoil. Nothing grows but clumps of switchgrass. Place is always barren and cold, and corroded chunks of industrial metal litter the ground like flint arrowheads.

They left behind a bulldozer, more rust than paint. An International, built in the sixties I reckon. Got a radiator sits up front and a fuel tank behind the seat. I got a box of tools and a torch wants to take em home.

These bolts take more WD-40 than I take likker. I bust the rusted sons a bitches and pull out the fuel tank. It'll hold maybe thirty gallon. I sever the fuel line and sit the tank in the truck. Got me a boiler.

Now for the work.

Hood comes off with just a little elbow grease, but it only covers the top, not the sides or the front. Sides is bolted on with lumps of rust fused to the frame. I chisel em off. Radiator mounts is fixed with half-inch bolts set back in under where I can't get a hammer, and while I study the radiator I see this won't work at all. Maybe if I was making elderberry brandy—but my condenser'll have to pull the weight. Man makes this kind of likker, he's got to coax every last drop. This radiator's all gummed up. I'd need ten feet of tube out the backside just to catch what steam the radiator let pass. Don't know what I was thinking.

But I got the cooker.

Odds of Stipe appreciating me poking around his garage at two in the morning is nil. But when I shot that Achilles dog I saw he had a row of oil drums lined on the garage back wall, and since he called the law and they filled my mash barrels with holes, he owes me.

I kill the headlights and drive within two hundred yard. Stipe's put up a chain-link fence. I get out and look along the line and see nobody. I figured Stipe would have added security, but this is just a fence. Whole joint's closed up, lights off. Only sound comes from nothing at all.

In the truck I head for the gate. It's got a padlock. I happen to have a torch.

In five minute I drive in easy like I'm supposed to be here. Head around back. The dog crates is maybe thirty yards off, and I imagine they's some noses pressed agin the link fence right now. I tap three fifty-five-gallon oil barrels before I find one empty. I hoist it to the truck bed and test the rest. The last in the row is mostly empty. I spill the gritty oil on the dirt and chuck the barrel to the bed of my truck. Two'll do the job.

I'm driving out and the front porch light goes on at the house.

By the time I get them barrels and the dozer fuel tank to the cave, it's light. I head back out.

I could find all the copper I want at Maple's Hardware in Gleason, but by now Maple knows my still's been hit and I don't want to answer questions. So I take 70 to Asheville and swing into the Home Depot. It's a big box, maybe two hundred thousand square mile. Need a helicopter to get from the lumber to the cinder blocks. Contractors everywhere look as haggard as me. I walk the edge of the aisles 'til I find plumbing.

I take two packs of fifty-foot copper coils inside a cardboard box. Grab a couple sleeves, solder, flux, a brush. A handful of connecting fixtures and a bunch of associated plumbing shit. I don't want to come back.

I take two five-gallon metal buckets, empty, and one five-gallon bucket of acetone, full. I spot six-quart packs of battery acid. I'll need ten.

Wait. These fuckers don't got lye.

I pick up thirty pound total from three grocers, and a heavy scrub brush and a straw broom at the last.

Cashier lady handles the lye and looks funny.

"Soap," I say. "Don't have time to strain my ash box."

Lady nods with all the polite she can muster, which ain't much.

I drive back to the trail that gets me close to the cave. It takes four trips, filling the duffel with as much as my back can handle. I stow supplies in the cave, acid and lye far apart, and head back down the hill.

I drive out to Stu Caldwell's cabinet shop. "Need a truckload of pine sawdust."

"Pine?"

"Uh-huh."

"I don't keep pine sawdust."

"What if we just took a couple boards and run em through your planer there, and I took all the shavings out that cyclone?"

He looks at the planer, a twenty-inch Delta from maybe 1950. His eyes follow the four-inch vacuum duct to the ceiling and over to the double cyclone, a vacuum that sucks like ten million hookers workin one knob.

"That's a little strange, Baer."

"What?"

"What you want with all that sawdust?"

He can't see my red. I lie. "Planting tomatoes come spring. Want to get that pH down. You know."

"Uh-huh. A truckload."

"Well, I bet you heard they busted my still?"

He nods. Getting right wary.

"I'm going straight. They's nothing so tasty as a tomato; figure I'll plant a couple acre."

"Tomato… wine?"

I grin.

"Can't you just take the sawdust I already got?"

"What is it?"

"White oak."

"Nah, nah. That'd never do. See, I don't want them 'maters smelling like cat piss."

"Well shit, Baer. I'm in the middle of a job here. I can't just buzz a truckload of pine into sawdust, for chrissakes."

"I'll do it."

"And then I got all this downtime. Why don't you pick up a planer at the Home Depot?"

Now I got a truckload of pine boards, a planer, a shovel, an electric generator, and a ten-gallon can of gasoline. All from the Home Depot. I haul em up to the cave and take a bite out a cold hamburger. I bought a bag of twenty Whoppers to hold me a couple day, but I don't think I'll eat more'n one. Not while all these trees got such tasty bark.

Takes an hour with the acetone and scrub brush to get the drums clean and rolled back up the hill from the crick. Another hour to cut a hole in the bottom side of each, and mount a mesh cone inside, and a water spigot on the outside.

I dig a hole, top off the generator, and rest it inside. Stretch a tarp across the ground and sit the planer on a corner. Start the generator, plug in the planer, and pass through boards, taking a sixteenth off each pass.

Them shavings look like snow, then drifts. Pine smells like Ma just mopped the floor.

By and by the planer gets hot and I shut it down. While it cools, I build two platforms out of flat rocks from the crick bed twenty feet downhill. Shaped like circles with a gap in the front. Time I get them rocks arranged and the gaps packed with mud, the planer's cool. I sit a fifty-fiver on each foundation, then gather all them shavings from the tarp, and fill the first fifty-five gallon drum. Start buzzing boards again.

I fill the second drum and it's dusk. I'm hungry enough to scrape bug shit off a window, and after a bite of cold Whopper I chuck the burger and the bag with eighteen more. I surely miss my old still site and wholesome food like cabbage. But this setup ain't permanent. I don't see this operation taking more'n a week.

I fill each barrel with crick water and eighteen quarts of battery acid. Mix that shit up good. Cover the barrels with strips of board too thin to run through the planer, and build a small fire inside the cave near my sleep sack. Pile a few logs nearby and settle in the bag. Bones pop as my back settles. I'm just about wiped out, but I never felt more purpose.

Stipe's right on the edge and I'm six inches farther out. That's what I think, heading into sleep. I'm six inches off the cliff.

What the hell…

Big old wet nose on my face, sniffing, grunting.

Fred?

He whines…

Fred!

I try and throw my arms around him and the sleeping bag holds me back. I unzip it from inside and Fred licks my face and eyes and I kiss him back, but he moves too fast to plant one firm. My lips hit his teeth.

"C'mere, you game son of a bitch!"

I get my arms out. The fire's dead and all the woods is silent beneath the husky sound of Fred slopping up my hair, the nylon bag zooshing with each motion. I throw a hug across his chest and pull him easy, and nuzzle into his neck.

"I love ya, Fred, God I love ya!"

He says I love you too, but I ain't Fred.

"Huh?" I mash the grime out of my eyes and adjust to the morning light. "Stinky Joe?"

It's the dog that jumped the fight circle that night and dashed off into the woods. He wags his tail, and that shakes his ass, and that shakes his whole body.

"I thought you was Fred."

Stinky Joe grins. It's all good, he says. Fuck it.

"You hungry? You had any food to eat?"

He mumbles something.

It's cold enough for frost and in my skivvies I'm a garden of goose pimples. I grab an eighteen pack of eggs. Dump a couple cups of dog chow in Fred's bowl—I took it because I'm a sentimental fool—and crack four eggs. Since it's getting cold out I got a block of New York extra sharp in the bag; I crumble some on top.

"You want a soda, something?"

Stinky Joe's got his head canted like he's looking past me. I look out the cave entrance. Grab Smith in one hand and carry Fred's chow bowl in the other. Damned if my feet ain't a couple of ice blocks. I look out on the hillside and nary a thing moves.

But they's about fifteen shredded Whopper wrappers spread all downhill.

"I'm glad you liked em." I head back and crawl in the bag for some heat. "C'mere." I reach to Fred's chow bowl and rest it on the dirt beside my bag. Stinky Joe dives in and finishes in three mouthfuls.

I sit up and Stinky Joe wiggles close, head low and ass high, like a pup knows I'm the rootinest tootinest dog on the porch. I grab him tight and drag him onto my sleeping bag, and he settles with his head on my lap. I'm 'bout to freeze. I pull the tail end of the bag over my shoulder like a toga, and we sit and talk like old friends.

"Where you been?"

Out in the woods. Nosed my way to a place seemed safe, from the sound and smell of it. Didn't have shit to eat—and I woulda. Then Stinky Joe says, You don't seem too chipper.

"Well, that's on account of Ruth."

Ruth?

"She's dead. Larry killed her."

Stinky Joe pauses, deep in thought. Larry. Well I don't know Ruth but it don't surprise me hearing Larry done her, the way him and his boys done me. I thought he was up to no good.

"Why didn't you find me at the camp and tell me? Maybe I coulda saved her."

I thought on that, but you scared me good. You was drunk.

"Well, shit. Hey, listen… my nuts is about to freeze and bust into little pieces. Lemme bring you a blanket over, and once I get inside this bag we can keep talking."

Sounds good, Stinky Joe says. He looks ready to shake apart if he don't get loved on.

THIRTY NINE

I lift a half-sheet of plywood from the first mash drum and stand back from a noxious blast. I look back at Stinky Joe. It's been two day slow cooking in chemicals on top a bed of coals. All that's left is to enjoy the mundane work of vengeance.

Insects that got inside float on top. I dip a stripped oak pole through the foam, into disintegrated pine fibers. I dump in a plastic container of lye. Stir with the oak pole.

The brew fizzes and froths. More acid yet. The reaction eases and I empty another container. I add lye until finally the fizzing ceases.

I look around the ground. Glance at Stinky Joe.

I dip my finger into the mash. Swirl it around and realize either the acid or the lye could've burned off my finger—but they's balanced.

"That's lucky."

Heading up to the cave, I wipe my finger on my pants. I grab a saucepan, clean it in the creek, and ladle a few inches of mash.

I crumble yeast into the pan, stir it with a stick. Watch. The familiar smell rises, and a layer of bubbles foams at the top. I'll give it a few minutes. Meantime I neutralize the second barrel.

I recheck the yeast—still alive, still foaming. Working hard. I dump the mix into the first barrel, add five pounds of yeast, and then test the second.

I convert the old International crawler's fuel tank into a boiler and situate it down by the creek. With the torch I fashion a doubler from the acetone can I emptied cleaning the fifty-five gallon drums. Rig a five-gallon bucket under a two-foot waterfall in the crick and run the copper coil through the bucket. Tube sticks out halfway down the bucket, goes two feet to a flat rock, and that's where I'll have a jug waiting.

Then I twiddle my thumbs and wait on the mash to ferment. Day after day.

Each night I carry a ragged washcloth to the stream and use a small pool like a sink. The rough cloth feels good. In spite of the cold I wash—sometimes so hard it's like I want to scrub off my whole life and send it floating downstream. Then I take what's left of me and step into fresh clothes. I linger at the stream before heading back to the cave, and then sit by the fire 'til it wanes. I listen to the trees. Pet Stinky Joe. Rub sleep from my eyes. All the while thinking they's no way to wash away what I am, what I done, what I'm about to do.

I stay awake late because each night I dream of corpses in trees. Each night I travel deeper on the trail. Close in on morbid terrain. Look in on death.

But each morning when the sun comes up I keep on.

I drop a cinnamon curl to the bottom of each gallon jug. It'll work like the worm at the bottom of a fifth of mescal—give the fuckers a goal.

First run, I put a five-gallon bucket at the copper's output end. The sqeezins will come out low-alcohol, and it won't be until I run them through a few times, even with the doubler, that they get any potency. I put two more buckets beside it.

I hold another bucket at the spigot on the first fifty-fiver, twist the knob and frothy, rank mash rushes out. I pour the mash into the boiler, back and forth until the boiler's three-quarter full. Can't touch the mash. Shit gets in through the skin, too.

"What you think of that, Stinky Joe?"

Stinky Joe's mum.

I sit on a log and gaze into the night sky. Prop my chin on my hands, elbows on my knees, and close my eyes. Burning logs pop. Steam spits through the tubes. The crick gurgles. The never-ending rumble of near-boiling mash—them sounds encourage thoughts that skirt agin the bare edge of divine justice. In a tooth-for-a-tooth way.

The first condensate spurts from the copper. I rock to my feet and kneel at the bucket. Dangerous to be so close… can't touch the shit directly. But I can't resist dipping my nose and whiffing the piney product. Smells like Ajax.

I'll tell em it's gin.

FORTY

I don't believe it, but Stinky Joe snores like Fred. Wakes me out of a godawful dream.

I sleep again and wake to Stinky Joe nosing around his bowl. It's dark out the cave front without a hint of gray. I fix some Alpo, eggs and cheddar. Before I sleep Stinky Joe comes back and licks my face, and that Alpo don't smell bad with cheese. I didn't eat last night, and without my usual likker treatment my stomach feels like an empty swimming pool somebody tossed an apple core in, and that was supposed to fill it. Come dawn I'll eat everything cached in the cave, and then hit the ABC for some store-bought likker. Yessir.

Can't sleep now Stinky Joe's got me woke. Today's the day I been waiting.

I lay thinking all kind of thoughts. Missing Ruth, thinking it'd be all right if I woke to her licking my face like Stinky Joe.

I lay in the sack 'til dawn turns the black woods gray. Climb out the bag, don my clothes. Grab crackers, apple, cheese, take my thirty-thirty and slip into the woods. They's a thicket grows down by the crick. I sit under a low-hanging hemlock and watch the sun turn everything into color.

That'd be something to wake to. Maybe not Ruth slobbering like Stinky Joe, but a nibble'd be nice. A soft sound with a powder smell. Don't take long 'til a doe comes along with her nose close to the ground. She stops—got my scent—and does this up and down thing with her head. She knows I'm here and her heart's got to be pounding. She steps forward and swings her head like to catch me in a false move.

I'm still.

I watch and she's beautiful. Liquid lines, and I can almost see lashes and mascara. Her ears flick. She leaps, stops.

I shift my weight ever so slight; get the posture; slip off the safety.

She steps away and I ease up the thirty-thirty. Line the sights on the back her head. She won't feel nothing.

Her ears twitch. Her tail's high—she's a little puckered, a little tense.

I keep the rifle trained though my hands tremble and the cold air blurs my eyes. A cool trickle spills down my cheek, one then the other, and the tremor in my hands moves to my arms. She's got one hell of an innocent position in the grand scheme. One day not long ago she was a fawn with spots, and just kind of growed into a world where armed shitheads like me hide in trees.

I think on Fred, lying there with a hole in his scabbed eye socket, and I close my eyes and can't breathe for the hate and pain. The best deer's got no personality compared to the worst dog. It ought to be easy. I blink five six times and half-hope she'll see, but the doe is motionless. I slide my finger up and down the trigger. Death, in such a small act.

"Ah, hell! Get out of here!"

She starts, then freezes. Stares. I wave. She bolts. Two huge bounds and she's thirty feet gone; another two and she's brown in the thicket.

Don't want to think on that doe. She was meat for a whole mess of dogs. I'll go the grocery instead. Involves risk, but hell, it ain't like I was going to get away with all this anyhow. I head back the still. Park the thirty-thirty agin the cave wall. Stinky Joe cocks his head. "What you looking at?"

Stinky Joe says, I didn't say nothing.

"I'll be back in a couple hours." I scruff his ears.

I walk down the hill with eyes and ears tuned. Crow farts in a beech tree, I'll hear it.

FORTY ONE

Joe Stipe sat on his porch with a sarsaparilla soda in one hand and a cordless telephone in the other. The delicate scent of diesel exhaust was in the air. He stared across the narrow lawn to the blacktop motor pool and the trucks awaiting maintenance, the forested hills beyond. Creighton was out there somewhere.

All morning Stipe had a nagging thought that he ought to know where Creighton hid. It was like a word on the tip of his tongue. The Gleason deputies had found no trail—the hound had tracked Creighton from toolshed to still site, back and forth three times, and finally sat down, confused. Stipe's men had no more success. Creighton had disappeared, almost as if he was in the burned Brown house. No dice there. The fire department found no remains.

Stipe had personally ransacked Creighton's camp and found no indication of where he was headed.

Anxiety didn't come close to it. On the afternoon before an extremely important dog match, his enemy with cannonball nuts was utterly unaccounted for.

Stipe had asked Stan to beef up security by bringing a couple nephews, bulky thugs who'd played high school football but hadn't gotten big until they joined the Local, but Stipe knew they wouldn't impede Creighton. He was impervious to ass-beatings.

When Creighton struck it would be for blood. The victor would be the man willing to risk all.

So far Stipe had held back. He could have finished off Creighton that very first night, but he'd intended to pressure Creighton into selling out and working for him. Why destroy a man when you could enslave him? Most men only bent so far, and just before they snapped, they'd relent. But not Creighton. Creighton had proved he would destroy himself for vengeance. That wasn't the kind of man to have running loose before an important match.

But for the moment a different problem had become more urgent. Stipe jammed his finger to the telephone keypad and sipped soda while the phone rang.

"Mort, this is Joe, up Gleason."

"Yeah."

"Got a special tonight. Need a favor."

"Halloween special."

"Uh-huh."

"Can't make it. Got the kids and the trick-or-treat."

Stipe exhaled into the phone. He was silent.

"Like to help, but I'm out of commission."

Stipe said, "You still got Rusty Nail?"

"Accourse."

"I want you to bring him tonight. I got boys coming in from Atlanta, and it's a big deal. Real big deal. Local hoodlum shot

Achilles right in the cussed eyeball and I need star power. I'll match Rusty Nail easy, and it'll give him another win 'fore you stud him."

"Look, Joe, like I said—"

"Mort, I don't ask a favor twice. You hear me?"

The pause was long. "Yeah, Joe."

The Atlanta boys had contacted Stipe earlier in the week on a telephone referral from a Georgia acquaintance Stipe knew only by his reputation as the best dog breeder in the state. Stipe was unsure if the two visitors were emissaries for the Georgia man or if they acted on their own. He hoped the former.

Truly superior genetic lines were difficult to find, but mixing them was the lifeblood of the sport. Breeding was always a balance between excluding inferior animals and keeping pairings diverse enough to prevent the line from stagnating. Pulling champion DNA out of Georgia would pay dividends.

If the Atlanta visitors represented a champion breeder, they wouldn't be interested in some redneck pairing labs and rotts. Stipe had decided to fight two of the bait dogs, the lab and the female pit, as an opening spectacle. But Stipe's Atlanta guests would be looking for true game, and for that, Stipe needed at least one uncontestable champion.

Champions were in limited supply, and none of Stipe's contacts had been willing to provide his top dog on short notice. A champion dog needed time to prepare. A month walking around with a chain wrapped around his neck. Hours swinging by his jaw from a rope.

None of the dogmen Stipe called took his bait. No amount of return favors secured their interest. It was almost as if word to avoid Stipe's fights had gotten out. It bothered him, and left no alternative but to flex muscle.

The last man on Stipe's list was Mort, owner of Rusty Nails, a four-year-old, sixty-pound Red Nose pit with an unbroken string of wins. The dog was so good Stipe had waited to match him against Achilles, hoping Achilles would improve and Rusty Nails would decline with the delay. If Achilles won, Rusty Nails's stud value would fall. Mort had called Stipe out on it a month ago, and all week Stipe had avoided making this call. Now his shenanigans were for naught and he needed his adversary's help.

"I've lined up five fights. I need six. I don't like to lean on you, but this is important. My boys coming up from Atlanta are big-time. Big dough. You ever want to match a dog in a sanctioned fight in Buncombe County again, you'll give me your word right now. What's it going to be?"

"You play hardball, Stipe."

"I'm backed in a corner. I need you in. So either sell Rusty Nails to me, or bring his ass down and fight him."

"I'm in."

"Good. Tonight. I'll put Rusty Nails last, and I'll make sure he looks good as a favor to you."

"I really appreciate that."

The phone beeped.

"I got another call, Mort. I'll see you tonight." Stipe pressed the button. He looked up and saw his security man Stan's GMC enter the motor pool drive.

"Stipe here."

"Joe. Dis's Ted."

"Hey, Big Ted, what can I do you for? You coming tonight?"

"Nah. Mebbe. Gotta mind the restaurant. You and Creighton square up yet?"

"Can't find him."

"Yeah. You oughta be lookin' a truck. Guilio—you know Guilio, up on Merrimon—he sold Creighton a '98 F-150."

"What color?"

"Brown."

Stipe raised his voice to overcome the sound of Stan's GMC, idling a dozen feet away. "Thanks, Big Ted. You come tonight and put money on Rusty Nails. That's the safe bet." Stipe drew his finger across his throat and Stan cut the engine.

"Eh, I appreciate that," Big Ted said.

Stipe disconnected the call. Stan exited the truck, crossed in front of the grill and stood on the steps below Stipe.

Stipe needed to replace Burly. The way things were heating up, he'd have to keep Stan and the other two deployable. Too bad Cory proved such an idiot. Come to think of it, Cory hadn't been around either.

Stipe waited for Stan to speak. For the last few days Stan had displayed a lack of imagination, almost as if he was glad Burly was gone and finding his killer meant nothing to him.

"We learned a little more. A little."

Stipe sipped sarsaparilla.

"I personally visited Larry's girl, Mae."

Stipe leaned. "Yeah?"

"He ain't been around, is what she said. I left Billy to keep an eye on the place until he had to go to work at the plant. Just to see if Creighton shows up."

"He won't. He's crazy, not stupid. He's holed up."

"Well, I talked to Ruth—you know there was history with Larry and Baer and Ruth? Well, took a while to find her. She's been staying with her father at the home. He's real sick and they was thinking he might keel over—"

"She seen Creighton?"

"Well, she's at her place now and says she ain't seen hide nor hair of him. She spent more time asking questions than answering. She don't know nothing. Then I stopped by to see Eve, since Larry said Baer put the moves on her."

"Larry's full of shit."

"Yeah, well, she said it was Baer putting the moves on her too."

Stipe laughed out loud. He rocked to his feet and stood at the porch rail. "So you got nothing."

"Not entirely. I started with the bad news, but we got a little good, too. Mechanic outside of Gleason, runs Gatchell's old body shop—he said Creighton tried to buy his welder, same day as Burly went gone. Kid sent Creighton to some guy named Craig Schlitz, like the beer or something."

"Was Creighton driving a brown F-150?"

"That's the other good news. Yeah. How'd you know?"

"Anything else? You've been digging how many days and that's all you got?"

Stan turned partly away. "Well, I turned up something else. What do you know about a couple boys poking around Gleason this week? Word is they're asking about you."

"Don't worry about them. What's your plan for Creighton? We're down to the wire and I want him found today. Right now."

Stan removed his ball cap and crumpled the bill in his hands.

Blood flushed Stipe's cheeks. "You fresh out of ideas, that it? Beat the bushes. I don't care if you have to go to Creighton's campsite and start walking circles. You find me that son of a bitch and you put him down. Now get the hell out of here!"

Stipe watched Stan's dense, dull, sad face. He'd pushed too hard. Stan was a dolt. But too much was riding on tonight. Sometimes a situation demanded strong leadership.

Stan retreated to the GMC. He climbed inside the cab and started the engine.

How could it be so difficult? Creighton wasn't a man to turn tail. He was hell bent on revenge, and Stipe knew in his bones that Creighton had stayed close enough to get it. He'd bought a truck. Tried to buy tools. He was rebuilding. Creighton thought he would win this war.

A man with the audacity to march into the enemy's stronghold, not once but twice... Creighton was in the woods somewhere, scheming. Each escalation proved him victorious. Achilles, dead. Burly and Ernie, dead. Cory, missing for a week almost. Creighton had even seen through Stipe's longtime associate Pete Bleau. Each time Stipe raised the stakes he found Creighton had already covered and raised. The only thing left was flat-out murder. No time for clever setups or covering tracks. He'd whitewash everything afterward. But you had to know where a man was if you wanted to murder him.

Stipe imagined Creighton sitting under a walnut tree, whittling a stick. Sipping moonshine. Staring blank into the trees, biding his time.

Ernie Gadwal had been certain Creighton would kife everything he needed to rebuild his still from the Brown farm. Stipe had seen it long before Ernie—it was in his mind when he told Smylie to tip off the revenue boys. But any chance of manipulating Creighton into a subordinate position vis-à-vis making shine was destroyed when Ernie went slam off his instructions and killed Creighton's dog. Stipe had Creighton right where he wanted him, and Ernie blew it.

Ernie. Another dimwit, thought he was smart. Followed Creighton everywhere, even...

Stipe lurched down the porch steps. Stan's GMC was at the gate.

"Stan! Stan!" Stipe crossed the lot with his hand against his chest. His heart thudded and flopped. "Stan!"

The GMC halted. Stan tumbled out and stood with his eyes revealing confusion.

Stipe looked at his watch. There was time. "Stan! Bring in the boys and tell em to fetch their guns. Now! I know where Creighton is!"

FORTY TWO

I back out the truck and head into town. It's early and nobody knows this truck, but I'm edgy. No way they ain't found Burly Worley and his sidekick.

Back in the day I'd tool along in my Nova nice and easy with the windows down. No radio. Just tires crunching dirt, aching to spin. Them days I didn't have a past, just a future. Now I'm old, I got no future so I brood on what's past. Feel like a kid started out with a hundred dollar bill and next I know I'm an old man with empty pockets, wondering how the hell I spent everything so fast.

I go to the Bi Lo so I don't see nobody I know.

I remember that dream.

Sometimes you don't know what the hell triggered the memory. Dreams is all bullshit anyhow, but the image smacks me upside the head and I stand numb on the sidewalk.

It's dusk, and the woods is a sketch of black and white, and the trail's emptied to a patch of land different'n any other. It's a land of horror. Stepping in means crossing a line. The trees is decorated with bodies. People—dead people—suspended with they backs agin the trees and they arms and legs sticking out straight. Each tree has fifty… it's like the trees is made of corpses instead of wood. This tree, that tree, the whole woods beyond the line is dead men and women. The air's tranquil, and though my feet strike crunchy leaves, they land silent.

I step closer the woods. The dead land.

I shake loose the image. Fuck dreams.

I stand at the cooler at the back of the grocery.

"Need ten pound of hamburg."

The man nods. Packs meat in plastic. I'm the grateful hypocrite didn't slaughter the doe-eyed cow going in that bag.

"You planning some kind of picnic?" he says.

I say "Yeah" by way of conversation.

He drops the wrapped meat to the counter. I grab it. "Take 'er easy." I leave.

I buy a jug of Turkey at the ABC.

"The liter?"

"Fuck liters. That big jug right there."

I pay with cash. His eyes go to mine but they's no red.

All these disaffected years—but no one ever surprised me.

"Everything good?" the man says.

"Things is about to get Wild Turkified. That's an improvement."

Ten-pound hamburg in the fold of my arm, Wild Turkey in the other. I put the meat on the passenger seat and break the seal on the Turkey. This Kentucky bourbon's smooth as goose shit but you got to drink twice as much.

I'm in the parking lot and two men come out George's Hot Dogs, other side of the street. They watch me and I gawk a minute back 'til they mosey toward the corner. They ain't from here.

Dressed like law that don't know how to fit in. I don't need another run to the jailhouse so I wait 'til they turn the corner, then gulp a long snurgle of Turkey.

I drive slow and halfways home a car passes. Inside the cab is the two fellas from town. My hackles is sky high, but I got no juice at all.

No harm comes, and back at the cave I treat Stinky Joe with a handful of hamburg, and dig out that melatonin I bought two week ago. I close the meat bag and set the pill bottle beside. Another gurgle of Turkey, and I stretch out on my sleeping bag and close my eyes for a nap.

See if I can steer clear of that land of corpses in the trees.

I wake and those dead stiff-legged bodies is still in my eyes but Stinky Joe's growling low and grumbly like he means it. I roll to my side and he's at the cave entrance, standing taut with his ass shaking. His floppy ears is up and a bad feeling shoots through me. I'm haunted by ghosts and deep shadows but living trouble's come to my door.

I grab Smith and scoot beside Stinky Joe. "What you see?"

Down there, he says.

I scan the brown landscape. I block Stinky Joe with my arm and he leans into it. I spot movement fifty yards off—a man flashes a go signal to someone on his right. He bears a rifle. Another man leaves the protection of a giant oak and advances to the next. His rifle barrel sticks out. I keep an eye on both of them and gather my scattered brain.

I got Turkey left in the bottle and two full flask. I slip to the back of the cave and grab the bottle, down it, and grab my thirty-thirty rifle. I pop the lever. Brass in the chamber.

Five jugs with cinnamon is lined on the cave wall, but they's no way out but them goons'll know and shoot. They've come for a showdown. I leave the jugs.

Wild Turkey hits the spot and starts pushing back the corpses in trees and the cold mist crossing my mind. The dream slips away but leaves the chill. Stinky Joe's moved to the entrance side. He shakes like he wishes I was there to hold him back.

"I'll show you how to fight, Stinky Joe. Just you watch this."

Back at the entrance I stay low in the shadows. It's early evening. Downslope is the fire circle, rocks stacked maybe twelve inch high. Got a boulder off to the side where I sit at nights watching the fire. They's trees all down the slope. To the right sits two mash barrels, each full of slaggy poison mush. I bet one of them barrel'd stop a bullet, but not as good as a big-assed rock.

I find the first fellow again, now forty yards away. He looks to his left at a third man. Three men, each with a rifle. They's the lugnuts was in town with Stipe that day. At forty yards I could drop any one of them but the other two'd hole up and the skirmish'd come down to which of us brought the most bullets. I got a bunch, that's for damn sure, and more on my pistol belt, but I got someplace to be in a couple hours. They could pin me down 'til dark.

I got one option: close work.

They'll converge on the cave. If they got any brains they'll send two up and leave one in reserve, covering them. If I got any luck they'll all three come up. I stretch on the dirt and wriggle 'til I got a clean view.

All three men is stopped and the leader's got deep thought etched on his face. His eyes is hell bent on the cave entrance but with the shadows he don't know if I'm a rock or a man with a gun trained on him.

Stinky Joe whimpers.

"Shhhh." I turn my head and signal him to slip to the back of the cave.

He steps toward me.

Man down the hill swings his rifle to his eye. I got no choice. I pull the trigger and the cave sounds like the middle of a thunderclap. I cycle a new bullet and take fresh aim. The man stands for a second, then fires his rifle. The bullet zings from the rock overhang. The man staggers and drops on his ass, then back.

The fellow on the left is hid but the one on the right is in the open. I throw elbow and ass left and grab a new sight picture. He skirts toward a tree. I lead him a couple inches and fire. The bullet catches his shoulder and he spins. I cycle another and pull the stock tight to my shoulder. The third man fires and the bullet zips by so close I want to comb my hair with the new part. I fire at the second man again and he goes down.

Dust falls like snow. I look up where the bullet hit and dirt falls in my eye. The more I blink the scratchier it gets. I wriggle back from the entrance and rub the heel of my hand to my eye. Grind a bit and the water cleans it out. I look deeper in the cave. They's a dark line on the cave floor where Stinky Joe squirted piss. He's in back trying to nose into my sleeping bag.

Now I got the exact situation I didn't want. I got a man out front liable to see me before I see him. I got a tangent—I know which direction to look, but if I do it's with the knowledge he might drill a bullet in my head.

I wriggle to the back of the cave. Stinky Joe shakes. I scratch his head and it's like giving him permission to come apart. He shivers deep and pisses all over my sleeping bag. He's forgot how to use his words.

"This'll be over in two minutes, Stinky Joe."

He nods but he can't hold my eye.

I pull Smith and check the cylinder. Full. I draw back the hammer. In my left hand is the rifle. I cock it too. I stand, then squat to test my knees. I twist a couple times and rotate my shoulders. All right—I'm loose by God here goes.

I run.

Just before the cave entrance I fire the rifle. I'm in the light. I hope it made him duck. I point the Smith on the tangent I remember and pull the trigger. Glimpse a man huddled behind a fallen log. I dive to the fire circle and claw behind the sitting boulder. A bullet zings off the rock and a fragment stings my leg.

That log he's behind is rotted pine. Hell, bears've clawed it for grubs. Still behind the boulder, I get on my knees and rest the rifle easy over the top. I pop up my head for a quick look. He's hid. I holster Smith and take up the rifle. Sight on the dead log where I think he is, and fire. I cycle another and fire again at the same spot. I do it again and again and again. Each shot blasts out a bit more log. Finally I'm out of bullets and I can see a hole through the log. It only took twenty seconds. I hope he was dumb enough to stay put.

I leave the rifle and draw Smith and start walking. Got a two-handed grip and the hammer's back. I got five more bullets to end this mess, then I'll have to reload. I stop and listen. The forest is quiet. Hair stands on the back of my neck. It ain't the electric; my hair stands because these woods is filled with dead mean. We's all dead, one way or the other. I come to the log and let Smith lead over the top.

I got him.

The last man dies with no dignity at all, hid behind a rotted log. He's one of Stipe's lugnuts all right. I got lucky and blasted out half his neck. Blood everydamnwhere. He's still got the rifle grip in his hand.

I leave him and find the next body—the first fellow I shot. He fell back with his legs crumpled beneath him. Whether he's in heaven or hell, it can't be comfortable.

The final body belongs to the man I winged then shot a second time. His face snarls. His eyes stare. His arms and legs is straight and stiff and all I'd have to do is tie him to a tree and I'd be in dreamland.

Never been exactly spiritual, but I can't shake that dream. All them bodies. Woods that looked like this or any other. I'm wide awake and feel like I'm still asleep. And just like in a dream where sometimes you know the real horror's about to start, and you can't wake, you can't move, you can't scream for help—you just lay paralyzed seeing red eyes and feeling the juice—that's here and now. The horror's around the bend.

FORTY THREE

Dark comes on the woods quick. Even under the big silver moon, distance vanishes and things up close get gray. The night goes from warm to cold. My fingers feel it first. I turtle my hands inside my sleeves.

I parked the truck deep off a side trail on the logging road leads to Stipe's fight circle. Got all my likker up close.

A hundred yards off, men stand wood shipping pallets on edge and pound metal stakes in the ground to hold 'em—they's the six-foot jobs used to string barbed wire. They've moved the fight circle left twenty feet. Must be the stink of rotted blood and gut grime gets on they nerves.

Man carries a stepladder inside the circle and hangs a wire jig on a limb. Fetches an orange-glowing lantern and suspends it, then several more. My stomach growls and I ease my flask north about eighteen inches, take a gurgle. I've carted five jugs, trusting the men won't notice the likker's discoloration. Not in the lanterns' half-light, anyway.

I study them jugs and think how Fred's eyes looked the night I found him.

Headlights cut through the woods, pointed my way. Evening's thick enough they can't see me, but I shrink anyway. This situation has me feeling I got to lay low, and I don't like it a damn bit. Like I'm wrong exacting revenge on Fred's behalf.

Accourse, it's no good introducing logic in the middle of a tactical situation. I got to keep my bearings. Keep the dreamland at bay.

A line of headlights arrives through the dusk. That'll be Stipe and his perverts. One by one they turn off they headlights and crawl past me in the twilight. The hatred fills me. These boys watched Fred get rent. Ahead is a small meadow where a giant hemlock fell and left a hole clear to the sky. Moonlight pours in and the trucks drive through it. Red, brown, brown, gray, white…

Tailgate is light on the left and a little darker on the right.

Something smoldering in my belly goes aflame.

That's him… that's Cory. That's the very pickup that hauled Fred to this fight circle and then hauled him out. I draw Smith. Aim on the back window, left side. I pressure the play out the trigger. I grit my teeth and see Fred with that bullet hole in his eye under a haze of black flies. But I ease on the trigger and holster Smith.

I picked a better way to end all this.

Man backs a truck close the circle, drops the tailgate and lands a jug on it. 'Nother fellow stands two sawhorses off the side with a sheet of plywood as a table. More jugs. Moths flap at the lanterns and bats chase em.

I creep closer.

Men drink and laugh. Larry's in the group with Pete Bleau.

Larry. I'm about to kill flesh-and-blood Larry. The one who give me the electric curse, the one who stole Ruth, and more than that, stole Mae. Made Ruth lie. And after all these years killed her.

I recognize the other faces but don't see Cory Smylie. I count twelve fellas and eight trucks. Maybe a couple brothers, a couple father-son, pass-the-sport-through-the-generations kind of instruction. Another reason to nip this shit right here. Man grabs a jug, wipes the mouth with his sleeve and drinks. But any man so uptight he got to wipe the mouth on a jug of shine—he ain't drunk enough.

A shadow crosses front of the moon and things go deep gray except over the fight circle, lit in lanterns.

Larry walks to a truck and opens the driver-side door, leans deep inside. He comes out with a fifth of store-bought likker and the cloud that crossed the moon cuts it loose. Everything's silver again—like the night I found Fred—and that truck, the tailgate cuts a glow on the left side. He's in Cory's truck—but Cory ain't here.

Unless—

I slink as close as I can get without entering the lantern light. I crouch and study with eyes that don't believe a damn word the picture says.

That's Larry's F-150.

Larry stole Fred.

I fall back on my ass and snap a twig.

No one minds me. They all drink. Every last one finds likker and gulps. Whoops and war cries cut through the woods and I speculate every animal around's already bugged out, save the ones in crates got no choice.

It was Larry. I can't quite ken it.

A pair of men don't seem so thirsty as the rest; don't tip the jug quite so far, or so long. They walk straight, no swagger. Got the faintest smidge of red I ever saw, like a star that disappears the longer you look.

The two circulate. One slaps a regular's back and carries on like they's deep buddies. Conversation ends and the other turns away, and the two red-eyes share a sober look like actors out of character.

These the two I saw in town, and again driving away.

I watch it all and struggle to get my mind around the fact Larry stole Fred.

Stipe finds the center of the group and looks about. He's slow to talk. A man stands beside him jawin and Stipe keeps his eyes to the trees beyond the men. He turns like he knows something's always behind him.

Two jugs of special likker in each hand, one in my elbow crook, I sneak closer, staying low and hid. Stipe raises his arm toward the two that's separate, and they nod. The revelers whoop. These boys come from someplace else, but this's my show and I'm vouching for 'em—that's what Stipe says.

I keep my eyes on the likker jugs they got everywhere. Larry's hitting it hard.

Scanning faces one more time, they's another one missing. No Sheriff Smylie.

I move closer.

"Let's get this shit rolling," Stipe says. "First off is Norm and Jeb. You boys gotcher dogs ready? Bring em out."

Men move. They avoid the side of the woods where previous fights was and cluster mostly on the other, with the trucks and the sawhorse table. I got vantage without getting up a tree. They's already acting drunk, talking shit and backslapping.

The men hush. Jeb leads his animal with a stick leash into the pit. Every man with money's already looked over the dogs but now they lean in close and study dog lines like they's chicken guts on a plate, tell which animal gets his ass licked.

I carry my five jugs. Sneak while I'm in the dark, and closer I get, straighter I stand. I expect every second some lugnut's gonna club me with a ball bat, but something mystical's going on. Stipe's surely got security, but it ain't just me here alone. I know it.

The men stare at the dogs in the circle and shout at first blood. I ease beside Pastor Jenkins. I land four jugs on the sawhorse table. Move the fifth to my hand. Jenkins eyes the jugs like they's naked titties. Finally he looks away.

"Never figured why you come here," Pastor Jenkins says.

"That's a question I'd never guess from you."

"Rough men need a rough sport. And the Lord says to go to the sinners."

"Well, Pastor, you're damn sure with us."

Jenkins frowns, looks into the crowd. Behind and between men, the silhouette of a fighting dog jumps. Jenkins glances at the jugs. "Stipe got you on likker duty, I see."

"Yeah. Get a load of the spirit."

Jenkins's eyes expand like he just realized it's me he's talking to. He opens his mouth like to shout a warning—but he stops. Lost his will, maybe. Gets all bug-eyed looking at me, and I unscrew the cap on each my four jugs. Pastor moves his hands to his mouth and his eyes is full of alarm. I grab the jug was on the table before I come, and stow it under the platform. Tip it over with my boot.

Larry ain't three feet away, but he ain't seen me. He's got the focus only comes with a good drunk; his eyes bulge and his face is drum skin tight. Ready to shout encouragement to a slave canine gladiator. Least he don't pay me no mind.

Stipes's got tunnel vision. His brow is furrowed and he looks past me to the trees like he saw the same dream as me. He's lost among corpses and smells and the cold. I'm here but the professed man of God is the only one who can see me. And the Lord's sealed his lips.

I keep my hat low and my mouth zipped. Though everything tells me to turn tail, I stay and imagine all them bodies suspended from trees by they spines, and everything's silent. I see each of these men, the gay face that he wears right now froze into his squawking, silent death mask as he dangles from gray tree limbs.

I understand it all. I'm the instrument. These boys made a bigger enemy than old Baer Creighton. I could gather my jugs and run and they'd still manage to drink em down. Nothing in the world could stop these men from the end they got coming.

I step back. Too spooky; too many things coming together and I don't have my wits. I'll wait in the trees—

"Hey!"

It's Larry. He steps closer but no one pays him any mind.

"You never learn," he says.

"Hey, asshole." I look him over and he's never looked worse. Got the rings under his eyes that come from distress, nights drinking booze and days of cigarettes and coffee. Slumped like he worked a sixteen-hour shift shoveling shit out an elephant stall.

Hate crosses behind his eyes, but no red. I don't get electric from nobody here, but Larry's looking like his rage'll be enough to deal with. Least we're at everybody's back.

I lift my last jug and show him.

I glance around the men. They's riled up watching dogs, shouting and calling names. But it's just uncanny how nobody knows or gives a shit I'm here. I sense them two fellas I saw in town's got something to do with it. They move like archangels, calm and all-seeing.

Larry growls. Throws his fist.

He's had a couple drinks. I swing the jug and clock his temple. He follows through, off balance, and I shove him. Ride him down. I drop the jug. He's face down on the forest floor and I jab his shoulder, his neck. That's for Fred, you bastard. That's for—well, let's keep this about Fred.

I got one of his arms pinned under my knee but his other's free; he pushes off and topples me. I lunge back and punch his cheek and glance another off his skull. His brow's crinkled. I'm ready to go round and round, but he's gone from drunk crazy-mad to drunk goofy-sorry. Looks like a ten-year-old ready to cry. His arms, holding me back, go weak. I sneak another punch and his teeth cut my knuckles.

The men shout and holler. I look but every one's got his head turned to the dog circle, where two animals with no past and no reason to hate have at the fruit of it.

"You stole Fred, you son of a bitch."

He takes another punch, no resistance. His eyes is wet.

"You killed Ruth… " I pull back my fist.

"Didn't kill Ruth."

His eyes is in the trees, loopy. Blood on his lips and nose, eye socket. His lungs heave.

I pop him.

"What?"

He spits blood sideways. "Didn't kill Ruth."

I grab his shirt with both fists. We's eye to eye, ten inches apart. He sees I'm about to bust total apeshit—least he better see it. Ruth, alive?

"You killed her."

"I should have thirty years ago, when she had your baby. That's when I should have killed her."

"Where's Ruth—you took her! Where is she?"

"Took her to her father's. She got a call while I was there. Home said he was dying."

"Neighbor said you hit her, on the lawn."

"She twisted her ankle. I caught her."

Nothing's right in my head. Nothing makes sense. I'm stuck without words or thoughts to string together. This's about Fred, not Ruth. Larry done some shit to her and that's the truth, but that's a separate matter between him and God. I got no standing.

All these years, it's been me that stole her first, and he got the right to steal her back if he could, and I don't grudge him that. Now he killed her and that's another story—or he didn't kill her and that's got my head mixed up—but what him and these boys did to Fred and a thousand other dogs is enough to seal they ends, far as I'm concerned. Ruth don't have a damn thing to do with it.

I look up and Pete Bleau gulps from a jug of wood likker.

I blink. Time is froze. Something flip-flops in me. I've had enough of the killing and the dying. Already I've had enough. It's the corpses in the trees. I'm weary of it.

"No!"

I wriggle off Larry. My legs is weak and my mind's half-blank but I dive into Pete. "Spit! Spit it out!"

He coughs.

"Stick your finger down your throat!"

I put my hand in his mouth and the son of a bitch bites. I pop him quick. He stares. The likker's hit him.

Someone takes a jug. Another. Some other has the third. All these men is dead men and whether it's God or me doing it I'm sick of it. Sick of Ruth and Stipe and Cory. Sick of a life seeing deceit in good and bad people alike. I got nowhere to run without seeing bodies in trees, and just like in the dream I can't shout, I can't move, I can't wake.

Don't drink that!

Did I even say it? "That's poison!"

The dogs wage battle.

I rush to the stinking ugly ground of the former fight circle, scoop a handful of shitty bloody pissy mud, and ten steps later tackle drunk Pete Bleau, rip the jug from his lips, and smack a fistful of shit in his mouth. He twists and wrestles and I shove as much of that shit between his teeth as he'll take.

His eyes is in a pleasant place.

Then Pete retches. Coughs and gags and vomit busts out. Still he smiles. I drip his bile and dead dog shit, all in a stew of cinnamon-flavored wood alcohol. Pete falls flat back and I look up and the other four jugs is each at some man's mouth, and they's no way I can get enough shit in these boys to make em yack up that poison.

It's out of my hands.

These little fights with Larry and Pete—it's like the other men see but don't care, or look but don't see. They drink from the jugs and pass them around.

"Smooth!" one says.

"Tastes real good. Real clean," says another.

"Gimme that jug."

The dogs fight. Grunt. Wheeze. Sounds arrive through the hoopla, but every body and thing sounds the same.

I ain't seen them two boys that kept themselves separate, like they's archangels only appear when they want. Angels of death, maybe. My jugs circulate from one pair of hands to the next. A man gulps as much as he can stand and they's another grabbing at the jug for his fill. On and on. Wood likker don't take long, and in a handful of minutes they's passed the jugs back and forth and all around and every man's had enough to blind a whale or drop a horse.

The dogs in the fight circle pull from each other and watch outside the pallets. One sits on his haunches and the other sniffs along the bottom the wood. Some kind of mystification going on, and the dogs ken it. They's stuck like me, outside the deluded group and not making any sense of it.

Off to the edge, the pastor's doubled over, yacking up his guts beside a tree trunk. "Woohoo," he says, and splashes his boots.

A man drops not five feet from me. Don't recognize the back of his head.

Pete Bleau walks with his arms stretched in front and his grin creeps closer and closer to fear. Men wander into the woods. Most groups, every man's aware of the others, and if you watch, they all sway together. One gets closer, the other backs; the whole group breathes together. But now they's each alone and separate. They's no coordination between them. Each man's stoned in his own world. Lost.

Stipe falls square on his ass. Looks like a mule right after a two-by-four got his attention. He faces me and his bony brow wrinkles like it takes all the concentration he got, but he sees me and knows all this means I tossed him over the ledge. I went one farther. They's no such thing as impunity, and he just drank justice. "You!" he says.

"Me."

He smiles at me then his brow contorts. Eyes go buggy.

"I cain't see!" Stipe yells. Got a hand raised in the air like some church lady filled with the Ghost. "I'm blind! Cain't see!"

Even as he says it, all four jugs is upended and dumping poison into one man or another. One of them jugs gurgles into Larry's piehole. Adam's apple bobbing like it's Halloween.

"Blind!" Stipe yells, then laughs. "Shit? This for real?"

A man lowers the jug from his mouth and says, "Open your eyes."

"Fuck."

He folds over.

Pete Bleau's legs rabbit-shudder. His face twitches. Eyes on nothing.

The dogs peer through the gaps. I keep my eyes on them. Rest of this makes me sick.

These men thought mercy was dropping a half-mauled dog in a field. How many other dog bones is spread through these woods? How many of these men go home and beat they women, poke they kids? This whole clique's a bunch of evil-ass heathen and if they got to die so be it, but I'll watch something else.

They hack. Cough.

Wail.

"Oh, Lord!" Pastor Jenkins says. "Lord have mercy!"

I look to the sky for the Lord.

Then I look back at Stipe. He's on his side, throwing up. Each burst weaker than the last, each grunt more pathetic. Clawing the ground and kicking back and forth with his feet in smaller and smaller arcs. He moans and whimpers and I bet none the dogs he killed died like such a wretched coward. Looking at Stipe is a painful thing but I miss Fred so much I can't pull my eyes away 'til Stipe don't shake anymore. He don't move at all and his eyes is wide open. I want to bust the fuckers and let em run—but the misery all around comes screaming and squealing back into my brain and shakes me loose.

Larry's crawled a few feet from the pit. He's half to his truck. I kneel beside him. "You know this's the end, brother. Why'd you go and drink that shit after I told Pete not to?"

He stops clawing the ground. His eyes is blank and bloody. I pass my hand in front of his face and he don't flinch.

"You blind, Larry? That it?"

He smiles.

I been chewed up over it for so many years I don't know what words to use. So I say, "Why'd you take my daughter from me?"

He wheezes. Inhales best he can. "I... come home from school... got Ruth back... "

"Easy, now."

"I'm a mule, Baer. Sterile since you crushed my nuts that day after school."

I drop back on my ass. They's men all around crying to God, 'cept Larry. "Why'd she go with you?"

"I took her. I couldn't have a kid. You took that from me. So I took yours."

His leg goes stiff, straight like a kick. Arm seizes up at his chest. Whole body rocks and shakes, and his crotch goes dark with piss.

I touch his elbow. He yells, but weak. Pure pain.

All these men got to suffer.

"Why'd you take Fred? Just tell me that, Larry."

His eyes tremble in they sockets and his drumskin face is pulled back. He's close.

I seize his hand. "Why'd you take Fred, brother?"

He whispers, "To hurt you."

I grab Smith. Close my eyes and exhale deep. Try to get a compass point leads out all this crazy evil, mine and all these men's, but the needle spins and spins and I don't know if the right thing's a bullet in his head or one in mine. Larry suffers. Though he got it coming for all the shit he did to me and Fred and Ruth and Mae, I done some shit to him, too. All this suffering here—all these men got it someplace else, first, 'fore they dished it on these dogs. The compass needle spins because they's no way out, no way to do right when everybody's compromised. You can look any direction but the dreamwoods is all around.

Larry groans. He shakes. He's seized up but the death won't come. His face is a frozen mask and his arms and legs is straight. All that's left is for them archangels to throw his ass in a tree.

I press the Smith barrel to Larry's temple.

FORTY FOUR

He shakes and drools, got his eyes turned back in his head. This's the brother that called our mother a whore, electrocuted me, gave me a life of visions and juice. Stole my girl. Stole my daughter. Stole my dog and fought him, and left him for dead where I scrounged apples every fall the last twenty years. He's tried to murder me deeper'n the way I'm about to kill him—tried to murder whatever soul I got.

I shake at the thought of pulling the trigger. He'll die without, and it'll be from my hand either way. Blowing his brains into the mud would be a favor but I can't do it.

Larry moans.

I got to end this. I stand Smith perpendicular to Larry's temple.

"Halt!"

I search the darkness.

"Halt, you!"

A man steps from the shadows with a pistol on me. One of the archangels. I pull Smith back, point at the sky, spin it to my holster. I stand. The man steps closer. His buddy's out there, covering him.

"Who're you?"

"Law."

Only a couple men moan. The rest is gone to the dreamland. Bodies contorted with pain, flexed and taut, faces scarred with horror. Men with straight limbs, so many ornaments ready to be hung from a tree.

"Higher law?" I say.

"FBI."

The other archangel comes from behind a tree. He dumps his pistol into a holster.

"Good of you to come," I say. "But the work's done."

"You made it quick at that."

"You saw me try and stop it."

"You the one got his ass beat two weeks ago?"

I nod.

"And two weeks before that? Fell out the tree?"

I nod again.

"Why you keep coming back? You ain't part of this group."

"You seen it. They stole my dog and left him blind."

"You did this for a dog?"

"Fred."

One looks at the other. "You're under arrest. I'll want that Smith 'n Wesson."

"I bet."

Larry seizes up stiff, his arms and legs like boards. He shakes and inhales slow like his lungs is a thimble already half fulla blood. He lets out the air and it carries a faint moan. He's still.

My brother is dead.

"Think these boys got some bad likker," the lawman says.

"Maybe."

"Something I can't understand," he says. He waves to the trucks, the crates. "What were you going to do with all these dogs? Kill them?"

"Got ten pound of hamburg in the woods, with sleep medicine. Thought that would mellow them out 'til I got em home.

"You planned to take all these dogs?"

"Where's the moral in leaving them to die in wood crates?"

"Where's the moral in killing fifteen men? No trial? No defense?"

I'm tired of yammering but I got to take a shot at making them understand. "All around us is dead men. Look at the lantern glow up in the trees—makes this whole place a cathedral. You got the circle there like an altar. These men come to the last service at the church of death, and they was struck down by the oldest law. An eye for an eye."

They look at me like I farted a goat. They don't see the dreamland, just death.

Ah, hell. I'm ready to go—except for Stinky Joe. He'll wait all night at the cave. Sometime tomorrow he'll figure he's got to fend for himself, and he'll sniff around after something to eat. He'll smell the paper bag carried the hamburg, and prob'ly spend a few hours learning I didn't leave it for him. Day after tomorrow he might figure the carton of eggs is fair game, and the cheese, and the bag of Alpo dry. Beyond that, he'll have nothing.

He'll be on his own, looking for a master who won't throw him in a pit.

"You boys prepared to shoot me in the back?"

"The back, the front. You're coming with us." He pulls his pistol but his eyes glow red and electric zips through me.

The other is silent.

"You better work on him. He's going to shoot me."

I turn my back and take one step.

"Mister, you walk and I'll fill you with holes."

No he won't. Not him. "Bullshit. You know these men got what they had coming."

I tramp into the dark. Behind me, dry leaves shuffle. "Freeze! You!" More rustling leaves. I got electric on my arms. But no bullets.

Ten paces.

Fifteen.

I break left and trot fast, scamper into trees. I raise an arm and rush on.

A pistol fires. "Halt!"

I keep on like a doe I remember, got away and blended in.

Can't help but see them deaths as the work of something beyond me. I stilled the wood likker rich enough to kill, and had murder in my heart every minute, though I didn't know I'd do it 'til I done it. Court of law, I'm flat guilty. But if and when I answer before the Lord, I'll tell him straight up. I wanted to go the other way. Events worked agin me, and that's how I mean it was a little beyond me.

But in this world I killed em and it might satisfy Fred to know.

Mae's my baby. Confirmed.

What the hell's a man do with that? Now that I know?

Ruth, alive? Yeah, and stuck on me. To hell with her. All this time I lied to myself about her being honest because if I didn't then all of us was liars. But they's no starting new and no avoiding the truth. We all lie.

My stomach goes tight and my throat's hot with bile. I choke it back once—the vomit charges again and I puke on a tree. I'm a cold-blooded killer.

Even a killer needs a drink. I rinse my mouth with crick water. It's good and clean, and I drink like I'm empty and never had water. Top it off from my flask of Turkey.

I get in the truck and head back to the old still site for two buckets of gold. I pass my driveway and a car sits in moonlight. Down the road I pull over without hitting the brakes and kill the lights.

I get out, slip my hand to Smith. Tramp toward the burned house, down a gulley and up the other side. They's a rodent, something in the brush, but nothing else.

I've been at the yard at night plenty times, but never since the house burned. Looks like a place to stretch a blanket and stargaze.

Moonlight glints off metal and glass in the drive, but most of the car's in shadows. I circle left along the yard, keep my body agin a backdrop of brush 'til I get the car lined with the opening to the road and the field beyond.

Figure sits on the hood.

I point Smith. Walk straight.

"Who's there? Baer? That you?"

A woman's voice. Mae?

"Mae?" I tramp fast. Into the clearing. She won't believe but I'm going to tell her I'm her daddy. I come out the shadow and into moonlight.

The car is shaped wrong. It's a chrome boat from the seventies. No electric, no red.

"Hey, Baer," she says.

Ten feet off, I stop.

"It's me," Ruth says. "The stars are beautiful tonight."

I'm still. Mouth tastes like yack again.

"What you want, Ruth?"

"I—"

Holster Smith. Hands on my hips.

"I—I'm sorry. That's what I want. I'm here to say I'm sorry."

"For Mae?"

"You know—*know*—about Mae?"

"You carried her ten month."

"Yes. I'm sorry about Mae too. I guess Larry told you everything."

"Didn't have to. You think I didn't see you at the house that time? You got my baby in your arms and standing plain as day saying they was no way we'd ever be together? Saying my baby was his? I could hardly stand to look at you."

"Well, if you knew—"

"What? Why pester you twenty-eight years?"

She nods. "Why?"

"I already give up on everybody else."

She slumps. Her smile is a flower got splashed in mud. I don't want to be mean. I don't want to go, but shit if I can take very much of this.

"You were such a wild man."

I turn half away.

"Going fast in your Nova. All souped up. Windows down. You still got that car? Is that it on blocks over there? I saw it with my headlights pulling in and I've been remembering things two hours now."

"You getting by, Ruth? Okay for money?"

"Daddy takes care of me, what the alimony don't."

I got a lump in my throat. "You here? For real?"

"For real," Ruth says. "Looks like you need a place to stay."

I look at the stars because they's there, convenient.

"I thought it might be time... " She pats the car hood. "I thought we'd ride somewhere. Ride all night and all day, until we come someplace pretty and quiet. Like you put in your letter."

I murdered fifteen men. I got no house. No still. I got a daughter and a lot of money. I got my talent.

"Go home, Ruth."

"Home."

"I'm calling quits."

I walk away. I can't ignore the lie and I surely can't forgive it. All mankind can go to hell. Way I see it I got two obligations. I'll take care of both and then bust out of Dodge.

"Baer?"

I stop. "Yeah?"

"Write."

I study her a long minute, then head for the truck. Grab an ax from behind the seat. Ruth backs out the drive in her old piece of metal. Her headlights flash off the ax blade.

Hand at my brow to ward off low branches, I head for the gold tree. They was in it together. Stipe, Larry, Cory Smylie, Pete Bleau—all the time I spent trying to figure who murdered Fred was wasted. They all wanted a piece of what was mine. Stipe wanted my operation. Larry wanted revenge. Pete wanted to be lazy. And Cory Smylie...

Sometimes you don't know exactly why you hate somebody. Maybe he did a hundred little detestable things over a long while, and in total they earn disgust for the whole man. Maybe Cory had it in for me like that. Maybe it's my simple ways, or looking out for my baby girl, or knocking that pistol to his head. Then Stipe saw he was eager, and give him money to take a couple shots at me.

Shit.

If I'm leaving, I better disassemble them mantraps at the Hun site so some kid don't wander in and get his guts tore out. Though I'm edgy approaching those traps in moonlight. Armed with ax and Smith I trek toward the Hun machine gun nest.

I step easy and slow, around the side, like when the sniper shots was coming at me two week ago. I stop and listen. The night is blank, almost no light, almost no sound. I look for red eyes but see none. I hear myself more than anything—the voice in my head says this is the end of the line. You done some pure-ass evil, killing all those men, and you can't blame it on God. He didn't make the likker.

They call it poetic justice when the bad guy is foiled by his own evil plans. That in mind, I tramp through the dark to my mantraps.

"You out there, Cory?"

I stop. Listen. Keep walking.

Fifty yard out, I creep slow. Ax in my left hand, Smith in my right. I stop, set down the ax, wipe my hand dry on my leg. Resume, each footfall gentle as I can on brittle October leaves. 'Cept for me the woods is silent. They's so damned much death all around. Bodies in trees. Bodies everydamn place. I hear them boys calling out, saying they's blind, and in pain. Hear em call out to God. See blind eyes searching. Open hands feeling, reaching for some unknown guide to take em home.

I stalk from tree to tree, pause. Hide. Lurk. Look. C'mon, Cory Smylie, I know you're hiding. I'm hunting you. My heart's about to pound a hole through my chest. My ears hear the seashell whoosh of blood, mingled with a ring sounds like too much coffee. I raise my pistol hand and wipe sweat from my brow. The Hun nest is twenty feet out; I come from the side.

I hear a faint tap sound—tink, tink, tink.

I lock up. I'm out in the open. Point Smith this way and that. I know I'm going to see a flash and feel a bolt of pain. I know it. It's God's way of business—he's going to strike me down. Evil is round and I got no impunity.

Tink, tink.

It's with the breeze.

I exhale hard. To hell with this. I got to reach down and find a pair. I tramp ahead. Fire into the Hun cave. Fire again. I head right to it, not on the trail, close under the rocks.

"I'm coming for you, Cory! It's quits this time. It's over to-night!"

I fire again. Stand still below the rock outcrop, looking up for motion. For a glint of silver or the sound of shoe leather. Rustling pant legs. Red eyes. The echoes fade and my ears still ring.

Tink. Tink. Tink.

The breeze turns and I whiff something recalls the scent of the fight pit. Death.

They's rocks everywhere. I drag my feet. That pungent smell gets strong down among the tree trunks. I ease up on the hemlock where I rigged the branch trigger and the branch don't cross the path. I stop. Hair stands on my neck, and I know what I'm about to find.

I holster Smith. Dig a Zippo out my pocket and flick. Kneel. Not five feet off is a black mat of bloody leaves. Furrows dug in the dirt, like from a boot—just one. The barbed wire I'd stretched across the trail is gone. The trap is sprung.

I touch the blood. It's dry.

I hold the light a foot off the ground and crawl, yard after yard. I weary of hands and knees, and stand, and continue at a half-stoop. The Zippo flame flickers and whips.

I see a boot.

I come alongside; kneel. His bottoms is black. I bring the lighter to his face. Cory Smylie.

His eyes is sunk, but fixed on the sky like he set his gaze on a star and tried to hang on while the darkness all around him swelled and blotted it all out. His face is gray-pale; I move the Zippo south and glance at his wounds. Barbed wire ripped out his pants, part his thigh, part his groin. All at once a breeze changes direction and I get a lungful of death.

I've had enough. Too damn much.

I tramp through the dark in footsteps I been setting twenty years. Cross the crick on slippy stones. Duck and weave through scrub, emerge in a grove of cherry and oak, and it ain't a minute 'til I'm at the rotted tree with two buckets of gold yet in the hollow. I'm going to swing this blade and cut down this tree. I'm going to grab a bucket of coin and take it to Mae tonight. Tell her I'm her daddy and I love her but she won't ever see Larry or Cory Smylie again. Tell her to take one coin each to a different dealer in a different town, 'til she has enough money to ditch Gleason, then keep the rest in gold. Tell her to make sure them kids go to college, and the next man she finds, he better have motor oil under his fingernails and smell like ten hours' sweat. Then she'll know she's got a man.

I'll come back to this tree, gather the rest of the gold. Come morning I'll take Stinky Joe—no, fuck that. His name's Joe from here out. I'll haul ass west with Joe in my brand new old truck. Keep the windows down and the radio off, and drive 'til I don't see dead men in the trees.

I swing the ax.

From the AUTHOR

Thank you for reading MY BROTHER'S DESTROYER. I hope you enjoyed it. The story continues in a series of fast-paced literary noir thrillers that take Baer Creighton (and you) to the American Southwest.

Book 2: *THE MUNDANE WORK OF VENGEANCE.*

Six days before Baer Creighton cut down a cabal of dogfighters, a sixteen-year-old girl disappeared while walking home from school in Asheville, North Carolina. Witnesses later claimed they saw her in the back of a police car.

Twenty-five years before that, an illegal fireworks plant blew up in Benton, Tennessee, killing eleven, and raining M100 firecrackers over half a county. A few days later, a thirteen-year-old boy learned his highest calling was murder.

The Mundane Work of Vengeance begins where My Brother's Destroyer ends: Baer Creighton taking buckets of gold to Mae, dreaming of driving west.

But Baer has no idea the treachery, blood, and misery in store. At his lowest with no one to trust, he'll have to decide whether to save a family who betrays him—or a kidnapped girl buried in a basement, a half state away.

If he can save anyone at all.

Book 3:   *PRETTY LIKE AN UGLY GIRL*

Luke Graves turned the family butcher business into an empire by cutting fat off the ledger as well as he cut meat off the bone.

He also learned many men sold beef, but few sold girls and boys. Demand was high—especially for the ones with brown skin—and supply, small.

Ten years later the family business included three sons and a distribution chain that delivered kids for any purpose throughout the western United States.

One evening, returning to Williams, Arizona from a pickup in Sierra Vista, the tire blows out. A chavo bolts the truck and runs for the plain. Cephus Graves takes him down with a deer rifle, then fires at a stray pit bull that catches his eye.

In the woods two hundred yards away, Baer Creighton looks up from his fire. He has a nose for evil men and he's found a clan of them. But he's met his match in Luke Graves.

Baer bleeds in Pretty Like an Ugly Girl.

Everyone bleeds.

Book 4: **THE OUTLAW STINKY JOE *(April 2019)***

Stinky Joe survives the wild Flagstaff winter alone.

But with first melt, he succumbs to warm broth and sleeping pills, placed at the doorstep of a scheming prostitute at the vortex of a politician looking for an issue, a money-launderer wielding leverage, and his 83 year old meth-dealing target.

Stinky Joe learned as a pup: don't ever bite a man. He'll beat you near death. But cornered in a bath tub by a pothead with a gun, Joe goes outlaw.

Within hours the best and worst of Flagstaff are mobile. Sheriff's deputies, the meth dealer and his tracking dog, news crews, and Baer Creighton—with the FBI after him, seeking vengeance for yet another agent down.

Joe has survived the wild, but civilized man is a different kind of devil.

Wounded, hunted, and holed up, there's no way out for **The Outlaw Stinky Joe**.

ABOUT THE AUTHOR

Hello! I appreciate you reading my books—more than you can know. If you've read this far, you and I are fellow travelers. I suspect you sense something is not quite right with the world. It's not as good as it's supposed to be. We human beings aren't as good as our ideals. Yet, we prize and want to fight for them.

I do my absolute best to write stories that portray the human situation with brutal transparency, but also I strive to tell stories that are not as bleak as the human condition sometimes seems. There's no limit to the darkness. Light is rare. But it exists, and I hope when you complete one of my novels, you find your values validated.

I'm grateful you're out there. Thank you.

Remember, light wins in the end.

CPSIA information can be obtained
at www.ICGtesting.com
Printed in the USA
BVHW041556020820
585229BV00009B/22

9 780615 938240